THE
CHILD
THIEF

THE CHILD THIEF

DAN SMITH

PEGASUS CRIME
NEW YORK LONDON

THE CHILD THIEF

Pegasus Crime is an Imprint of
Pegasus Books LLC
80 Broad Street, 5th Floor
New York, NY 10004

ISBN: 978-1-60598-571-8

10 9 8 7 8 6 5 4 3 2 1

Printed in the United States of America
Distributed by W. W. Norton & Company, Inc.

For Mum and Dad.
And for my brother, Mike,
who always shared the adventure.

Winter 1930

Village of Vyriv – Western Ukraine

1

The distant figure was little more than a dark smudge on the steppe. The land was flat and white and cold; a vast sea of nothing with just that single blemish on the landscape, drawing the eye. During the war, an imperfection on the horizon would have halted a company in its tracks. Boots would have ceased their struggle, and the chatter of rifle slings would have fallen silent. Fear and curiosity would be felt in equal measure.

And in that silence, would be the long wait to see what might come of the lonely fault in the otherwise faultless beauty of the steppe. A single stain that could multiply into an army, bringing with it only violence and ferocity and death.

But the war was over, and red had crushed all colours that stood in its path, yet the blurred stain in the distance still brought fear and curiosity. It shouldn't have been there.

Staring against the wind, bitter tears welled and clouded my sight. I wiped them away and squinted against the few flakes that had started to fall. I contemplated the figure, watched it shift and blur, then I moved to the edge of the tall grass, wading through snow as deep as my calves, dropping to one knee and resting my elbow on my thigh. I blinked hard, touching a cheek to the cold stock of my rifle, and brought one eye close to the scope.

Magnified as it was, the dark spot was still just a stain on the brilliance of the drift, but I could see it moving towards us as the wind blew across the surface of yesterday's fall, whipping the soft snow into a powder that floated in a swirling mist.

'You see something?' Viktor said.

My sons moved behind me, but I kept my eye to the scope.

'What *is* that?' Petro asked, coming alongside. 'Some kind of animal?' His face was almost hidden, his hat pulled low, and only his eyes were visible above the scarf that covered his mouth and nose. Petro was just a few moments younger than his brother. Two boys, seventeen years old and almost men; born together, raised together but as different as the seasons. Summer and winter. One coarse and hardened, with an outlook that saw no subtlety. The other younger, more complex, more in tune with who he was.

'Could be.' Breath clouded around my face as I spoke, misting the scope lens. I wiped the glass with a finger of my glove.

'Let me see.' Viktor slung his own rifle over his back because it was without a scope and useless at this distance. He squatted beside me, his thick coat moving against mine.

I nodded, letting him take the rifle, and Viktor remained silent as he watched the magnified shape.

'What's it look like to you?' I said. 'An animal?'

'Hard to tell. The wind's picked up again; it looks like there's a storm coming.' He took a breath and steadied the rifle as the icy wind gathered strength, making him shiver despite his thick clothes. 'No, wait. I think it's . . . yes, it's a man. I'm sure of it.' He took his eye from the scope and stared out into the oncoming blizzard. 'Someone's coming,' he said.

'Who?' Petro asked. 'You think it might be activists? Red Army?' It was the threat hanging over Vyriv: that one day the activists would come with soldiers to our village and take everything we had.

'There's just one person,' Viktor said.

'Give me that.' I took back the rifle and scoped the figure once more.

It was closer now. Not just a dark stain, but a person; the movement was clear. A shambling gait, head down, shoulders hunched, bent at the waist. A solitary figure without an army to

4

follow it, but I eased back the rifle bolt and reassured myself that a cartridge was pushed home.

'Petro, I want you to go back,' I said. 'Warn your mother first. Then tell the others.'

'What about you?'

'We're going to wait here. See who's coming.'

Petro didn't want to go, but he knew argument was useless, so he went without another word, raising his knees high as he lifted his feet from the snow.

I watched him until he was gone, disappeared below the lip of the hill, then I turned to watch the figure once again.

'Take this.' I handed my rifle to Viktor, knowing the rare scoped weapon would be more effective to cover me from a distance. 'I'll use yours. Watch from the trees.' I nodded in the direction of the forest which grew along the steppe to the right. A line of leafless trunks, dark and barren against the grey sky. Their crooked fingers were heavy with icicles which glinted in the rare days of sunshine but now hung in shadow. The uppermost branches of the trees at the periphery were filled with the black spots of clumped twigs and forest detritus the crows had used to build their nests.

Viktor didn't take the rifle. He looked across at the trees, then back at me, indecision in his expression.

'You'll be safe,' I told him. 'Stay at the edge of the forest, that's all.'

'I'm not afraid. I just don't want to leave you alone.'

'I won't be alone. You'll be watching me with this.' I put the rifle into my son's hand. 'Do as I ask, Viktor. I need you to watch for me.'

Viktor sighed and nodded before he turned away and struck out for the edge of the trees.

When Viktor was gone, I adjusted my scarf and took up my son's rifle. To the right, crows shifted in the trees, snapping their bleak cries into the afternoon as Viktor approached, but it was cold and they were as embittered by it as we were. Once they had

5

voiced their displeasure, they became quiet, and the only sound was the wind against the wool covering my ears.

Out on the steppe, the figure approached.

2

The progress of the figure was sluggish. His legs dragged through the snow, barely lifting, and his head hung like a beast of burden. His body was bent almost double, his arms hanging limp at his sides. He was like a walking corpse, kept alive by nothing more than the determination to push on.

Swathed in thick clothes and with his face covered, he wore a stout rope around his waist, running out behind him to a sled covered with a tarpaulin thick with ice and snow. When I called out for him to stop, the man kept coming, stopping only when his head was just a few inches from the barrel of my gun. He spoke one word before dropping to his knees. He said, 'Please.'

I followed the man's movement, keeping the weapon pointed at his head, but the stranger remained as he was, as if in prayer, with his head bowed and his shoulders slumped.

When he finally looked up at me through the narrow gap in his coverings, I could see there was almost no life in his eyes.

I lowered the rifle a fraction and the man spoke again. 'Thank God,' he said, and fell face first into the snow at my feet.

I waited for a moment, then released my finger from the trigger and prodded the man's back with the rifle barrel. There was give in his clothing, as if the man beneath was thinner than he appeared to be. I shoved him again, but he didn't move, so I raised a hand to Viktor, hoping he could still see me despite the fall of snow in the air.

I turned the man onto his back and worked my fingers through his clothing to find the skin of his neck so I could feel for a pulse.

'Is he dead?' Viktor asked when he arrived at my side.

I shook my head. 'Not yet. Check the sled.'

Viktor went to the sled while I put my hands under the man's armpits and prepared to drag him.

'Anything?' My voice was almost lost to the wind when I called out. I looked back to see Viktor standing with a corner of the tarpaulin in his fingers, lifted so he could look beneath.

Viktor spoke without turning in my direction, his shrouded face angled down towards what was concealed beneath the waterproof covering. His voice was muffled. 'I think you should see this.'

I released my grip on the stranger and went over, stopping as soon as I saw the children lying on the sled. Immediately I looked away, lifting my eyes to the barren trees. But I didn't see the black branches. Instead I saw the image of the children fixed in my mind, as if they had been burned into my thoughts. It had been a long time since I had seen anything like it, and it probed at my darkest memories like the tip of a hot needle.

I took a deep breath and hardened myself, prepared myself to look once more. And when I was ready, I turned back to them.

The boy's hair was as black as the winter night that moved through the trees, and his head was turned so that, were he alive, he would have been looking to the right side of the sled. But this boy saw nothing because his eyes were dry and dead and stared at only whatever comes after death.

Accompanying him on the sled was a girl. Her hair was long, frozen hard against her face and neck so her features were less visible. She was lying on her back, staring wide-eyed through the stiff strands of tangled hair. Her small, undernourished body was naked and pale, and I estimated she was no more than ten or eleven years old, just a few years older than my own daughter. There was a long and wide laceration from the top of her thigh to just above the knee. From one side to the other. The whole of the front of her thigh had been removed so the white of the bone was visible.

I had seen many wounds, but few like this. Wars did not

fashion violence in this way. I was accustomed to the ragged shredding of explosions and the punctured flesh left by bullets, but these cuts were clean. Precise. And whenever I had seen injuries like these, they had been made with much darker intent than that of soldiers fighting soldiers.

'Papa?' Viktor's voice cut into my thoughts. 'What happened to them?'

I glanced at my son and shook my head.

'So what do we do?'

I went back to the man lying in the snow and crouched beside him, staring down into his face, wondering who he was and why he had come here. 'This man is dying,' I said. 'He needs our help. We should get him back.'

'You mean take him back to the village? Is that safe? He might—'

'If we leave him here he'll die. Do you want that?'

'And what about them?' Viktor inclined his head towards the children. 'What do we do with them?'

'We take them with us.'

Together, we pulled the man aboard the sled, mindful of the terrible cargo hidden beneath the tarpaulin. I hitched the reins around my waist and leaned my weight forward as we began the trek home. Soon my legs were burning with fatigue. I wasn't getting younger, and my muscles were weakened by age and circumstance. I had lived just less than half a century and my bones and muscles were feeling the strain of the wear I'd forced on them.

Once we peaked the summit of the low hill, we could see Vyriv nestling in the shallow valley below, and as we began to descend, we saw smoke trailing and could already feel the warmth and the light the homes held within.

We moved into the village of only twenty or so buildings, many of which were now unoccupied. Some people had left because they couldn't cope with the hardship, thinking life would be better in the cities, and some had moved on to Karkhiv

9

or Kiev, others hoping to enter Russia. And there were those who had gone west, looking for Poland, going back to the place where I had fought not fifteen years ago when General Brusilov led the Russian army into disaster in Galicia. But now the country was being closed off. There was no way out.

Last year the government introduced collectivisation, and defined the kulak. The use of labour, ownership, the sale of surplus goods – these were all signs of a kulak. Any man who could afford to feed himself and his family was to give his property over to the state, and when people resisted in numbers, Stalin declared war on us and his great machine swept across the country, liquidating, collectivising and appropriating. Homes and possessions and people all now belonged to the state, leaving only three fates for the kulak – death, deportation or the labour camp.

It was as if we were simply waiting for execution or the march to the trains. We lived in constant fear of the soldiers' arrival; of being forced into wagons and taken north to Siberia, south to Kazakhstan, packed so tight our feet wouldn't touch the wooden floor. And already there were signs of hunger like there had been before the famine of 1921.

For those of us who still lived in Vyriv, there was nothing left but a slim hope of survival; a small chance to avoid starvation if we kept our heads bowed and remained there, unnoticed in the valley for as long as possible.

'What do you think?' asked Viktor as we walked. 'Where's he from? I mean, there's nobody close. Uroz is the closest and that's more than a day's walk in this weather. And what do you think happened to *them*?' He looked over at the shape of the tarpaulin. A range of hills in miniature, hiding something unspeakable beneath. 'You think some kind of animal did that?'

'Some kind.' I kept my head down, staring at the ground beneath my feet.

'Wolves?'

'No.'

Viktor sighed, his broad shoulders rising high as he drew air into his lungs. 'You think a person did it, don't you? I'm old enough to know the truth.'

I lifted my head and stared at my son, and Viktor stared back as my equal. Viktor was wilful and determined, like me. He had inherited my obstinacy and, as he grew older, he was learning to apply it. 'Yes, I think the wounds are man-made.'

'It looks . . . well, it looks like an animal.'

'That was no animal. The cuts are too clean.'

'No. I mean it looks like when you butcher an animal. When you take off the meat.'

'I've seen something like this before.' I swallowed hard. 'There are people,' I said. 'Desperate people who'll do anything to survive. Hungry people. There were times – during the wars and the famine – when people would eat whatever they could. And there are bad people too, Viktor; people who've forgotten what it is to be human.'

Viktor shook his head and ran a hand across his mouth. 'You think that man did that so he could . . . ?'

'I don't know. Him, someone else, I don't know.'

'But they're *children*. Is it safe to take him with us? What do you—'

'I don't know,' I cut him short. 'Wait until he can tell us himself.'

3

The heart of the village was a circular area now covered with snow that had drifted into the shallow valley on a bitter wind. And in the centre an oak stood old and hard and dark, unclothed for the winter. I had no idea what this village elder had witnessed through the years of war and revolution, but I knew this small collection of houses, close to nowhere, had seen little of the bloodshed. The fighting on the eastern front had been far enough from here, and the revolution had happened in another world. The civil war had ridden past Vyriv, not noticing the tiny village crouched in the dip of the land. I had passed it myself without realising; marching down to the Crimea, the Black Army advancing to defeat another that called itself White. Even the famine of ten years ago had barely managed to rake its fingers across this small village. It was as if God turned the heads of men who passed it, so they looked away to the horizon. But the clouds were darkening now, and our great leader had dispatched his eyes and his ears to scour the land, and perhaps even God wouldn't be able to blind those eyes.

For now the oak stood silent, refusing to give up its secrets, and as I passed it a thin memory of the summer came to me. A *bayan* accordion and a violin playing together, music drifting in the warm air. The women in their best dresses, singing to the breeze.

Close to the centre of the village, my home stood with open wooden gates hinged to a broken fence erected to define ownership in a past that allowed it. In more recent times it had become something to fall into disrepair or else it might denote the presence of a kulak.

As we made our way through the gate, dragging the sled, we saw shutters opening and cracks appearing in doorways as curious eyes looked out into the oncoming night.

We went to the front of the house and I unhitched myself and banged hard on the front door. 'It's us.'

Bolts were drawn back, and the door opened.

Natalia's cheeks were red and her dark eyes were worried. 'What's going on? Are you all right? Where's Viktor?' Petro was standing behind her, holding a knife. My daughter Lara was by the table, her cousin Dariya beside her. Both girls looked excited and afraid at the same time.

'Everything's fine,' I said, pulling down my scarf. 'There's a man, though; he needs our help.'

'A man?'

'We need to get him inside.' I looked over Natalia's shoulder at my daughter and her cousin. 'What's Dariya doing here? She should be at home.' Dariya was a year younger than Lara, just eight years old, but she was bold and inquisitive, not afraid to speak her mind.

'And miss this?' Dariya said, coming forward. 'It's the most exciting thing to happen in years. Everything's so boring.' She was a little taller than Lara, despite being younger, and her manner was more confident. She had dark hair braided on either side, the plaits reaching her shoulders. She wore them so they fell across her chest.

'Boring is how we like it,' Natalia told her. 'Boring is good.'

'Boring is boring,' Lara said.

'You've been listening to your cousin too much.' Natalia nodded to me and beckoned with her hands, telling me to bring the man into the house.

So Viktor and I lifted him between us and carried him to the door while Natalia snatched up some blankets and cushions and put them by the fire.

'Put him here,' she said. 'It's the warmest place. There's a little food; you think he'll eat?'

13

'I don't think he'll do much of anything.' We put him down and watched Natalia cover him with blankets.

'Who is he?' Dariya asked, squatting beside the man and peering into what she could see of his face. She put out a finger and poked him, but Natalia caught her hand and pulled her away.

'Did you bring meat?' she asked. 'We have some mushroom soup, a little milk and oats, but, like this, a man needs meat.'

We set our rifles by the door and Viktor went for the rabbit we'd snared, coming back and handing it to his mother, holding it up by the ears.

'This is it? A small rabbit? I send my husband and twin sons to find meat and they bring me one small rabbit and another mouth to feed?' She took it in her fist and held it up to inspect it. 'How do I feed a family with one rabbit?'

'We have potatoes,' I said. 'A few beets.'

'And not much else.'

'Be thankful. The activists come here, we'll have nothing.'

'One rabbit.' She shook her head and turned her attention back to the man.

'Petro, stay with your mother.' I touched Viktor's shoulder, indicating he should come with me.

'I can help you, Papa.' Petro came forward but I shook my head.

'I said stay with your mother.' I looked at Petro for a moment, softening my expression, but my son tightened his jaw and turned away. I sighed and stepped outside, pulling the door closed.

There were one or two men standing by their homes now, armed with pitchforks and sticks, and I knew they'd be worried about Petro's warning, wondering if men had finally come to take their belongings. Sticks and farm implements would be no match for the rifles of a Red Army unit, but some of the men would fight with their bare hands if they had to.

I told Viktor to let them know everything was safe. 'But don't mention what's under there.' I glanced back at the sled. 'Don't tell them what else we found.'

'Why not?'

'Because I don't want to scare them. They're scared enough already.'

Viktor nodded, and when the men saw him approach, they began to wander out to meet him. I waited until there was a group of them, clustered in the twilight, then I went back into the house and closed the door behind me.

The room was small but it was large enough for one family. There was a table and a *pich* – the clay oven where Natalia did her cooking. There was a woven mat in front of the fire, a couple of chairs to soak the heat, and above the fire an *obraz* hung on the clay wall. The icon was unremarkable, just paint and wood, an image of the Virgin embracing her child. It had been in Natalia's family for as long as she remembered, and the last time it had been taken from its position was when her mother lay dying, outliving her husband by just a few weeks, and she had held it in her fingers while she breathed her last.

The *rushnyk* draped over the top of the icon had also been in its place for many years because we'd had no reason to take it down. Before the revolution, the *rushnyk* was always on the table, put out to welcome guests. The colour of the embroidered flowers on the towel was a rich and deep red, and the family would display it with pride and put out bread and salt as an offering for visitors. But now it gathered dust and the flowers had faded. No one visited any more. No one trusted anyone now.

Already, Natalia had discarded the man's scarf, opening his jacket and removing the clothing that would become damp now he was inside where it was warm. What I could see of his face was bright red, the blood resurrecting in his veins, but his cheeks and his chin were covered with a thick matting of beard that hid his mouth from view. The hair was clotted together in places, twisted and clumped.

'I'll have to take everything off him,' Natalia said, looking up when I came in. Petro was standing beside her, still holding his knife, reluctant to let it go. Lara was sitting in one of the comfortable chairs, squeezed beside her cousin Dariya, both of them watching the man with curiosity. Lara jumped down and came over to me, putting her arms around my waist and holding herself tight against me. I leaned down to kiss her hair.

'Who is he, Papa?' she asked.

'Is he one of *them*?' Dariya said. 'A twenty-five-thousander?'

Natalia and I shared a glance over the top of Lara's head.

'Where have you heard that?' I asked.

'I don't know. Someone was talking,' Dariya said. 'Some of the men.'

'And you were listening in? There's a word for children like that,' Natalia told her.

'They said they're coming to take our land, is that right?' Dariya asked.

Word had reached the village about the party activists. Twenty-five thousand young communists dispatched by Stalin, bringing with them the ranks of the Red Army and the political police, spreading out across the country, searching for anything of value, anything that could sustain life. Already there had been word of other villages garrisoned and occupied, families broken.

'That's not for you to worry about,' I said. 'You let the adults think about that.'

'But when are they coming?'

'Perhaps they won't come at all,' Natalia told her. But we knew they would reach Vyriv eventually. It was inevitable that some time soon the soldiers would look down into the shallow valley and see the smallholdings, and the purge would come.

'But Papa said—'

'Enough, Dariya,' Natalia stopped her. 'We have other things to think about right now.'

'You need to go home.' I went to where Dariya was sitting and squatted in front of the chair. 'Your mama and papa will be worried about you.'

'Please, Uncle Luka.'

I shook my head.

Dariya pouted, but when I tickled her ribs she laughed and knew she was beaten. I went to the door with her and waited for her to put on her boots before letting her out. 'Straight home,' I told her as she ran out into the cold.

I watched her go, then closed the door and headed to the room where we slept.

It was dark in there, but I could see well enough to find the chest of drawers that had once been white but was now a greyish colour. I opened the bottom drawer and looked at the few clothes folded into neat piles. Lara had one dress, the one she was wearing now, and there was another in here, ready for her when she grew into it. Beside it there were some clothes my boys had outgrown long ago, in a time when I hadn't even known their faces; a time of bloodshed and filth.

I picked up a shirt, the material worn so thin I could barely feel it between my hardened fingers. There was still use in the clothes, but I needed something and they could be spared, so I took a pair of trousers to go with the shirt, tucked them both inside my coat, then slipped back into the adjoining room.

As I headed to the front door, Natalia spoke to me, asking, 'Where are you going?'

She was leaning over the man by the fire. Lara was beside her, taking his clothes as her mother passed them back to her. He was wrapped in many layers, each one a surprise, as if, when they had all been peeled back, the man beneath would be nothing but a skeleton robed in slack skin and matted hair.

'I have something to do,' I said. 'Outside.'

Natalia continued to watch me for a moment and I looked away so she couldn't read me. When our gaze met again, I knew she had seen something in my eyes, stored it in her memory, ready to bring it out at a more appropriate moment. I nodded once to her, an understanding passing between us, then forced a smile and turned to the front door.

Outside, I dragged the sled around to the small barn behind the house. The sky was heavy with cloud, the moon failing to do much more than break the odd patch, but the ground was white and reflected what little light there was.

Pulling the barn doors wide, the smell of animals came out on a waft of warm air, and I hauled the sled inside. The cow watched from its stall, its dark eyes like glass.

I studied the tarpaulin, seeing its shape, knowing what was beneath the ice-encrusted material.

'I can help,' Viktor said, surprising me.

'I didn't hear you coming. You better close the doors,' I told him.

While Viktor pulled the doors shut, I lit a lamp and hung it from a nail on one of the supports. 'You spoke to the others,' I said.

Viktor came back and pulled down his scarf. 'They wanted to see him, but I told them to wait until tomorrow.'

'And they listened to you?'

'Of course.'

I showed my son a rueful smile. 'They listen to you. It's good.'

Viktor gestured in the direction of the sled. 'What are you going to do?'

I replied by taking the clothes from beneath my coat. 'I need to cover her.'

'You want me to do it?' Viktor asked.

'We'll do it together.'

Viktor hesitated before reaching down to take the corner of the tarpaulin and peel it back. I took the corner nearest to me and did the same, both of us moving the length of the sled so we could draw back the covering and whip it off.

I had to force myself to look at what lay beneath.

4

The low light was a blessing; it cast a gentler hue on what we were seeing. The sled was packed with the man's few belongings. A bale of clothes, rolled and tied with rope. A couple of waterproof coverings. A leather satchel and a Mosin-Nagant rifle like the one Viktor had been carrying on the steppe. There was also a wooden case for a Mauser pistol.

And there were the two bodies. A boy and a girl.

It wasn't so easy to make it out in the incomplete darkness, but I had seen the boy's face when we were on the hillside, I had seen the precise laceration on the naked girl's leg, and I saw those things now, just as clearly in my mind.

Looking at the two bodies lying in shadow, I closed my eyes and thanked God I couldn't see better in the dark.

'We have to cover her,' I said. 'Give her some dignity. And nobody else needs to see this. You understand that, don't you? People have enough to scare them. They hide in their homes and pray for deliverance, and something like this . . .'

'I understand, 'Viktor said. 'But how do we keep it from them?'

'We'll bury them tomorrow. In the right place.'

'The graveyard? People will see.'

'We'll go early.'

'They'll see where we've been digging.'

'By then it won't matter. We'll tell them something they'll believe.'

Viktor reached out to take the clothes, but I tightened my grip. Viktor tugged once. 'Let me.'

'No.' I pulled them back and opened them out, laying them beside the girl.

I gritted my teeth and leaned down to slip the trousers over her feet. My hands were dumb inside thick gloves, and I fumbled and failed. I shifted, straightened the trousers once more, and tried again, but her feet were at right angles to her ankles and they refused to slide into the legs of the material. I cursed and breathed out hard, preparing myself for another attempt, this time jamming the child's feet in the trousers so hard I had to tug to remove them for another try.

'Damn it.' I put the trousers aside, knowing I'd have to break the joints.

'I'll do it,' Viktor said, but his voice was weak, almost a whisper.

'No.' I took off my gloves and stuffed them into my pockets. I put my left hand on the girl's frozen shin and looked up at the ceiling of the barn.

My hands were still warm from having been inside the gloves, but I felt the heat draining away when I touched the girl. Her skin was smooth and cold as stone.

I put my right hand on her foot and squeezed my eyes tight before I leaned all my weight down and felt the ankle crack. And as it did, a lump rose to my throat and I fought hard to retain my composure in front of my son. Our world was not a world for weakness. It was a world for strength and survival. Those were the most important lessons I could teach my son. And yet I couldn't bring myself to look at the girl as I felt for her other foot and prepared to do the same the thing again.

With the second crack, I turned away and bent over, putting my hands on my knees and breathing hard. I fought the urge to vomit, swallowing hard, drawing on all my reserves of strength. 'Damn.' I punched my own leg. 'Damn, damn, damn.'

I had been in terrible places and I had seen terrible things. As a soldier I had been responsible for many deaths, and in my life as a farmer I slaughtered animals and I butchered them. I had broken bones many times over, but nothing had ever sickened me like this. The sound was close to that of snapping away a lamb's leg, and I knew I would never be able to do that again without thinking of this moment.

'Let me finish,' Viktor said, putting his hand on my back.

I straightened and looked my son in the eye. 'No, I—'

'You don't have to do it all yourself.'

I wanted to tell him how much that meant. 'Dry that. It'll freeze.'

'Hm?'

I pointed at my son's face and Viktor rubbed his eye with the heel of his palm, taking away the tear. 'I'll do the rest,' he said.

I let him take the trousers, and I watched him slip them over the girl's loose feet and pull them over the wound on her thigh. I tried not to think of my own daughter.

When he was finished, we stood side by side and looked down at the two small bodies on the sled.

'You think we should have left them up there?' Viktor asked.

'On the hill?'

'Not just on the hill, but out of sight, somewhere—'

'For the wolves? Or for the crows to take their eyes?'

'No, I just meant—'

'This is someone's daughter. Someone's son.'

'I didn't mean that.'

'Then what *did* you mean?' It wasn't Viktor's fault, but I could feel anger building anyway. I'd gone out this morning to find something to eat to keep my family alive as long as possible in this hateful, murderous weather, but I'd come down with the bodies of two children and a man who was no use to anyone.

'I just meant it would have been easier. No, not easier. *Better*. Maybe it would have been better. We wouldn't have had to do this. People don't need another thing to worry about. This will scare them. It scares *me*.'

I swallowed my anger, forcing it away, battling it back inside me to feed and grow. 'That's why we have to keep it to ourselves.'

'We shouldn't have him in the house.'

'We don't know he's done anything wrong.'

'Does it matter? Is it worth the risk?'

'Of course it matters,' I said, trying to feel my own humanity; trying to find my own compassion. 'We're still human. Whatever we do, whatever we see, whatever's happening to this country, we have to remember that. We're still human. We always have to remember that. Because once we forget *that*, it will all be over.'

Coming back to the house, we stopped at the front door. 'Viktor . . .' I pursed my lips, wanting the right words to come.

My son looked at me. 'I know,' he said. 'You're welcome.'

I nodded and reached out to rub his shoulder. 'You're a good boy.'

We went in and removed our coats and boots, stamping the snow off by the door.

The stranger was lying in front of the fire with a blanket over him, but if anyone had walked in, they would've thought him nothing more than a pile of rags. Petro was sitting in the far corner, settled into one of the old chairs, a rifle propped against the wall beside him. The room was lit only by the fire that burned in the grate, and three half-burned candles wedged into a chipped clay holder on the table.

'Has he said anything?' I asked.

'Nothing.' Petro blinked hard as if he'd been falling asleep. 'Not even moved.'

'But he's alive?' I went to the man, my knees popping when I crouched, and put my fingers to his neck. 'Yes. He's alive.'

'You think he's an activist?' Petro asked.

'No.' I glanced at Viktor, letting our knowledge of the man's cargo remain a secret between us.

'From a *kolkhoz*, then?' Petro pushed himself out of the chair and came closer. 'You think he's from a collective, running from the OGPU? Maybe they'll follow him here.'

22

'It's possible,' I said, opening the flap in the wooden case I'd taken from the sled. 'But unlikely.' I tipped it so the pistol slipped out. 'I don't know. There's something about him.' I turned the pistol over in my hands, looking at the number nine burned into the handle and painted red.

'Some kind of mark?' asked Petro. 'Does the number mean something?'

'To remind you what ammunition to use,' I told him. 'It means this weapon belonged to a German.'

'He's German?'

'Or he took it from someone who is. Was.' I slipped the pistol back and put the case on the shelf. I left the boys talking and went to where Natalia was standing over the stove. Lara was sitting at the table, playing with a piece of wool. I tousled the top of her hair and sat down beside her, watching her smile as she twisted the wool.

'Hungry?' Natalia asked, without turning around.

'Starving.'

She banged a metal spoon against the rim of an iron cooking pot and laid it on the worktop beside her. 'Lara, put that away now.'

Lara groaned and rolled her eyes at me, but did as she was asked, winding the wool into a ball as she pushed back her chair and called to Viktor and Petro.

'Is everything all right?' Natalia asked as soon as Lara had turned her back. 'You want to tell me about it?'

'Not now.'

She glanced at Lara, then lowered her voice further. 'That man's been shot, Luka, who the hell is he?'

'Shot?'

'Right through here.' She put a finger to her abdomen, just below her last rib. 'Straight through. Someone's dressed it – maybe he even did it himself, I don't know, but he's lucky to have lived *this* long. I don't think he'll last much longer.' She put her hand on mine. 'I'm scared. We can't keep him here.'

'What else can we do with him? We can't leave him to die.'

'He'll probably die anyway; he must've lost so much blood. There's some infection too, I think. And he looks like he hasn't eaten for days.'

'Then we have to help him.'

'We can't, Luka. What if he's being followed? What if someone finds him here—'

'You'd want someone to do the same for me. For one of our sons.'

'Yes, but—'

'He stays here for now.'

'You know what they do to people who help enemies of the state. They'll call us counter-revolutionaries.'

'Who says he's an enemy of the state? And if they come here, they'll call us kulaks and take everything anyway. But at least we'll still have our humanity.'

Natalia made a sound of disapproval and turned away, reaching up to take bowls from the cupboard. She stared at me as she put them on the table, placing them harder than she needed to. 'I've left his things for you to look at,' she said.

'Where?'

'In the basket by his clothes.'

I started to stand, but she stopped me, saying, 'Later. Food's ready.'

Natalia ladled rabbit stew into the bowls, putting only a little into each. It was bulked out with some of the few potatoes and beets we had left, and we ate it with dented spoons and we drank water from dented cups.

'When will he wake up?' Lara asked. She was excited to see someone new. Vyriv was small and isolated. Newcomers were a rarity and it was better that way but, in Lara, the advent of a stranger stirred curiosity and adventure.

'Soon, I hope.' I looked across the table at my daughter and couldn't help but see the image of the mutilated girl in my mind. I tried to ignore it, but it fought against my better thoughts, tainting them and forcing them aside so I saw the cold white face, half hidden by matted hair. I saw her blue lips, her tiny limbs, and the whiteness of the bone in her leg.

 I put down my spoon and pushed the bowl away with the back of my hand.

Natalia turned to watch me. 'Not hungry?'

'I lost my appetite.'

After we'd eaten, my sons turned in and Natalia chased Lara to bed. When they were gone, I blew out the candles and took the pistol from the shelf. I collected the basket containing the man's belongings and went to sit by the fire, stretching my legs so my feet were close to the man's head and I could feel the warmth of the fire.

The man lay still, as if he were already dead, and I had to watch him for a long time before I detected the slightest indication he was breathing.

There was little to speak of in the basket. A small piece of sausage wrapped in cloth. A knife, a handful of cartridges of different calibres, and a heavy revolver. I opened the revolver and pulled out a single spent cartridge, turning it over in my fingers before replacing it with a fresh one. I set the revolver back in the basket and put it down, turning my attention to the pistol that had been on the sled.

Once again I took the German pistol from its wooden case, but this time I set the case on the floor and checked the weapon. It was in good condition, and when I drew back the slide I could see it was loaded. I ran a fingertip around the red number nine and remembered how I had looked into the barrel of a similar weapon, in the days after we were betrayed by the Red Army.

In those days everything was tainted with one colour or another. Black, red, white, green. Every army gave itself a colour, as if they were teams preparing to meet for some purpose other than to murder each other. With the anarchist Black Army under Nestor Makhno, I had fought hard against General Wrangel's White Army, eventually joining forces with the Red

Army that I'd deserted just a few months before. In 1920, with our tenuous bond holding, the cavalry and infantry of the two armies pursued Wrangel south through Ukraine to the Crimea, but after our combined victory that winter, the Red Army renounced its agreement and broke the weak alliance between black and red. The communists were ruthless in their treatment, more so of those of us who'd once been among their number, and the palette was washed clean. The only colour that remained was red, and few of my brothers in arms escaped the executions.

Just days after Wrangel fled, Bolshevik communications were intercepted: orders for all members of Makhno's organisation to be arrested. All staff and subordinate commanders were apprehended and executed. Makhno escaped, taking his soldiers, fleeing north into Ukraine and then disbanding, heading west for the places Lenin had signed over to the Polish.

I was with a small group of men who, like me, had no intention of leaving Ukraine. Natalia and I first met in my home town of Moscow, but she was from Ukraine, and when the war with Germany began, she returned to the village of Vyriv to raise our sons. So that's where I intended to go – I had a wife and children I hardly knew and I wanted to make a new life with my family.

I and a few stragglers shed any sign of allegiance and headed north, hoping to find provisions in villages along the way, but at one settlement a small unit of Red Army soldiers had already been to requisition grain and food. The villagers had protested so the communists retaliated by burning them out of their homes. As we approached, we saw the smoke from the fires and chose to skirt around the area, but the reds had already left and we ran straight into them.

The communists were fuelled with the destruction and death they'd left behind, and they confronted us without fear. Their commander drew his pistol and nudged his horse forward so he could point it down at me, the barrel close to my face. I was younger and faster in those days. Battle-hardened and fearless. I reached out and took the pistol in my fist before the mounted soldier could fire. I pushed it aside, dragged the soldier from his horse and took the weapon from him. I shot the commander twice, pressing the pistol against his chest, and red and black emptied their weapons at each other until there was silence once more.

Two of my friends were killed in the fight, but when the rest of us left on horseback, taking the communists' weapons, all five red soldiers lay dead.

Now I rested the pistol in my lap and stared at the flames. The room was filled with flickering orange light, the only sound was the crackling and snapping of the wood. The ticking of a clock.

'What are you doing?' Natalia asked, making me blink and rub my eyes.

'Sitting,' I said, looking up to see her standing in the doorway. 'Remembering.'

She came in and eased into the chair opposite.

'How long were you standing there?' I asked.

'Long enough. You going to tell me about it?'

I watched the fire reflected in her eyes. 'He wasn't alone. There were two children with him. A boy and a girl. Both dead.'

Natalia put her hands up, cupping them over her mouth and nose, her thumbs sliding under her chin. 'How?' Her voice sounded hollow, held in like that.

I tried to find the words but nothing felt right. There was no good way to say what I thought.

Natalia pulled her chair closer and turned it to face me, sitting so our knees were touching. 'Whatever it is, you can tell me.'

I nodded, thinking it was a hard thing to tell a mother, but I relied on her to help me carry my dark thoughts. She needed to know. 'The girl had wounds like her flesh had been taken off,' he said. 'Like she'd been butchered.'

Natalia knew the stories as well as I did. She hadn't seen it first hand, but she'd heard that in the famine ten years ago there were those who were so hungry, so deranged, they'd taken to eating their dead.

'Not now,' she said. 'Not any more. People aren't that desperate.'

I ran a hand across my beard. 'Do you think a man could find a taste for it?'

Natalia sat back. 'That's too horrible to even think about.'

I had seen it before. After we'd fought the small detachment of red soldiers, we'd entered the skeletal village to look for food and survivors. The *povolzhye* famine was not yet in full swing, but grain requisitions, disruptions to agriculture and drought had squeezed everything from the Volga-Ural region, and disease and starvation was spreading. First the war with the central powers, then the civil war had taken the heart and life from the country and it was beginning to die. People were so hungry that seed grain was eaten before it could be sown. Farm animals had all been butchered, as had dogs, cats, anything that would provide meat. People foraged for whatever sustenance they could find because their cellars and their bellies were empty. They ate rotten potatoes, grass, nettles, bark from the trees. They filled themselves with water, distending their stomachs, swelling their legs, making their eyes bulge and their skin sag. And finally they dropped in the streets with no one strong enough to bury them or take them away. Then came rumours that people had begun to eat their own dead.

I had found evidence in that unnamed village. A place with no more than a few homes scattered around smallholdings which had been ransacked and burned, the charred wood blackened and bleak.

We had checked each home that was still intact, knocking on the doors and going inside to search for food, but we didn't need to open cupboards because they were already left open to display their emptiness. We looked beneath tables and searched cellars, stepping over the wasted bodies of women and children left to rot. We covered our faces and noses, searching only because we were desperate and because desperate men will do almost anything they have to do to survive. And then I discovered the one thing I would not do.

In one house I found an emaciated man standing by a large pot that boiled on the wood-burning stove. He was like a dead man animated, a corpse dressed in rags. And, at his feet, a naked body with slices of flesh cut from the backs of its legs.

'Luka.'

'Hmm?' Once more Natalia jarred me from my memories. 'What?'

She drew her arms around herself and stared at the wall. I didn't know if she was looking to where our children lay asleep or simply trying not to look at the stranger smothered in blankets by the fire. 'You really think someone might do that when they didn't have to?'

'Are there people who like it, you mean? I don't know. Maybe it's possible.'

'We can't have him in our house. We have to get him out.'

'Right now he's harmless.'

'So why are you watching him? And why do you have that?'

I smiled without humour and lifted the pistol. 'To be safe.'

'You should have left him,' she said. 'Out there.'

'That's what Viktor said.'

'So maybe he was right.'

'He would have died.'

Natalia shrugged.

'Would you want that?' I asked. 'Would you want to go to bed each night, knowing your husband and son had left a man to die?'

'You were a soldier,' she said. 'I manage to sleep knowing you've done the kind of things soldiers do.'

'This is different. What kind of a person would I be if I didn't do something to help? What kind of a human being would I be?'

She remained silent.

'There are things on his sled,' I told her. 'Things he has with him that make me think he's a veteran.'

'Of what? Which war?'

I looked down at the pistol. 'I've seen weapons like this before.

29

Some of the German soldiers carried them. The Bolshevik commissars used something similar during the civil war, but this one came from a German. The number on the handle tells me that. This man might have fought the Germans, Natalia, and that means he was in the Imperial Army like me. It's like he's my brother.'

'Unless he's Red Army.'

'We have to give him the benefit of the doubt. We have to let him speak for himself and *then* we can decide what he has and hasn't done.'

Natalia folded her hands in her lap, pushing them between her knees. 'And if he's running from something?' she asked. 'Someone shot him, so they might be following him. What if he brings the communists?'

'They'll come eventually; we both know that.'

'Later rather than sooner is the way I'd like it. What do you think they'll do when they come here? They'll take everything we have. Force us onto a collective if we're lucky or send my children away to Siberia if I'm not. Take my husband out in the night and I'll never see him again.'

I stared into the fire. 'We should think about leaving,' I said. 'Soon. There are ways into Poland.'

'We've talked about this. The borders are closed and we don't have papers.'

'We'll find somewhere if we go across country – stay away from the roads.'

'We can't take Lara across country in this weather. No, all we can do is stay here, and when they come do whatever they ask of us. If we do that, we can stay together.'

'I'm not so sure they'd allow it.'

We sat for a long time without speaking, both of us lost in our thoughts. We watched the fire weaken in the hearth, and I threw on another piece of wood when Natalia went to bed. And while she drew the blankets against the cold, I stayed in my chair, watching the stranger.

I barely closed my eyes all night. My whole being was alert to the sounds of the house, my ears strained for a rattling at the locked door. I considered Natalia's concern that someone might have followed the stranger – that he might have been running from something – and I knew that when the activists first came, they always came at night. To take the men away.

5

It was still dark, but I guessed it was between four and five because I was roused from an ill doze by the lilt of a lonely black-bird's song. It continued to sing, oblivious to my troubles, and I looked at the man still lying in front of the fire. The flames were long since dead and the room was cold, but the man was well covered.

I stood and rubbed my eyes. I arched my back, feeling the stiffness working out of my muscles.

The man had hardly moved. He was in more or less the same position he'd been in last night, his thin frame tucked beneath a pile of blankets and sheets. I could hear him breathing – a slow, heavy sound. Laboured and shallow breaths, each one accompanied by the rasping wheeze of a dying man. I waited, listening to the awkward drawing in of air, the weak exhalation, then I went through to the bedroom.

'What's the matter?' Natalia whispered.

'Nothing. Go back to sleep.'

'I haven't slept all night.'

'I'm going to take Viktor up to the cemetery,' I said. 'Bury those children. You can take care of the animals?'

'I can manage.'

'Take Petro and Lara with you.' They would make Natalia's job easier and it would mean they were out of the house. I wanted to show our guest some care and hospitality, but I didn't want to put my family at risk by leaving them alone with him.

Natalia pushed back the bedclothes and swung her legs out.

Beside her, Lara stirred. In the other bed, Viktor and Petro, men now, not boys, too big to have to sleep together. Perhaps, when times were better, they could have their own places.

I shook Viktor awake. 'Come on. I need your help.'

'Is he still alive?' Natalia asked.

'Still alive.' I nodded. 'Still asleep. He must be exhausted. I wonder how far he's come. What he's been through.'

'Or what he's *done*.'

'We'll wake him when I come back. Give him something hot to eat, find out who he is. Then we'll know what he's done.'

'Will we?'

I looked at my wife.

'If he's done something to those children, do you really think he's going to tell us?' she asked.

'We'll know if he's lying.'

'How? How will we know?'

'He'll be tired,' I said. 'Confused. Exhausted. He won't be able to think straight.'

'Then maybe we should talk to him *before* we feed him.'

'Could you do that? Just let him starve?'

Natalia came close. 'Yes. Maybe.' She shook her head. 'No. Oh, I don't know. I just want him gone. Out of this house. He's brought trouble with him; I can feel it in the air like I can feel it when winter's coming.'

'It'll be all right. *We'll* be all right.'

'Can you really say that?'

'Yes.'

'Really?'

I sighed and turned away from her, telling Viktor to meet me outside. I went to the front door, Natalia coming from the bedroom as I put on my coat.

'You should eat something before you go,' she said as I pulled on my boots. 'I'll make porridge.'

I shoved my foot hard into my boot and straightened up, putting a hand on my belly. 'I can't eat before this,' I said.

'You'll need your strength.'

'I'll regain it afterwards.'

'Please,' she said, unfastening my coat. 'It won't take a minute.'

I slumped my shoulders and thought about it before nodding.

'And Viktor will need something,' she went on. 'Think of your son if not of yourself.'

'OK,' I sighed. 'But not too much.'

I sat while she prepared something for us, Viktor and Petro coming out of the other room. Petro was carrying Lara, dressed but still sleepy.

'You said you'd wake us,' Petro said. 'You watched him yourself all night?'

'I slept a little.'

'So now what?'

'So now we see to one or two things. Viktor and me. Outside.'

'You want me to help?' Petro asked, putting his sister down and coming to sit in his usual place, opposite me.

'You can help your mother.'

Petro mumbled something under his breath.

'What did you say?'

He looked at me. 'I said "woman's work". You always give me the woman's work.'

'Woman's work? Looking after the animals isn't woman's work. Taking care of your family is not woman's work.'

'But you always take Viktor,' he said. 'You give Viktor the rifle when we hunt—'

'He's a better shot than you. We can't afford to waste ammunition.'

'And now you take Viktor with you when you could take me. Or both of us.'

I sat back and ran a hand across my beard. 'Trust me, son, you don't want to do this. That's why I'm taking Viktor.'

'I'm stronger than you think,' Petro said, looking at his brother.

'Maybe you should let him come.' Viktor shrugged. 'He's as strong as I am.'

I watched my sons sitting side by side at my table and

wondered how they had grown to be men without me noticing. I allowed myself a moment of pride, looking at my family. My strong wife, my two sons and my beautiful daughter. I was a lucky man to have come so far and still have so much. Behind me there was death and hardship, before me there was blood and horror, but here, now, I had everything a man could want.

I nodded. 'All right, Petro. We could use your help.'

There was still no sign of the sun when we went out into the cold. A greyish half-light had graced the air, but it was subdued by a mist that hung like a veil. We trudged around the house, disturbing a pair of magpies that flew up into the naked branches of an apple tree. The birds watched us from their perch, chattering their staccato cackle and dropping back to the ground as we passed.

'How d'you want to do this?' Viktor asked as we came round the old barn.

I unlocked the door and we went in, disturbing the animals, a chicken running for cover.

'What's under there?' Petro asked, nodding his head at the shape under the tarpaulin.

'Children,' I said.

'Children?'

I looked at Viktor. 'We'll take everything else off the sled.' I crouched to untie the ropes that held the tarpaulin in place. 'Then we'll take them to the cemetery and bury them.'

Viktor and Petro helped unload the man's belongings, piling them in one corner of the barn. It wasn't much to account for a man's life. A few odds and ends, items one might collect on a long search to survive. I imagined what it must have been like to pull that sled, with its ugly cargo, across the snow for so long that it had wasted a man to almost nothing. I asked myself what could drive a man to that kind of task, and I remembered what Natalia had said about the man's injury. A single shot that had pierced and exited his body. An expertly dressed wound. I'd seen evidence this man might have been a soldier, maybe even fighting the

Germans before we pulled away from the war, so perhaps he had learned to dress a wound. But I wondered who he'd been running from and who might be following him. It didn't occur to me that the stranger might not have been running from anything. Someone might have been running from *him*.

I watched Petro's eyes trying to look away from the small bodies, and was dismayed he'd been adamant about coming with us. He was strong, but he was more sensitive than his brother. Viktor had a harder heart, a stronger constitution. What Viktor saw, he took at face value, but his brother always looked deeper. Petro had his mother's understanding of the world, and a thing like this would haunt him. I could see the sadness and the revulsion in both their faces, but I knew it was Petro who would see this when he closed his eyes at night.

When everything was unloaded, we covered the children once more and Viktor and Petro took up the reins and dragged the sled outside.

I grabbed a couple of shovels and a pickaxe from the barn and jogged to catch up with them.

'Put them on the sled,' Viktor said, but I rested them against my shoulder like weapons and walked alongside my sons as we left the gates and headed out to the cemetery that lay behind the church.

I scanned the doors and windows as we passed among the houses, but I didn't notice anybody watching us. It wasn't that I wanted to keep secrets, but I didn't want the other villagers to worry. They didn't need to share this. Burying a child is hard, and they'd had their fair share of hardship.

The people of Vyriv had endured the shortages of the famine ten years ago. They had kept their heads low and survived on what little they could produce themselves, afraid they would be noticed in their small valley. They had been spared the cholera and the extreme starvation, but it had been no easy time for them and many had died. Natalia's parents had been among those who were too weak to survive the hardship. Her father collapsed in the field, at the handles of his plough. His heart failed and he fell into the freshly turned soil, dying on the land he had sown for most of his life. Natalia's mother saw him fall, but she was old and her painful joints made her slow. He was dead by the time she reached him, and his death weakened her will to go on.

Seeing the destruction caused by the famine, Lenin abolished grain requisitioning, allowed free trade and the country began to recover. Vyriv, like other villages in Ukraine, enjoyed a brief period of prosperity, and the culture was allowed to flourish for a short while. The Ukrainian language was freely spoken once more. But Lenin's successor was more ruthless and his demands were higher. Stalin was threatened by the prospect of an independent Ukraine. He wanted the country's food, its blood and its sweat, so he sent his soldiers to take it.

The arrival of the stranger in the village would put the people on edge. They would be full of fear, sense the advent of something terrible, and I wanted to keep this from them because I was afraid of what they might do. Especially if they saw what he had brought with him. I wanted to bury the children, put them to rest without them ever coming to the villagers' notice.

The church in front of the cemetery was small, nothing grand. A simple building of wood and stone, the walls painted white. There were no gold spires, no bright colours, not even a bell tower. Nor was there a priest to tend it; he had left more than a year ago when he heard about the fate of other priests. The state had tolerated the Church for a while, but now there was only the advance of Stalin's vision. Like the kulak, priests and poets were a threat to the common way of living so they were sought out and they were deported. Some were executed for their beliefs or for the words they put on paper and the thoughts they had in their heads. Churches were broken and torn down. Bells were cast down from their towers.

Our priest saw it coming and he ran. No one knew where he'd gone; all we knew was that one day he was simply not here. He told no one of his flight.

Since then we had kept the church clean and in as good order as we were able, but there are things that can change a man's faith, *mould* a man's faith, and there are other things that can't. For me, a building and an effigy were not enough to make up for all that had happened and was happening to this world, and that was even truer as I walked alongside a sled that carried the bodies of two small children. But I understood the value of ceremony for some people, and I knew the importance of life and of ritual.

We passed among the broken headstones, and found a spot at the far end of the cemetery, by a crumbling wall, where we could dig.

'One hole,' I said, using a shovel to move the snow. 'They can go in together.'

Viktor took the other shovel, helping to clear the snow, and when we had outlined a big enough plot, we took turns swinging the pick to break the ground, which was hard with cold. And when that was done, Petro shovelled out the dirt until the hole was deep enough.

As we worked, the mist dissolved around us and the sun struggled to the edge of the sky, occasionally breaking through the cloud to catch on the icicles that stretched down from the overhang of the wall. The graveyard was filled with a bleak beauty that was not lost on me.

It was hard working like that, and after a while we stopped to take off our coats, Viktor nudging me to attract my attention.

'What?' I asked, glancing up.

Viktor inclined his head in the direction we'd come from, and I looked across to see someone approaching.

'Dimitri,' I said under my breath. 'Shit.' I jabbed my shovel into the loosened soil and leaned a forearm on the end of its handle to watch him approach.

'What are you up to, Luka?' he said. 'I came over to do some repairs on the church and I spot you three skulking round the back. What are you doing?'

'Dimitri,' I replied and raised a hand to my head in mock salute.

'What are you up to?' He grinned as he spoke, but there was

no humour in him. He thought we were doing something he should know about and he was making it his business to find out.

Fate had related Dimitri Petrovich Spektor and me. We were family by marriage because our wives were sisters. My daughter Lara played with Dimitri's daughter, Dariya, because they were cousins and of a similar age, but Dimitri and I had never managed any bond of friendship. Dimitri made no attempt to conceal his dislike of me and his opinion that I sullied the family blood. I had lived in Vyriv for over six years, my wife and children were Ukrainian, and I had fought for the Ukrainian anarchists, yet Dimitri found it hard to see beyond the fact that I was Russian and had once been a soldier of the Red Army. To him, all Russians were thieves and drunkards, and his brash rudeness was always amplified when he addressed me. He used harsh tones and often spoke quickly, running his words together, making it more difficult for me to understand him. I spoke good Ukrainian, but it was not my first language.

Now I sighed and looked at Viktor before waving a hand at the sled. There was no point in trying to hide it from him. The man was like a ferret and would find out whether we wanted him to or not.

'What you got under there?' Dimitri asked, putting his hands on his hips and tilting his head. He wore an old cap, the kind his father used to wear but, like everything else, it was worn in patches, the material fraying.

'Maybe you'd better just take a look,' I said, thinking it was easier than trying to explain.

Dimitri nodded and stepped forward, reaching out to take hold of the tarpaulin. 'I'm not going to get a surprise, am I?'

'Probably,' I replied as Dimitri pulled back the cover to reveal the two bodies.

Dimitri dropped the corner of the tarpaulin and stepped away. 'Shit. Why didn't you just tell me? What kind of a trick is that?'

'No trick,' I said. 'It's what it is.'

Dimitri puffed his ruddy cheeks and breathed out hard. 'Who

39

are they? I've never seen them before. And what the hell happened to her feet?'

I shrugged.

'They were with that man you brought in yesterday?'

'Yes.'

Dimitri stood silent, shifting his eyes to the open grave. I knew what he was thinking. His brain would be churning under his cap and his thinning scalp, coming to all the wrong conclusions. I knew what Dimitri's words were going to be before they even tripped off his thick lips and puffed into the cold air around his red-veined cheeks.

'Did *he* kill them?'

'I don't know. I don't know what happened to them.'

'Nothing natural, that's for sure.' He stared at me. 'And you brought him here. Where is he now?'

'Safe.'

'Safe where?'

Dariya obviously hadn't told him what she'd seen the day before and it surprised me that she'd kept it to herself. It showed restraint I wouldn't have expected from her. 'In my house,' I said.

'In your *house*?'

'Yes. He's very sick. Unconscious.'

'And if he wakes up? What's he going to do? Murder all our children? Put his hands on my little Dariya? She is forbidden from coming to your house again. What kind of idiot are you?'

Viktor stepped forward but I put out a hand to stop him. 'Nobody said anything about murder. We don't know what happened to these children. All we can do is bury them and wait for the man to speak for himself.'

'He must've done something to her. Look at her feet for God's sake.'

'Perhaps she fell,' I said.

'Fell?' Dimitri's face was gaining heat, the veins becoming more prominent as his mood heightened and his words tripped over one another. 'What about the boy, then? Did he fall too?' His whole body shook with emotion. 'And you took him into your house.' He looked down at the grave again, his eyes lighting up. 'I'll have to tell the others.'

'No, Dimitri. Let me tell them. As soon as we're done here, I'll tell the others. They don't need to see this. Let me give these children some dignity.'

'Wait right here,' he said, turning around and hurrying away. 'Don't do anything. The others need to see this *now*.'

'That went well,' said Petro when we were alone again.

'Of all the people . . .' I pinched the bridge of my nose. 'It had to be him.'

Viktor put his hands in the small of his spine, leaning back. 'What now?'

'Bury them?' Petro asked.

'No, we should wait,' I said, whipping the tarpaulin back over the children. 'What else can we do?'

Viktor and I were sitting on a broken piece of the wall, Petro standing, when Dimitri returned with some of the other men. We saw them coming around the side of the church and making their way through the grave markers.

We had put our coats back on now we were still, but the day was growing to be a good one. The sun had risen in Dimitri's absence and burned away the low-hanging cloud, to give us a light blue sky that was as clear as any I had seen. The brightness was reflected from the snow and the gravestones glistened with encrusted ice which had begun to thaw at its outer edges. I could even hear a gentle drip from the branches of the trees.

I squinted as I watched the men approach.

'There,' Dimitri pointed when he reached us. 'Under there.'

We greeted each other with short nods and grim faces.

'What's going on, Luka?' Ivan Sergeyevich stepped forward, holding out a hand for me to shake.

Ivan Sergeyevich Antoniv was well into his sixties, but he was strong and healthy. I knew him as a man who believed in fairness. We had spoken many times about the revolution and what we had expected of it, and I knew our views were similar. Both of us were disillusioned by what we had thought would be a better way for us all. He was a sensible man, and I knew he would see this the right way, so I shook his hand with some relief.

'Why didn't we know about this last night?' Ivan said, and I remembered he'd been one of the men in the square when we had returned from the hillside. 'Viktor told us you'd found a man. There was nothing about bodies. Nothing about children.' He put a pipe to his mouth, clamping it between yellowed teeth and sucking hard.

Behind him, Dimitri shuffled, glancing at the other two men he'd brought with him. Josif Abramovich Fomenko and Leonid Andreyevich Tatlin. All of them men who had grown together and survived together. I was an outsider here, but they were men I respected. Men who worked hard and took care of their families. And they didn't look at me the way Dimitri did. They didn't see my history the way Dimitri saw it.

'I thought it would scare people,' I said, looking at Dimitri.

'They're already scared.' Ivan let the smoke fall from his mouth rather than blowing it away. It shrouded him, hanging in the air. 'Someone said OGPU—'

'Who said that?' I asked. 'Why would they say that?'

'I doesn't matter,' Ivan told me. 'You know how rumours start. What matters is now people think he's either running from them or that he's one of them. And whichever way they look at it, they think activists are coming to murder their husbands or take their wives and children from them.'

'I didn't want people to think the wrong thing.'

'They already do.'

'Maybe we should have a look,' Josif said. 'Would you mind?'

Josif Abramovich had been the first man to come to our door when I arrived in Vyriv after the war. He had welcomed me before any other, bringing bread and Ukrainian vodka – *horilka*. Natalia had laid the *rushnyk* on the table and we'd drunk the whole bottle together. Josif drank himself into a good mood and told me he had been disheartened when Natalia's parents died, but was glad for her and our children now our family was together again.

'It's not a good thing to see,' I told him. 'Are you sure you want to look?'

'I've seen bad things before.'

'Maybe not like this.'

'You'd be surprised.'

'All right.' I nodded to Viktor and my son pulled back the tarpaulin to expose the bodies once more.

Josif studied them for a few moments, his breath audible as he crunched around the sled, his boots crushing the snow. He beckoned the other two men, who came over and looked. They seemed immune to the death right before them. As if they saw not the bodies of children, but an object to confirm or otherwise the theory of an irate man.

Ivan and Leonid shook their heads almost in unison.

'You see?' Dimitri said. 'The man's a killer.'

'Or perhaps it was the cold?' Josif suggested.

Ivan looked closer. 'These marks here.' He pointed close to the girl's face. 'You see these around her nose and mouth? Maybe she was suffocated.'

'What does it matter how he did it?' Dimitri said. 'The man's a killer.'

'We don't know that,' I said. 'Not for sure.'

'We should do something about it,' Dimitri went on.

'Like what?' I asked. 'Think about what you're saying, Dimitri.'

'I *am* thinking.' He looked round at each of us. 'I'm the *only* one thinking. That man is too much of a risk to our own children.'

'He's dying,' I said. 'He's not a risk to anyone.'

'Then let him die,' Dimitri said.

'What?'

'Let him die. Leave him out in the cold and let him die.'

'Hold your tongue, Dimitri Petrovich,' Josif snapped at him. 'And calm yourself.' He put a hand on my arm and took me to one side, walking away from the others, speaking quietly so they wouldn't hear.

'What are you hiding?' he asked as we walked.

'Hm?'

'Come on, Luka. We've known each other long enough to be honest with one another. You may think you're a closed book, but some of us have learned to read you better than you think. There's something you're not telling me.'

We stopped at the place where the wall formed a corner. There was a large oak there, its roots bulging beneath the bricks, pushing them up and out.

'You have always been honest with me,' Josif said. 'Please don't stop now.'

'There's a wound on the girl's leg,' I sighed. 'I didn't want anybody to see it.'

'Why?'

'Because it looks like she's been cut and I thought people would react exactly the way Dimitri is reacting now. They'd want to murder the man before they even knew what's happened. People are scared, they're afraid of outsiders.'

'With good reason.'

'The man in my house is a soldier, Josif. The things he has with him tell me that. And I mean an imperial soldier, not a communist soldier. I don't think he means any harm.'

Josif stared at me, his eyes dark beneath the brim of his fur hat, and I knew what he was thinking. To Josif there was no difference. The tsarists or the communists – they had all tried to crush him and his kind. The pogroms against the Jews were no different from the drive to wipe out the kulaks.

'He could have stolen them,' Josif said.

'Maybe. But . . . I don't know; I have a feeling. He's a veteran, I'm sure of it. A brother.'

'A brother? And what if you're wrong? What if he's red and a whole unit follows behind him?'

'That's not very likely, Josif, and you know it. That man was alone.'

44

'Did he say anything?'

'He said, "Thank God." '

'That's all?'

'That's all. Look, this is why I wanted to keep it quiet. To avoid people like Dimitri getting riled up and doing something stupid.'

'Dimitri's an idiot,' Josif said. 'But you could have come to me.'

'What for? What would that have done? I thought it best to cover her up and bury them.'

'And leave us not knowing? You're not our protector, Luka.' Josif looked me in the eye. 'Perhaps we should see the child for ourselves.'

'Can't you just take my word for it? She has a wound on her leg, right down to the bone. It looks as if she's been carved.'

'Carved?'

'As if she were an animal. It looks as if someone has taken some of her flesh.'

Josif made a fist and put it to his mouth. He tapped it against his chin as he thought, then he nodded. 'Perhaps you're right, my friend. I have no desire to see the child's mutilation, and Dimitri doesn't need to see any more than he already has. As you say, we don't want to get people excited. They're frightened enough already. I—'

But he stopped when we sensed movement and heard Viktor's protest. Josif and I both turned together to see what was happening over by the sled, and we could only stare at what we saw.

Dimitri was standing back, knife in one hand, the other held to his mouth in horror. The girl's trouser leg was cut from cuff to waistband.

The sun was weak, but it gave enough warmth to melt the crust of the snow and the smallest icicles just as it could thaw blood. And so it had done. The blood at the outer edges of the girl's wound had softened as we talked and, once liquid again, had soaked into the trousers and blossomed in a butterfly pattern across the well-worn material.

Josif and I had been too busy to see it, but Dimitri had spotted it, watched its ethereal resurrection blooming on the material. He had pushed Viktor aside to put his blade into the cuff and split the trousers lengthways, and now he gaped, looking around at the others until his eyes settled on me and narrowed.

'You,' he said. '*You.*' The accusation was thick in that single word. 'You brought this man into our lives. And you give him shelter in your home. This man who does . . . *this* . . . to children.' Dimitri shook his head. 'You have children of your own.'

'It doesn't change anything. We don't know he did this,' I said, beginning to doubt my reasons for protecting the man lying by the fire in my home. I wanted to do what was right, but perhaps Dimitri spoke the truth. Perhaps I was a fool.

'Of course he did this,' Dimitri said, spitting on the ground. 'Who else? *You?*'

'That's enough.' Josif pointed at Dimitri. 'That's enough from you. I don't want to hear any more.'

'So he told you?' Dimitri asked. 'He told you about this, did he?'

'Not until just now.'

'Then he kept it from us all.'

I glanced at Viktor standing silent by the sled. He was watching Dimitri, and I could see the distaste on his face. His hands were clenching and unclenching, fists that turned his knuckles white. Dimitri had pushed past him, forced him aside to get to the girl, and it had angered him. He didn't like to be beaten in anything, and he didn't like to be treated as an inferior. Viktor was seventeen and considered himself to be a man. He expected Dimitri to treat him with the same respect he would have given to any of the others, but instead he had pushed him aside as if he were a child.

Petro, on the other hand, had taken a step back. He had removed himself from the potential flashpoint and was watching as if he were a spectator at this event.

'Why would he do that?' Dimitri went on, directing his words at Josif and the others, then turning on me once again. 'Why keep it hidden, Luka?'

'So people like you wouldn't get so excited,' Josif told him.

'I'm not excited, I'm angry. Angry that he brought a killer into our village. A man who kills children and eats their flesh.'

'No one brought a killer anywhere,' Josif said. 'Luka did the right thing.'

I looked at Josif, glad to hear him coming to my defence.

'I agree.' Leonid Andreyevich stepped forward, shaking his head. 'Something like this could cause a lot of trouble.'

'You're right about that,' Dimitri said. 'That's why we need to get rid of him.'

'No,' Leonid said. 'That's not what I meant. I meant we should keep this to ourselves.' Leonid was a taciturn man who might have seemed timid to an outsider, but he was a man who listened and spoke only when necessary. He was younger than Ivan and Josif and, like me, he had fought in and survived the civil war. But, unlike me, he was a native of Vyriv, and that, coupled with his reputation, earned him the respect of the others in the village.

He spoke quietly now, his eyes averted from what was on the sled. 'Bury these poor children and be done with it.'

'Be done with it?' Dimitri raised his voice. 'What the hell does that mean? What about the man in Luka's house? What about *him*?'

'We watch him,' Leonid said. 'As soon as he's well enough, we talk to him. Find out what happened.'

'He'll deny it.'

'Of course he will,' Josif said. 'But we'll have to decide for ourselves if he's lying.'

'A trial?' Ivan was using the heel of his palm to bang the used tobacco from his pipe. 'Interesting. Like one of the communist *troikas*?'

'Something like that,' Josif said. 'But fairer. We have to give him a chance. We don't know anything about him.' He turned to look at me. 'He had belongings? Something that might tell us who he was?'

'Or maybe we should just let him go when he's well enough. Make him leave,' Leonid offered.

'So he can kill again?' Dimitri said, looking around at us. 'What are you talking about? Have you lost your minds? This man kills children and you're talking about making him better and setting him free.'

'What would you do?' I asked.

'I'd string him up.'

'I bet you would,' I said.

'Damn right.'

'I vote we keep it to ourselves for now.' Ivan held up his hand, the stem of his pipe pointing to the sky. 'Bury them and don't speak of it until we've decided what's for the best.'

I put up my hand in agreement. Leonid and Josif did the same.

'This is bullshit.' Dimitri spat his words. 'Bullshit.'

Now they all looked to Viktor and Petro.

'Since when do they get a vote?' Dimitri asked.

'They're men now,' Ivan answered. 'And they're here. That gives them a vote.'

'Men?' Dimitri scoffed. 'Boys who are seventeen. One of them a brute like his father, and the other . . . I don't even know what the other is.'

Petro raised his hand. Viktor looked at me.

'Don't look at him,' Josif said. 'This is your decision now.'

But Viktor wasn't asking for my direction regarding the vote. He wanted to punish Dimitri for his actions and his words, and he wanted me to sanction it, but the look in my eyes told him this was not the place for it.

Viktor nodded and slowly raised his hand.

'Then it's settled,' Ivan said.

'It's bullshit, that's what it is.' Dimitri turned to walk away. 'There's nothing settled here at all.'

I took the back of Dimitri's coat in my fist and stopped him. 'Where are you going?'

'Home,' he said, looking me in the eye, pushing my hand away. For a moment we stood close, faces level, searching one another's thoughts. I could feel Dimitri's breath on my skin, see the air whiten and cloud between us, sense the heightened tension in my brother-in-law.

'What are you going to do?' Dimitri said. 'Hit me?'

I considered it. I thought about doing what Viktor had wanted to do, and I fought the urge to ball my fist and slam it into Dimitri's nose. Instead, I held up my hands. 'Go home, Dimitri. Go home and annoy your poor wife.'

The six of us watched him leave, and then finished burying the children.

6

We walked in silence, coming back from the cemetery. The crunching of our boots in the snow, and our heavy breathing, and the cackle of the magpies. Leaving the church behind, though, I could hear raised voices from the heart of the village, and I shared glances with the others as we quickened our pace.

We all suspected. We all *knew*. As soon as we heard the commotion, we knew what it was, and when we came within sight of the centre of the community, we saw it for ourselves.

There was a group of people there, close to the oak that stood within its low circular wall. A dense nucleus of fifteen or twenty people, with as many again standing around the edges, undecided if they were a part of what was happening or if they were just spectators. Those in the centre were nodding their heads, gesticulating, raising their hands in the air. They were shouting agreement, being whipped up by the man at the centre of it. Dimitri.

'What the hell does he think he's doing?' I said to no one in particular, catching sight of Natalia coming in our direction. She was without her coat, as if she'd come in a hurry.

'He's been knocking on doors,' she said. 'Shouting and ranting about our children not being safe. Is it true? Are they not safe?'

I stopped to speak with her, Viktor and Petro staying with me. The other men went to where the villagers were standing.

'Where's Lara?' I asked.

'She went out after she helped me with the chickens. Said she was going to play with Dariya.'

'Dimitri's forbidden her from coming to our house.'

'That's what Dariya said. But she told me that if they play outside, they won't *be* in our house. And who am I to argue with such a sly girl?'

'You don't know where they are now?'

'In the field, rolling snowballs. Are they in danger?'

'No. She's probably better off not being here.'

'You're sure?'

'Not really.'

'What's going on?' she asked. 'Has something happened?'

I could see the crowd was growing as more people joined Dimitri, arms raised, voices raised, tensions raised.

'Petro,' I said, 'go find your sister.'

'Why me? Why not send Viktor?'

'Because I might need Viktor here. Find your sister and bring her home. Keep her inside.'

'Papa—'

'Don't argue with me, Petro Lukovich.'

Petro shook his head and stayed where he was, deciding whether or not to defy my wishes. But the hesitation was short and he rolled his eyes, moving away. I watched him go, disappearing around the rear of our home, before I looked back at the crowd.

'Has something happened?' Natalia asked again. 'Why is he saying our children aren't safe?'

'Because he's an idiot,' I said. 'Nothing has happened.'

Dimitri was drawing more people in now, addressing those who had gathered round him, telling them they were unsafe, that a child-killer had come among them. Ivan, who had been at the burial, had gone to intervene, but he was not a strong man and he pleaded quietly, his voice lost in the growing cacophony. He was respected, but he had no voice in this confusion. He had no control over a mob like this. Josif and Leonid too tried to reason with the people, but when Dimitri pointed towards me, raising his voice, directing the stares of the other villagers, I could see how this was going to turn out.

'Natalia, you need to go inside.' I stepped back and took her arm, drawing her with me through the gate, pushing open the front door with my foot. 'Into the back.'

Viktor followed us inside and shut the door. Together we pushed the bolts across and closed the wooden shutters over the windows.

'Papa? What's going on?'

I went straight to the shelf and took up the revolver Natalia had found among the stranger's belongings. 'Here.' I pressed it into Viktor's hands before grabbing the pistol that had been on the sled, dropping the wooden holster onto the table.

'Papa?'

'Viktor, I've seen crowds before. I've seen what they can do.'

He held up the revolver. 'I don't even know what to do with this.'

'You won't need to. As long as they see it, it should be enough.'

Viktor nodded, a grim expression on his face. He was scared but he knew how to push it down inside him and hide it. His mother though, Natalia, I could hear her breathing. Heavy. Panic was tight in her throat. 'What's happening?' she asked, the words constricted.

I pulled her close and told her it would be all right. 'Go into the back room. Stay there.'

Outside there was shouting. It might have been Dimitri but it was hard to tell. There were other voices too. A sea of voices that grew with tension. More and more of them, building, the crowd becoming a mob of fearful peasants who needed something to strike at.

'Listen to them,' Natalia said. 'What are they going to do?' She looked down at the bundle lying by the hearth, where the flames had weakened. The man was still asleep, oblivious to the trouble he had caused.

'Nothing,' I told her. 'They're not going to do anything. Please – go into the back room.'

She looked up at me, a kind of understanding dawning on her, and I knew what she was thinking.

'Lara,' she said. 'Lara and Petro.'

'They'll be fine,' I reassured her. 'I haven't forgotten them. Petro will see what's happening; he'll keep her away.'

'No, we have to find them. Make them safe.'

I saw the fear in her eyes. We lived in fear. Always there was fear, but never had it been so close to the surface. Never had it been so threatening. I looked at the man on the floor, then at my son, the revolver in his hand.

'I'll find them,' said Viktor, but even as he spoke, the sound of the mob outside increased. There was shouting, the heavy fall of many footsteps, then the front door rattled in its frame and the crowd bayed before their noise abated and fell into a lull.

'Bring him out, Luka.' It was as if Dimitri was alone outside our door.

Natalia gripped me closer.

Again, banging.

'Luka! Bring him out.'

I could feel Natalia tremble. She looked up at me and whispered. 'Let them have him, Luka. For God's sake—'

'We don't know he's done anything wrong.'

'We don't know he *hasn't*. I'm scared, Luka. Let them have him.'

'He can't even protect himself.'

'Luka!' Dimitri again. 'Open the door or we'll come in and take him.'

'You'll break down my door, Dimitri?'

'If we have to.'

'*Natalia's* front door?'

'We'll do what we have to. She's not safe with him in there.' His reply was spoken with determination and followed by a murmur of consensus as the crowd grew restless.

'Please,' Natalia begged me. 'Just—'

'I'll speak to them,' I said, breaking away from her. 'I'll make this right. Don't worry.'

'Luka . . .'

I ignored her and glanced at my son, nodding at the revolver in his hand, then I took a step towards the door and drew back the heavy bolts.

Dimitri was standing with his chest out and his fists on his hips. Behind him there were at least thirty men and women with red faces and fearful eyes.

'Go back to your homes,' I said, scanning the crowd, trying to look each of them in the eye. 'Go home and think about what you're doing. I understand your concerns. I *know* your concerns, but I don't share your wishes. Please. Don't bring shame on us. Don't bring shame on your children.'

'Children.' Dimitri seized the word from the air as if it were a solid entity. He snatched it with his fist and he threw it back at my face. 'Children. That's who we're trying to protect.'

'Bring him out,' someone said.

'So you can kill him?'

'So we can judge him.'

'And who will be the judge? You?' I looked at the crowd, singling someone out with a pointed finger. 'You?' I pointed at another. 'All of you?'

No one spoke.

'You think you can know what this man is? What he's done? You think you can know him without even speaking to him?'

'Then let him speak,' someone called out.

'He can't,' I said. 'He can hardly even breathe.'

'Bring him out!' Another shout, this time louder, joined by others as the people began to work themselves up again.

Dimitri had told them what he'd seen. He'd told them about the bodies and the butchery. They were old enough to remember the pain of ten years ago, the terrible hunger. They knew how it could turn men into monsters, and they knew what Dimitri had seen on that child's leg. By telling them, and stirring them to his own cause, he had infected them with his own brand of anxiety and bigotry. It settled deep in them, pricked at the fear they all

54

kept buried just beneath the surface. And now they had found something to strike at, someone to punish for their situation. A way to release their demons into the open.

'You tried to keep it from us,' someone called out. 'Keep a child-murderer hidden. A monster.'

'No.'

'And then the police will come,' a voice called. 'So they can take *all* our children.'

'And our wives.'

Another uproar from the people. Another mess of voices and shouting, and then a tentative surge, not actually moving forward but a testing of the water, as if the crowd had, as one, decided to try my resolve.

Dimitri was pushed forward by the swell so that he fell against me. I stopped him with one hand, pushing him back and raising the pistol into the air. I fired a single shot – a sharp, clean crack in the morning air – and the people fell silent once more.

When the sound of the gunshot had settled I spoke again.

'Go home. All of you.'

And now there was a different kind of movement among the people standing at my front door. A softer movement as someone pushed through them to come and stand beside me.

Josif nodded once at me and turned to look at the others. 'Luka's right. We have to stop this before it goes too far. We don't know anything about this man—'

'Then why do we keep him among us?' Dimitri said.

'We need to calm down.' Josif held up his hands.

'You wanted to keep this from us too, Josif. You, Leonid, Ivan. All of you respected here, trusted, and yet you wanted to keep it a secret. Those children out there in the cemetery were murdered by that man. Is that what you want for our children? To be butchered and eaten?'

'We don't know that for—'

'I saw what I saw, Josif. That man is a murderer.' Dimitri turned to the crowd again and they responded by raising their hands into the air. 'Bring him out!' he shouted, and the villagers began to chant those words: 'Bring him out! Bring him out!'

Then a snowball came from somewhere within the crowd. A hard ball of ice and snow crushed into a vicious projectile. It struck Josif and he bent at the waist, putting his hands to his face. When he stood straight again, there was blood running from his nose.

He held up his gloved hands to show the people what they'd done. He shook his head at them. 'Is this what you want?' he shouted over their chanting. 'Blood?'

'Yes,' someone yelled back. 'Blood.' It wasn't the answer he had expected. Josif had wanted to shame them, but the people had moved beyond that emotion. They were angry and they were becoming frenzied. There was an approaching wickedness that threatened to harm all of them, and this was the only thing they had to aim their anger at. They had found something upon which to focus all their dark emotions, and their collective mood was moving them to act without reasoned thought. If there was to be any chance of stopping them, I knew I had to break them apart, restore their individuality if they were to see sense.

I fired a second shot and pointed my pistol at the crowd. 'Move away. Now. I want you all to leave my home.'

'You're going to shoot us?' Dimitri asked.

'I've shot many men. You'd be no different.'

'And women? You've shot women too, Luka?'

I didn't reply.

'And you'd shoot *us*?' Dimitri looked behind him. 'Your friends and neighbours? To save a man you don't even know?' Now he showed me the defiant expression of a victor and he pointed to the corner of the house. 'In front of your own daughter?'

Petro was standing far back from the crowd, with his arm around Lara, pulling her close as if for protection. She in turn had squeezed herself into the folds of his coat as her older brother watched with interest. I held a hand out to them, indicating they should remain where they were.

'What about you, Dimitri?' I turned my attention back to my

56

brother-in-law. 'You want to drag that man out into a mob? In front of your wife? What does Svetlana think of this?'

'She wants to protect the children as much as I do.'

'Then where is she now?'

'Where she should be. With our daughter.'

I shook my head. 'Don't do this, Dimitri. Please. Don't do this. We're still human.'

Dimitri stepped forward so the barrel of the pistol was against his chest, but it wasn't the act of a brave man. It was the act of a coward who knew he'd won. I had shot men in this way before – pressed the barrel of a gun against the cloth of their coat and fired right through them – felt their bodies become heavy and watched them fall aside. But Dimitri knew I wouldn't shoot him in front of my wife and daughter. There was nothing more I could do to save the man in my home.

I lowered the pistol, putting my free hand against Dimitri's chest. 'Don't do this.' But I knew I'd lost my ability to control this situation. Dimitri had weakened me and now he looked down at my hand, shoved it aside and pushed past me. Others followed him, the chanting beginning again as Natalia's own kin poured in to defile our home.

'Put it down, Viktor,' I heard Dimitri say, and I nodded to my son, who was standing beside Natalia, the revolver held out in front of him. Viktor lowered it and moved to protect his mother.

I continued to protest as the villagers lifted the stranger from his resting place. I appealed to each of them, pulling them back, trying to make them see what they were doing. It was as if I were trying to wake them from a trance, and they neither saw nor heard me, and I knew I was beaten even as I went on pleading with them.

They put their hands under the stranger's arms and they pulled him up, his head lolling to the side. People crowded in to touch him, to carry him, to be a part of what was happening. The blankets that fell from his body were cast aside and they saw his nakedness. His bloated belly. Skin tight around his ribs, clinging to the bones. His legs so thin, his arms without any fat on them.

Seeing him like that, I knew the man was close to death. Perhaps, with food and rest and warmth, he might survive, but otherwise he was already almost gone.

'What are you going to do?' I asked as they set upon the stranger.

'What needs to be done.' Dimitri gestured to those who were holding the emaciated man and they dragged him to the door, his feet trailing the floor. The man made no effort to help himself. He didn't even make a sound.

'We should help him,' I said. 'Look at him. This man needs our help.'

'We don't help child-murderers,' Dimitri answered before turning to follow the others out of my home. 'Not in Vyriv.'

'Stop this.' Josif remained by the front door as the men dragged the outsider into the snow. 'Please. Stop this now.' His nose was still bleeding, the blood running across his lips and down his chin, following the line of his neck. 'Stop.'

But their furore was high. There was no stopping them now.

I hurried out and beckoned to Petro and Lara, telling them to come inside at once. Lara went straight to her mother. Her eyes were wide with confusion and fear. Tears welled and fell across her cheeks. She held her mother tight, wrapping her arms around her waist and burying her face in her stomach.

'We have to stop them,' Josif said, standing in the doorway. 'Luka?'

'What can we do?' I said. 'You saw them.'

'There must be something.'

'Would you have me shoot them?'

'No.'

'Then what else? You're the man of words, Josif. What else can we do? You heard me try to reason with them, but a crowd like that? That feeling? It's powerful.'

The crowd had passed through our gate and was now at the centre of the village, beneath the old tree.

The man was in a bundle on the ground and I knew he wouldn't last long. He might even be dead already.

They were shouting at him, spitting on him. These were people I had known since the end of the civil war but now I hardly recognised them. They were no longer men and women; they were a pack of wild beasts, savage and raw.

I pushed the door shut behind me, to spare my daughter the sound and sight of people beyond their own control. Even Dimitri was holding up his hands now, trying to bring them to order, but he had stirred a beast. He had awakened the animal that slept in these people and there was no soothing it now.

When the first kick landed on the stranger's bony ribs, a cheer went up. Another kick, another cheer. Then feet came in from all angles, prodding at him, striking him. People who had never harmed a person in their lives were aiming tentative blows, becoming more confident, more intoxicated by the crowd.

And I watched from my doorstep.

I watched as a rope was thrown over one of the tree's strongest boughs. Thick and rough and black. The living wood dusted white and crystal on its leeward side. I watched as it was tied off and a crude noose was formed. And I watched as the starving man's head was slipped through the thick rope and he was hoisted into the air. His body didn't resist. His untied arms didn't struggle. His legs didn't kick. He simply rose into the air like a bag of grain and he swung, his body rotating slowly on the rope as the last of his life escaped into the cold air.

A naked man hanging from a naked tree.

7

With death came a stiff silence. Their mania was now in a trough; their madness fallen into a hush of contemplation and realisation. It was done. The intoxication had passed and reality had slipped back into their world.

They stood and watched as if they were one. Heads inclined upwards to gape at what they had done, breath tangible in the air around them. They huddled close to one another, feeling the weight of their actions, before their humanity returned to them, wanting to distance them from this and from each other. The first of them to step back was a woman at the edge, Akalena Vernadsky. She crossed herself and turned to walk along the road from the place where she had sung traditional songs last summer. She looked at the ground and trudged the frozen mud.

Then others began to peel away from the pack. Like a serpent shedding its skin, the layers stripped back as the villagers woke from their trance and edged away in silence.

They left their agitator until only Dimitri was left before the tree, looking up at the naked body twisting on the rope. A gentle rotation. The man's head tipped to one side, his eyes bulging, revolving until his back was visible, his narrow torso, the spine clear under thin skin, his emaciated buttocks, the red marks where he'd been kicked. Then he swung round to show his face again, the ragged beard covering most of his neck and face. More marks on his chest and legs. His genitals exposed. No dignity. No mercy. No pity.

I left Josif to wonder at what his people had done and I stepped away from the door. There was no sound but for the breeze that brushed the surface of the snow and skimmed the gentle valley. The sun still shone low in the sky, a faded orange arc made ill defined by a thin layer of cloud. The world was still a beautiful crisp blue and white. My boots made hardly a sound as I stepped in the prints of those who had come to my door that morning. I walked in their footsteps without being one of them, and I went to the place where they had brought dishonour and humiliation upon themselves.

At Dimitri's side I looked up at the hanged man, at peace on the end of a rope. I considered cutting him down, taking him to the cemetery and putting him in the ground – the stranger deserved some dignity at least – but I chose not to. The man's body had another purpose now: to act as a reminder to the people who had done this. I knew as well as anyone that people are capable of terrible things but must recognise the things they have done. Without that recognition, they are nothing more than animals, empty of any feeling.

'Shame on you,' I said. My voice was hoarse and my words were quiet. 'Shame on you, Dimitri Spektor. Shame on your family. Shame on this whole damn village.'

Dimitri continued to stare up at the hanged man.

'Is this what you wanted?' I asked him. 'Is it?'

Dimitri opened his mouth, but whatever words he intended to say were caught in his throat. They stuck there and refused to come out.

'Does this make our children safe?' I asked him.

He stared as if no thought could pass through his mind, then he blinked, shook himself and refocused. 'I didn't do this.'

'You were part of it. You led it. You *caused* it.'

'Don't be so damn self-righteous. I didn't want this. I—'

'What *did* you want? What did you *think* was going to happen? You knew what you were doing, Dimitri; don't pretend this was an accident.'

He swallowed hard. 'What now?'

'Now? Now you have to live with it.'

I left Dimitri standing alone and went back to my family. Viktor and Petro were at the window, their faces at the glass as I approached.

When I went into the house, Viktor was still holding the revolver. Lara was clinging to Natalia.

'What the hell is happening to them?' I said.

'People are afraid of what's coming,' she told me. 'And who can blame them?'

'It's no excuse.'

Natalia looked down at our daughter, but Lara showed no sign of understanding.

'Close the shutters,' I told my sons. 'I don't want Lara to see what Uncle Dimitri has done.'

'But . . . all those people,' Petro said. 'How could they do that?' He was even paler than usual. His brow creased so tight in bewilderment that the bridge of his nose wrinkled. He looked as if he'd woken in the night and forgotten where he was.

'I don't want to talk about it,' I said.

'To do that to another man. They just—'

'Not now.'

'But, Papa . . .'

'I said I don't want to talk about it.'

'Shouldn't we cut him down or something?'

'Petro!' I turned on him. 'I don't want to hear about it.'

'He's only asking,' Natalia said. 'He's—'

I slammed my fist hard on the table and raised my voice so it filled the small room. 'Don't talk about it. I don't want to hear it. Don't talk about it any more.'

Natalia pulled Lara closer, placing her arms so they covered the child's ears.

'Please.' I lowered my voice. 'I don't want to talk about it.' I held up a hand and bowed my head. I closed my eyes and took a deep breath. When I looked back at my wife, I nodded an apology before glancing at my children, each in turn. Then I went to the door. I hesitated, took hold of the old iron handle and pulled it open.

I stepped out into the cold and glanced at the hanged man as I yanked the door shut. I let my gaze linger on the body for a moment, then I turned and headed round the back of the house.

Entering the barn, the chickens complained at my intrusion but soon settled. The ones which had ventured out from the coop scurried back inside to the warmth.

I went to the pile of belongings from the man's sled and took up a milking stool to sit down before them. A small collection of essentials and a few items that meant nothing.

The fact that he had the weapons though told me something important. There had been so much gun registration and con-fiscation – the last being just a year ago – that few farmers were armed. Unauthorised possession of a gun was punishable by hard labour. It was a way of pulling the peasants' teeth – take away his weapons and you remove his ability to fight. It made life easier for the authorities when they came to enforce collectivisation if the farmers had no means of striking back. But this man, like me, had kept his weapons, and that confirmed my belief that he was a soldier. Because whichever army the man had fought for, our recent history was so filled with war and violence that no man who had ever been a soldier would willingly give up his arms.

Searching the rest of his belongings, I felt even more kinship with this unknown man. An aluminium water bottle, heavy and hard with its frozen contents. It was the same as the one I owned, issued to those of us who fought in the Imperial Army. A trenching shovel still in its leather sheath. Just like the one I owned. A black spike bayonet. And a leather satchel almost identical to the one I used to carry ammunition for my own rifles. There were other things too, essentials for a man who intended to live away from civilisation, but it was the satchel which took my eye.

I leaned down and lifted it to my knees, where I let it rest for a moment, feeling the cold of it against my legs. Putting my hands on top of it and turning my face to the ceiling of the barn, I paused to give a thought for the dead man, then I nodded to myself and opened the satchel.

Inside there was a handful of ammunition for the weapons he'd been carrying, the brass casings loose in the bag. There was a flat tin bound with a black and orange striped ribbon. When I turned the tin in my hands, I saw that in the place where the ribbon was knotted, a medal hung from the material. I had never seen one like it, but I knew what it was and what it meant. If the man with the sled was the owner of this medal – if he had *earned* it – then this man had not been my brother. He had not been my kin. He would most probably have been an officer.

I had fought on the front with many different officers during the Great War before the revolution. Men who'd been bred for self-sacrifice and honour. Men who'd had those things so thoroughly ingrained in their personalities they were unable to turn and walk away when they saw death coming for them. I had stood in bloody water up to my knees with them, lain in the mud among the bodies of my comrades, thrown myself at enemy lines for them. They were men who became outraged at the growth of battlefield committees and were confused by soldiers who refused to fight without committee agreement. The words and status of the officers was useless against the growing feelings of inequality among their men, and many of them were lynched by revolutionary squads refusing to fight.

I had been a supporter of the changes and I had embraced the revolution when it came. I had even seen the failings of the officers who drove us into a futile war, but I had never condoned their slaughter at the hands of revolutionaries, and I still maintained my respect for any man who was prepared to fight for his beliefs. A hundred men like Dimitri turning on officers who gave their lives to their country and had earned the honour of dying in battle was not my view of justice. I felt both anger and sadness conflict in me when I thought this stranger in our village had come away from that nightmare, survived the sweep of the revolution and the civil war that followed only to be hanged by Dimitri and his cruel pack. I wondered if I had tried hard enough to stop them; if there was anything else I could have done to stop Dimitri.

Outside, I went back round the barn, dragging the sled upon which the children had been lying. The old black oak came into view, its naked arms reaching for the heavens, presenting its grotesque decoration still twisting and swaying. I had left him there to shame the people who had done this, I didn't want to spare them their guilt, but now I knew I had to take him down. Such indignity was no end for a man who had once fought for his country. And whether he'd been tsarist or communist or anarchist it made no difference. They were just names that meant nothing.

Natalia was sitting at the table with the children when I pushed open the door. They all looked up at me, but I barely acknowledged them. I put down the items I'd brought from the barn, laid them with the man's rifle, then collected one of the blankets Natalia had used to cover him. There was a fresh fire in the hearth now, the flames just beginning to pick up, and the blanket was tinged with its warmth.

Natalia watched me, unspeaking, but when I went back to the door, she stood. 'Where are you going?'

I stopped with my fingers on the handle and spoke without turning round. 'To cut him down.'

'And then what?'

'I'm going to bury him.'

'The blanket . . .'

'We can spare it.'

A chair scraped the floor behind me. 'I'll come with you,' Petro said.

'No. Viktor can help.'

'*I* can do it, Papa.'

'I said, Viktor can help.' I pulled open the door.

I took the sled to the centre of the village, where the tree stood unmoved by the death in its fingers. I pushed the tarpaulin to the end of the sled and moved the shovels and pick. I had a pocket knife which I handed to Viktor before stepping up onto the wall and wrapping my arms around the naked man's legs.

Viktor didn't need any instruction. As soon as he saw I had hold of the man, he went to the place where the rope had been secured, and began sawing at it with the knife. The rope was thick, but the knife was sharp, and within a few passes it was cut.

I took the weight of the body and struggled for a moment before Viktor came to help lift him down and onto the sled. With that done, I put the blanket over him. It was a good blanket, but this man deserved some respect in death.

'Petro could have helped,' Viktor said. 'It would be easier with three.'

'This isn't for him. He's not as strong as you.'

'You might be surprised.'

'I think I know my own son.'

Viktor opened his mouth as if he were about to speak. Perhaps he was thinking of telling me that no one knew Petro like he did. They were different, but they were twins and they had spent their lives together. In those terms, I was a relative stranger. But if those were the words on his lips, he kept them for another time.

Instead he just sighed, so I took up the reins. 'Come on. Let's get this done.'

I pulled the sled along the street towards the small church. Many feet had been on the road and the snow was trampled through to the hard mud beneath. The runners dragged on the dirt. I sensed a few faces at windows, and I swept my gaze around, letting each one of them see my eyes.

'Look at them,' I said. 'Hiding away like frightened animals. Afraid of what they've done.'

'You think it's what they wanted to do? Do you think they meant to kill him?'

'Who knows what they meant to do. But when people come together like that, it's hard to control them. It's hard for them to control them*selves*.'

66

'They were so angry, Papa. It was frightening. I've never seen people like that. And when Dimitri came to the house, I thought . . .'

'What, Viktor? What did you think?'

'I thought you were going to shoot him.'

'Maybe I should have.'

'Could you?'

I looked at Viktor, the two of us walking side by side.

'Maybe,' I said. But I *knew* I could have. Were it not for Lara and for Natalia standing close by, I would have fired a bullet straight through Dimitri's heart. I had no love or respect for my brother-in-law, and I had taken enough lives for one more to make little difference. The first time it had been as if someone had shaved away a tiny piece of my soul, but so many pieces had gone now that I sometimes lay awake at night and wondered if there was any of it left.

Viktor continued to watch me. When he spoke, his breath washed around his face and drifted back behind us. 'You fought in the army.'

'I fought in many armies.'

'You don't talk about it. How old were you?'

'The same as everyone else,' I said. 'I was conscripted when I was twenty.'

And it was as a new soldier in Moscow that I met Natalia. So young and beautiful and full of hope. And she'd given me two sons before I was marched to war for the first time.

'You must have seen some things.'

'I've seen many things, Viktor. Many *bad* things. Soldiers can do terrible things, but this? Today?' I shook my head. 'Today is the worst I've seen. Proud people falling into shame.'

'I think I understand why they did it though. Why they were afraid.'

I took a deep breath and looked at him. 'Me too.' And that made it so much worse.

*

67

The digging was harder the second time. The ground was a little softer, but we were tired from the work that morning, and we were drained by what had happened. The grave was shallower than it should have been, but we laid the corpse with its bulging glassy eyes and we put the blanket over his face before piling the cold dirt onto him. The pitiless thump of shovels full of earth fell heavy on him.

No one else came. No words were said.

We settled the soil, flattening it with the backs of our shovels, and we threw the tools onto the sled before dragging it home.

We were exhausted when we finally sat at the table and Natalia put hot food in front of us. Soup made from beets and what was left of the meat from yesterday's rabbit. It felt good and warm.

When we had eaten, I asked Lara to bring the satchel from the corner of the room, and I opened the flap, taking out the contents and laying them on the rough surface of the table. I unwrapped the medal from around the flat tin and held it up for them to look at. I pinched the end of the ribbon between finger and thumb, letting the cross twist and turn until it reminded me of the hanging body, then I laid it down on the table. The orange and black ribbon was striking against the dark wood of the table. The white cross was edged with gold and the colourful depiction in the circle at the centre of it was still vibrant.

'What is it, Papa? It's pretty.' Lara leaned across the table for a better look.

I pushed it towards her so she could touch it. She picked it up and hung it around her neck, letting the medal hang down her chest. She stood so we could see how it looked on her.

'It's the Order of St George,' I said. 'Awarded only to officers, and only for exceptional bravery.'

'And what's the picture?' Lara turned the enamelled white cross, twisting the ribbon to see it better. The colourful representation in the centre of the medal was of a man sitting on the back of a white horse, driving a lance down into a dragon that cowered at the feet of his mount.

'It's St George,' I said. 'Killing a dragon.'

'There's an icon in the church,' she said. 'It looks like this but the horse is black.'

'St George is one of the martyrs. He was a brave man who died for what he believed in.'

Lara turned the medal this way and that, seeing the way the light from the window caught on the colours.

'But it means something else too, Lara. It's not just a man killing a dragon. The icon reminds us of our struggle with ourselves. With the evil inside and around us.'

'Luka.'

I looked at Natalia. 'What?'

'She doesn't need to hear about that.'

'It's what the priest would tell her if he were here.'

'Well he isn't here.' She turned to our daughter. 'Take it off, Lara. It's not for you to play with.'

'Can't I keep it?'

'No.'

'Just wear it then? Please, Mama, just for a—'

'No.'

'Let her wear it for a while,' I said. 'What harm is there?'

Natalia looked at me, deciding. When it came to Lara, it was Natalia's decision that was final. She sighed and nodded.

'Thank you, Mama.' She hugged her mother. 'Can I go and show Dariya?'

'Not now,' Natalia said. 'I don't think that's a good idea.'

'Tomorrow then?'

'Maybe not tomorrow either.'

Lara's demeanour changed, her shoulders dropping. She sulked and left the room, going into the bedroom to look at her prize; cherish it while she still had it.

I smiled as I watched her go. 'She's like you, Natalia. So much like you.'

Natalia shook her head and reached across the table to touch my hand. 'Perhaps as I used to be.'

'What about the tin?' Petro asked. 'Have you looked inside?'

'Not yet.' I contemplated the tarnished tin lying on the table. I touched it with the tips of my fingers and pushed it from side to side looking up at my wife.

'Open it,' Viktor said.

'It feels wrong,' I replied. 'Rifling through his belongings.'

'There might be something in there that tells us who he is,' Petro said.

Or perhaps it would confirm something else: that this man was indeed a killer of children. That these things did not belong to him. That Dimitri and his mob had rightfully hanged him from the boughs of their tree.

I pinched the lid of the tin, pulled it open, and looked at a piece of paper inside. There was nothing on it but a date, written in slanted script. The date was eight years ago, 1922, after the end of the civil war, around the time I came home to be with my family for good. I knew straight away that I was looking at the back of a photograph. I owned none of my own, but I had seen others.

I took it out of the tin and placed it face up on the table to see the image of a young woman, seated, with two children. The woman was neither beautiful nor ugly. She was plain. In her arms she cradled a baby. A second child, maybe two years old and dressed as an adult, stood beside the chair.

I took the other photographs from the tin and put them on the table.

'They might not be his,' Natalia said.

I nodded and began to spread the photographs out. There were more pictures of the same woman – some alone and others with the two children. There were also single portraits of the children. There were as many as ten photographs, some creased as if they'd been kept in a pocket, or damaged as if something had been spilled on them before they had been placed in the tin for safe keeping.

I stopped and stared.

This photograph was small, no larger than a packet of cigarettes. It was not a good picture, but it was more recent than the others, not faded or damaged at all, and the faces of the people in the sepia tones were clear enough. It looked to have been taken in some sort of garden, for there was a tree out of focus in the background. There were two people seated. A patriarchal man, wearing a dark suit that contrasted with his heavy white beard and moustache. His left elbow was resting on a table covered with white lace. On the other side of the table, a woman, similar in age, wearing a heavy dress. Her head was covered with a light-coloured headscarf. Standing behind them, a younger couple. This woman was the one from the other photographs. She wore a plain black dress and her dark hair was drawn back on her head.

The man beside her had been in our home just a few hours ago. He stood straight, as if a plank of wood had been inserted into the back of his double-breasted jacket. The high white collar of his shirt was tight beneath his closely bearded chin. He looked fuller in the face, and far healthier than the man who was now buried in the cemetery behind our church, but there was no doubt it was the same man.

And on the floor, at the feet of the seated grandparents, two children. A boy and a girl, just a year or two between them. Their features were more developed than the children in the other photos, but I was certain they were the same two.

'He was their father,' I whispered.

Natalia took a deep breath. 'We don't know that, Luka. This doesn't mean . . .' Her words trailed away.

'It's enough for me,' I said. 'This man was no child-killer.' I tapped my finger on the picture. 'He was a soldier. A decorated officer. And he was a father. No father could do that to his own children.'

'All you have is a photograph, Luka. You don't know anything. He could be, I don't know, an uncle.'

'Look at the similarities,' I said. 'The man and woman in the photograph. These children have their features. They *look* like them. And they're the same two we buried this morning. Look at them, Natalia. Dimitri and the others murdered an innocent man.'

I laid the picture down and said nothing more, understanding

71

that she wanted there to be some doubt; she wanted there to be a chance the others had done the right thing.

I reached over and squeezed her hand, then returned the photographs to the tin, but even as I pushed the lid tight, I heard footsteps outside, heavy boots approaching the front door, followed by a rapid banging.

'What now?' Natalia started to stand, but I stopped her.

I took the revolver and went to the window, looking out to see Dimitri's wife, Svetlana Ivanovna, standing on our doorstep.

'The coward has sent your sister,' I said. 'Perhaps you should speak to her.'

'What will I say?'

I drew the bolts and stepped back to let Natalia answer the door. 'I don't know; she's *your* sister.'

I put the revolver behind my back, so as not to frighten Svetlana, and stood behind Natalia.

'What is it, Sveta?' Natalia asked when she opened the door.

'Have you come to see who else you can drag from his house?' I said. 'Or have you come to express your shame? Your husband has sent you to hang your head for him?'

'No,' she said. 'We can't find Dariya.'

8

For a moment, no one spoke. In my mind, I saw the two children lying on the sled. I saw them in the bottom of a cold hole, waiting for the soil to be thrown over them.

'When did you see her last?' Natalia broke the spell.

'This morning. Before . . .' But Svetlana couldn't say it. She didn't even want to think about what she'd been a part of.

'And you haven't seen her since?' Natalia asked.

'You probably scared her away,' I said. 'Frightened the poor child with your hanging.' I shook my head and turned my back. I went to the table and sat down with my sons.

'Do you think she saw what happened?' Natalia asked her sister.

'I saw,' I said. 'The shame you must feel. Do you know who that man was? He—'

'Enough.' Natalia cut me short. 'Sveta has lost her daughter. Your niece. Have some sympathy.'

'I'm not sure I have any left.'

Natalia tutted. 'Come in, Sveta. Come out of the cold.'

The little warmth we managed to conjure with the small fire was escaping through the open door, so Natalia invited Svetlana inside and closed it behind her.

Svetlana Ivanovna was a large woman. Not fat though, nobody had enough food to be fat. She was tall and strong; from a long line of farmers. She had strong shoulders and strong hands, a large frame beneath the extensive dress. She wore a plain dark headscarf which covered black hair, and she watched with dark

73

eyes. Svetlana and Natalia shared some features – they had the same sharp nose, the same prominent chin and searching eyes – but they were different in more ways than they were similar. Svetlana was more insular, she had grown up and outlived her parents in Vyriv, spent her whole life in this village, marrying Dimitri and working the same land for years. Natalia, on the other hand, had forged away from rural living and farming. She had travelled to Moscow to find a life other than farming. She became a worker and could recount stories of the first revolution, the unrest spreading from Petersburg to Moscow in the year after I was conscripted. I was a soldier when we met in Moscow, and she became pregnant with our sons, but my life as a soldier gave little support so she returned home to Vyriv before the outbreak of the war with Germany. For many years we saw little of each other. First the Great War and then the civil war kept us apart. But when they were done, I came home to her and my sons. A woman and two ten-year-old boys I barely knew. But our bond grew strong, and when Lara was born, our family was complete.

'Lara might know where she is,' Petro said, looking at me and shrugging. 'They were playing together when I found her. Maybe she knows where she was going.'

I didn't want Svetlana in the house. After what she and her husband had participated in only a few hours earlier, I wanted to turn her around and push her through the door, and the only things stopping me were Natalia and a small vein of sympathy just below the surface of my anger. She was worried about her daughter, just as any mother would be, and I had to tell myself it was Dimitri who had instigated the hanging, not Svetlana.

I put the heavy revolver on the table and pushed it away before waving a hand. 'Ask her.'

Natalia called to her, and when Lara came from the other room, she was still wearing the medal around her neck. The orange stripes in the ribbon stood out against the black of her dress, and the colours depicting the slaying of the dragon were vibrant. 'What is it, Mama?'

'Do you know where Dariya is?'

Lara thought about it for a second, pursing her lips. 'No.' She shook her head.

'You sure?' I asked. 'There isn't somewhere she goes?'

Again she shook her head.

'If there's something, you must tell us,' Natalia pressed her. 'Whatever you can think of. Your aunt is worried about her.'

'Anything.' Sevetlana's eyes pleaded. 'Anything at all, Larissa.' She was willing her to know where Dariya was.

Lara tightened her lips and shook her head.

'Where did you go with her this morning?' I put out a hand and brought Lara to me. I lifted her to sit on my knee and I put my face against the back of her head, above the place where her hair was gathered into a bun. I could see the pale skin of her scalp in the parting and I breathed the scent of her hair and rubbed my hands on her shoulders.

'Just at the back,' she said.

'In the field?'

'Yes. Where Petro came.'

'And when Petro came, what then? What did Dariya do then?'

'She stayed.'

'You're sure?'

'Yes.'

I looked up at Svetlana and opened my hands to her. 'She doesn't know.'

'I'm sorry,' said Natalia.

Svetlana watched us as if she thought we might be hiding something from her, then she nodded and turned to the door.

As soon as Svetlana was gone, Lara jumped down from my knee and went to the other room without looking at any of us.

'Is there something she's not telling us?' Natalia said in a quiet voice. 'Do you think she knows where Dariya is?'

'No, why wouldn't she tell us?' I said. 'She can see how upset your sister is.'

'Because she's nine years old?' Natalia said. 'And because children sometimes have secrets.'

'She's probably just worried about her cousin.'

'Maybe.'

'I'll talk to her,' Petro stood up. 'Sometimes she talks to me.'

I looked at him. 'Really? About what?'

Petro shrugged and there was the trace of a smile in his eyes. A small victory for him. A moment of subdued pride. 'Nothing much,' he said. 'Sometimes we talk, that's all.'

'Fine. Talk to her.'

Outside I could hear voices.

'It's Dimitri,' Natalia said, going to the window. 'He's with some of the other men.'

'Coming here?'

'Looks like it.'

Viktor went to stand beside his mother, but I remained where I was, wondering what else could happen today.

'No,' Viktor said. 'They're going round the back. Where Lara said they were playing.' He looked at me. 'Maybe we should help.'

The sound of voices outside grew quiet again as the group of searchers moved away.

'They'll find her,' I said. 'They don't need us.'

'You mean they don't deserve your help?' Natalia said. 'That's what you mean, isn't it?'

I picked up the photograph on the table and studied the family burned onto it. A trick of light that captured an image and stored it as if it would exist for ever. A family that had no inkling of what the future held for it. 'Yes,' I said. 'That's exactly what I mean.'

'She's your *niece*.'

I could feel their eyes on me as I stared at the photograph. 'They don't need my help.'

'Of course not,' Natalia said. 'There are enough of them.'

'Right.'

'And they're good men.'

'Are they?'

'Mostly, yes, I think they are, Luka. You've said yourself that

76

they're afraid, and people do bad things when they're afraid. Rash things.'

'*We* didn't.' I looked at her.

'No, but I know you too well, Luka Mikhailovich. I know what's in your heart, even when you try to hide it from me.'

'What are you talking about?'

'I can see it,' she said. 'You think you should've done more to stop them. You feel like it's your fault too.'

'It isn't.'

'No, it isn't. And that's what makes you even more angry – they put you in that position.'

I opened my mouth to reply, but caught my words when Petro came out from the other room, holding the door wide. 'I think they've found something.'

'Found what?' Natalia asked after a moment of silence. 'What have they found?'

'Come and look.'

Standing at the back window, my knees against the bed, I could see much of the area behind the house. To the left, the side of our barn. There was a small yard, the snow trampled and kicked into furrows and tracks that came from everywhere and went nowhere. So many times had the ground outside been trodden over the past two days. The sled, the animals, the mob that had lynched a man from a naked tree, and now this.

The group of men, I counted seven of them, had gone through the yard, looking for the place where Lara and Dariya had been playing. Beyond, there was an open field, white, glistening in the orange light from the falling sun. There was a patch of disturbed snow just on the other side of the fence where Lara must have been because I could see how the snow had been built up into balls, and I knew she and Dariya liked to roll the snow.

But the men had moved beyond that and were now hiking away, seven dark stains on the glorious white. They were heading up the back of the shallow valley towards a line of poplar trees that stood on the crest like a regiment of well trained soldiers.

Tall and straight they stood; their branches reaching upwards, their narrow bodies proud. In the summer they would be a soft green against the pale blue sky, and the field would be filled with red winter wheat moving in waves. The gold and green would ripple as the breeze moved through it. And just below the window, around the base of the fence, flowers would spring with colourful life.

'Where are they going?' Lara asked.

'They must have found something,' Viktor said. 'A trail maybe.'

I turned to look at Lara, but she wasn't watching the figures advancing on the poplars. She was sitting with her back to the window, scrutinising the medal. Or at least that's what she wanted us to think, because as I watched her, she dared a sideways glance at me and I saw the secret in her eyes.

She quickly looked away, creasing her brow, inspecting the medal.

'What is it, Lara?' I asked her. 'What's the matter?'

She didn't answer.

'I want you to tell me,' I said, going to sit beside her. 'I know there's something.'

Again the sideways glance.

'Larissa, if there's something you know, I want you to tell me right now.' And I sensed something move in to replace my anger at Dimitri and Svetlana and the others. I felt my own urgency before I realised it was there. An unease crept in, like cold fingers slipping around the back of my neck. Seeing those figures moving up the valley, and with the impression that Lara was hiding something, I began to wonder if there was more to this. Something was wrong.

'Lara.' I softened my voice.

She looked at me. She was deciding, struggling with her thoughts.

'You're not in any trouble,' Natalia said. 'Do you know where Dariya is? Her mama and papa are worried about her. Something might have happened to her.'

A glistening redness washed over her dark eyes. She tightened her lips, her chin rising a touch.

I ran a hand over her head. 'You're not in trouble, my angel, I promise, but you must tell me—'

And with the compassionate tone from both mother and father, the tears came as they inevitably would. And to accompany them, the words of confession to a crime that was no crime at all.

'We sometimes go up to the trees,' she said. 'We have a place where we play.'

And I didn't need to ask why she hadn't told us. She wasn't allowed there, that was all. She had been forbidden to go that far from the village.

'And you think that's where she may have gone?'

Lara nodded.

'Why do you think that?' Natalia asked, sitting beside us. 'Did she *say* she was going?'

She shook her head. 'I saw.'

'You saw?'

'I saw her go. After Petro brought me back and you made me come inside, I was sitting here and I saw her run around the house. She ran around and went straight up. I watched her all the way to the trees.'

'Where those men are now?' I pointed at the window and the dark smudges on the snow beyond.

Lara nodded.

'OK,' I said. 'Good girl.'

'Am I in trouble?' she asked.

'We'll talk about that later.'

I took Natalia's elbow and beckoned her through to the front room. 'Do you think Dariya saw what they did? What her father did?'

'Perhaps.'

'Why else would she run away like that?'

'I don't know.'

'Dimitri's such an idiot. What he did. Trying to do it to make his child safe, and now he's damaged her for ever. Imagine if you saw your father do a thing like that. String a man up from a tree and—'

'That's enough.' She glanced over my shoulder at the bedroom door. 'We have to live with these people. They're our friends, Luka. Svetlana's my sister. And Dariya is safe.'

'If she hasn't frozen to death up there, have you thought about that?'

'Luka.'

'You imagine how that idiot will feel if he's driven his daughter away to freeze to death on the rise. Hanging a man to make her safe, while frightening her away to die.'

'Luka!' her voice harsh but quiet. The words hissed. And her eyes were over my shoulder again.

I turned to see Lara behind me. Fresh tears in her eyes. 'It's my fault,' she said. 'I killed Dariya.' She ran to her mother and threw her arms around her.

'No, angel, she'll be fine. You'll see. The men will find Dariya.' Natalia narrowed her eyes at me and stroked our daughter's hair, running her hardened fingers over her head.

'Will you go?' Lara turned to look at me. 'You'll find her.'

I forced a smile. 'If Dariya is there, your Uncle Dimitri will find her. They don't need me.'

'Please,' she said.

'Lara, it's not your fault.'

'It *is* my fault, Papa. I should have told you I saw her, but I was afraid I'd get into trouble.'

'You're not in any trouble.' Natalia held her tighter.

'Please, Papa. Please find Dariya.'

'Of course he will, won't you, Papa?' Natalia glared at me.

I sighed and nodded. 'OK, angel, if it's what you want. I'll help them look.'

To my daughter I was still a hero. I was still a figure of strength and adult wisdom. She had not yet grown to understand that even fathers are fallible. That even fathers make mistakes, just as everyone else does. And even fathers cannot beat all the odds.

80

'Thank you, Papa.'

I sat on a chair and pulled on my boots before taking my coat from the hook by the door. I stood for a moment and looked at my daughter. 'Don't worry,' I said. 'We'll find Dariya.'

'Promise?'

'Yes, my angel. I promise.'

9

Adding my own footsteps to the many stale ones which now littered my land, I went round the house and climbed over the fence, starting up the gentle slope towards the line of poplars and the dark smudges that lay within. In the field beneath my feet, winter wheat seedlings lay in the stubble of the last harvest, buried beneath the snow.

To the west, the sun was low on the horizon, spreading a muddled amber glow across the steppe. A beautiful sight for eyes that had never seen it, the sign of approaching darkness to those that had witnessed it countless times. It would drop within the hour, orange turning to red, like blood spilling across the snow, then it would bow its head and be gone from our world for another night. And the most bitter cold would sweep in to replace it.

The snow was deep here but I tried to move quickly as I crossed the field I would harvest and re-sow next year. At least, that's what I had done in past years, but I knew this year might be different. By then the land might not be mine any longer. It might belong to the state and I would be forced to work on it for nothing or be sent away to Kazakhstan, Siberia, somewhere they could wring the sweat from my body and make me work until my heart refused to beat any longer.

I followed to one side of the mess of tracks, while the men before me had walked directly in Dariya's footsteps. The poplars cast shadows that fell long and dark across the snow-covered steppe, and I headed towards them, wondering what the men had found. Maybe Dimitri was scolding his daughter right now, telling her she shouldn't have run away, bearing accusing looks from eyes that had witnessed her father's cruelty. Or, worse, they might have found only her cold body, her blood frozen in her veins, her eyes hardened. But the truth was worse than that.

As I came closer, I could hear voices and see the shapes of men among the trees.

Here there were tufts of long grass which protruded from the carpet, their stalks heavy with the weight of ice. The line of poplars with their long, naked legs, evenly spaced and regimented as if planted by men. Behind them, a wooded area of stark black trunks and branches. Trees that would only come to life when the snow was gone and the air began to warm. Dark branches harsh against the white of the snow, icicles hanging from them like wild and strange fruit. And the ground was laced with the shadows of those wretched limbs.

'Dimitri,' I called, and the voices ahead of me stopped. Only the sound of my boots in the snow. A soft crunch and squeak. 'Dimitri.'

'Who's that?' came the reply, and I saw the shadows moving. Shapes coming towards me in the darkening day. The blood now seeping from the sun, the final strength of that light shining as if to burn out the very last of its energy before falling from the earth.

I didn't reply. I didn't shout my name. I continued on until I could see the men, and Dimitri came forward and, for a moment, we stood like that. Them on one side and me on the other.

'Have you found her?' I asked.

'She's not here,' Dimitri said.

'Any sign?'

'There are tracks,' he said. 'All the way up to here. We followed them into the woods.'

'And?'

'Nothing.'

'Nothing?'

Dimitri looked at me and I held his stare. Our breath reached out, merging around us. The other men stayed behind Dimitri, not speaking, and when I looked over at them, none of them met my eye. They knew their shame.

'You walked over the tracks,' I said.

'What?'

'You followed Dariya's tracks up here?'

'Yes.'

'But you walked over them. I could see your boot marks all the way up here. All of you.'

Dimitri stared.

'You ruined her tracks; they're no good any more.'

'Why didn't she tell us?' Dimitri took a step towards me.

'What?'

'Lara. Why didn't she tell us where Dariya had gone?'

'You're trying to blame Lara? Why the hell do you think she didn't tell you? She was afraid.'

'Afraid of what?'

'Of what? I can't believe you even need to ask after what happened today. She's afraid of *you*, Dimitri. Of *them*.' I waved a hand at the men behind him. 'Afraid of what was happening in our village. She was afraid of the same things your own daughter was afraid of; the men and women who were shouting like animals.'

'*He* was the animal. What he did to those children. If that man did—'

'That man didn't do anything to those children. They were his own children, Dimitri. His *own*. That man you murdered did nothing more than serve his country. He fought for us. For you.' I could feel my anger rising again, my breath coming heavier now as Dimitri tried to shuck the weight of blame from his shoulders. 'And you strung him up from a tree.'

Dimitri stared. 'I . . . she . . . she should've told us.'

'This is not Lara's fault. Don't blame *her*.'

'She should've told us.'

I struck out with a gloved hand and hit Dimitri hard in the

84

face. My limbs were stiff with cold and heavy with the weight of my coat, but I hit him hard and Dimitri had to step back to stay on his feet. The cold would have numbed Dimitri's pain, but his nose was bleeding when he came back at me, trying to rush me in the deep snow. I had no time to move away and the farmer struck me, knocking me from my feet, taking us both to the ground.

Dimitri was a big man and he used his full weight, but I put my arms around him and rolled, raising my hands to punch him in the side of the head, over and over again as he struggled. I moved so I was on top of my brother-in-law and I hit him again and again before I felt hands grabbing at my coat and I was yanked back, falling in the snow.

I sat like that, the sun almost gone, the air so cold the snow didn't even melt beneath me, and I looked across at Dimitri. I watched him push himself up to look back at me, his face bloody and blotched from the weight of my punches, his eyes wild and staring like a horse's when it's exhausted from a hard run.

'Don't try to blame Lara for this,' I said to him. 'Dariya ran away because she saw you killing a man.'

'She didn't see anything.' Spittle came from Dimitri's lips as he spoke. The hate was thick in his words.

'She saw you take him and string him up and she came up here to get away from it,' I said, getting to my feet and standing over Dimitri. 'While you were trying to save us from a killer, you were failing to protect your own child.'

Dimitri looked away.

'And if you ever say it again,' I told him. 'If I ever hear you blame my daughter for this, I'll kill you. I swear to God, I'll bring you out here, right *here*, to this place, and I'll kill you.'

The other men said nothing. They stood in the failing light, among the dark trunks of the naked trees, with their breath circling their heads like wraiths, and they said nothing. I looked at each of them and let them see what was in my eyes; let them see that if any of them repeated Dimitri's thoughts, I would take the words as an insult.

One of the men nodded, his face barely visible beneath his

fur hat and his thick beard, but I saw that it was Leonid. The respected war veteran who had been in the cemetery earlier that day. One of the men Dimitri had brought with him. He had seen it my way; he had tried to persuade Dimitri to keep what we'd seen to himself, but later he had been in the crowd.

I had always thought Leonid Andreyevich to be strong – a man who knew his own mind – but today he had proved himself fickle and indecisive, following the majority, afraid to step forward from the line. He'd listened to Josif, a wiser and stronger man than he would ever be, but faced with the strength of numbers he'd merged with the majority, following them like a sheep that follows its flock to the place of slaughter.

He opened his mouth as if to speak.

'You have something to say, Leonid Andreyevich?'

He held up his hands to my challenge, a defensive, calming gesture.

'There are tracks,' Stanislav offered, trying to ease the moment. He was a young man, just a few years older than my own sons.

'What kind of tracks?' I asked, still staring at Leonid.

'They could be the girl's.'

'Show me.' I was already thinking it would be a miracle if any tracks had survived all the activity up here. When the men had come up the slope, they had walked in Dariya's prints, and now all that was left was a deep trough from my house to this point. It looked as if a small army had marched there. And where we were standing, the ground was a mess of crushed snow from our fight. We had destroyed what might be the quickest means of finding Dariya.

Stanislav turned and led me further among the slender trunks of the trees. They were widely spaced, but they were confusing; the many bare trunks against the white snow in the failing light of the day made it hard to focus on anything in particular. The last of the sunlight was showing, a glimmer that reached from the horizon and felt its way among the trees. A mesmerising babble of colour and image that could easily confuse a man lost in this place.

Above, visible through the gnarled and empty tree branches, the spectral image of the waxing moon as it drew its strength from the sun, waiting for the short day to come to an end.

The other men began to follow, but I turned and held out a hand. 'The rest of you stay here. You've disturbed enough.'

Leonid spoke up. 'What makes you think—'

'Leonid.' I stopped him. 'I saw you there too. Did you bring the rope? Or maybe you tied it off so he swung like that from the tree.'

'No.'

'Or did you just kick him when he was lying in the snow?'

'Don't judge me, Luka.'

'Like you judged *him*?'

'You've no right—'

'Rights? That's a joke. What? You suddenly grew some balls after you lynched a man? It gave you the strength to step forward, did it? Or are you speaking because you think these men stand behind you?' I looked at the others, but none of them made any sign of wanting to join Leonid. They looked at one another and I could see they knew what they'd done. Finally, there was shame.

Leonid looked at the ground.

'I thought so.' I watched them before turning back to Stanislav. 'Show me the tracks.'

'Maybe Dimitri should come too?' he offered.

I nodded. 'Of course.' I had no love for Dimitri, but I hadn't lost my ability to empathise with him. His daughter was missing, and I couldn't think of anything that would burden my heart more than if Lara were taken from me.

The three of us moved away from the mess of the scuffle and the destructive tracks of the searchers until we came to the pristine snow, and Stanislav pointed.

We stood in a line at the first print. A clear footprint in the snow, followed by another and another, moving away into the trees until they were too far away to see any more.

'Could it be Dariya?' Stanislav asked.

Dimitri moved to step forward but I put out a hand and

stopped him. 'Keep them fresh,' I said. 'For once the snow is our friend.'

Dimitri resisted a moment, then stopped. He shouted Dariya's name into the woods and waited for a reply.

There was no sound. Nothing. Not a bird call, not a flutter of snow from a branch, not even the whisper of the wind. He called again, and when there was no reply he stepped forward once more, pushing against my hand which was held to his thick coat.

'Please,' I said. 'For Dariya's sake. Stay still.'

I felt him relax.

'You think they're her tracks?' Stanislav asked.

I already knew they weren't Dariya's tracks. Dariya was eight years old. A young girl with small feet and a short stride. These tracks were large and deep and far apart.

'What do *you* think?' I said as I continued to study the marks, crouching in the snow for a closer look, blowing away the sprinkling of soft snow that had fallen into the prints. The tracks were recent enough to call them fresh. They had sharp edges, the bottom packed hard but not frozen to crystal. Older prints would be less defined, crumbled around the edges, glazed with ice. These were clear; the snow had captured them perfectly. I could make out the shallow tread of the boot that had made them, a place on the bottom of the right foot, close to the toe, where a piece of the sole was missing. This was what I'd use as a signature track. That defect on that particular boot made its print unique. I could follow it.

'I think they're too big,' said Stanislav. He crouched beside me and we looked at each other.

'We should follow them,' Dimitri said.

'These aren't Dariya's tracks,' Stanislav said.

'What?'

'He's right,' I told him. 'Anyone can see these aren't your daughter's tracks.'

'Then whose?' He started to move again. 'We have to go after—'

I stood and held him back once more. 'There might be other tracks,' I said. 'Something to show us where Dariya has gone.'

'And you're an expert?' Dimitri said.

'I've followed tracks.'

'Rabbits,' he said. 'Squirrels. That makes you an expert?'

I ignored him and went back to the other men, taking no notice of them watching me as I went to the boundaries of the disturbance we'd made and began walking around it, looking for other signs. It wasn't long before I found them.

I called to my brother-in-law, but Dimitri wasn't alone when he came to where I was crouched in the snow. The others followed, keeping back.

'The same tracks,' I said without looking at them.

I sensed Dimitri step closer and I put out a hand to take hold of the hem of his coat. I tugged, indicating he should come down to my level.

'I have tracked more than rabbits and squirrels,' I said quietly. 'They're what I track here, because they're what we have. Maybe a wolf from time to time, but I've been way north of here, right into the Carpathians, and I've tracked bear and deer and elk.' I looked at Dimitri. 'And you're forgetting the things you hate about me. I've followed armies through the snow and the summer forests, across steppe and river, and they've followed me. I've tracked and killed men – experts at concealing themselves – sharpshooters hiding in the forest. I've hunted deserters and enemies, anarchists and revolutionaries and tsarists.' I leaned close so Dimitri could feel my breath in his ear. 'Don't doubt that I know how to track a little girl.'

Now I looked back at the others standing behind us and I raised my voice. 'Any one of us can see these tracks were made by the same boots as those tracks back there. And even my daughter Lara,' I glanced at Dimitri, 'even my daughter *Lara* could tell me these prints were not left by an eight-year-old girl.'

I pointed into the track. 'The light's not so good, but see how deep this is?' I took Dimitri's hand and pulled off his glove. 'Put your finger in it,' I told him. '*Feel* how deep this track is.' I let go of his hand and waited for him to put it into the impression in the snow, nodding at him when he hesitated. 'Go on.'

When Dimitri had done it, I stood and walked away, beckoning him to follow. We went to where the other tracks led away and I told him to do the same thing.

'What?' Dimitri said looking up. 'What am I supposed to be feeling?'

'They're different,' I said.

'For God's sake, we're wasting time. My daughter is out there, maybe she's—'

'These tracks are leaving,' I said. 'The others were arriving.'

Dimitri looked at me.

'And they're made by the same boots. There's a defect in the right sole, close to the toe.'

'Dariya's?'

'No. You followed her tracks. You wiped them out with your own; otherwise you'd be able to compare them. These are a man's boots. And the prints are much deeper here. This man was carrying something when he left. Something heavy.'

'Something heavy like what?'

'A child.'

Now the realisation came to his eyes. Dimitri's whole face changed as he stood and looked out at the tracks that disappeared into the trees. 'We have to follow. Now.' He began to move, but once again I stopped him. Dimitri pulled against me but I dragged him back.

'This is going to be difficult for you, Dimitri, but you can't go now. Unprepared. In the dark.' The sun was gone now and the sky was darkening quickly. It would be black in just a few minutes. 'Only an idiot would go into the forest at night in just their coat and boots.'

'But we have to go after her.'

'We can't leave her out there.' Leonid came forward.

'I'll go,' Stanislav said. 'Together we'll find her.'

'You'd die,' I said. 'That's what you'd do together out there, and you know it. You'd get lost in the dark and you'd freeze to death.'

'What about Dariya?' Leonid said. 'She—'

'She'll be fine. Whoever she's with, he'll have to stop. There's nothing out there for a long way. It'll be too dark, too cold. He'll *have* to stop. He'll have somewhere. Shelter of some kind.'

'Then we'll catch up with him. Come on.' Dimitri turned to the others. 'Come with me.'

Stanislav nodded, but the others stood and watched. Uncertain.

'How can you be sure this man has shelter?' Leonid asked.

'Because if he didn't, he'd freeze to death just like any of us. We have to go back first,' I said. 'We have to collect a few things. Then we'll follow. At first light.'

'That's too late,' Dimitri said. 'She might be—'

'She's not,' I said. 'She's not.' But I couldn't be sure Dariya wasn't already dead. I could only hope.

'I can't wait till first light. I'm going now,' Dimitri said, pulling away from me and rushing out into the snow. Almost immediately he stumbled and fell.

I hurried out to grab hold of him. 'You're destroying the tracks. We'll never find her if you do that. We have to wait until first light,' I said. 'We have to *wait*. I understand your pain and your impatience, but we have to wait. We can't follow at night, unprepared.' I felt Dimitri's fear and his anger. I felt it seeping from every pore, washing him with its stink. I could smell it all around him. Dimitri was afraid for his daughter as any father would be afraid for his child. As I would be afraid for mine. And he had come fresh from the scene of two murdered children and a wrongly hanged man. He would be thinking what we were all thinking.

'We'll find her,' I said. 'I promised Lara, and now I'm promising you. We'll find her and we'll bring her back.'

Dimitri continued to struggle, but he began to weaken and I felt the fight drain from him. He knew I was right. There was no point in following her in the dark. The moon was dying behind the clouds and the night would be black. We'd see nothing of the tracks, and the cold would break us. It would slip its fingers beneath our coats and it would wrap itself around our hearts. I could feel it now, already nipping at me.

'We'll fetch a lamp,' Dimitri said. 'Begin searching tonight.'

'A lamp's no good,' I told him. 'A few candles in the forest at night? You'll see nothing but your feet. At best you'll destroy any tracks, and at worst you'll lose yourself and be dead from the cold before morning. I've seen it before.'

I pulled my brother-in-law to his feet and turned him in the direction of home. Pushing and pulling him back down to the village.

'First light,' I said. 'I promise.' I was already thinking about what we would need to take with us.

The other men walked in silence, all of them feeling Dimitri's pain.

'You're a believer,' I said to Dimitri.

'Hm?'

'You believe in God.'

'Of course.'

'Then pray.'

'I already am. Every second.'

I nodded, watching what I could see of Dimitri's face in the falling darkness, then I lifted my eyes to the stars and a made a quiet prayer of my own. I thought about those tracks in the land, leading away from Lara and Dariya's secret place, and I prayed that God would do just one thing for me. I prayed the tracks would stay fresh. I prayed it wouldn't snow tonight.

10

Natalia was at the window, lit by the weak flame of a candle, when I returned. She and the children had been watching for me, seeing the dark shapes up on the slope before the sun dropped and took them from their sight. But now she was at the door, helping me with my coat, waiting for me to remove my boots.

'Did you find her, Papa?' Lara came forward without hope in her eyes.

I put my hands on my daughter's cheeks and squatted so our eyes were level.

I wanted to tell her that Dariya was safe at home, that I had climbed the gentle hill with my head high and I had shown the other men what to do. I wanted to prove to my daughter that I was the brave and perfect father she believed she had.

But I shook my head. 'No, my angel.'

Lara swallowed and nodded because she knew that would be the answer. She'd been at the window with her mother, and she'd seen that Dariya was not with me when I returned to the village. 'Did the Baba Yaga take her?'

I smiled, but it was a forced, tight-lipped expression caused by sadness rather than amusement. 'No, my angel. There is no Baba Yaga. That's just a story.' A story with which we teased the children, a way of keeping them from wandering too far into the forest. It was a dangerous place if they became lost, but it was sometimes hard to make children understand that. Frightening them with tales of the old hag worked better. There were even grown men who shuddered in the forest when they remembered the tales they'd heard as children – tales which they now recounted to their own sons and daughters.

Alone in the forest, with nothing but the trees, a person raised on folk stories of the old witch can find it hard not to imagine the bone fences, each post topped by a human skull except for the one left free for the head of the next weary traveller. There were savage dogs and a terrible house that moved on chicken legs, creaking and groaning, screaming as it turned to face the traveller. And the twisted old hag herself, spewing from that house, cackling, flying in her blackened pestle. The stories varied from telling to telling – the keyhole filled with teeth, the witch who ages a year each time she answers a question – but the one thing many of the stories had in common was that the Baba Yaga's favourite food was lost, vulnerable children. And thinking about it like that, I wondered if Lara wasn't half right. Perhaps the Baba Yaga *had* taken Dariya.

'Then where is she?' Lara asked. 'Is she lost?' Her eyes widened as she considered something even more terrible than the broken teeth and the crooked back of the old witch. Lara had heard Natalia and me talking. She had assimilated words and emotions she knew nothing about, but they had become her fears. 'Did the Chekists come for her?' she asked.

I glanced up at Natalia standing close, the word hanging between us as an invisible entity. It was an old word for an organisation that no longer existed under that name. Lenin's Cheka was once responsible for grain requisition, the interrogation of political enemies, running the Gulag system and putting down rebellious peasants, workers and deserting Red Army soldiers. Its name was so ingrained in the consciousness of the people that even though it had a new title, OGPU, many people still referred to the political police as Chekists. And just that one word was sufficient to capture the essence of everything the organisation stood for.

For Lara, the word held special power. She was afraid of the Baba Yaga, but the adults were afraid of the Chekists.

'No, Lara. Not them either,' I said. 'Dariya is lost, that's all.

But I'm going to find her. Her papa and I are going to look for her and we're going to find her.'

'You promise?'

'Didn't I already promise?'

Lara nodded and I hugged her tight, grateful she was here and not out there in the dark and the cold. I felt a great sadness for Dimitri, and I felt fear and sympathy for Dariya, but I couldn't help also feeling relief for my own daughter, and for the other people standing around me in that room.

I held Lara for a while, the hard floor painful on my knees, and I wiped the palm of my hand across my eyes before I released her. 'Time for you to sleep now.'

'But, Papa, I—'

'Now,' I said, looking up at Natalia again. 'And no stories tonight. Straight to sleep.'

Natalia nodded and took Lara's hand, leading her into the bedroom.

I watched them go and stayed on my knees. My legs didn't work like they did when I was a young man. There was a stiffness in the joints, aches in the places where they had been broken or injured. I'd survived two wars, fought for three different armies, and I counted my blessings I'd come away alive, but I hadn't been free from injury.

I pushed up, ignoring the pain, and stretched the discomfort away before beginning to gather the things I'd need.

'You're leaving now?' Viktor asked.

'No, not in the dark. Not now. I'll go at first light. Dimitri will be waiting, if he isn't stupid enough to try going now.'

'But you don't think he will?' Petro said.

'No.' I shook my head as I tipped an assortment of cartridges onto the wooden table. The brass and lead rolled together, forming patterns. 'He knows it's no use. He'd never find her in the dark.' I looked up at my sons. 'You want to help; sort these out.'

'You're going to need all these?'

'Who knows what I'm going to need.'

I took the two handguns that had been among the hanged man's belongings and placed them on the table along with other things I intended to take.

'You don't think she's just lost then?' Petro asked as he began to sort the cartridges, standing them upright on the table.

'No. Dariya's not lost. Someone has taken her.'

'Taken her?' Petro looked up from what he was doing. 'Why do you think that?'

'There were tracks.' I sat down and put my elbows on the table, but my hands were in fists and they pushed down on the wooden surface.

'But who would take her?' Petro asked. 'Who would want to take Dariya?'

'I don't know.'

'Someone from the village?'

'No.'

Natalia came out from the bedroom and closed the door behind her. 'Speak quietly,' she said. 'Lara's not sleeping.'

'I wouldn't blame her if she didn't sleep at all tonight,' I replied.

Natalia went to the *pich* and put a pot of water on to boil. She made black tea, weak to preserve what we had left.

'Tell me what happened,' she asked as she put four cups on the table, clicking her tongue at the mess I'd made. 'And move some of these things away.'

I told her about the fight with Dimitri at the edge of the forest and I described the tracks I'd found.

Natalia listened in silence, her hands wrapped around her cup. Not once did she sip her tea.

'You're sure about this?' she asked.

'Of course I'm sure. There's no doubt at all. Dariya's been taken.'

'And you think it's the same person who did that to those poor children you found yesterday.' It wasn't a question. It was what we were all thinking, but Natalia was the only one with the

96

courage to say it aloud. And then she voiced the second thing we all had on our mind: 'Do you think she's still alive?'

'I hope so, but . . .' I put my face in my hands and rubbed hard before speaking again. 'I'm afraid for her.' I stared at the tabletop. 'I'm afraid that when I find her she might already be dead.'

'Then why wait until morning to go after her?' Natalia asked. 'Why not straight away?'

'Don't you think I'd have gone straight away if I could?'

'It's just a question, Luka, not an accusation.'

I sighed. 'The tracks I found were at least a few hours old, but we had less than half an hour of daylight left and you can't track with lamps. If we'd gone unprepared, we'd have ruined the trail and been lost and cold within two hours. We'd probably be dead by morning. It wasn't an easy decision to make.'

Natalia reached across the table and put her hand on mine. She held my fingers in hers. Two hands that had been apart for so much of the time they should have been together.

Viktor and Petro stayed quiet, watching us.

'Every time I think of Dariya, I see those two children.' I took a deep breath. 'But beneath it all, a part of me is glad.'

I looked around the table and saw confusion in Viktor's eyes, but in Petro and Natalia's I saw only understanding.

Natalia nodded, her face softening. 'You mean you're glad it isn't Lara.'

'Yes.'

I went back to gathering what I'd need tomorrow while Natalia remained in her seat, drinking her tea and watching me prepare. She didn't touch anything, and she didn't protest again at the mess I was making of her table. She lifted her cup to make room for me and when I'd put everything on the table, I stood back to look at it all.

'So much to carry, Papa,' Viktor said. 'One man couldn't carry all that for long in the snow.'

'Two men,' I said.

My sons both looked at me, but my eyes were on Viktor. 'I want you to come with us.'

Viktor nodded. 'Of course.'

'But not me?' Petro asked.

'I want you to stay here. You need to look after Mama and your sister.'

Petro shook his head, clenching his jaw, the muscles bulging and relaxing.

'Why not both of them?' Natalia said. 'Three are stronger than two, and Petro's a strong boy.'

'That's why I want him to stay with you,' I said. 'If they both come, who's going to take care of you and Lara?'

'We can take care of ourselves,' she said. 'You shouldn't be gone more than a day or two, and there's not too much for us to do.' She stared at me as if she were looking right inside me, trying to see what gave me my thoughts. 'We can manage on our own for a while.'

Petro looked hopeful, his eyes meeting mine.

'No. Petro stays.'

Petro turned away, going to the bedroom, closing the door behind him. The three of us stood in silence for a moment before I spoke again. 'You should sleep too, Viktor. It'll be a long day tomorrow.'

When Natalia and I were alone, I asked her to put out some food for me to take, so she gathered bread and sausage, a small piece of *salo*, wrapping each in a square of clean cloth. The *salo* was from our own pig, which I'd slaughtered in the summer. Nothing had been wasted. I'd cut the fatback myself, smoked and salted it, and Natalia had made *kovbyk* with the flesh from the beast's head. That single animal had fed us for some time and the smoked *salo* had lasted well, but there was very little of it left.

She put the wrapped packages on the table with the other things and looked at the neat rows and piles I had laid out.

She spoke to me in a whisper. 'So much to take. More than enough for just one day.'

'It might take longer. I have to be ready for that.'

98

'But I've given you only enough food for just one day. Hardly even that. I could give you more—'

'No. Keep it. We haven't enough, and, God knows, if the Bolsheviks make it here, there'll be even less. I can hunt if I need to. I'll find something.'

'You should take Petro with you.'

I snatched a box of *papirosa* cigarettes from the shelf and sat down, taking one out and pinching the wide filter. I lit it with a match and leaned so my forearms were on the table, letting the smoke drift around my head.

In front of me, the photograph I'd found in the man's tin. I picked it up and held it out so I could see it in the light of the candle. The family posing for the picture. All of them so serious. The children captured in that instant as if they would live for as long as the photograph remained.

'This man lost everything,' I said, tapping his face in the photograph, covering it over and rubbing my finger across his features. 'Everything that made him who he was.' I took a drag on the cigarette. 'I think he was following the person who murdered his children.'

'Why do you think that?'

'It's what I'd do if someone did that to my children. I'd want to find him and kill him. And you saw how weak he was. Shot. Starving. What else could make a man in that condition keep going? What else would make him drag that sled and keep on?'

I looked up at my wife and remembered the nights I'd woken her with my shouting; how she'd held me, repeating my name over and over, telling me where I was. Even in the winter, when there was ice on the inside of the window, I'd sweat in my sleep and she'd have to fetch water to cool me. I didn't speak much of the things I'd seen or the things I'd done, but when I first returned from the fighting in the Crimea, she said she hardly recognised me. I was thin and hard and seemed barely alive. There had been a darkness in me, and I felt that same darkness now.

'I think he was following someone who came close to Vyriv,

and now that person has taken Dariya. And when I find him, I'll kill him.'

Natalia watched me.

'That's why I don't want Petro to come. He doesn't need to be part of that,' I said. 'He's strong, but he's not like Viktor.'

'No, he's not like Viktor, you're right. But he's stronger than you think he is, and the way you treat him, he thinks you favour his brother. He thinks you don't love him as much.'

I dragged on the cigarette, the harsh smoke tearing down my throat and soaking into my lungs. I allowed the smoke to leak from my nostrils before I pushed out the chair beside me. 'Sit with me.'

Natalia sat down, and I turned to face her.

'I think . . .' I tried to find the right words. I rolled the cigarette in my fingertips and lowered my voice to a whisper. 'I think I love him *more*, Natalia. Because he's like you.'

Natalia was surprised. 'You can't love one son more than the other.'

'It's not like that.' I rearranged my thoughts. 'Not more, that's the wrong word. *Differently*. I love him in a different way. I want to protect him from things that are . . .' I sighed. 'The kind of things I'd protect you and Lara from. He's got so much goodness in him, I don't want it to be ruined by all the shit that's happening around us. I don't want him to be hardened by it like you were.'

'I'm hardened?' She feigned surprise.

'We've seen so much, Natalia. War, famine, winters that want to freeze our souls. You remember how I was when I came back? I couldn't rest. The nightmares, the fevers. I felt like I didn't belong anywhere, and if it hadn't been for you I'd be . . . well, I don't know what I'd be. *Where* I'd be. Maybe like that man they hanged today.'

'This is different. And Petro feels guilty about what happened to Dariya, I see it in his face. He was the last person to see her and he thinks he should've brought her home. You have to give him a chance to find her.'

'Viktor is strong enough to endure it, but Petro?'

'*I* endured it. All of it. The fighting, being without my husband and then calming his sleepless nights. You weren't the only one who had nightmares.'

'I know. I'm sorry.'

Natalia made a dismissive gesture with one hand, then raised her eyebrows and chuckled. 'And what about the revolution? We *all* endured that. How we thought it would make things better.' She swallowed her bitter amusement and looked at me in her searching way. 'I endured and so will Petro. Lara too. They all will; they have to. It's life.'

'Maybe you're right.'

'Of course I'm right; I'm always right.'

'Mostly, that's true.'

'So take him with you. Show him he has your love and let him help find Dariya.'

'What if something were to happen to him?'

She put her hands around her cup to soak in its warmth, but it had grown cold. 'Nothing will happen. He'll be safe with you.'

'I don't know . . .'

'Luka, I don't want *any* of you to go but, together, the three of you are so strong. This is no different from one of your hunting trips. You'll be back in a day or two and Lara and I will be fine.'

'There are other things to think about,' I said. 'I don't want you to be alone when the Chekists come—'

'*If* they come. Maybe they never will.' She was trying to sound hopeful, to reassure me. 'We're so far west. So far from Moscow. And we're not even close to Karkhiv; why would they ever come this far?'

'They're getting closer. Every day they find a new village. They're everywhere, collectivising our farms, and each one they find leads them to another. They'll find us eventually.'

'Perhaps there'll be another revolution before then, and everything will change again.'

'I don't think so. Not this time.'

'We're hidden away where almost no one can see us.'

'But the other villages know.'

She let go of her cup and leaned back. 'Then let them come, Luka. What will they do other than take what little we have? And what could Petro do to stop them, anyway? What could *you* do? Is it not more important to concentrate on one problem at a time; to find a stolen child? To give your sons some respect?'

I sighed and closed my eyes.

'I don't want you to go, Luka, but you're the only chance Dariya has. Dimitri would never find her alone – he's a farmer.'

'So am I.' I looked at my callused hands.

'You were never a farmer. You were always a soldier. And now you're a soldier pretending to be a farmer, and I can see in your eyes it isn't who you really are. It's why you go hunting and spend so much time outside. You're happy to be with us, but the farming is a burden to you.'

'No.'

'I know you too well, Luka. On the outside you're a family man, a farmer, but inside? Inside you're still a soldier. So go and do *that* for a while. Put your knowledge to some use. Keep the promise you made to Lara.'

'I didn't promise to take both her brothers with me.' I dropped my hands to my knees.

'Take Petro,' she said. 'Let him see he has your love and your respect.'

'He already does.'

'Then show him.'

We sat together for a while before washing and going to bed, moving silently so as not to wake the children. It was cold – the fire had done little to heat the house – and we pulled close to one another to keep warm. Lying face to face, Natalia kissed me as she hadn't done for a long time, and we pressed our bodies together, feeling the security and comfort of skin and scent and flesh. We made love, not as we had done when we were young and first together, but as two who are intimate in ways that reach beyond the physical, and, as we did, there was something that felt final in our act. We moved together that night as if it were the last time we would move in that way.

And when Natalia slept, I held her. I listened to her breathing in the night, and I felt the cold at my face. She turned in her dream, putting her arm across my chest, curling her leg around mine. I memorised the softness of her skin and I closed my eyes. But I did not sleep for a long time. I stared at the darkness and thought about Dariya, wrestling with the decision I had made not to follow her into the forest at night.

11

Rest came in broken shards. Glimpses of tracks in the snow, of blinding white, of children lying naked in their graves. And Natalia's words repeated in my head as I reconsidered taking Petro on the search for Dariya.

My eyes were open long before the dawn came, and I was out of bed before the sun had begun to rise. Natalia sensed my movement, and the speed with which she rose told me that she too had not been granted a deep sleep that night.

While I prepared the last of my things, Natalia woke the boys and made a breakfast of eggs and bread toasted on the stove. She laid it on the table and sat down to drink hot water and watch us eat.

Viktor and Petro came from their bedroom, both of them yawning and rubbing their eyes.

'Come and eat,' I told them. 'We'll need our strength.'

Petro looked at me, waiting for me to go on.

'I want you both to come,' I said. 'Three will be better than two. And if we need to hunt, Petro is the best shot. You'll keep us fed, won't you?'

'I thought you said Viktor is the best shot.'

'Did I?' I shrugged. 'Then you must both shoot well. That's good.'

Petro looked at Natalia as if for confirmation that I was telling the truth; that he'd heard me correctly. Then he turned to me. 'You want me to come?'

'Yes. Now eat. We need to leave soon.'

Petro smiled at his brother, who nodded to show his approval they'd be together, then he sat and pulled his plate towards him. 'Thank you, Papa. I won't let you down.'

Natalia was looking into her cup as if hoping it would tell her our fortune. There was both worry and satisfaction in her expression.

When I was done, I pushed my plate away and lit a cigarette, pinching and bending the cardboard filter before smoking it. 'I've packed you each a bag – you should have everything you need. It's your responsibility to look after it.'

'How long do you think we'll be?' Viktor asked.

'I don't know, but we need to be prepared. You don't walk too far from the village without the things you need to survive. And if we find Dariya . . . well, she might not be alone.' I watched Petro for any kind of reaction, but he guarded his feelings well. He kept his eyes down as he finished the last of his breakfast.

'Each of us will be armed,' I said. 'Petro, you can take the rifle we found on the sled yesterday. Viktor will carry my old rifle. If I'm right, if someone has taken Dariya, there's a chance he might not want us to catch him. Do you both understand?'

Both boys nodded.

'Petro?'

'Yes. I understand.'

'Good.' I finished the cigarette then crept through to the other room, where Lara was still sleeping. I sat on the very edge of her bed and leaned over to brush away her hair and kiss her cheek. She smelled warm, and she moved slightly under my cold face.

'I'll find your cousin,' I whispered. 'I'll bring Dariya back. I promise.'

I kissed her once more before slipping from the room.

We wore our heaviest coats to keep out the worst of the cold and we put on our boots before Natalia stopped us.

'Wait.' She called us back. 'Sit for a moment.'

I nodded to the boys and we sat at the table in silence, a traditional few minutes for luck, and when Natalia stood, we went to the door. Like a hunting party moving out at dawn to catch the trickiest prey, we were quiet, lost in our own thoughts of what the day might bring. We put our rifles over our shoulders and our packs on our backs. I slung my leather satchel across me so it hung at my side, and I waited for the boys to kiss their mama.

As I watched them, I thought how much they looked like men, soldiers perhaps, standing with their rifles and their firm intent, but they were still Natalia's sons and they were not too old to show affection for their mother. I liked to see how much they loved and respected her, and I knew it was she who had made them strong.

When I opened the door, the cold swept in, bringing with it the first glimpses of light in the sky. Viktor and Petro stepped out into the snow and I stayed back to kiss Natalia.

'Come back soon,' she said. 'Find her.'

'We will.'

She put a hand on my face, nodded once, and stepped back, closing the door.

I stared at the wood for a moment, then turned towards the approaching dawn. I looked up at the sky and took a deep breath before studying the snow around the front of the house. It was grey and brown, trodden down to the mud in patches, frozen in places where men's boots had crushed it, and it had set hard in the night.

'That's good,' I said. 'There was no more snow last night.'

We didn't need to go to Dimitri's place; he was already on the road, making his way towards us. He had his head down as if he were watching his own boots rising and falling in the snow, but he looked up as he approached the gate, seeing us standing there, waiting.

'Luka,' he said, nodding to me and looking at the boys.

'Svetlana all right?' I asked.

Dimitri shrugged. 'Worried.'

'Of course.'

'She was surprised you're going to help, after . . .' He looked away.

'What kind of man d'you think I am that I'd just sit back and do nothing? And it's not just because Dariya's my niece. Not *just* because I promised Lara I'd find her cousin. I'd do this for any child here, no matter who her father is.'

Dimitri's face twisted and he took a step forward. 'Is this how it's going to be?'

'It's how it usually is with you, Dimitri. But you're right – we should put our differences aside for now. Agreed?'

'Agreed.'

'You brought what I told you?'

'Yes.'

'Good.' I turned and headed round the house, Viktor and Petro either side of me, Dimitri behind.

Like that, we made our way up the slope towards the trees, following the furrowed path the men had made yesterday. When we reached the top, I showed Viktor and Petro the tracks I'd found, and I instructed them to test the depth of them, just as I'd done with Dimitri, then we set off into the trees.

The day was beginning now, one or two blackbirds coming to life in the branches as if they'd been frozen during the night and were beginning to thaw. The trunks were spaced wide enough for us to walk two abreast, leafless limbs tangling together above our heads. In the summer, when the snow was gone and the sun was stronger, the ground would be shaded where we were walking now. The leaves would be rich and green, and the shrubs would be vibrant with colour and smell. The black soil would be soft under our boots and the scent from it would be rounded and earthy. Right now the whole area was a dark and lifeless scrub, but this barren form would make the search easier. During the summer it would be more difficult to track a man on this ground. The signs would be harder to read, easier to hide.

I stopped and looked at the tracks leading away into the trees. A long line of footprints heading only in one direction.

'We should be able to follow him easily,' said Viktor.

'For now,' I agreed.

'Those are his tracks?' Petro asked. 'Just like that? He didn't try to hide anything?'

The same thing had been in my mind. It was strange that someone who would take a child – *steal* a child, Natalia had said – wouldn't try to cover his tracks.

'He probably didn't have time,' Dimitri said, speaking the words as if to an imbecile. 'He was in a hurry.'

I glanced at my brother-in-law but let the comment pass. I could think of a different reason why the thief might not have covered his tracks – because he had already killed Dariya and left her somewhere further along the trail. The stranger who had come to Vyriv two days ago had not been searching for his children; I believed he had been looking for the man who murdered them, and this might be what the future held for us.

'Keep your eyes open,' I said as I began walking again. 'There may be other tracks. Other people.' I turned to look at Dimitri. 'And keep off the prints. Keep them fresh.'

We continued to trek east for close to a kilometre before I noticed a change in the markings and held up a hand for the others to stop. 'Don't speak,' I warned them.

I moved forward to where the disturbance was and crouched to examine the area. There were two sets of footprints here. One set was the same as those we'd been following, but the other was smaller. The prints were in a haphazard pattern, scuffed, as if the feet that had made them had kicked at the snow or been dragged through it. I stood and scanned the ground among the trees.

'Come closer,' I told the others. 'But be careful.'

When Dimitri was beside me, I pointed at the smaller prints. 'These could be Dariya's. You recognise them?'

Dimitri shook his head. 'They're smaller. They could be hers but . . . What happened here?'

'Maybe he got tired,' I said. 'He must be strong to have carried her this far, but no one can carry the weight of a child for ever. He must've put her down so she could walk herself.'

'And?'

'And maybe she tried to get away. See these?' I pointed. 'It looks like she tried to run back.'

'She got away from him?'

'He caught up with her.'

Dimitri grimaced and looked away. He twisted around, searching in every direction. 'You sure? Maybe she's here somewhere. Maybe she's hiding. We should check.' He started to move away from them.

'She didn't get away,' I stopped him. 'They left here together, both of them walking. Look, you can see.' I pointed at the trail beyond the place where the snow was most disturbed. I knew that Dimitri could see it – all of us could – but I understood Dimitri's desperation and I knew *I* would have had to control myself if it was Lara who had been stolen.

'But it means she's still alive?' Viktor asked.

'Yes. It means she's still alive.' Or at least, I thought, she was still alive when this happened. 'Come on, let's keep going.'

As we continued to walk, Petro came alongside me. 'This is too easy, isn't it?'

'Hm?'

'Why wouldn't he try to hide his tracks? You think there's more to this?'

I was surprised to hear Petro asking the question, not Viktor. I thought it was Viktor who was most suited to hunting, but I could see that Petro looked at a situation in a different way. He thought more deeply and, in his mind, he had extended our situation to anticipate what might be ahead, rather than only what we could see.

I looked down at the footprints in the snow. These were messier now, not so crisp. These were Dariya's footprints, stepped in by larger feet, the two sets of marks disturbing each other, fighting for room. 'How would he hide them out here?' I asked. 'He could try to disguise them, I suppose, try to mislead us, but it would take time. No, he knew we wouldn't follow at night so he took his chances.' And for a second I felt a stab of regret that we hadn't come out in the dark.

'Do you think, if you'd come last night, you would've caught up with him?' Petro asked.

I was shocked by the question. It was as if he had read my thoughts.

'I don't mean you *should* have,' Petro said. 'I just mean . . . *if* you had.'

'I don't know.' I glanced back at Dimitri, who was walking in front of Viktor. 'I don't know.'

But I knew the man had been carrying the weight of a child for some time and would have been tired. We would have been fresh and free to move quickly. Perhaps when the man had stopped here, and Dariya attempted to escape, perhaps *then* I might have been there for her, to scoop her into my arms and take her home. I clenched my teeth and experienced a loose feeling inside when I considered I might have made a wrong decision. But I pushed the thought away. I could think only of what was and what would be. We would find Dariya alive and we would take her home.

'No,' I said. 'It was the right decision not to look for her in the dark.'

With those words repeating in my mind, we moved on in silence as the sun rose higher, casting itself through the trees so it lay ahead of us, skimming the white land and dazzling us. I kept my head down, and told the others to do the same, but the light was harsh and began to blur my vision, so I looked for a shaded spot and we stopped for long enough to dig down to the soil.

We warmed and moistened the dirt, rubbing it on the skin around our eyes before pulling our hats and scarves back over our faces. We all knew that men could be blinded by the sun's reflection on the snow, their eyes burned sightless, so the dirt and coverings would give us some protection. As a soldier I had learned to cut slits in birch bark and wear it like a mask, but we didn't have time to look for the right tree nor to construct masks from its skin, so for now the coarse dirt would be enough.

And with the earth drying and hardening on our faces, we moved on, following the tracks which carried on before us. The large prints, with the section missing from the right foot; the smaller prints that scuffed alongside them, the stride of their maker too short to clear the surface of the snow with each step.

The density of the forest tightened and expanded so that in some places we could walk only in single file: me at the head of the line, followed by Dimitri, his breath heavy and regular, his footfall clumsy. It was in such an area, three or four hours after we had begun our journey, in a place where the hornbeam grew close, that the tracks took a sharp turn to the left, striking into a place where the trees grew thick and tight.

I removed one glove and pulled the revolver from my pocket, raising my other hand, looking back and putting a finger to my mouth.

'What is it?' Dimitri asked, coming close.

'You see that?' I pointed to a place where the ground swelled in an unnatural way, as if something large had been lying there when the snow fell, leaving a distended bulge.

'What is it? Is someone there?'

'Let's have a look.'

The shelter was crude but I knew it would have provided cover and warmth. It was a mound of snow, brought together in a patch where the trees were just wide enough apart to take its size. It wasn't large, and would be almost invisible if it weren't for the tracks that led to it and around it.

'He made this?' Dimitri asked.

'I think so.'

I walked around the shelter, seeing how well it had been put together. 'It's good,' I said. 'Strong.' I'd made shelters like it before, collecting snow into a mound and hollowing it out to make a space to sleep in, away from the cold. Whoever had built this one had even built a low breaker in front of the opening, to stop the wind from coming in. I looked in, seeing the ventilation hole in the top and the compacted snow where someone had slept.

I lay on my stomach and dragged myself inside, searching for anything that might be left behind, turning onto my back and spotting something stuck to the uneven ceiling. I picked off the long black hair that was stuck to the snow, the end hanging like the thread of a spider's web.

'How long would it take to make this?' Dimitri asked.

'It's not big,' I said, turning onto my stomach and pushing myself out. 'An hour maybe. The snow should be left to harden, stop it from collapsing, but . . .' I stood up and shrugged. 'He would have been in a hurry; perhaps he would've taken a risk.'

'Over here, Papa. A fire, I think.'

I went over to where Viktor was standing, kicking at a place where the snow had been disturbed. There was blackened wood beneath.

'He had to keep warm,' I said. 'Eat something.' As I spoke, I looked up at Dimitri. What we had both seen on the sled was now in our minds, the way the girl's flesh had been cut, and I wished I hadn't said anything about eating. 'She's safe,' I said. 'I know it. Look.' I held up the single hair.

'Is that Dariya's?' Dimitri asked, coming closer.

'Unless we're looking for someone else with long black hair,' Viktor said.

I waved a hand to silence him, let him know he'd spoken out of turn. 'And this man knows how to survive out here,' I said. 'He kept her safe last night. He built a fire and a shelter. She's alive and we'll find her.'

Dimitri took the hair between his finger and thumb. 'It's hers. I know it.' He removed one glove and touched the hair with his own skin. 'I know it.' He snapped his head up to look at me. 'We should go; come on.'

'Wait. Let me—'

112

'Wait?' said Dimitri. 'We haven't got time to wait.'

'Another minute,' I said. 'Let me look for any more signs.'

'Like what?' Dimitri put the hair in his pocket and pulled his glove back on. 'What kind of signs? There are the prints.' He pointed. 'Let's go.'

'Those aren't the prints. Not the right ones, anyway. Those are the tracks he left when he looked for firewood.'

'How do you know that?' Dimitri asked me. 'How can you be sure?'

'Because they come and go?' Petro suggested. 'And because you can see places down there where wood has been snapped away from dead branches.'

'That's right,' I said.

'Well, we can't wait any longer,' Dimitri said. 'We have to go. We've delayed long enough. I shouldn't have listened to you; we should've gone last night. If we'd gone last night we'd have found her by now.'

I didn't answer him.

'Already he stopped back there.' Dimitri looked behind us. 'And now this? An hour he was here, making this? We would have found him, right here.'

'Maybe,' I said. 'Or maybe we'd have lost our way in the dark.'

'*He* didn't get lost coming here.'

'No. But he wasn't following tracks. We made the right decision.'

'And he had a fire,' Dimitri went on. 'We'd have seen it.'

'The fire is right back here, away from the shelter. It would have been almost invisible in the trees.'

'I would have seen it,' Dimitri said.

'We probably wouldn't have even got this far,' I told him.

Dimitri stared at him. 'You're enjoying this, aren't you?'

'What?'

'*This*. Being out here. Tracking. It's what you like to do. All that hunting. I know you go out alone, sometimes for days. It's in your blood – the only thing that makes you happy.'

'You don't know anything about me.'

'I know you're a brutal Russian who fought in more armies than you can probably remember. Killed more men than hunger. This excites you. You're enjoying this. It's probably the only thing that makes you feel alive.'

I stared at him, angry and guilty because there was a scent of truth in his words.

'And you're enjoying making me look stupid.'

'If you look stupid, it's nothing to do with me. Even if we *had* got this far last night, this fire would've been deep in these trees. Why d'you think he came in here, where the trees are so thick? We could've walked within five metres of it and not known it was there.'

'We would've seen the tracks.'

'In the dark?' I pushed my doubts aside. 'At best we'd have ruined the trail, killed any chance of following, and at worst we'd be lying frozen in the snow, dead, while he walks away with your daughter.'

'You're punishing me,' Dimitri said. 'Punishing me for what happened yesterday.'

'Punishing you? You're punishing yourself, Dimitri. What happened yesterday was shameful, but has no bearing on this. You think I'd delay finding Dariya because of what you did yesterday? This isn't about you.'

He said nothing.

'Don't ever doubt that I will do all I can to find your daughter,' I told him.

Dimitri nodded.

'OK, then, come and look at this.' I grabbed his coat and pulled him, but Dimitri knocked my hand away.

'Don't pull me around.'

'Then stop being an ass. Now, come with me.'

I took him round the shelter and into the trees on the other side from where we had come into this place. I stood on the edge of the disturbance where our prey had dragged the snow into a pile to make his shelter and I pointed at the ground.

'You see,' I said. 'Still alive. And my guess is they set out just before dawn – like we did.'

In front of us, leading out into the trees, the trail continued. Two sets of footprints. One large, one small.

12

We followed the prints which led on and on through the trees, avoiding the open spaces. The trail remained within the forest wherever possible, staying where the snow was most shallow, and we were glad not to have to venture out where it would be much deeper. On the open steppe, the snow would be over our boots, maybe higher in the places where the wind had swept it into drifts and whipped the land into a pale desert of dunes and ripples so beautiful and white one could hardly believe this weather could kill a man in just a few moments.

We'd been walking most of the morning and were all tired now, wondering if we were gaining on our quarry. Dimitri was silent, and I knew his mind would be focused on Dariya, so that all other thought would be consumed. I'd hoped we would find her early, while all the tracks were fresh and we were well rested from a good night's sleep, but the child thief had been more resourceful than I expected and I was worried there was too much distance between us.

The shelter had surprised me. That the child thief had found a good spot for a fire, well hidden, concerned me. Whoever we were following was knowledgeable and able to survive outside in conditions that would close around most people in no time at all. And yet, with all his ability, he had left an easy trail to follow, and that troubled me. Putting myself in the place of the kidnapper, I knew that covering the tracks would be difficult. The only sure way to erase them would be under another snowfall, but even then it would need to be heavy. Under light snow, prints are still distinguishable. It would be possible to create false trails, but that would take time and I guessed the man must have decided to move quickly, keep ahead of us until he found a place to adequately erase the signs he left behind. It made no sense, otherwise. There hadn't been any attempt to confuse potential pursuers.

We had come a few kilometres from the village, and there were other settlements in the area where we were travelling. North of our position now, the village of Uroz hid in a shallow valley much like our own, but it might as well have not existed at all. For us, there was only the snow and the trees and the wind. Nothing else. Whoever we were following, he had stayed clear of anywhere there might be people. He had skirted around Vyriv, seizing an opportunity, and then continued into the wilderness.

'We should stop,' I said.

'Stop?' Dimitri was by my side and I sensed his tension increase. He needed an enemy and, although I was helping him, I was the closest he had.

'Rest for a moment, regain our strength. We've been walking all morning.'

'I'm not tired,' Viktor said. 'I can walk further.'

'Me too,' Petro agreed as the boys came to join us.

I pulled the scarf away from my mouth and nose, allowing the cold air to bite at my face.

'We can't wait. We don't need to rest,' Dimitri said. 'What we need is to find Dariya. How can you even—'

'Is anybody thirsty?' I asked. 'We need to keep fresh.'

Dimitri turned and walked away from me. Just a few steps to show his displeasure.

I looked at Viktor and Petro. 'Thirsty?'

They shook their heads.

'All right then. We'll go on.' I pulled the scarf back over my face and began moving again. I could feel the cold creeping into my joints. My knees were stiff and there was a faint pain with each step, but my resolve was strong.

I went on ahead, walking alongside the marks in the snow, watching the land in front, squinting into the distance, trying to see any sign of movement in the trees. I knew the kidnapper would be well out of sight, but I watched anyway. Something might have happened to slow him down, and if that were the case, I needed to be vigilant.

Behind me the others followed in single file, keeping the disturbance to a minimum.

I turned when I heard footsteps quicken behind me and I nodded to Petro, who fell in step with me, walking by my side. His back was straight despite his pack and the heavy rifle he carried over his shoulder. As if he were showing me how strong he was.

'Do you think she's all right?' he asked. His voice was muffled behind his scarf and he spoke quietly so Dimitri wouldn't hear.

'I hope so,' I said. 'I can't do anything more than that.'

Petro was quiet for a moment.

'There's something on your mind?' I asked, shifting the weight of my rifle. The strap was catching on the shoulder of my coat, pulling it to one side.

Petro looked at me. 'Does Dimitri blame me?'

'Blame you for what?'

'For what's happened?'

'Why should he blame you?'

'Because I brought Lara home but left Dariya to play.'

'No one blames you for anything. And I don't want you to blame yourself. No one is to blame but whoever took her. No one.'

'And you really believe we'll find her?'

'Yes, I really believe that.'

'And this man. Or whoever it is . . .'

'Yes?'

'What will you do?'

'What would *you* do?'

'I don't know.'

Petro and I were alike in many ways – many more than I understood – but this was something that made us very different. Petro didn't know what he would do. I, on the other hand, knew exactly what I would do. I would take whatever weapon was to hand, whether it was my rifle or my fingers, and I would take the man's life from him. I would punish him for what he had done to the two children I buried yesterday. I would punish him for taking Dariya. And I would punish him for turning the people of Vyriv into frightened animals.

Petro lowered his head to watch his feet. 'I hope she's all right, Papa.'

I shifted my rifle again and stared ahead.

When we came to the edge of the trees and emerged onto the open steppe, the first thing I noticed was the red stain on the ground. It lay there like an insult. A single splash, no bigger than a man's fist, surrounded by spots that had sunk just below the surface of the disturbed snow. It was striking, the bright red against the bright white. Like the bold red of the communist flag flapping against a white winter sky.

From this spot, the land sloped up for a short distance, coming to a ridge, concealing the rest of the steppe beyond. There were tracks moving up the ridge, but there was also a mess of tracks running off to the right, along the line of the trees.

I held up a hand to stop the others from coming closer, waving them to one side, showing them not to disturb the tracks.

'Is that blood?' Dimitri asked, stepping forward.

'Stay back.'

'Is it blood?' he asked again.

'Yes, but it's not much.' I moved closer for a better look. The ground was a mess here, much like it was back at the shelter.

'Is it Dariya's?' Dimitri said.

'I don't know.'

'You think she tried to get away again?' Viktor asked.

'Maybe.' I studied the area. 'But if she did, that's good. It means she's still strong.' I looked up at Dimitri. 'She's a strong girl. The more I see, the more I know she'll be fine. I think—'

'You're enjoying yourself.'

'What? Not this again, Dimitri.'

'I can see it in your eyes,' he said. 'This is thrilling for you. That could be my daughter's blood and it's exciting you. If you could see yourself . . .'

'I'm just trying to find Dariya.'

'But it makes you feel alive, doesn't it? Being a farmer could never be enough for you. For God's sake, how many times did you change sides in the war? Imperial, revolutionary, anarchist. You were looking for excitement.'

I wasn't sure what to say. There was truth in his accusation. There were times when being a farmer wasn't enough for me. It was a very different life from the one I'd had before coming to Vyriv, and, as much as I hated to acknowledge it, I sometimes craved the exhilaration of adrenalin, the closeness to danger and the camaraderie that had carried me through the worst of times. There was no bond like the one between men who had fought together; no other experience could sharpen and focus you the way combat did. But it was more like a drug than anything else. My rational mind wanted to distance itself from those things, to think only of family and duty, but a part of me needed that stimulation.

'You're wrong,' I said. 'I joined the revolution because I believed in it, but when I saw what they did to their own soldiers, I couldn't be a part of it.'

'Don't expect me to feel sympathy for you . . .'

'I don't.'

'. . . or to respect you . . .'

'I don't care what you think.'

'. . . and don't pretend you're not enjoying this. Hunting. The excitement. You're *enjoying* it. I can see it in your eyes; hear it in your voice.'

'Then make the most of it,' I said, remaining calm. 'Take advantage of what I know and what I can do. Stop moaning and let me find your daughter. Or do you think you could do it alone?'

Dimitri stared.

'Now, instead of wasting time with this, have a look that way.'

I pointed north along the line of the trees. 'See if you can find anything else. Viktor, you go with him.'

'And me?' Petro asked.

'You stay with me.'

Dimitri stayed where he was. 'This isn't a game.'

'Do you want to find Dariya or not?' I asked him.

'Of course.'

'Then go that way and look for her.'

Dimitri hesitated, shook his head once, and turned away. I watched him and Viktor move off before I went back to looking at the marks in the snow.

'What the hell's wrong with him?' I said.

'Maybe he feels inadequate,' Petro suggested.

'Inadequate?' I crouched, took off a glove and felt the tracks, put my finger on the place where the boot sole was damaged, as if I were making a connection with the man who wore it.

'He doesn't want to rely on you. He wants to be able to do this himself.'

'He's a farmer.' I stood and shifted my rifle and pack. 'He grows potatoes.'

'He's a proud man. And he's Dariya's father. He wants to be able to do what you can do, but he hates you, and that makes him angry.'

I looked at Petro, not sure if I understood what he was saying. 'I'm doing everything I can to find Dariya. It should be enough for him.'

'He's always treated you with disrespect and now he needs you. I think he's ashamed he had to ask for your help.'

'He has a lot of things to be ashamed of, but that isn't one of them.'

'Maybe you're too hard on him, Papa.'

For a moment I thought how grown-up my son sounded. Almost like Natalia, trying to understand why people did the things they did. 'I'm not hard on him. Not hard enough.'

'You—'

'He killed a man,' I said. 'He and the others, they hanged a

man right in the middle of our village, and *that's* why he's angry –
because this is his fault. While he was murdering the wrong man,
the real killer stole his daughter. *That's* why he's ashamed.'

'I suppose they were afraid.'

'That's what your mother said, but she knew it wasn't an excuse
– just like *you* know.' I took a deep breath. 'Men like Dimitri are
cowards. They stir people's thoughts, swell their anger, and when
the mob does something wrong, they distance themselves from it
and say it wasn't their fault.'

'He wasn't alone.'

'No, but he whipped those people into a frenzy. What happened was *his* fault, and that man they hanged deserved better.' I
stared at the blood in the snow. 'You know, I once saw a mob of
revolutionaries turn on their officer in Galicia, and it wasn't much
different from what they did to that stranger.'

'What happened?'

I thought about telling my son what I'd seen. My own unit
was refusing to march because the committee hadn't yet made a
decision, so our officer had climbed up on an ammunition box
and tried to reason with us. When that didn't work he tried
threatening us. I could see what was happening – the men
beginning to taunt the officer, throw pieces of bread at him,
insult him, spit at him – and I told him to go while he still could.
The officer refused, so I dragged him down from the box and told
him to run, but the men misread my actions and they cheered as
the officer stumbled. They moved closer, jeering, pushing him to
the ground. I tried to stop them, just as I'd tried to stop Dimitri,
but when the first man put his bayonet in him, the others
followed, and I could only stand by and watch, as helpless as I
had been in Vyriv two days ago.

'It's not important,' I said to Petro. 'It doesn't matter any
more. We have other things to worry about now. These are their
tracks.' I indicated the disturbance in the snow. 'But it's hard to
tell what happened here.'

Petro watched me, perhaps wondering what it was that gave
me such a pained expression. 'Maybe he's tried to confuse us.

Leave a trail in each direction so we don't know which way he went.'

'Mm. Maybe. But I don't know.' I shook my head. 'It's as if he wants us to follow him.'

'What?'

'It's just a feeling.'

'But you still think Dariya's all right?'

'She's a fighter,' I said. 'Who would think an eight-year-old girl would have such fight in her? Look at all this mess. I think she tried to run from him, push him away maybe, run out into the snow. She went that way.' I pointed at the tracks that led away in the direction Viktor and Dimitri had gone. 'That's why it's so messy – they were both running. But he caught her and brought her back to this spot before heading across the steppe.'

'If that's what you think, then why send Viktor over there? Why don't we just go on ahead?'

'Because I need to be sure there's nothing that way,' I said. 'And because there's blood. I'm afraid of what we might find over this ridge, and I don't think Dimitri should be here.'

'Maybe this isn't her blood; maybe it's *his* blood. She might have hurt him.'

'Let's see if we can find out,' I said as we began following the tracks, cresting the ridge that led out onto the open steppe. 'These marks were made by people moving quickly. See how the snow is dragged and pushed rather than pressed underfoot?'

Petro followed, both of us walking twenty metres or so out onto the steppe where the land swept away on all sides, open and clear. Here, out in the open, we came to another area where the snow was disturbed.

And here there was more blood.

Like before, it was concentrated mainly in one place, but there were also spots of it splattered around the surface of the snow.

I could sense Petro waiting for an answer.

'I don't know what to say,' I told him. 'There's no way of knowing whose this is. No way. But it looks like someone had a

fight. Like a bloodied nose or . . . I don't know . . . like someone's been spitting blood.'

'Maybe he hit her.'

I shook my head and turned to look at the place we'd just come
from; survey the line of trees behind us. 'It looks wrong.'

'What?'

'It's not right. As if someone intended to make this mess here.
Back there, that looks to be where something happened, but
here?' I searched for an answer. 'This here looks *deliberate*.'

'I don't understand.'

'I'm not sure I do either, but whatever happened here, they
went that way.' I stared out at the land ahead. 'I'm sure of it.'

'Doesn't he get tired?' Petro asked.

'Are you tired?'

'A little.'

'Then he will be too. Don't worry; we'll catch him.' I took my
binoculars and scanned the clear expanse of white, broken only by
a single line of tracks. To the left and right, the country looked
almost identical. In the distance, perhaps four hundred metres
away, there was a low hedge, almost buried on this leeward side.
The snow had drifted against it, piled thick and heavy, and I
could just about make out the place where the tracks led to it.
Beyond that another stretch of open steppe before more trees.

And as I watched, something caught my eye. A movement.
Not much, but enough to make me look again. A slight disturbance in the natural order.

'You see something?' Petro asked.

I focused on the spot, inspecting every inch of the land, then
began to sweep the binoculars from side to side, looking for
anything that broke the clean lines of the snow. A bird in flight
low over the steppe, or on the ground searching for food. A
rabbit, a wolf, anything. Perhaps a man leading a child.

I watched, expecting more movement but seeing nothing.

'Is there something there?' Petro strained to see into the
distance. 'You see something?'

I took the lenses away from my eyes and stared out at the

steppe hoping to sense movement again. 'I don't know. I thought I saw something. Maybe a bird.' I continued to watch a while longer. 'Must be all this snow playing tricks on my eyes.' But I was sure there had been something.

If it had been a man leading a child, perhaps I'd had a glimpse of their movement as they entered the treeline in the distance, beyond the hedge. At this distance, with the snow as it was, maybe that's what I had seen. Not something close to the hedge, but something further away. That would explain why I couldn't see it now.

Petro looked up at the sky, turning, seeing the grey clouds moving in from the west. 'I think it might snow,' he said.

'You're right; we need to go,' I agreed, telling Petro to move forward with me, away from the blood, before I called to the others to join us.

'Dimitri doesn't need to see more blood,' I told my son. 'Keep this to yourself for now.'

Viktor and Dimitri arced in from where they had been searching.

'Anything?' I asked.

'Nothing,' Viktor said.

Dimitri shook his head. 'No sign.'

'Looks like they went this way, then. He'll be headed for those trees, trying to keep out of the open.'

'We're wasting time,' Dimitri said. 'Let's go.'

'And he's still not trying to cover his tracks,' Viktor said.

'No way of doing it,' I told him, and I wondered if the man knew we were following him; wondered why he wouldn't try to hide himself. 'It looks like it might snow again. Maybe he's hoping it'll cover his tracks. In the forest that would take longer, but out here his prints will be gone in minutes.'

'Then we have to move faster,' Dimitri said. 'We haven't time to stand around.'

'Or maybe . . .' And then I understood why the child thief hadn't tried to cover his tracks. I understood why the disturbance in the snow had been staged here, on this side of the ridge.

The child thief had *expected* someone to follow him. This was his game. We were following him just as the man who had come to the village yesterday had been following him. But we hadn't just been following, we had been led. Whoever had taken Dariya had brought us to this place: left a clear trail and enticed us out into the open to stand on a ridge, four dark figures against a perfect white background.

And as the realisation struck, so Dimitri jerked beside me. A sudden movement and he fell to his knees, a plume of blood puffing out behind him. He tottered for a second, his head turning to look up at me, his eyes wide in wonder, his mouth open as if he were about to speak, but all that emerged was a rush of breath. And then the sound of a crack reached us, carried by the wind, and Dimitri fell forward onto his face.

'What the hell—' Petro started to say, but I stepped over Dimitri, grabbed Petro's shoulder and shoved him to the ground, shouting at Viktor to get down.

'Lie flat.' I dropped onto my stomach, pressing low. I felt the air over my head change in a way that was impossible to understand and I heard the zip of something moving through it at speed. Somewhere behind us a bullet smacked into the field and, once more, a sharp crack cut into the late morning.

'What's going on?' Viktor asked. 'What the *hell* is going on?'

'He's shooting at us,' I said. 'He's shooting at us.'

'What? Who?'

'Drew us out into the open. That's why he didn't cover his tracks. That's what I saw. He was waiting for us to come out into the open.'

I looked at Dimitri, whose face was turned towards me, his mouth biting at the snow as he tried to draw breath. I could hear the wheezing gasp of a chest wound, the gurgle of blood in his throat as my brother-in-law gagged and grasped at his own soul. His face carried a confused expression. Even in his last moments of life he wouldn't understand what had happened. One moment he'd been standing, and the next he was on his face, drowning in his own blood, unable to keep the air in his body. I held his eyes for a moment, seeing the fear that consumed him. Blood had begun to leak out of him, pooling around his chest, melting into the snow.

When I looked away from his eyes, glancing across his body, I saw the place where the bullet had exited his back. A hole in the fabric of his coat, the tattered strands of fabric torn outwards, tipped with flecks of blood and tissue from the body it had sought to protect from the cold weather. I stared at the hole and thought about the way he had fallen without a sound. It had been a good shot, probably at the limit of the accuracy of the rifle that had fired it. No. Not a good shot. It had been a *perfect* shot. I was sure the bullet had struck Dimitri exactly where the shooter had wanted.

It was not a shot intended to kill immediately. I'd seen men shot this way before. I remembered that the first German sharp-shooters we had encountered – armed with magnifying scopes and silent tactics – had used a similar technique. They used camouflage and patience, steel masks and a well placed bullet to wound men with the intention of drawing out further targets. They enticed us out to try to save our comrades, and I was sure that's what this man was doing now.

'Stay as low as you can,' I said. And as I spoke, something hit the ground beside me, pummelling into the snow, kicking it up in a small plume.

'He's fixed on us.' I looked across at my sons. 'We have to move away.'

Petro was breathing hard. He was looking to me for answers, perhaps an easy way out of this.

'Stay calm,' I told him, but I knew it was almost impossible.

'What about Dimitri?' Petro asked.

'There's nothing we can do for him.' I looked at Dimitri again, his pale face, his mouth still moving. 'If we try, we'll be shot too.'

Dimitri's pupils were wide, the sucking sounds now coming less regularly. He moaned a low and lamenting sound – a sorrow for his inability to save his daughter, for his guilt at having murdered an innocent man and for his fear of death and whatever might lie beyond it. Dimitri's life was escaping into the cold air, and he knew it. It was leaking out of him as an icicle melts away when the season changes. Fragment by fragment. Drop by drop. And soon it would be gone.

'Nothing we can do?' Petro asked, but he didn't look at me. He couldn't tear his eyes from Dimitri. 'You mean he's going to—'

'Yes. Even if we could get to him, there's nothing we could do. We have to move. Now.'

I was certain the marksman knew where we were. He had watched us from his spot, waited for us to line up just below the crest of the rise, and he'd taken his first shot. Why he had chosen Dimitri, I didn't know, but he had seen the rest of us drop into the deep snow and would have a rough idea of where we were. He was continuing to shoot, perhaps thinking he might catch another of us. Pierce the deep snow and hit whatever lay behind it.

I turned my focus to my sons, remembering what Natalia had said: that the boys would be safe with me.

'Stay low,' I told them, keeping my voice measured. 'And stay calm. That's very important, do you understand?'

Another shot hit the ground in front, and all three of us flinched.

'Take off your packs, keep your rifles, and roll, crawl, whichever is easiest. He can't see us – he's guessing where we are – but we have to move away from here.'

Lying as we were, in our elevated position, we were deep enough in the snow to be out of the marksman's line of sight, and I knew that if we moved away and back, he would have no way of knowing where we were.

'Go now,' I said as a fourth shot hit the ground to Dimitri's right, smashing into his hand this time. It was a probing shot, but it had found a target. A spray of blood fanned across the snow, whipped across Petro's face. Dimitri managed only a moan, all feeling faded, but Petro pulled back with a sudden movement.

'Stay low!' I said. 'Ignore it. Be strong.' I looked right at Petro, trying to reassure him. 'It's going to be fine. We'll be fine.'

Petro stared, spots of Dimitri's blood glistening on his scarf and hat, flecks of it on his eyelids.

'Tell me you're all right,' I said.

'I'm all right.' Petro nodded.

'Then start moving back. Away from here. But stay low.'

I shuffled back and to the side, moving away from Dimitri, following Viktor and Petro away from the spot where my brother-in-law was dying.

Another shot, this time closer to Petro, making him cry out in surprise and fear. The shooter was trying his luck, placing shots to either side.

'He's going to shoot us,' Petro said. 'He's going to kill us all. We have to hurry, we have to *run*.'

'No,' I told him. 'Stay low. Don't try to look. Don't run. If you run, he'll kill you.'

I continued to move sideways, keeping my head low, my face to the ground, and when I was a good ten metres or so from Dimitri's body, I stopped.

Two more shots hit the earth between me and Dimitri, confirming that the shooter couldn't see us. If he could, the way he shot, he would have killed all four of us by now.

Viktor and Petro stopped moving when they saw me halt, and they looked to me for instruction.

To my left, Dimitri was lying in a wide stain of dark blood. He was looking at us, his eyes still alive, his mouth still moving, but he would die soon. I didn't think about my sister-in-law Svetlana, waiting for her husband to come home. I didn't think about Dariya, taken from her parents, terrified, hoping for her father to come to her rescue. I thought about how I was going to get my sons out of this situation alive. I needed to get them back into the line of trees and find some protection.

'Where is he?' Viktor asked. 'You see him?'

'Quiet. We don't want anything to give away our position.' I closed my eyes for a moment and thought about what I'd seen just before the first shot. That movement at the line of the hedge. I'd thought it could have been a bird, some kind of wild animal, but I didn't think so any more. It had been our assassin, settling for his shot.

In my mind I saw the lie of the land, imagined the spot where the man had been. I considered looking, taking a shot, but I knew it would be a mistake. The shooter had a good idea of where we were, and he would be watching. There was a chance he had moved to another position. He had continued to fire probing shots at us, but he had also forced us to keep our heads low as he perhaps found a new place to conceal himself.

If I were the one pointing a rifle at this place, it's what I would have done, and now I would be waiting. If I had a partner, he would be scanning the distance with his glasses, or if I were alone, I'd be watching the area, keeping the stock close to my face, my eye close to the sight. I would be looking for any movement. Movement is the key. Movement is visible.

'What do we do?' Viktor asked, trying to conceal his fear.

'Nothing. Do nothing. Stay low, that's all.'

I put my head in my arms and thought about what I was going to do. The man who I believed to be the child thief had every advantage except one. Just a couple of metres behind us there was a shallow dip in the land, providing a natural shield of frozen dirt beneath the snow. If we could get to it, we would have some protection from his bullets.

Dimitri called to me with a weak voice. He spoke through his own exhaustion, his chest wheezing, the blood frothing at his mouth as he tried to form the words. I watched him struggle, his mouth biting at the deep red snow.

'Why is he making that noise?' Petro said. 'Why is he—'

'He's trying to talk,' I said.

'What's he saying?'

'I don't know,' I looked away from him. 'It doesn't matter.'

And then Dimitri began to moan, as if he had managed to draw some of that escaped life back into his body. Louder than before. Gurgling and moaning. He even mustered the strength to move his arm, his broken hand fractured and useless at the end of it. 'Please,' he groaned. 'Please.'

'Make him stop,' Petro said. 'Make him stop.'

Dimitri's voice grew louder and I half expected another shot to come, but none did. The child thief would be waiting.

'Make him stop.'

'Shut up,' Viktor told his brother.

Dimitri called again. 'Please.' The last strength of his voice calling through the blood and into the snow. 'Please.'

I didn't know what he was pleading for. Forgiveness? Life? Or perhaps he was asking us to find his daughter and keep her safe.

'Make him stop.' Petro put his hands to his ears.

I looked across at Dimitri, our eyes meeting for the last time. 'I'll find her,' I said. 'And I'll kill this man.'

Dimitri nodded, the tiniest movement of his head. He allowed his mouth to relax, the words to die, and he continued his laboured breathing. No more calling now, no more pleading, just the rasping and the wheezing. As if he were breathing water into his lungs, sucking it down and exhaling it.

'He'll die soon,' I said to Petro. 'Then he'll be quiet.'

I began to shuffle back, aware that to get to the dip I would have to move higher, into shallower snow, and there was a chance I would be exposed. The only alternative was to wait for the sky to darken, but there were still a few hours until that would happen, and if we stayed still for that long, we might freeze to death. During the war men had succumbed to the cold that way. Strong soldiers, made weak. Sometimes we'd find them when the watch changed, frozen in position at their posts.

I inched backwards, pushing with my hands, sliding my body through the snow, making sure I scraped the dirt beneath the snow as I moved.

'What are you doing?' Petro asked.

'Quiet.'

I continued back until I felt my boots come to the ridge and hang in the air, not touching the ground. I turned sideways on to the dip, then took a deep breath and rolled quickly to the side, dropping down. Another shot thumped into the ridge, in the place I'd been only a second ago.

Out of sight, I scrambled along the depression so I was in line with the place where my sons were hiding.

I spoke quietly. 'Are you all right?'

'Where are you?'

'Right behind you. *Are you both all right?*'

'Yes. I think so.' It was Viktor who spoke.

'Is he still there?' asked Petro.

'Don't be afraid. I know what you're feeling, but you need to stay calm. If we stay calm we'll be fine. We'll find a way to get out of this. Do you understand?'

'Yes,' Petro said.

'You need to get back here,' I said. 'But we've got to draw his attention away from you. He'll be watching for any movement. Any movement at all.' And I remembered how many times I had waited like the child thief was waiting now. How many times I had remained motionless, my cheek pressed to the stock of my rifle, the smell of its oil and its powder in my nostrils, my eye focused on the iron sight. Waiting for the sun to arc behind me; waiting for the slightest movement in the distance.

In Galicia there were times when we'd lived like rats in flooded holes in the ground, the enemy not more than a few yards across the wasteland that lay between us. As a sharpshooter, I had shot soldiers who made the mistake of lifting their heads above the parapet of their trench on the other side of that corpse-strewn landscape. I wondered if the child thief had been in similar places, learned his patience and skill in similar circumstances. If that were so, then I would know how to confuse him; how to draw his attention and force him to expose his position.

I stayed flat and took the rifle from my shoulder. Keeping low, I moved it in front of me and pulled back the bolt, bringing a cartridge into the chamber. I looked at the brass casing lying in the open port, then pushed the bolt forward.

'Viktor,' I said. 'Take off your hat.'

'What?'

'Take off your hat. I want you to be ready to hold it up. Put it on the end of your rifle and hold it away from you. You too, Petro.'

I thought about what the shooter would be expecting to see. The child thief knew there were three of us, perhaps only two if he'd hit his mark with one of the probing shots.

'When I call, I want you to lift your hat, Viktor. Just enough to make a movement.' It was a weak trick, but it was one that had worked for me before and was all we had to draw the man's fire. If my sons had been more skilled, I might have offered myself as a target, but if something happened to me, they would be left alone with the child thief. I had to try this first.

'And you Petro, I want you to count to six and do the same thing. Remember to hold it out and away from you, though. He *will* shoot.'

'What about you?'

'Don't worry about me.'

'What are you going to do?' Viktor asked.

'I'm going to see where he is. And then I'm going to shoot him. Be ready to move, though. When I say so, I want you to get back here as quickly as you can. Bring only your rifles.'

'What about Dimitri?'

'Leave him,' I said. 'He was dead the moment the bullet hit him. If we try to help him, we'll die too.'

'Can we do something to make him stop that noise?'

'We can't do anything that will give away our position – not until we *want* to give it away. Don't worry about Dimitri,' I said. 'He will die soon, and then he won't make any more noise.'

It was their first taste of violent death. They were too young to remember the losses of the civil war with any clarity, even though it had touched their lives, and Vyriv had been spared much of the violence and suffering. They had never been this close to the horror, and although both understood my intent, they were shocked by my coldness.

'You know what you're doing?' I said.

'Yes.'

'Good, then there's no need to be afraid. We'll get out of this.'

But I couldn't be sure we wouldn't all die here on the steppe with snow in our mouths and holes in our hearts.

I took a deep breath and moved beyond the place where my sons were pinned down. I wanted to move further south, follow the curve of the ridge so I was at a better angle and in a place where I wouldn't be expected. My enemy had positioned himself well, but the sky was darkening now, a thick blanket of grey cloud blocking the sun, and I was thankful for that. The child thief had no advantage of light.

When I was far enough away from my sons, I stopped and opened my satchel. I took out one of the bundles Natalia had wrapped for us and opened it out in front of me. I put the bread and the sausage back into the satchel and, using my teeth, made a rip in the white cloth, tearing it lengthways into two pieces. The first piece I wrapped over my rifle scope, turning it from black to white. Then I took off my hat and tied the second piece around the top of my head. When I rested the rifle on the ridge and aimed down the sight, these were the two things that would be most visible. The telescopic sight provided magnification, but it also meant I had to raise my head a little higher to take a shot. The cloth was by no means perfect camouflage, but it would help reduce the impact of my movement on the stark white horizon the child thief would be watching.

With that done, I turned so I was face on to the ridge, and shuffled closer to the edge, pushing the rifle in front of me, keeping it sideways on so all I had to do was swivel it out, raise my head and put my eye to the scope.

I carefully parted the snow directly in front of me so the ground was clear for the weapon. I took a long breath, closed my eyes and said a short prayer. Then I spoke quietly but clearly.

'Ready.'

For a moment I heard nothing, then a crack. A familiar sound that split the air at almost the same time as Viktor swore, and I turned my rifle to point down the steppe, resting it on the ridge. From my slightly elevated position, I could see Viktor and Petro lying several metres to my left.

I estimated where I thought the shot had come from, some-where in the line of the hedge, and I imagined the shooter lying prone, working the bolt of his rifle, preparing for his next shot. I hoped his attention had been so focused on Viktor that he hadn't noticed me add my profile to the land.

And then Petro raised *his* hat. The shooter would think he had hit his mark, that we were panicking, moving erratically, looking to help our comrade. He would see the second movement as a mistake upon which he could capitalise, and he fired again.

This time I saw him.

I saw the muzzle flash from the rifle, and I put my eye to the scope, magnifying the spot where the child thief had chosen to wait for us. But I had been wrong. The shooter wasn't by the line of hedge that marked the end of this field. He was much further away, hidden in the treeline beyond. A small pile of dead wood, a fallen tree trunk with protruding branches. And behind it, the outline of a man either dressed entirely in white or half-buried beneath the snow.

I eased the rifle back so the snow on either side of it would hide the muzzle flash as much as possible, then I took another deep breath, let the air escape slowly as I steadied the rifle and squeezed the trigger.

The German rifle kicked against my shoulder and in my scope I saw the snow rise in a fountain beside the prone man, many metres away. Without taking my eye from the scope, I chambered another round while calculating the adjustment I'd need to make to hit my target. But already the figure was moving, the snow breaking, the dark shape rolling away from the spot where my bullet had hit the ground. This was not to be a shooting com-petition; we were not going to trade shots. Escape was the child thief's intention now.

'Get up,' I shouted as I prepared for a second shot. 'Quickly. Over here. Now.' I had to keep shooting, keep the man sup-pressed while I brought my sons to safety.

'Now!'

I heard Viktor and Petro's movements in the snow, heard their heavy breathing as they dropped into the trough beside me, but I ignored them, concentrating on the figure down there in the trees.

Hitting a target at this range was difficult enough, but now he was moving, it was an impossibility. I fired again anyway, seeing the snow erupt close to the rolling figure, then the child thief took his chance. He knew I would be working the bolt, ejecting the spent cartridge, pushing a new one into the chamber, so he rose to his feet, rushing back into the trees.

I fired once more at the escaping figure, seeing a plume of snow and bark tearing away from one of the trees, and then he was gone.

13

'Did you get him?' Viktor asked. 'Did you shoot him?'

I withdrew my rifle and ducked back behind the dip. 'No.'

'Did you even see him?' Petro said.

'I saw him. But he was too far away. I missed him.'

'But he's gone?'

'If it was me, I'd be looking for somewhere else to shoot from.'

'Then we should move?'

'Let me think.' I had been shot at before, but this was different. There were factors I'd never had to deal with. I had to consider my sons and their mother waiting for them at home. And I had to think about Dariya, whose father now lay on the steppe, his remaining blood freezing in his veins.

I took the cloth from my head and put my hat back on, telling Viktor and Petro to do the same. 'We may be here a while; we can't afford to get cold.'

'Shit, look at this.' Viktor showed me his hat, put his hand inside it and poked his finger through the hole the bullet had made. 'I never saw anyone shoot like that. He has to be using a scope like yours, Papa. No one could shoot like that without one.'

'Even with a scope, he's good.' I said. 'Impressive.'

Petro inspected his own hat, holding it out so we could see there was a hole in that too. 'He meant to kill us like he killed Dimitri. Why would he do that, Papa?'

'Put them on,' I said.

Petro hesitated, thinking what would have happened if the hat had been on his head. He looked at me and took a deep breath, blowing it out with puffed cheeks. 'Shit,' he said, putting it onto his head, grabbing the flaps and tugging it tight. 'Shit.'

'Don't worry,' I told them. 'We'll get out of this.'

'How?' Viktor asked.

I didn't reply.

'You don't know, do you?'

'I'm thinking about it.'

'We're stuck here until dark,' Viktor said. 'It's the only way we can be safe. We have to wait here until dark and then we have to go back.'

'Go back?' Petro said.

'That's what you're thinking isn't it, Papa?' Viktor asked. 'We have to go home.'

'No,' Petro said to his brother. He was shocked by what had happened and he was afraid, but he was surprised at Viktor's words. 'We have to keep going. Dariya needs us more than ever now.'

'We can't walk out there, onto the steppe, while someone is waiting to take a shot at us,' Viktor said. 'And the way he shoots . . .' He shook his head. 'He shoots even better than Papa.'

'No one shoots better than Papa,' Petro replied. 'Anyway, I didn't mean walk down there *now*. I meant wait until dark, then follow.'

'You don't think he'll be waiting somewhere in the woods?'

'It's too hard in the trees,' said Petro. 'That's why he waited until we reached the open field.'

'He can shoot us just as easily in the woods as he can in the field,' said Viktor. 'Isn't that right, Papa?'

I nodded but I was only half listening. I was trying to think of a way out of this spot. We couldn't afford to stay here for too long because there was a possibility the shooter was looking for a better position – perhaps one from which he could see us where we were right now – and if that were the case, it was only a matter of time before he was able to take his shot.

The other problem was the cold. The temperature was low but

not low enough. A few degrees colder and we would have been all right, but at that time of day the temperature was just on the wrong side for us. The snow was not dry and powdery, but wet, and I could already feel it soaking into my clothes. Our bodies were warm enough now to melt the snow beneath us but it would drench us and we'd grow colder and colder. We couldn't afford to wait for that to happen.

'We can't go back. We can't leave Dariya,' said Petro. 'We have to bring her home.'

Viktor spoke quietly: 'Maybe we *do* have to leave her. There's no sense in us all being killed. 'I mean . . . maybe she's already . . .'

'What?' Petro would know how his brother was feeling because he felt it too. Viktor was looking for the right thing to do. He was weighing our options, just as Petro was doing, but they'd each come to a different conclusion. 'Where's your fighting spirit? It should be me wanting to go home and you wanting to go on.'

'I'm as willing to fight as anyone, you know that,' said Viktor, 'but I'm not stupid. I won't run into a bullet.'

'No one's running into any bullets,' I said. 'And I'm not going back without Dariya. I promised Lara I'd bring her back, and that's what I'm going to do. We need to take things one step at a time. Right now all we have to think about is getting away from here. If we stay here until dark, we'll freeze to death.'

'And if we try to move, we'll be shot,' said Viktor.

'If he's still waiting,' I said. 'And we don't know that he is.'

'We don't know that he's not.'

I turned over onto my back, immediately feeling the cold air on my damp stomach.

I looked back at the woods we'd come from. The trees were close, maybe twenty metres away, at the top of the ridge, but twenty metres might as well have been twenty kilometres if that scope was still sweeping the area, looking for us. I didn't agree with Petro – I believed the man who had shot at us *was* a better marksman than I was, and I wondered if the child thief could still hit us at this range if we were moving. It would make it much harder for him, but he had shot Dimitri as good as dead with one bullet, and he had put holes in both Viktor and Petro's hats with almost no time to make any calculation.

But we had the weather on our side. The grey clouds had been rolling in over the morning and now the wind came and the first flakes of snow began to fall. As I looked back at the dark trunks of the trees standing sentry in the snow, I watched the air fill with light flakes, drifting and turning as they floated from the sky.

'Someone's watching over us,' I said. 'We'll let it build, and then we'll move. Snow and wind will make it almost impossible for him to hit us.'

'Are you sure?' Viktor asked.

I took hold of my rifle and looked at my son. 'Yes, Viktor. I'm sure.'

We waited for half an hour, maybe more, it was hard to tell. Immobile, lying prone, the minutes felt like hours. I lay on my stomach rather than expose the wet part of my clothing to the cold air. I tried to insulate myself against the ground, told my sons to do the same, but the snow was falling on our backs now, too. If we stayed there much longer we'd be buried beneath it, three unidentifiable shapes on the ground, hidden until the winter began to thaw.

Just a few metres away, Dimitri would be dead now, his unseeing eyes staring at nothing as his corpse lay in his own frozen blood. I imagined Svetlana's tears and wondered what we'd tell her when we returned to the village without her husband.

We hardly spoke, but I could almost hear what my sons were thinking. I knew them well enough for that. Petro's fear had subsided in the cold, probably replaced by an aching anger at the man we were following. But I knew there would be a quiet voice in his head telling him none of this would have happened if he had only brought Dariya home with him and Lara yesterday.

Viktor, on the other hand, would be thinking how it would feel to return to Vyriv as a hero. Like his brother, his fear had dulled, as fear does when it has been present long enough for it to become usual, and now he'd be picturing a scenario in his mind in which he was the one to take the final shot, to execute our prey and rescue the child.

That was the difference I saw in my sons.

My own thoughts took a contrasting course as I considered the way Dimitri had jerked and dropped at the sudden impact of the bullet. I tried to picture it again, to calculate how far away the shot had come from. Maybe six hundred metres. The person we were following had stopped, turned and waited with his sight trained on the place he had chosen for his killing ground. He had watched us discover the bloodstains, waited for us to line up along the ridge, silhouetting ourselves like dumb animals.

I speculated what kind of a man the child thief was. Perhaps he was a veteran like me – like the man Dimitri had hanged. War is an intense experience, and for some who fight long enough there's no other way for them to live. I knew something about that. Maybe this man was disturbed, lost without the thrill and excitement of sanctioned murder, and this was the only way he could re-create it. I believed there were those for whom fighting became their nature, and I believed it because I'd sometimes felt it overcoming me. I understood that war can sit in a man's heart and taint the blood that fills his body. For me, there had been nightmares, sleepless nights calmed only by Natalia's presence. There had been other feelings too, more complex and harder to understand even though they ran through my own mind, and sometimes I needed to leave everything behind. Dimitri had been right about that. There were days when the life of a farmer was not enough, and I would leave the village to hunt, and for a while I would be free of everything. Perhaps this man's need for release was more intense, and his response to it was darker. Perhaps he needed a different kind of hunt, so he would steal a child and wait for his pursuers. He was a man intent on provoking his own battles. And despite my misgivings, there was something in this situation that made me feel alive. Dimitri had been right: a small part of me was enjoying this. It was as if the child thief had challenged me personally, and I was torn between accepting his challenge and protecting my family.

'It should be safe now,' I said, lifting my head to see how the snow filled the air, the flakes swirling around us. 'He won't see us in this.'

'What if he's watching?' Viktor asked.

'We have to take the risk. This is our best chance. Right now. We'll stand and move as quickly as we can. Bring your rifles if you think you can carry them. If not – leave them.'

'I don't think I can move my legs,' Petro said. 'They're so cold.'

'Then start moving them. Shake them. Rub them. Whatever it takes. Viktor, do the same.' I didn't want them to turn and run if their legs weren't going to do what they expected of them.

So for a few minutes we rubbed our legs and shook the life back into them.

We ran like drunks running from a fight. Our legs wanting to seize and cramp, our cold bodies moving as if in slow motion. We zigzagged as I had instructed, but our progress was so slow it hardly made any difference. If the air had been clear, we would have been dead before we reached the treeline. We would have lived only as long as it would have taken Dimitri's murderer to draw back the bolt of his rifle and squeeze the trigger with the tip of his finger.

But nature stayed with us and visibility was poor. We could barely see the trees just a few metres ahead of us, so it was impossible for our hunter to see us at all. Not even three dark streaks drifting backwards and forwards in the storm.

The wind rushed around us, pulling at the weaknesses in our clothing, freezing the dampness and probing any unprotected area. I carried only my satchel and my rifle, both of them banging against my back as I ran. And even under the cover of the storm, I found myself dreading the singular and unmistakable sound of a gunshot. But none came.

Petro was the first into the trees, just a smudge in the blizzard ahead of me and Viktor. His shape disappeared among the stumps, followed by that of his brother, and then we were all in safety, coming out of the worst of the weather and into the relative quiet of the woods.

We moved further in before I called to them to stop.

'We'll make a fire,' I said. 'Dry out.' I put my hands on my knees, almost bent double, trying to catch my breath. There was pain in my legs and an ache in my hips, and I waited for it to ease.

'Won't he see?'

'He won't come out in this.' My words were laboured, coming between breaths. 'Anyway, it doesn't matter. We need to get dry. It's the most important thing.'

Both boys were huddling themselves with their arms, their teeth chattering. They had scarves across their mouths and noses, I could see the movement beneath, and I could see the colour of the skin that was exposed. They needed warmth, just like I did.

'Find some wood,' I told them, 'but stay close. Don't get lost.'

While they collected wood, I took my entrenching tool and used it to shovel snow into a pile in front of the place where I intended to build the fire. Petro was right to be worried about Dimitri's murderer, but not because he might follow us. I suspected he was not a man who would tackle us by coming close; experience suggested he would always look to take a shot from a distance, and that's what we had to concern ourselves with. So I built a wall high enough to hide the light from the fire, forming an arc to shield us.

The trees were not close together in this wood, and their branches were naked, but they still offered protection from the storm, allowing me to work without too much difficulty, and it was calm enough for the boys to find wood.

By the time they returned, I had dug a shallow pit and laid a small bed of tinder made from wood shavings and pieces of cotton which I kept in a tin in my satchel. I also had a handful of fire sticks I'd made earlier in the winter and always took when I was hunting. These were short tubes of thick paper packed with woodcuttings and sealed with fat. I placed one on top of the tinder and used a knife to make shallow cuts in the driest pieces of wood the boys had brought, propping them against each other in a cone over the bed of tinder. When that was done, Petro and Viktor crouched beside me, protecting the area from the wind as I struck a match, putting it to the cotton.

Within a few seconds the flames had given enough heat to light the fire stick, which burned well and long enough to light the kindling.

The three of us sat around the fire, desperate for its warmth, willing it to succeed despite the weather. We protected it as best as we could; feeding it as it grew, developing it until we had to sit back from it so we didn't burn ourselves.

Under other circumstances we might have undressed, given our clothes time to dry, but it was unthinkable that we'd sit here without any protection, so we stayed as close to the fire as possible, offering the wettest parts of our clothing to its drying heat.

The flames rose and cut into the grey, sawing in the wind, crackling, giving the fire's lightest embers to the storm. And we held our hands to it, praying to it, begging it to keep us warm.

After a while, the three of us sitting in silence, I reached into my satchel and took out the sausage and bread that Natalia had packed for us. I had tried to wrap it back into the cotton, as she had done, but the cloth was in two pieces now and my hands had been too cold to do as I had asked them. The sausage had come loose from the cloth and it was covered with lint and dirt from the inside of the satchel. I brushed it off and cut it into three pieces. They were small, no longer than my thumb and not much thicker, but it was better than nothing. I tore the bread into three chunks and passed one to each of the boys.

'What now?' Viktor asked as he finished the last bite of his bread. He clapped his gloved hands to dust away the crumbs, his palms making a hollow banging sound as they came together.

'You think he'll come after us?' Petro said.

'No. I think he's the kind who waits.' I took a packet of cigarettes from my pocket. The card was soggy, the lid wrinkled and ill-fitting because the weather had penetrated it. It came away in my hands when I opened it and I could see the cigarettes inside were wet. It didn't matter. I needed to smoke. I removed one glove and picked out a cigarette, fumbling with numb fingertips. The tobacco was damp and there were brown spots on the paper.

'What makes you think that?' Viktor asked. 'That he's the kind who waits.'

'He works like a sharpshooter.' I took a burning stick from the fire and touched the tip to the cigarette. 'Wounding a man and trying to draw out his comrades was a trick we all used.'

'We? You were a sharpshooter? You never told us that.'

'It was never important.' I threw the stick back into the flames.

'I bet you were good, though,' Viktor said. 'The best.'

'The Germans were the best. We were good, but their rifles were second to none. And they had scopes, like this one.' I clamped the cigarette in my mouth and lifted the rifle onto my knee. 'That man out there has to be using something like this; otherwise he could never have shot like that. Not at that range.'

'Where would he get a rifle like that?' Petro asked.

'Where did *you* get it from?' Viktor said.

I dragged on the cigarette. 'A German.'

'You shot him?

'Yes.'

'Where?' asked Petro.

I hesitated, then put a fingertip to the side of my head.

'No,' he said. 'I meant where were you? When was it?'

'Does it matter?'

'I just wondered, that's all. You never say much about it.'

I ran my hands along the stock of the German rifle, feeling the smoothness of it. 'It was in Galicia in the summer of 1917,' I said. 'Our final offensive against the central powers, which would make you . . . just four years old at the time.'

'You'd never seen us,' Petro said. 'Did you even know our names?'

'I knew your names. Your mother wrote to me, and I thought about you all the time.'

'You never thought about coming home, though?' he asked.

'Sometimes. But I was a soldier; I had a duty.'

'You must have been afraid.'

'How was it?' Viktor said. 'Being in the army.'

'Not good. Morale was low, officers always being demoted and replaced, soldiers refusing to act without discussing everything with their committees.' I looked at Petro. 'Some soldiers *did* just go home. They abandoned their posts and left their brothers to fight alone.'

'The beginning of the revolution,' Petro said.

I smiled. 'We thought it was going to be utopia. No more oppression, no more rich and poor.'

'So tell us how you got the rifle,' Viktor said.

I thought for a moment, taking myself back. There had been times when these things had filled my thoughts, but the years had moved on and I had learned to put many of the memories away. I kept them behind a strong door in my mind that was rarely opened now.

'Well, when the artillery began to fire in the last days of June, we knew something big was happening. They only ever fired like that when they were going to make us push hard. They went on for two days, driving some of the men so mad they screamed and screamed.'

I shook my head to dispel the sound of those guns and took another drag on the cigarette. I watched my sons by the fire. Viktor was sitting on a small log, his forearms resting on his thighs, his body leaning forward as he listened. His eyes were alive, the flames reflected in his pupils.

'Go on, Papa.'

'On the first morning of July we came out of the trenches and advanced on the Austro-Hungarians, driving them back. It was the first time we'd been out of our holes in many days. We were the first into the ruins of a town I don't even know the name of, a place with buildings smashed and blown apart by our shelling. We thought it was deserted, but we were wrong. Shots fired from somewhere in the rubble took down two soldiers before the rest of us had time to find protection.'

'The sharpshooter,' Viktor said.

'Mm. The shots were well placed and both men were still alive. They lay in the open, calling for help, dying slowly while the rest of us stayed hidden.'

Petro stared at the flames as he listened. He would be remembering how Dimitri had called to us as he died.

'I was ordered to find him.'

'Why you?' Viktor asked.

'Because I was a sharpshooter. Three men were sent out to act as decoys while I looked for him. Three men, my brothers, all shot dead so he wouldn't see me coming, but I found him. A German, lying prone on the roof of a half-demolished building. He'd made a barrier of bricks around himself, leaving just enough room for the barrel of his rifle and the height of his scope. He was firing at us from so far away it was almost impossible to imagine how he could hit his target, but when I was close enough, I put a bullet right here.' I touched the side of my head once more. 'Just one. With that rifle you've been carrying all day.'

Viktor glanced at his Russian-made Mosin-Nagant.

'This was the first telescopic sight I ever looked through,' I said. 'And my officer gave it to me as a reward.' I tapped the weapon on my knee and looked at my sons, seeing their different reactions. Viktor was entranced by the story, seeing the heroism and the adventure, while Petro saw the suffering and the loss of life. One story, two different interpretations. For me the events of that July were neither one thing nor another; they were just a part of my past told now so the words could evaporate by the fire.

'This man, though,' I said, 'the one who shot at us today – I've not seen shooting like that before. And he was so well hidden. He's very dangerous.'

No one spoke. Petro and Viktor stared into the fire, dry sticks popping and crackling in the flames that rose and fell, rose and fell, snapping and twisting in the wind. Somewhere out in the darkness a wolf howled, but none of us reacted to the sound. We had heard wolves before.

'So what are we going to do?' Viktor asked, breaking the silence. 'Are we going back?'

Both sons were watching me again, waiting for an answer.

I sighed and looked down at the cigarette in my fingers, as if I'd forgotten it was there. I wished I had something to drink. A mouthful of *horilka* to take the edge off my thoughts.

'Yes,' I said.

Petro was surprised. 'Yes? You mean we're going to leave Dariya?'

'That's not what I said.'

Now Petro was confused. 'What then?'

I passed the cigarette to Viktor.

'We can't leave her,' Petro said.

'She's not your responsibility,' I told him. 'It's not your fault.'

Petro shook his head. 'I should have brought her back with me.'

'Stop feeling sorry for yourself.' Viktor passed him the cigarette. 'No one blames you.'

Petro snatched it from his brother without looking at him and sat for a while with it between his finger and thumb before lifting it to his mouth. 'If I had—'

'If you had nothing,' Viktor told him. 'Papa said it isn't your fault and he's right. You didn't know what was going to happen. We all thought the man we found did . . . *that* to those children.'

'You too?' I asked, looking up.

Viktor shrugged. 'I didn't want to. You were so sure about him, but . . .' He searched for the words. 'There was no one else.'

'You thought I was wrong?'

Viktor nodded. 'Yes, Papa.'

I smiled at that. I put my head back and laughed, releasing some tension.

'What's funny?' Viktor asked.

I patted his shoulder. 'You're a good boy.'

'Why?'

'Because you stood by me anyway. You thought I was wrong but you stood by me.' I smiled and wondered how many years, maybe months or days, it would be before Viktor would no longer trust my judgement or respect my decisions. What would it have taken for him to tell me he thought I was wrong?

Petro stood and leaned over to hand me the cigarette. I took it with cold fingers, and while Petro was leaning towards me like that, I spoke, saying, 'What about you, Petro? What did you think?'

'I thought you were right.'

I waited for him to sit down again, put his hands towards the fire for warmth. I finished what was left of the cigarette and threw it into the flames. 'I want you two to go back,' I said. 'I want you to go home. I'll find Dariya.'

'Alone?' Viktor looked up.

'It's better that way.'

'Better?'

'Safer. It doesn't make sense for all of us to head on.'

'I want to come with you,' Petro said. 'Viktor can go back if he wants to, but I'm coming with you.'

'You have nothing to prove to me, Petro. You're a good boy. A good *man*. You already make me proud.'

Petro looked away.

'I can't take you with me. Not with things as they are. That shot might have hit either of you today and I don't want to have to take that back to your mother. It'll be bad enough seeing Svetlana's face.'

Petro stared at the fire. He was listening but he didn't want to hear.

'I'm coming too,' Viktor said.

'No. You need to get away from here. Go back to the shelter we saw. Stay there until first light, then make your way home. You know the way?'

'Of course.'

'So wait for me at home. And if anyone comes to the village, give them what they want.'

'You mean communists?' Viktor asked.

'We're all communists,' Petro said.

'Communists, Chekists, Bolsheviks, whatever you want to call them.'

'Whoever it is, don't put yourselves in any danger,' I said. 'Just give them what they want, and when I come home we're going to leave this damn country.'

'We're not going to leave you alone.' Viktor looked at his brother, and I knew they both wanted to come for different reasons. Petro felt responsible. He thought it was his fault Dariya was missing and he felt a duty to her. He had failed to bring her back once, and he was determined not to do it again. Viktor, on the other hand, was drawn to the fight. He wanted to find Dariya and he wanted to help his father, and the promise of action excited him.

'I've already told you, it's safer for me alone. Don't argue with me.'

'What about you, then?' Petro said. 'If we go back, what will you do?'

'I'll cross the fields tonight, when it's dark. I'll find his trail in the morning and follow him.'

'And if he's waiting?'

'I don't think he will be. Not there, anyway.'

'But later. In the forest. Or maybe when you come out into another field. He'll be waiting then, won't he?' Viktor said.

'Yes.'

'And you'll be alone.'

'Yes.'

'Then it's better to have us to help you.'

'No.' I shook my head. 'I'll move faster on my own. I know what I'm looking for.'

'Then teach us,' said Viktor.

'And I'll be harder to see if I'm alone. If we're together, we're easier prey.'

'We'll keep apart.'

'Stop.' I held up a hand and raised my voice. 'I said no and I mean no. I'm not taking you out there for that man to put a bullet in your belly like he did with Dimitri. I'm not going to listen to your screams. I can't do that. I won't go home to your mother to tell her I couldn't keep you safe.' I closed my eyes and remembered the times I had done the same as the child thief had done that day. The times *I* had waited for the moment to take the shot. *I* had dropped a man alive so his comrades would try to help him, and I had taken them too, when they came into the open.

'Everything has changed,' I said, my voice quiet. 'We're not just hunting him now; he's hunting us.'

14

By the time the wind dropped and the snowfall subsided, night had come to the steppe. We huddled by the fire, our clothes more or less dry now, our stomachs empty and grumbling.

'We need to find our things,' I said, standing. 'You two wait here.'

I didn't give them time to object. I took the revolver from my satchel and stuffed it into my coat pocket before breaking a solid stick, half my height, from the pile of firewood. I put the satchel in the snow where I'd leaned my rifle against a birch and walked through the trees to the place where they formed a line along the edge of the field. It was dark, the sky still clouded, but the snow brightened the open ground. My silhouette would stand out, but I kept low, hoping it would be enough, knowing that if the man was still watching, his telescopic lens would be unable to take in enough light. I was invisible to him now.

I moved down to the place we'd escaped from earlier, where everything was now under a thick covering of snow, and began poking the stick into the soft undulations. I pushed hard, moving from side to side, searching for our packs, and within a few moments the end of the branch touched something solid but with a little give in it. This was not frozen soil but something else, so I knelt down to brush the snow aside.

This wasn't where I had left my pack. This was the place where Dimitri had died.

I squatted and cleared away the fresh snow, revealing a patch of dark cloth, moving my fingers around the edge until I made out Dimitri's shoulder.

I paused for a moment, imagining him lying beneath the covering, his face frozen in that expression of fear and confusion and begging. I heard the ripple of his dying sounds in my mind, shook them away, and continued to dig. I knew I could let nothing go to waste; nothing useful should be left behind.

I followed the line of Dimitri's leg until his feet were un-covered, digging down and lifting them in turn, pulling off his boots and socks. I stuffed the socks into the boots, tied the laces and then strung them around my neck so they fell against my chest. With that done, I removed Dimitri's coat, wrestling with his frozen limbs, before I reburied him and stood up.

Dimitri would stay there until spring, hidden just below the surface, but when the temperature rose and the snow melted, he would thaw and lie in the open, by the forest which would be freshly adorned with leaves and new life. And then something would find him and make him its meal.

I intended there to be one more body to join him.

Continuing to search, I found all of our belongings before going back to the trees, looking for the vague glow of the fire. The windbreak I'd made had done its job well, and the fire pit helped to keep the flames hidden from sight as well as from the wind. It was hard to spot anything, even this close.

When I came back to the fire, both Viktor and Petro were pointing their rifles in my direction. Viktor kneeling behind a fallen tree, Petro standing close to the trunk of another, the barrel of his rifle resting on a low branch. Shadow cast from the flames flickered across his shape.

'It's only me,' I said, feeling a touch of pride that they'd thought to take up a defensive position. They had been alert to the sounds in the forest, and that was a good sign. Despite everything that had happened, they were still thinking. I was certain they would make it home without me.

My sons came back to the fire as I rummaged through the

packs, making some things more accessible than others, ensuring I had everything I'd need. The situation had changed now; my priorities were different. Before, there had been three of us to carry everything, but now there would be only me. And when we left the village this morning we were just following tracks, chasing a thief. But now the thief had turned on us and I saw his intention was not as I'd first thought. There were some items I'd need to have close to hand.

'Let us come,' Viktor said as I finished packing the bag.

'Don't make me talk about this again.' I checked the red nine pistol was loaded, and put it into my satchel. I closed the top and fastened the buckle.

'I'm not planning on taking too long,' I said. 'I'll be over the fields in no time, pick up his trail in the woods as soon as it's light. I'll be fine. And if the sky clears, and I can see the tracks at night, it'll be easier for me to follow if I'm alone.' If I could, I would go on in the dark, as I had failed to do the previous night. There was a chance the child thief would do as he had done before – find a place to rest – and if that were so, I might discover him as he slept and be able put an end to this hunt.

'And if it *is* too dark to go on?' Petro said. 'Where will you sleep? What will you eat?'

'I have wire, I can make a snare. I'll find tracks and catch something. I have enough guns to shoot something – I'm a hunter for God's sake. And anyway, how will it be any easier if *you* come? Will I be less hungry? Less tired?'

Petro didn't answer. He didn't even shake his head.

'Please,' I said. 'Do as I ask. Go home to your mother. Tell your sister I'll bring her cousin back soon.'

'And Dimitri?' Viktor asked. 'What do we tell them about him?'

I stared down at my feet and thought about Svetlana. I couldn't ask my sons to carry that news. 'Tell them he's still with me.'

'What about his coat? And his boots? You want us to leave them?'

'No,' I sighed, 'they're too valuable.'

'So how do we explain—'

'Petro will do it,' I said, looking up at my youngest. 'I want you to tell Mama what happened. She'll speak to Svetlana.'

Petro didn't ask why I had chosen him.

I stared after my sons as they left the small circle of light and walked into the darkness with their reluctance and their annoyance clear in their eyes. I watched the place where the night had taken them and I warmed myself one last time by the flames before I kicked snow into the pit and suffocated the fire. It flickered and fought to survive, hissing and spitting, but it quickly succumbed to the snow and gave up the last of its light and warmth.

I threw the pack over my back, kept my satchel close to my side and took up my rifle before moving away in the other direction. Once again I stepped out onto the open field and headed across the steppe.

I had a fix on the place I wanted to go. I remembered the direction of the tracks and I remembered the place where the man had run into the trees. The sky was without stars, but the field was white enough to collect just enough light for me to know where I was going.

I tried to be aware of the land around me, of movement and sound, but I had to concentrate just to put one foot in front of the other. The snow was deeper now, and the rise and fall of the land beneath it was invisible. I stumbled a few times, but kept on going until I reached the hedge. I had only travelled a few hundred metres, but it felt longer and I was beginning to sweat beneath my clothes. As a younger man, I could have crossed that distance in half the time and hardly felt it in my chest and legs, but years and circumstance had slowed me.

Pausing at the hedge, I allowed my heartrate to return to normal, giving my body a moment to rest. I didn't want to sweat, to dampen my clothes with moisture that would freeze and steal my warmth. I stood and looked out at the wood beyond, seeing nothing but the trees and the darkness. Dariya was out there somewhere. Alive or dead, I had no way of knowing.

As I moved along the line of the hedge, looking for a way to pass through, I imagined the man with the rifle doing the same. I pictured him dragging Dariya with him, perhaps tied, or maybe she followed him because she had nowhere else to go, or because he had tempted her with some kind of promise. And it struck me that the child was now dependent on the thief. The kidnapper had provided shelter and warmth, perhaps even food, and without those things Dariya would die in that wilderness. She was now reliant on the child thief to keep her alive and protect her. She was damned if she remained with him, and damned if she managed to escape. I was her only hope.

Coming to a place where the hedge was thinner, I turned sideways, pushing through the branches, knowing this was where my enemy would have passed through. His clothes would have touched these branches. His hands.

Within the woods on the other side of the field I spotted a number of burrows, cleared and left open, suggesting they were still inhabited. There were small prints in the snow, droppings on the surface, and I guessed my approach had disturbed the rabbits back to their holes. These signs were visible in the natural light, but once I was deeper among the beech and oak and hornbeam, everything became more obscure, and I knew I wouldn't be able to track this man during the night. There was some light here, but not enough. I could see disturbances on the ground, the spot where the man had waited to take his first shot, and I found the marks where he'd crawled back to his place by the tree, unsettling the dusting of delicate light green moss on the bark, but the fresh snow had made an impact on the tracks. The marks were smooth, the footprints barely discernible. Here they were almost impossible to spot; even further into the woods and they would be invisible.

I cursed my fortune and tried to find some reassurance in my inability to track Dariya at night. It meant at least that yesterday's decision had been the right one. I also consoled myself with the suspicion that this man wanted to be followed and would therefore ensure it was possible to track him. It was the only thing that made any sense and, as twisted as it seemed, it felt as if this was all part of a macabre game. He had taken Dariya as bait and he was leaving a trail that was easy to follow. He seemed to be doing everything he could to invite me to go after him so, resigned to waiting until dawn, I decided to make camp.

I moved away from the place where I had found the tracks and set about building a quick shelter for the night. It was something I had learned as a soldier, mostly through trial and error rather than training, and had put into practice many times. I had shared my observations with comrades, and they had shared theirs with me, until I had found the best way to provide shelter under many different circumstances. And I had practised many times, both at war and later while hunting to feed my family.

I used the trenching tool to pull together as much snow as I could, piling it into a mound along the length of a fallen tree. I packed it hard and used the small shovel to hollow it out. As I worked, I imagined the child thief doing the same. The shelter he had made for himself and Dariya had been efficient and uncomplicated, and it reinforced my belief that the man I was hunting had also been a soldier.

When I was finished, I built a low windbreak close to the entrance of the shelter, leaving me enough room to shuffle inside. It took me no longer than an hour to build, but I was exhausted when it was finally ready. It was small, compact, and would keep me warm during the night. I thought I might even be able to sleep for a few hours, but it was unlikely, knowing what was out there.

Before settling, I took a couple of wire snares and returned to the place where I'd seen the burrows. I collected some twigs and set the snares close to the entrances of two of them, hiding the base of each noose in the snow. The air was quiet, almost no wind, and there was a strong sense of being alone in the world, and when my mind wandered from the task an unnerving sensation crept in. As if something was out there, in the birch scrub and the darkness – something that was part of the forest – and I couldn't help recall Dariya's fears of the Baba Yaga.

Satisfied I'd set the traps in the best places, I took a tree branch and swept it across the surface of the snow as I backed away. It wasn't a perfect way to hide my presence, but it was the best I could do. In the morning it would be obvious where I had swept the snow, but for now, in the near dark, it was good enough. If the man I was hunting came this way, he would have to look very closely to see what I had done.

Back at the shelter I placed a canvas sheet on the floor for insulation, and climbed in feet first, keeping my head close to the semicircular entrance. I turned onto my back, so I could see the roof of the cave, not even an arm's length from my face, or so I could see the treetops if I shifted my gaze. I stared at the blank white surface above me and wondered about the man who had taken Dariya. I imagined him lying in a similar shelter. Perhaps Dariya was beside him, shivering and frightened, praying for her papa to come looking for her. And it occurred to me that maybe Dariya wasn't even with him any more. Maybe she was already dead. And I might have believed it if not for the tracks in the snow. The small footprints alongside the larger ones.

Removing my right glove, I put my hand in my coat pocket and drew out the revolver. I lifted it to my chest and gripped the handle tight, closing my eyes and praying that Dariya was still alive.

Sleep didn't settle itself over me. It circled me, moving in and away again, always threatening to take me but never doing so. I dozed in and out, warm enough in my shelter, always aware of the revolver in my hand, the cold air blowing against my face. There were vague snatches of dreams, visions of Lara and Dariya, of the children on the sled, of the man hanging from the tree, of

Dimitri lying face down in the snow. These images taunted me, like the muddled dreams of a drunkard, but I persevered, determined to rest – trying to will myself to sleep, to not be afraid of the man who was out there in the forest with his rifle and his keen eye.

But somewhere in the darkness, somewhere in the plague of images that riddled my thoughts like an incurable disease, a sound broke through. A single terrifying sound. From far away the unmistakable sound of a scream.

Immediately my eyes were open and I was turning onto my stomach, bringing the revolver out in front of me, pointing into the night. I held my breath without thinking, making not a sound as I watched the night. My eyes were wide, my head turning, looking for anything.

I thought of Lara's concern once more, the Baba Yaga, and I remembered the stories from my childhood. How real they had felt then, as a young boy. The thought of the witch in the forest, waiting to bring her victims to her pot. And now they seemed real again. During the hours of daylight nothing was more frightening than the threat of those who would come to break my family apart, but now, at night, roused from the broken dreams, something unearthly seemed more possible.

I listened to my heart beating and I felt both absurd and afraid. I had seen things not meant for human eyes. I had done things no man should ever do to another. I had killed and killed and killed, all in the name of one cause or another. I had seen men on the battlefield with their bodies turned inside out. I had seen artillery vaporise flesh and bone, and I had heard battle-hardened men sob for their mothers with their last breaths. But that scream in the night was unlike anything I had ever heard before. A single awful sound that could only have come from a child. And I had to remind myself who I was before I could force myself to crawl forward, to leave my small space of safety and emerge into the wood.

Once outside, I crouched by the low windbreak. I raised the revolver and searched the darkness once again.

The second scream made me jump. Almost an exact repeat of the first, like an echo, but a third followed it within a few seconds, this one longer. I tried to gauge the direction from which it had come, but it was difficult to be sure. There was almost no wind now and sound carried well over the flat ground. It might have been as close as a few hundred metres, but it might have been much further.

For a long time I crouched behind the windbreak with the revolver in my hand. I considered striking out into the forest to search for the source of the scream but knew it would be a mistake. The child thief might be trying to draw me out. So I remained where I was, alert, eyes wide to draw the light, listening. The forest listened with me.

The screams were long gone. The only evidence of them having existed was the echo of them in my head. And then I heard movement. Close.

Boots in the snow. The gentle scuff and crunch of someone moving in the forest. Footsteps pushing through the soft surface covering, breaking through the icy layer beneath. I turned the revolver towards the sound and squinted into the gloom. The trees stood unmoved by the screams and the secretive movements, like silent witnesses. Unjudging and unconcerned with the affairs of men. Their silhouettes against the snow, laying shadow where I needed there to be light, and among those shadows something demanded my attention.

A shape. Close to the base of a tree. A mound that broke the evenness of the area. As if something lay covered. I narrowed my eyes, pushed my head forward, studied. The shape of a man, perhaps. A killer in the night, lying concealed beneath a camouflage of snow, his rifle barrel pointed directly at me. I dropped lower, holding the revolver out, my finger tightening on the trigger. And, for a moment, the clouds above me parted. As if they had been looking down at me they split and allowed me the light of the moon. In that light my mind saw the child thief revealed: his face intent, his eyes hard and cold, his aim steady and true.

But all that my eyes showed me was a mound of snow covering a decaying log. And when the clouds reformed, shutting out the light, I continued to stare at that place. I stared and stared until something else took my attention. The briefest of movements. Something passing among the trees. Too tall for it to have been a small animal. It had to be something larger. A wolf. A deer. A man.

Then another exclamation. Not a scream. Not a child's scream as before, but a more guttural sound. And then a loud bang, less than ten metres away from where I was crouched.

The muzzle flash lit up the area around the shooter, a man, his weapon pointed somewhere to my left, the orange-yellow flare exploding from the barrel of his rifle. A few metres away I heard the crash of a bullet as it struck something solid. I ducked lower, kept the revolver pointed at the figure and hunched so I was looking directly along the barrel, lining up the sight.

I was sure I hadn't been seen. The shot had been a blind one. Something had startled the shooter and he had fired at it, but I had not made a sound. I had not moved. I had hardly even taken a breath.

I raised my eye from the sight and looked out at the dark shape, thinking this erratic shooting didn't seem like the behaviour of a man who had led me to a killing place. This had less purpose and was less professional.

The figure moved now and I could see its shape more clearly. Then something was moving beside it, coming close, the two shapes crouching low in the forest, moving back to the cover of a tree, blending with its shape, becoming part of its shadow.

An urgent whisper.

The sound of breathing.

I raised my head further and took a risk. There was a danger to revealing my position, but I had to be sure. 'Viktor?'

Silence.

'Viktor?'

I kept the revolver pointed at the place where the shadows had merged. 'Speak now or I'll shoot.'

'Papa? Is that you?'

15

Viktor and Petro had walked back in the direction of the shelter we found earlier that day, but their quiet conversation had focused solely on what they were going to do. Neither of them wanted to return home. For different reasons they both wanted to be by my side, so when they reached the shelter, instead of settling down, they turned round and headed back the way they had come. At the open steppe they found my tracks and followed them to the line of the hedge and across the field, but once inside the trees, they had lost sight of them.

'We stayed together,' Viktor said. 'Looked for signs, but we couldn't find anything. It was like you just disappeared, and then we heard . . .'

They were sitting by the shelter, backs to the low wall, talking in whispers. I clasped my hands together, my fingers held tight to hide that they were shaking. There had been a moment when I had almost shot my own sons.

'What was it?' Petro asked. 'What made that noise? You think it was Dariya?'

No one answered. We all thought it was Dariya's scream. We knew of no one else out there who would make such a noise.

'We'll find her.' I put a hand on my son's shoulder and Petro looked at me. I could hardly see his face in the darkness, but the light reflected from the snow into his eyes.

I told them to try to get some sleep. There was enough room in the shelter for both of them if they lay close and didn't move around. It would work well: we could take turns staying awake, watching the forest. It made sense, and I felt more comfortable. I'd at least be able to close my eyes for an hour or so later on, knowing one of my sons would be watching.

'I'm glad,' I said to them. 'I'm glad you came back.'

'You're not angry?' Petro asked.

'That you disobeyed me?' I smiled. 'Of course, but you're not children any more. It's good to have your company and I feel safer having you here. We can watch each other.'

As my sons slept, I watched over them, the revolver never leaving my hand. I sat until my legs were numb, then I moved slowly, keeping to the shadow until it was my turn to sleep.

At first light Viktor woke me and Petro as instructed. I handed them my satchel, telling them to make a fire, and trudged back towards the hedge, through the area where I had brushed the snow last night.

Up close, I could see the forest edge was a tangle of brambles and briars, the perfect place for rabbits to build their winter burrows, and there were fresh tracks where the animals had come to forage in the early morning. I was disappointed to find the first of my snares empty, and I took it up, removing the stakes and putting the noose into my pocket. As I came to the spot where the second snare was, however, I saw movement in the snow and hurried to grab the rabbit struggling in the trap. It must have been a recent catch because it still had plenty of energy, jumping and fighting to free itself, but the stake and the noose held tight. I took the animal's back legs in one hand, gripping it tight, before removing the noose and holding it behind the ears. A quick pull and the rabbit's neck was broken.

'It's not much for three,' I said putting the carcass by the fire, 'but it's better than nothing.'

Viktor cleaned the animal and we cooked it over the flames, sharing it equally. As I ate, I glanced over at the place where I'd seen the mound last night.

'What is it, Papa?' Petro asked, seeing me stare.

Ignoring the question, I got to my feet and took the revolver from my pocket.

'You see something?'

Both boys reached for their rifles as I advanced on the place where the snow had collected over the fallen log. Only there was no longer any mound.

There was no fallen log.

All that remained was a slight disturbance in the snow. Enough to tell me that someone had been there, concealed just a few metres from our camp.

'Someone was here?' Viktor asked. 'Last night? Right *here*?'

'It seems so,' I said.

'Was it him?' Petro couldn't hide the fear in his voice.

'Who else?'

'How the hell did we not see him?' Viktor said. 'How did we not know?'

'I thought I saw something, but . . .' I stared at the place where the child thief had been lying.

'You thought you saw something?' Viktor asked. 'So why didn't you come and look?'

'I thought it was nothing.'

'There're no tracks,' Petro said. 'Coming or going. Nothing. How did he do it?'

I shook my head and scanned the trees. I studied the branches, searched for any sign.

'Who is he that he can come and go without leaving tracks?' Petro asked.

'When he wants,' Viktor added. 'Otherwise he leaves enough tracks for any idiot to follow. Who is this man?'

I looked at my sons, understanding what this meant. The question now was not whether the child thief could kill us whenever he wanted, but why had he not done so already? And how long did he intend to wait before he tried to take another of us?

16

It didn't take long to find the trail he had left for us, two sets of prints, one large one small. For the most part it looked as if Dariya was walking well. There were places where she seemed to have fallen, perhaps been dragged, but they were brief.

'She's strong,' I said aloud. 'To be walking like that. He must be feeding her, keeping her well.' And even as I said it, I saw a meaning I hadn't intended. Like the Baba Yaga fattening up children before they were ready to be eaten.

'I still don't understand how he left no tracks,' Viktor said. 'We're following tracks right now, aren't we? So why has he left these but didn't leave any last night?'

'He *wants* us to find these ones,' Petro said. 'He wants us to follow. He didn't want us to follow last night so he covered his tracks.'

'Why?'

'Because he had a camp,' Petro said. 'Somewhere he was keeping Dariya.'

'Right,' I agreed. 'He wanted us to know he'd been there, but not to follow him. Nothing else makes any sense. I should've gone to look. Last night. I should have investigated what I thought I saw. We might be going home with Dariya right now.'

'If we'd caught him, though,' Viktor asked, 'you think he would've told us where Dariya was?'

'Yes.'

'How can you be sure?'

'There are ways to make men tell you what you want to know.'

Both boys were quiet.

'He must've used the trees,' I said. 'I've been thinking about how he could have done it and it's the only way. He must've climbed across the low branches and that's why there were no tracks.'

'You sure he didn't fly?' Viktor asked.

I smiled that his thoughts had followed the same pattern as my own. 'I'm sure. He's just a man.'

'Who comes and goes as he pleases,' Viktor said. 'Like he's playing a game.'

'He *is* playing a game,' I said. 'That's why we have to be vigilant if we want to win. I've let us down once; I won't do it again.'

We followed the tracks for another hour or so, veering close to the edge of the woods, passing the houses of another village.

'That looks like Uroz,' I said. 'Which means we've come almost fifty kilometres. We're still going east.'

'Maybe we can go down there,' Viktor suggested. 'Maybe they'll have something for us to eat.'

'And maybe they won't,' I said. 'Maybe the place will be under the control of the OGPU. No, we have to keep going while we still have daylight.' I thought about the screams during the night. 'We have to keep going.' And I thought about Dimitri, that first night, wanting to go after Dariya straight away. I wondered if maybe the child thief had been watching us then, ready to shoot the first person to follow him.

'Papa.' Petro stopped and grabbed at my coat, disturbing my thoughts, making me look up. 'Something there. Someone.'

Immediately I crouched, dropping my rifle from my shoulder. Viktor and Petro did the same, but I damned myself for day-dreaming, for not being as observant as I needed to be. Not much more than an hour ago I had told myself how vigilant I needed to be, and already I was failing. My instincts and senses were dulled by the cold and the hunger, and by age. I was growing old, and each day was taking a little more of my steel. I should have seen the shape through the trees before either of my sons saw it. It was my duty.

I looked to where Petro was pointing his rifle and lifted my own weapon, pulling the stock against my shoulder, wrapping the sling around my left hand to steady it. We were just past Uroz now, half a kilometre maybe, the houses behind and out of sight. A single figure was standing close to the trees, facing our direction. It was lighter out there, so he was only a silhouette, and to him we would be shrouded in the murk of the forest, but he was stationary and he was staring in our direction.

I put my eye to the scope, bringing the man into focus. It was hard to make out his features. His demeanour was that of an old man, though. He stood hunched, his shoulders slumped, his back bent, his head low.

'Did he see us?' I whispered.

'I don't know,' Petro answered. 'I just saw him there and stopped.'

'You didn't see him do anything?' I asked as the man moved. He shuffled to one side, leaning forward as if looking into the forest.

'No.'

'Viktor? What about you?'

'No.'

I tried to get beyond my anger at not having seen him. I was a soldier, a hunter. I was accustomed to seeing the slightest movement, always watching for signs of life. But tiredness blunted me, and now there was anger to distract me. I couldn't allow any of those things to prevent me from finding Dariya. I had to be without exhaustion, without emotion; I had to lock those things away. There was only one purpose and I had to let it drive me. If I faltered from that, even for a moment, it could mean a child's death.

'Is it him?' Petro asked.

I continued to watch through the scope. 'I can't be sure.' But I couldn't help thinking that if it *were* him, if he had allowed us to come this close to him, then his game was over and we'd all be dead. If he had concealed himself, he could have shot each of us three times over before we could have worked out where he was.

'Shoot,' Viktor said. 'It's him.'

'And if it isn't?'

'It *is*, Papa, it's him. Trying to sneak up on us like he did last night.'

I continued to watch the man peering into the trees as if looking for us. 'It doesn't feel right. If it's him, why is he out there?'

'Who else would it be?' Viktor said. 'We have to shoot him before he shoots us.'

'No, Viktor, it's not him.'

'Isn't that what you thought last night?'

'But why would he wait here and not far ahead? Remember how he shot Dimitri.' I whispered my thoughts, reasoning aloud why this was not our child thief. I wanted Viktor and Petro to see the logic in his thinking, to understand that the man we were following would not present himself in this way. But that wasn't the effect of mentioning Dimitri's name. Instead, the word was like a hot knife to Viktor, bringing back memories of blood and death. The sounds Dimitri had made as he struggled with his life out on the steppe.

And while those thoughts cascaded through Viktor's consciousness, they brought with them a powerful instinct to survive. In his mind he saw Dimitri dying, and he responded in a way that was only human. He knew he did not want it to happen to him. His reaction was all instinct. The instinct to survive.

So when the man took a step forward and raised his hand, Viktor fired his rifle.

The man at the line of the trees stopped mid-movement and his head snapped back. His body relaxed as if a hand had come from the sky, taken hold of his soul and ripped it out of him in one movement. He simply ceased to be. In an instant his life was gone, his body now vacated, and the empty vessel collapsed into the snow.

'No.' I lowered my weapon and looked at Viktor and Petro,

both of them with their weapons still aimed, their expressions of surprise. 'What the hell are you doing?'

'He was going to shoot at us,' said Viktor. 'You saw it. He was going to shoot.'

But I saw doubt in my son's eyes, and when I looked across at Petro, I knew he saw it too.

'What?' Viktor said. 'Why are you looking at me like that? I'm telling you, he was going to shoot.'

'All right.' I looked back at the dark shape in the snow as I put my hand on the warm barrel of Viktor's rifle and lowered it to point at the ground. 'All right.'

For a few moments nothing happened. No sounds. Nothing. Then I rose to my feet and slung my rifle. I took the revolver from my pocket and glanced at Petro and Viktor.

'Wait here,' I said. 'No more shooting.'

'He was going to shoot,' Viktor said. 'He *was*.'

'Stay with him,' I told Petro, and he nodded, glancing at me briefly before looking at his brother again.

Viktor could only stare at the shape lying in the snow.

I made my way to the edge of the wood, keeping close to the tree trunks, trying to give myself as much cover as possible. I kept the revolver pointed ahead and I hunched low. As I came closer, so the body became clearer, and when I reached the last trees I could see we had reached the road between Uroz and Sushne. The narrow track that ran alongside the forest was covered with snow, just as everything else was, but it had been used some time since the storm yesterday. There were hoof prints, two sets from first glance, and ice had formed in the bottom of the prints so I guessed they had been made either last thing yesterday or first thing this morning. Someone had ridden this way on horseback.

At the side of the track the man was lying face up with his arms by his sides, like a child playing dead. His head was twisted sideways so his cheek rested in the snow. Viktor's shot had been a good one: the man had died instantly. The bullet had struck him in the face, just above his mouth, and had torn up through the back of his head, releasing his life. There was a large stain around his head, and the track behind him was sprayed with blood and brain.

And I could see, straight away, the man had not been alone. A few metres further along a second person was crouching at the side of the track, looking around in fear, hands raised to shoulder level.

I stepped from the woods and pointed the revolver at her.

'Please,' she mumbled. 'Please don't shoot me. Please.'

She was young. Not much older than my boys, maybe nineteen or twenty, and she wasn't clothed for winter weather. She wore no coat, no hat. Her dress was dirty and there were red marks on her face that could have been first-stage bruises or might have been caused by the cold biting at her skin. Her hair was long, but not tied back as I would have expected. It was loose around her shoulders, tangled and wild. Like a young Baba Yaga, but her features were too soft for her to be mistaken for a witch. She had pale skin which heightened the flushed patches on her sharp cheekbones, and she had dark eyes.

When I told her to stand up, she shifted in the snow and I could see her feet were bare. And when I glanced down at the dead man I saw that he too had nothing on his feet. He was wearing a shirt and jacket but no winter coat.

'Who are you?' I asked, staying where I was, keeping the revolver levelled at her. I looked past her at the road, seeing nothing in the distance, risked a quick look into the trees to make sure Viktor and Petro were hidden.

'Who are you?' I asked again.

'Aleksandra.'

'And him?'

She didn't look down at the body. 'Roman.'

'You knew him?'

She nodded.

'Where are you from?'

'Uroz.'

'And what are you doing here? Like that – no shoes, no coat.'

'They made me,' she said.

'Who?'

But she just stared.

'*Who* made you?'

The shock was leaving her now. It was lifting from her like a dark shadow that had fallen over her but was now snatched by the wind and blown away into the trees. I saw the change in her face, saw the difference in her eyes, and then there were tears on her cheeks.

I lowered the revolver and went to her, putting an arm around her and leading her to the side of the track. She walked like she was just learning, her steps awkward and hesitant.

'How long have you been out here?'

'I'm not sure.'

'Can you feel your feet?' I asked her.

'No.'

'They look all right, but we need to get them warm. If they get too cold, there's a strong chance of frostbite. You know what that is?'

'Of course.'

Taking her into the trees, I called to Viktor and Petro, and spread Dimitri's coat on the ground for her to stand on. I wrapped it around her feet.

'Stay with her,' I told Petro. 'See if you can rub some warmth into her feet. And when they're warm, make sure she puts these on.' I put Dimitri's boots and socks on the ground beside Aleksandra. 'Viktor, you come with me.'

'Is it him?' he asked. 'Did I get him?'

'No, it isn't him.'

Viktor looked at me. 'It must be. He was going to—'

'It isn't him.'

'But he's armed.'

'I don't think so.'

'He was going to shoot.'

'No, Viktor.' My son had been afraid and his mind had showed him what he expected to see. But the man he had shot was unarmed. I sighed and shook my head. 'Come on. We have to move him before someone comes. Before someone sees.' I began walking back to the place where the man lay by the road, but Viktor stayed where he was, staring.

'Come on,' I said to him. 'Now.'

But Viktor just stood and stared. As if something was keeping him from moving his feet. He wanted to follow, he wanted to help, but something wouldn't let him. He was still processing my words. He had killed a man, but it was the wrong man.

'You have to try,' I said. 'You have to—'

'I can't.'

'Go and help the girl, then. Her name is Aleksandra.' I looked back at where she was standing beside a tree, her body turned away as if she were trying to disappear into the cracks in the bark. She hung her head, her hair falling across her face. 'Petro, you come with me.'

While Viktor went to stand with Aleksandra, neither of them speaking, Petro and I dragged the man away from the road. We each took an arm and pulled him into the trees, leaving a flattened mark in the snow, and a wide streak of blood. I could see how it turned Petro's stomach, handling the body like that, but he didn't complain. He averted his eyes from the man's face and did what was necessary, and when we had dragged the corpse far enough, Petro let go of the man's arm, leaving it to flop across his chest and slide away.

'What Viktor did—'

'He was scared,' I told Petro. 'We all are. He thought this man was going to shoot us. Kill *you*, maybe. Me.'

'I know. I understand.'

'Good. So he needs to accept it and get on.'

'Just like that?'

'Just like that.'

'Is that what you do? Pretend it hasn't happened?'

'If that's what it takes, yes.'

'How do you do that?'

'I don't know. I lock it away.'

Now Petro looked down at the body. He put all his effort into forcing himself to see.

'I think if Viktor hadn't shot first, I would've killed this man,' he said. 'I was going to shoot him.' There was fear and revulsion in his eyes as he connected with his brother's emotions. He almost knew what his brother was feeling, because he was almost the one who had murdered this man. But there would also be a kind of relief that it hadn't been him.

'When people are scared,' I said, 'they'll do almost anything to survive. Like what happened in Vyriv . . . He'll be all right,' I told Petro. 'Give him some time.' I looked across at Viktor and Aleksandra. Like two more trees in the forest.

'She needs clothes,' I said, bending down to remove the man's jacket.

'Will *she* be all right?' Petro asked.

'Of course she will. We don't breed weak women. And our men can turn their hearts to stone, so your brother will be fine too. Now, help me with this.'

Petro swallowed hard and helped with the other arm, pulling it from the sleeve of the jacket, keeping his eyes away from Roman's face, not wanting to see the trauma inflicted by Viktor's bullet.

We stripped the man naked, taking every scrap of clothing he had, and went to Aleksandra, giving her the shirt and trousers. 'Your feet warm enough now?' I asked, and when she nodded, I told her the socks and boots were for her. 'They'll be too big, but they're better than walking barefoot in the snow. And you can keep the coat.'

As she was dressing, I took my entrenching tool back to the road, shovelling away the bloody snow, throwing a fresh covering across it while Petro brushed it smooth with a branch broken from a tree.

Coming back to Aleksandra, she refused to make eye contact. She kept her head down, her hair falling over her face, keeping it hidden. Close by, Viktor remained silent, staring into the woods.

'We don't have time to feel sorry for ourselves,' I said. 'I need to know why you were out here dressed like that.'

She said nothing, so I went to her, took her shoulders and shook her until she looked up at me. 'Why are you here?'

She stared at me, her eyes widening, then her muscles tensed and she raised her arms, trying to break my grip and push me away. I held her tight as she struggled, and when she began to weaken, I let go and stepped back.

'Well, good luck,' I said, collecting my pack, slinging it over my back. I picked up my rifle and nodded to Petro. 'Come on. Let's get your brother. We don't have time for this. The longer we wait, the further away they'll be.'

'They came a week ago.' Her voice was hoarse.

I stopped and turned to look at Aleksandra. 'OGPU?'

She shook her head, creased her brow like she didn't understand.

'Soldiers?' I said. 'Chekists.'

'Yes.'

'And they made you come out here like this?'

'Yes.'

'Did they . . . did they do anything else to you?'

'It isn't enough they took my father? That they took our food?' There was anger in her eyes now, in her voice too, as if she was letting out something she'd kept inside. She saw we meant her no harm, and that had released the pressure inside her, but when she mentioned her father, her voice cracked and she squeezed her eyes tight.

'How many men?' I asked her.

Aleksandra shook her head and I gave her a moment to settle her feelings. 'Four or five, I don't know. They came on horses, went to every house and searched them. Took everything. Lermentov.' She spat the word out like it tasted bad in her mouth.

'Lermentov?'

'The leader. That was his name.'

I looked at my sons. Petro was listening to what the girl was saying, but he had one eye on his brother, who was leaning against a tree with his head bowed. Viktor was still disturbed by what he'd done, turning inwards now, keeping his thoughts to himself. I knew he needed something to take his mind from it. Keeping him busy wouldn't erase what had happened, but it would make him less numb. He needed to get back on the trail as soon as possible. The longer we waited, the further away Dariya would be, and the more Viktor would retreat into himself if he had nothing to occupy him. And with soldiers already in Uroz, it was only a matter of time before they discovered Vyriv. I had to find her and return home.

'Communists,' I said, turning back to Aleksandra. 'There'll be more of them somewhere. This man Lermentov, he'll be the party man, or the police. The others will be Red Army. Were they armed?'

Aleksandra nodded.

'And what did they do?'

'There were meetings. My father went to them. He said they wanted to take our land and our cow. For the glory of the collective, he said, but he refused.'

'And where's your father now?'

Aleksandra looked away. She hung her head in the same way that Viktor was doing, and I couldn't help feeling impatient. I didn't need this. I wanted only to be on the trail, closing the gap between me and the man who had taken Dariya. I didn't want to be dealing with disturbed girls and a boy who couldn't face the fact that he'd killed a man. Viktor's reaction was disappointing, and I needed to bury that too.

I closed my eyes and took a deep breath. The longer this took, the further away Dariya would be. But I had to know everything before we could go on. If someone was looking for Aleksandra, following her as we were following Dariya, we may need to leave her behind.

I put a hand on her chin and lifted her face to look at me. 'I need to know where your father is.' The bruises were more obvious now, whether from the light or from their further development. Purple-red, angry marks on her right cheekbone and just below her eyes.

She pushed my hand away. 'What do you care? Who are you anyway?'

'No one.'

'And what are you doing out here, shooting at people? How can I trust you?'

'How can we trust *you*? How do we know you're who you say you are?'

'Look at me.'

'Look at *us*. We're just like you. And you have to trust us – what choice do you have?'

She sighed and looked away.

'What happened to your father?'

'I don't know. They used Pavlo Kostyshn's house as a prison, took my father there and beat him with sticks and revolvers until he was swollen and blue before they released him. Then they demanded grain we didn't have, so they took him away again. They came in the night when we were asleep and . . . I tried to stop them, but they hit me.'

'When?'

'Three, no, four nights ago.'

I felt no guilt at being firm with her, but I knew she would never see her father again. He was either dead or had been loaded onto a cattle truck and shipped to a labour camp.

'They took others too,' she said. 'And when I asked where he was, what they had done with him, they just pushed me away. And they came to our houses and took everything we had. They took the food from our cellars and our cupboards and loaded it onto carts. Left me with nothing but a spoon and a saucer.'

'You have anyone else?' I asked her. 'Family?'

'No one.'

'And when did you last eat?'

She shook her head. 'Yesterday, I think.'

'You think?' Petro spoke now, coming closer, looking at

Aleksandra and then giving me a questioning glance. 'You don't know when you last ate?'

'They kept me in the dark,' she said. 'I don't know for how long. And they hit me.'

'Why?'

'They think I know who slaughtered the animals.'

'Your animals were slaughtered?'

She nodded. 'And many things were burned. Food, seed grain. People from the village did it to stop the soldiers from taking them. They said if they couldn't keep their own animals, they would rather cut their throats. And the soldiers thought I knew who did it.'

'Did you?'

'Of course. Everyone knew. I think they even knew it themselves, but they wanted to shame us, make an example. But I wouldn't tell them, so now they make me walk to the next village. In the snow. Without shoes or a coat.'

'What about Roman? What did he do?'

'Hid food.'

I thought about the horse tracks on the road. 'And they've gone ahead to wait for you,' I said. 'Two men on horseback. They're expecting you.'

'Yes. So they can ask me more questions. But I don't think they want any answers. I think they just want me to die.'

'How far away is your village from here? Two kilometres?'

She nodded.

'And to the next one?'

She shrugged.

'Four or five kilometres?'

'About that,' she said.

'That gives us a while before they're expecting you,' I thought aloud.

Petro shifted. 'And when she doesn't arrive, Papa? Will they think she died on the road?'

'Maybe. Or maybe they'll come looking for her.'

*

178

I walked away and fumbled a cigarette from the packet, only three left, and lit it with a match. The phosphorus smell was tangy, but it lasted only a second or two before the tobacco smoke smothered it. I stood for a while, just looking at the trees, seeing the snow, letting my eyes drift out of focus so all I could see was white.

'What is it?' Petro spoke from just behind me.

I took a long drag on the cigarette, long enough for me to have to stifle a cough, and blew the smoke out, letting it mingle with the heat of my breath.

'We should leave,' Petro said. 'Go after Dariya; get away from here in case those men come looking. We can take Aleksandra with us.'

'Or we could leave her here.'

'What?'

'If they come looking for her, maybe we should make sure they find her.'

Petro opened his mouth to speak, but he had no words.

'We could put her back on the road and let her walk.'

'And if she tells them about us?' Petro finally found his voice. 'If they ask about the coat and boots? And when the old man doesn't show up?'

I offered Petro the cigarette and he looked at it for a second before shaking his head.

'We could take the clothes from her,' I shrugged. 'Let her walk barefoot—'

'No.'

'Or we could kill her.'

'*What?*'

'Just possibilities, Petro, that's all.'

'That's not an option. I couldn't . . . *we* couldn't do that.' He looked at me, probably persuading himself I would never do that – murder someone to cover my tracks – but at the same time he doubted his own thoughts. 'It would be so wrong.'

'Would it?' I hadn't given much thought to killing Aleksandra – I had spoken the words aloud as they came to mind – but now I was asking myself if I would do it. And it made me feel sick to realise I would. If I thought it would help our situation, I really *would* consider it.

'Of course it would be wrong. How can you even think—'

'Don't worry; we'll take her with us. We'll just have to hope no one follows.'

Petro shifted where he stood, moving from one foot to the other, breaking the stillness. 'I don't know what it's like,' he said.

'Hm?'

'To be like you. To fight like you have. I can't imagine what you must have done, how you must have felt.'

'Where's this coming from?'

'I think you pretend it hasn't happened.'

'What?'

'You harden yourself and pretend it hasn't happened, and that's how you live with it. And that's what you expect from Viktor, isn't it?'

'We should go.'

'Am I right?'

I stood where I was, cigarette in hand.

'Am I right, Papa? Is that how you live with it? Is that what Viktor must do?'

'Viktor must do whatever he can.'

'And you? You do things and then make yourself believe they haven't happened? Is that how you could leave Aleksandra behind?'

'I don't want to talk about it now.'

'When?'

'Come on, let's get moving. We can't waste any more time.' I went back to Viktor, sensing Petro's eyes on my back. Petro knew I'd been thinking about what I was going to do, and he knew that if I thought we had to leave Aleksandra behind, I would do it.

'You all right?' I asked Viktor.

He nodded.

'I need you to say it.'

'I'm fine.'

'Good. One more thing to do and then we're leaving. Come and help me with this.' I went to the body of the old man and took his arms, starting to drag him deeper into the woods. 'Help me, Viktor. I can't do it on my own.'

But Viktor remained where he was, looking away.

'Viktor,' I called again. 'Help me.'

Still he remained.

I felt my impatience rise. I was disappointed by my son's reaction. I thought him stronger. I called him once more, louder this time, but again he didn't move. Instead, Aleksandra turned towards me. She seemed to harden herself as she took a step forward, only to be stopped by Petro.

'I'll do it,' he said, putting a hand on her arm, holding her back. 'It's all right.'

So Petro helped me drag the old man further into the trees, and together we piled snow over him.

Once the body was hidden, I took Petro back to the road, casting a glance at Viktor. I told Petro to take off his boots and socks.

'Why?'

'We need to make more tracks,' I said, crouching to remove my own boots, looking across once more at Viktor.

'He'll be all right,' Petro said. 'He just needs a moment.'

'He's had a moment. We don't have many more left.'

'He'll be fine.'

'Right.' I took off my boots, blocking out the pain when I put my naked feet in the snow. 'When Aleksandra and . . .'

'. . . Roman.'

'Mm. When Aleksandra and Roman don't arrive in Sushne, they'll come to look for them, and we don't want them to find a body. If they find tracks ending here, they'll go into the trees, maybe find where we buried him.'

'So we make more tracks,' Petro said. 'Further down the road.'

'Exactly.'

Petro nodded and removed his boots, wincing when his bare feet touched the snow. 'It hurts,' he said.

'Let's do it quickly then.'

With our boots in our hands, we walked barefoot, trying to continue from the place where Aleksandra and Roman had been walking. At first the cold was painful, then it began to feel more like burning, as if we were walking over hot coals.

'Some people can do this for a long time,' I said, trying to keep my mind off the feeling in my feet.

'How long?' There was tension in Petro's voice.

'Half an hour, maybe.'

'Half an hour? What about frostbite?'

I clenched my teeth. 'We'll stop soon. Walk faster.'

'Will we get frostbite?'

'No. If your toes go white, we'll stop and rub them. As long as they're pink you're fine.'

'That's the rule?'

I shrugged and looked at Petro. 'I don't know.'

Petro had pulled his scarf away from his face and I could see the redness of his cheeks, the mud smeared beneath his dark eyes. His features were contorted with pain and determination. Like some kind of twisted clown. And, despite our situation, I felt myself smile.

'What?' Petro asked.

'If someone could see us now, they'd think . . .' I began to laugh.

'What?' Petro started to smile, his expression turning to one of confusion. 'They'd think what?'

'That we're mad,' I said, laughing out loud.

Petro began to laugh with me as we hurried along the road, barefoot, like two insane vagabonds, and when I finally signalled to Petro to stop, we rubbed warmth back into our feet and put on our socks and boots.

We left the road, heading back into the trees, covering our tracks as we went, then doubled back to where Viktor and Aleksandra were waiting.

'You think it'll be enough?' Petro asked.

'We'll have to hope so,' I told him. 'A fresh fall would help cover it better.'

'But then we'd have no way of following Dariya.'

'I think we'll be able to follow her whatever happens. It's part of his game.'

'You really think this is a game to him?'

I nodded. 'Take a child, provoke a hunting party and turn the tables on them. I'd bet the stranger who came into Vyriv wasn't alone when he started out to rescue his children. I'd bet this man killed them one by one, just like he wants to do with us.'

'Why?'

'Because it's exciting? Maybe he enjoys it.' I looked at my son. 'But this time it's different. This time it's me who's after him – and he won't get away.'

Coming to where the others were waiting, I took up my pack and handed Viktor's to him, saying it was time to be strong again. Beside him, Aleksandra was swamped by the coat we had given her, the warmth bringing colour to her face and hardening the intent in her eyes. She no longer looked cold and afraid, but had the air of a woman who was watching closely, assessing her options, deciding what she had to do to survive. There was something almost animal-like in the intensity of her expressions. I had told Petro that we did not breed weak women, and the look in Aleksandra's eyes proved it to me.

Viktor took the pack from me and put it over his back. He hesitated when he was about to pick up the rifle, but he grasped it tight, fighting his guilt as he slung it over his shoulder.

'I would have done the same thing,' I said, glancing at Aleksandra, looking for a reaction.

Viktor turned to look at me.

'I would have shot him the way you did.' I gave him my full attention now. Aleksandra had not reacted to my comment, but she was watching us closely.

'But you didn't.'

'No.'

'So you wouldn't have.'

'I just hesitated a little longer than you, that's all. It's experience.' I shrugged. 'Or maybe it's age, I don't know. Maybe I'm just slower than I used to be.'

Viktor said nothing.

'It's no small thing, killing a man. Taking a life. Taking away everything someone is.'

'It's not that,' Viktor said.

'What then?'

'It's taking the *wrong* life. If it had been *him*, if I had been right, I would be pleased.'

'You're sure about that?'

'I'm certain.'

I nodded. 'Good. Then I need you to take care of Aleksandra. She's your responsibility now.'

'I'm not anybody's responsibility,' Aleksandra said. 'If you take me with you, I won't slow you down. I'm strong.'

I looked her up and down, seeing how much her demeanour had changed since we first saw her. 'Yes, you are. But back there you were afraid.'

'Of course.'

'There will be more of that,' I said. 'Are you sure you want to come with us? You don't even know where we're going.'

'What choice do I have?'

'You could stay here. Try to go home.' I shrugged. 'It's up to you now.'

'You'd just let me go?'

'If it's what you want.'

'But you know I'm going to come with you. That's why you hid Roman. That's why you made the tracks. What else can I do?'

I looked directly at her and saw that she knew her father was gone. She had accepted it as a fact because it was the only way she could move on and survive. Aleksandra had nothing to go back to; she had already told us she had no other family. The only thing waiting for her in Uroz was death or exile. Perhaps both. We were the only hope she had now.

I reached out and put a hand on her arm. I said nothing, but I let her see what was in my face, in my eyes. We were together now. She was with *us* now.

Aleksandra nodded gently. 'I won't be a burden.'

'I know.'

And with that we began walking again.

17

Noon came and went. We sat to make a small fire and brew tea to warm us but there was nothing to eat. Aleksandra was weak and hungry, but we had nothing to give her. If we were still tracking Dariya by nightfall, I'd set more snares, but otherwise there was little we could do for her. Even so, true to her word, she did not slow us down. She walked as strong and hard as any one of us.

For the most part we were silent until Petro aired his worries once more.

'You think they'll find Vyriv like they found Uroz?' he asked. It was an hour or so since we had left the place where Viktor killed the old man. None of us had spoken in all that time, each of us lost in our thoughts and exhaustion.

'That's where you're from?' Aleksandra asked. 'Vyriv?'

'Yes.'

'They'll find it,' she said.

Petro looked across at her, sitting an arm's length from Viktor. 'Maybe not. We're small and remote. It was hardly touched during the civil war. Even during the famine there was enough to eat.'

'Hardly enough,' Viktor said.

'Maybe.' Petro nodded. 'But it survived. It's well hidden.'

'It's different now,' Aleksandra said. 'The communists are different. They want everything.'

'But if they can't find it . . .'

'You think they won't find it?' Aleksandra said. 'You think someone won't tell them?'

'Why would they do that?'

'Why would a woman denounce her own husband?'

'What?'

Aleksandra shook her head at Petro's naivety. 'A woman in Uroz gave up her own husband because they threatened her children. So she gave him up. Denounced him like a criminal. And you know what they did? They arrested them all. Him they executed. She was taken away with the children.'

'Taken where?'

'Who knows?'

'Siberia maybe,' Viktor said. 'Or the White Sea. Papa said there are prisons up there.'

'Labour camps,' I told him. 'They don't call them prisons.' I spoke to Petro: 'They *will* find it – Aleksandra is right. Perhaps they're in our village now, as we sit here.'

Petro looked at me with alarm. 'Now?' And he saw our dilemma. While we were scouring the countryside for Dariya, his own mother and sister had been left to fend for themselves in the shadow of an approaching danger.

'We have to get back,' he said.

'Get back?' Aleksandra looked confused.

'We will, as soon as we can,' I said. 'We need to find Dariya and we need to get home.'

'And then? What can we do?' Petro asked.

'You mean about the communists taking our belongings?' I said. 'Nothing. There's nothing we can do. In the end they'll take what they want.'

'Who's Dariya?' asked Aleksandra. 'What's going on here? Why are you talking about going back? I thought you were running *away*. I thought you were afraid and trying to escape the communists.' She looked around at each one of us, not under-standing. 'But you're looking for someone?'

Petro turned to me and I thought for a moment before nodding. 'All right. Tell her.'

'A girl was kidnapped from Vyriv,' Petro said. 'My cousin. We've been following the trail since yesterday.'

'Kidnapped?'

'There have been others too,' Viktor said. 'Two dead children brought into the village. One of them butchered as if—'

'Enough,' I stopped him.

'—to eat her.'

'That's enough.'

'I want her to know. I want her to know why I killed that man.'

'Not because you thought he was a communist?' Aleksandra asked.

'No.' Viktor rubbed a hand across his mouth. 'I was afraid he was the one we've been following. This man, he's . . . he's like a ghost.'

'A ghost?'

'He's there and then he isn't,' Viktor said. 'Shooting at us from the shadows, watching us at night.'

'He's just a man,' I said.

'A man who eats people.'

'Maybe that's not what he does.' I watched Aleksandra for a reaction, wondering what she would make of this. 'Maybe he cuts them for another reason.'

'But people have done it before,' Aleksandra said. 'I've heard of it.'

'We don't know it for sure,' I told her. 'And it doesn't make any difference. He's just a man who's taken my niece. We'll find her and we'll bring her back.'

'You really think we can, Papa?'

'Of course we can, Viktor.'

'And you thought Roman was this man?' Aleksandra asked.

'I was . . . I thought . . .' Viktor looked at the ground. 'I made a mistake.'

'You weren't to know,' I told him. 'You saw a man; it could have been any man. I would have done the same thing.'

We fell silent, all of us staring into the flames of the small fire.

'Roman was old,' Aleksandra said. 'I think he may be better off now anyway.'

We crossed the steppe like wild animals, scanning, watching for movement, stopping to listen. For a while we saw nothing but trees and shadow. The sky had darkened again and the snow began to fall in thick wet flakes, obstructing our vision and filling the tracks we followed. We increased our pace as much as we could, trying to keep up with the trail before it was swept away, but we were wary of what lay before us, and we were able to see only a few metres ahead.

'We'll lose the tracks,' Viktor said.

'We'll keep going,' I told him.

And then I saw the child thief's second gift and I wondered about the man who'd been hanged in our village – about him not being alone when he first set out to find his children. Perhaps the child thief had taken them one by one, taunting them, tempting them, murdering them. I imagined others lying out there in the ice, their lives gone.

The first gift had been a bloodstain on the land. A violent streak of crimson that might have been drained from Dariya's small body or from the carcass of a trapped animal. It had been both a gift and a trick, a means to draw us into his sights so he could kill the first of us.

The second gift was much worse. It was so much more than a stain on the snow. There was no doubt what kind of animal this trophy had come from.

The child thief knew we would be following his tracks. He had made it easy for us, so he knew we'd come this way, passing through this part of the forest, and he had chosen the perfect place for his display.

We came to a stretch which formed a natural path among the barren trees. An open space of perhaps fifty metres, like a scar in the forest, where nothing grew. The disappearing tracks led directly through this area, along the centre of it, the two sets of prints which I was certain belonged to our quarry and, I hoped, to Dariya.

Towards the end of the scar, where the trees closed ranks once more, a single branch stretched across the natural pathway at head height. And, from the centre of the branch, something hung. A dark shape that may have been a fallen nest, its broken pieces dangling like tendrils from the nucleus of the construction. Or perhaps it was a bird, its body caught on the branch, its wings dropping, the feathers splayed out.

I stopped.

'What is it?' Petro looked up. He had been walking with his head down for a while now, too tired to lift it.

'Get into the trees.' I hurried them into cover, moving so there were thick trunks between us and the object. From there we looked again.

'Is it an animal?' Viktor asked.

I shook my head and slipped my rifle from my shoulder.

I pulled the stock tight to me and looked through the scope at the dark shape, but still couldn't be sure what I was looking at. The light was all wrong. The object was in shadow and I could see nothing more than its shape.

'It's hard to tell,' I said. 'Could be animal fur. A bird. Maybe just twigs and leaves. I'll have to get closer.'

Petro put his hand on my arm.

'It's all right,' I said. 'You and Viktor watch carefully.' I glanced at Viktor. 'You're all right?'

'I'm fine.'

Petro released my arm and unslung his rifle.

Viktor did the same, and the vacant look that had been in his eyes had disappeared. He had something concrete to occupy his thoughts now. Something to take his mind from what he had done. 'I'll go,' he said.

'I need you to watch. From that side.' I pointed. 'Aleksandra, stay with him.'

'Let me go. *You* watch,' Viktor said.

'You're not ready.'

Viktor closed his eyes tight, knowing there was no point in arguing, then he sighed and went to the place I had indicated, crouching and steadying his rifle.

'You on this side,' I told Petro. 'And don't take your eyes off the forest. This might be another trap.'

When they were in position, I made my way towards the object, scanning the forest ahead, looking for anything out of the ordinary. If the child thief was out there, he would be stationary. He would have chosen the perfect place and he would be prepared, so I stayed in cover, kept to the shadow, and moved to a protected spot beside the tree with the protruding branch.

From there I could see blood on the ground directly beneath the hanging object. There was a great deal of it, and I was sure it had been spilled right there. It had been warm when it touched the crust of the snow, had sunk into it, the body heat melting the surface ice. Much of the snow here was flattened, something we hadn't noticed from where we were standing before, and I could see that while two sets of tracks led to this spot – a man's and a child's – only one set led away from it. Only one person had walked away from this carnage.

I was almost afraid to look up at the branch, but I forced myself to raise my eyes from the blood and see the horrible tangle that drooped from this naked tree.

And now, from this close, I knew exactly what it was. The matted hair, clumped together with frozen blood, the underside of the skin glistening as if still wet. I turned away from the child's scalp and put my back against the ragged tree, sliding down it until I was sitting in the snow. I put my hands over my face and blamed myself for being too slow. I had failed in my promise to Lara. I had taken too long. I was too late. I was no longer looking to rescue a child. Now I was searching only for justice and revenge.

18

'Maybe it's not Dariya,' Petro said. 'Maybe it's . . .'

'Who else would it be?' I asked. The others had joined me as soon as they saw me fall back against the tree. They knew right away something was wrong and they came across, keeping in the cover of the trees.

They had each stared at the clump of hair and flesh that hung from the twisted branch, but now all their heads were turned away.

Petro's face was pale. He was scared and concerned in equal measure. He was wondering, once again, if there was something he could have done to stop this from happening.

'Could anybody survive a thing like that?' Aleksandra asked.

'It's possible,' I said. 'It's just skin and hair.' It sounded dismissive – as if I was suggesting that scalping a child was nothing. An irritation. 'But all that blood.' I put a hand to my mouth and saw Dariya's face in my mind. I saw her small round face, her dark eyes and her white skin. I saw her standing at my door, looking up at me, smiling, asking if Lara was allowed to come out, and I heard myself teasing her, telling her Lara still had work to do – there were chickens to feed, a harvest to take in – and Lara was behind me, calling me Papa, telling me not to joke.

I went to the tracks leading away and took off a glove, putting my finger into one of the prints. 'He was carrying her when he walked away,' I said.

'Alive?' Petro asked.

'There's no way of knowing.'

'So what are you going to do now?' Aleksandra asked.

I took one of the two last cigarettes from the packet and put it between my lips. I lit it with a match and sucked the smoke deep. 'Keep going,' I said, looking at the boys. 'I'm going to find this man and I'm going to kill him.' And I knew I wanted it more than ever now. Never had I wanted to take a life as much as I wanted it now. Until this moment I had been intent on finding Dariya, and the fate of the child thief was always secondary, but now I wanted him dead. I wanted to see his life fade. I wanted him to look into my eyes as his own glazed over and became dry.

'Maybe it's time to go back,' Petro said. 'Maybe it's time to go back to Mama and Lara. I want to find Dariya, but I'm worried about Mama. And if Dariya's already . . .' He took a deep breath. 'Maybe we should go back to them.'

'They're fine,' I told him. 'They're strong.'

'The Bolsheviks might be there already. In our village. Taking our—'

'They won't do anything to your mother or Lara. It's the men they want. It's our belongings and it's the men.'

Petro looked at Aleksandra, who stared at him for a moment and then turned away. Her mouth was tight, her lips pressed together, her hair falling about her face. She knew different. We all did.

'I don't know,' Petro said. 'I just can't help feeling we should go back. I want to keep looking but . . .'

A part of me wanted to listen to him. I wanted to go back and be with my family, to protect them from the oncoming storm, but the truth was that there was little I could do to protect them from the Bolsheviks. When the party officials and the OGPU and the Red Army were upon Vyriv, there would be nothing anyone could do other than cooperate with them. They could have our chickens and they could have our field and they could have our grain and what few potatoes were left in the cellar. Natalia and Lara were no threat to them, but they might think I was. A veteran of the Imperial Army. A former Red Army soldier who defected because he grew to despise an army that treated its soldiers with disdain, executed young soldiers who were afraid to fight, dragged men from their homes to fill their ranks. If they came to Vyriv and they found out who I was, they would take me out in the night and they would shoot me. They would murder my family as counter-revolutionaries.

'Maybe we should go back,' Petro said again. 'There's no point if she's already gone.'

'No. We should follow him.' Viktor spoke now, and I could see myself in my son's eyes. He felt what I felt. He felt the rage and violent necessity for retribution. For Viktor this was a direction for his feelings, something to obliterate what he'd done back on the road. It was his nature to deal with it this way. 'Papa's right. Mama and Lara will be fine.'

'And if someone denounces them?' Petro said. 'What then?'

Standing out there in the wilderness and the cold, my heart faltered and it was my turn to look at Aleksandra. I knew Petro was right. There was nothing to stop one of the other villagers from denouncing them in order to make themselves look more loyal. Aleksandra had already made that clear. In their delusion, they would try to deflect the horror onto others rather than accept it upon themselves. The truth was that we would all suffer, and in the years to come millions would lie dead in the streets with their bones pushing through paper-thin flesh and their eyes bulging in their skulls. But human instinct is to survive, and if someone in our village saw a way of making their own situation less severe, there was a strong chance they would use my history to save themselves.

I looked back at the way we had come. Then I looked forward at the single track leading away. Ahead, the child thief was increasing his lead. Behind, there might be soldiers already following our trail, searching for Aleksandra. And, further back, our village hid in the dip of the valley, trembling at the approaching terror. I could see no right decision. There were too many possibilities and too few certainties.

Viktor and Petro waited, but I didn't know what to say. For the first time since we had left, I didn't know what was the best thing to do. I had made a promise to Lara that I would return with her cousin, but the blood and the scalp suggested I had failed in that already.

It was Aleksandra who gave me the answer. 'You said she could survive this.'

I tried not to look at the scalp. 'I said it's possible, but . . .' I blew my breath out, puffing my cheeks and shaking my head.

'Then maybe you should give her a chance,' Aleksandra said. 'You have friends in your village?'

'Of course.'

'And your wife is with your daughter.'

I could see what she was saying. She was weighing the options, trying to find who needed me most right now.

'But this girl . . . she has no one. She is just a girl, alone. With a killer.'

I took the last drag of the cigarette and dropped it into the snow.

'Maybe we should separate,' said Petro. 'I'll go back to—'

'No. That's the thing we should *not* do,' I said. 'Not now. You'd never get back alone.'

I could see Petro was about to protest. I'd seen the expression enough times to know what was in his head. 'I trust you, Petro. It's not that. I know you're strong and I know you're capable. You've proved that. You can hunt, build a shelter, keep warm, but it's a mistake to go alone. We should stay together.' I gestured at the forest behind us. 'There might be soldiers out there searching for Aleksandra. Or maybe this man we're hunting wants us to split up, so he can pick us off alone.' I looked my son in the eye. 'If we separate, we can't take care of each other.' I felt as if we were being led, drawn into the child thief's trap, but I saw no alternative other than to press on. And it troubled me that, while we discussed our options, the child thief had left his trail, knowing before we knew ourselves that we would follow. There was no choice.

'I'm afraid for Mama,' Petro said.

'So am I. But I'm afraid for Dariya too. If she's still alive, then she's alone and afraid and hurt. We have to keep after her until we know for sure.'

'For how long?' There was relief in his expression. He had voiced his concern, but the decision was out of his hands. I had chosen to go on and I had told him to follow. He wanted to find Dariya, appease his guilt for what had happened to her, and he had spoken aloud his worries about his mother. I had made the difficult choice for them, and the decision had been prompted by Aleksandra, the only one of us who had any objectivity.

'We'll keep going until nightfall,' I said. 'After that, we'll rethink if necessary.'

So we walked in silence again. Petro to my left, the faint remainder of the child thief's lonely tracks to my right. And behind, Viktor and Aleksandra kept up, all of us forging through the snow until we came to the edge of the forest, opening onto another clear area. But this was not like the fields we had come across before. Here the ground was rocky and undulating. And unlike the flat fields of fertile black soil where Dimitri had been shot, this area was on a steeper incline.

'Stay close to the trees,' I said, crouching at the trunk of a large maple and taking out my binoculars. The snow had begun to ease off now, just a few light flakes falling from a translucent sky.

'You see anything?' Viktor asked.

There was almost nothing to see on the plain of white, other than the places where black rocks broke through. Without the trees for protection, almost all trace of any track was gone, smothered by the heavy fall of snow. Close up, I could see the child thief had come to the spot where we now stood, but further out in the open I saw nothing.

I looked across towards an overstood coppice of hornbeam just less than a kilometre away. And there, among the cluster of trees, I could see a small, primitive building.

'Shepherd's hut?' I passed the binoculars to Viktor for him to look.

Viktor wiped the lenses and held them to his eyes. 'I don't know.'

I called Petro, asking, 'What do you think?'

Petro hesitated before taking the binoculars and looking into the distance. 'Where're the sheep?'

'Hm?'

'Sheep. If it's a shepherd's hut, where are the sheep?'

'On a collective?' I suggested.

'And why would there be a hut this low?'

Petro had a point, but a shepherd's hut wasn't impossible down here.

'It doesn't matter,' I said. 'It's where the tracks lead us.'

'No sign of life at all,' Petro said. 'Nothing.'

'We can't go that way now,' Viktor said. 'Cross open land in daylight. That hut's a perfect place to watch from: he'll see us coming.'

'You're right.' Viktor was thinking now and I was pleased he had something to occupy his thoughts other than what he'd done on the road. 'What would you do?'

'Wait until dark?'

I nodded. 'Or maybe just one of us going up there would be hard to spot. Keep low. There are rocks,' I pointed. 'I could use them to stay hidden.'

'Maybe an hour ago,' Viktor said. 'The way it was snowing, you could have tried it, but now? No, you'd never get up there without him shooting at you. Some of those rocks are too far apart. It'll take too long to get from one to the other.'

I studied the way the land rose and fell, wondering if I could make it to the hut without being seen. But there wasn't a direct route to the crest of the hill that would provide sufficient cover.

'You could follow the forest,' Aleksandra said. 'It curves around that way.' She indicated north. 'Maybe if you come from that direction, he won't be watching.'

I looked at the arc of the forest edge, the way the trees hugged the hillside, embracing it. 'I thought of that already,' I said, 'but it would take too long.'

'Longer than waiting for dark?' she asked.

'No.'

'And you already decided there's no direct approach.'

'Right.'

'Then what choice do you have?'

'You think like a general,' Petro said. 'Outflank him. I like it.'

'All right, you three stay here,' I told them. 'If I move fast, it shouldn't take me more than an hour to get around there. Make yourselves visible from time to time. Not for too long, but if he's seen us already, it'll be enough to make him think we're still here. If we're lucky he'll think we're trying to decide what to do and it'll keep him focused on this place. I'll signal if it's safe to come.'

I took the rifle from my shoulder, removed my pack and placed it on the ground, thinking I'd move better without it. The others could bring it with them, or I'd collect it on my return. I adjusted the way the satchel was hanging and retrieved my rifle.

'Keep watching,' I said, handing the binoculars to Viktor. 'If there's anything that looks like trouble, fire two shots.' I wanted to keep Viktor busy, give him something to do. He had been quiet for a while after we'd left the place by the road, and I was glad to see him regain some of his spirit. What he had done would haunt him, but he needed to accept it, and if he had something else to share space with those thoughts, he would get some perspective.

Viktor hesitated with the binoculars in one hand, then shook his head and offered them back. 'Why don't you let me go?' he said.

'What?'

'I'll go up there.' He glanced across at the hut nestling in the trees. 'Let me.'

I watched him, looking to see what was in his eyes.

'Please. I want to do it. Let me go.'

I knew it was his guilt talking. The kind of guilt that could make a person stoop with the weight of it on their back, sitting like a devil on his shoulders, whispering in his ears, pulling at his cheeks. 'Your head's not clear,' I said.

'It's clear enough.'

'You've nothing to prove. Nothing to feel guilty about.'

'I don't—'

'You need to stay here. You're not ready for something like this.'

'What do you mean I'm not ready? I can shoot. I can walk. I can go up there just as easily as you can. Maybe better. Let me go and I'll find this man and kill him. Let it be *me*.' He began to walk away, so I took his arm and pulled him away from the others.

'I'm not letting you go out there on your own, Viktor. I can see what's in your mind. It's in your eyes, the way you move and talk.'

'What?'

'There were men,' I said. 'In the war. Soldiers who survived their comrades. Soldiers who took the last reserves of food from a village and left the children to starve. Soldiers who killed women when they—'

'Why are you telling me this?' He tried to break away but I held him tighter, gripping his coat with both hands and shaking him.

'Because they had the same look in their eyes,' I said. 'They weren't strong enough to live with what they did, so it ate at them until they were mad. The first to run into battle when there was no chance of survival; the first to charge through artillery fire, raise their heads above the parapet, go over when the time came for attack. They fought beyond the call of duty and they were doomed men, Viktor. Doomed because they couldn't live with themselves.'

Viktor stared at me.

'That's why you can't go. Because I see that in your eyes, and I'm afraid that if I let you go, you'll do something rash.'

I put my arm around him and held him so our cheeks were touching.

'Look after Aleksandra,' I said. 'That's your duty now. I know how you're feeling, and I know you want to do something to make it feel right, but this is not the best thing for you. Going up there instead of me isn't going to make you feel any better. It won't rub out what happened. You have to just accept it. Live with it.'

'Let me try,' he said.

I shook my head and stood back. 'What you did, Viktor . . . I would have done it too.'

'But you didn't. And last night, when we followed you, you didn't shoot. You called out to us.'

'It was a mistake,' I said. 'One that could've got me killed if it hadn't been you. I should've shot.'

Viktor took a deep breath and blew it out into the cold air. 'You don't mean that. I know you don't.'

'Do what I asked. Look after Aleksandra. I'll go up there and I'll let you know if it's safe. We'll talk about this later.'

Viktor turned away, anger rising in his eyes, but I liked that better than seeing the guilt.

19

Circumnavigating the base of the hill, I remained in the forest, keeping the hill to my right. The snow was deep where it had been drifted by the wind and rippled like the dunes of a desert. It was difficult to move, my feet sinking until I was knee-deep, my legs feeling heavy. My stomach was empty too, a sensation that added to my weakness, amplifying my exhaustion. I was a tired and hollow man, wishing I'd prepared better for this journey, but I pressed on, dragging myself through the snow, trying to find the places where it was shallow, or where a firm crust had formed over the top so it made movement easier.

Reaching the far side of the hill, I came to the edge of the trees and looked up at the crest of it. There were rocks here too, but the drifts were deeper on this side so they weren't much more than just black tips like islands in the vast sea of snow.

I used the scope of my rifle to inspect the hilltop, but saw nothing that gave me any reason not to move on.

There was no cover, so I marched straight up, exposed to anyone who may have been watching, but I almost didn't care any more. I was cold and hungry and tired. My feet were sore and my shoulders hurt. The muscles in my thighs were burning from the strained walking, lifting my knees high or dragging them through the snow. My eyes stung from the harsh white of the snow.

And still I kept on. Head down, shoulders slumped, I kept on and I waited for the impact. As I climbed the incline, my body anticipated the penetrating bullet; my ears listened for the crack of a rifle shot. But my mind was hardly aware of that expectation.

My mind worked only to drive my legs, to push me on towards the cluster of trees and the hut within them.

As much as I could, I kept the rocks between me and the hut, trying to break any line of sight. From time to time I stopped to take a breath and look up, but now the hut was hidden, obscured by the closeness of the coppice trees growing thick and multi-trunked.

I rested when I reached the first tree, a single heavy stump with several ancient and gnarled stems thrown up and out from it like the fingers of a witch's hand. I sank to my knees – my legs already too numb to feel the cold – and took shelter in those fissured knuckles, breathing heavily, wishing I was younger and fitter.

The hut was just a short distance ahead; I could see glimpses of it through the trees. I sniffed hard and looked around, taking the revolver from my pocket. I double-checked it was loaded, ensured the cylinder revolved when I cocked the hammer, then I stood and propped myself against the tree for a few seconds, taking a few last moments to regain my strength before I went on.

Movement was easier here. The trees were dense and they had protected the ground from the heaviest of the snow. And now I was rested, I felt a renewed sense of urgency, a greater need for caution.

I kept my movements quiet, sliding my feet to avoid crunching the ice crust. I looked for tracks but saw none. And when I was closer, I stopped and took stock of what lay ahead.

A rudimentary fence had been constructed from branches of similar size, stripped of leaves. The wood was dusted with snow and ice, and was faded and grey as if it had been here for a long time. At the front there was a gap where there may have once been a gate.

The hut itself was small and in bad repair. It looked to have been built from trees like the one I was standing beside, the trunks cut, stripped and laid on their sides. In places I could see gaps in the walls where the crooked trunks didn't quite come together. There was one window facing me, just a hole in the side of the building with nothing to protect it.

There was no sign of life, nor was there anything to suggest there had been any life here in the recent past. If there had been tracks, the recent snowfall had covered them. It was as if no one had been here for years.

I stayed back, inspecting the area, looking for the best way into the hut, but could see nothing other than the open window on this side. I considered where I would be if I were the child thief. The open window was the most obvious place. The building was poorly built but it would be warmer inside, and a sharpshooter can lie in wait for a long time, so it would help to be warm. But the roof would also be a good spot. From there he would have an excellent view all around him.

I looked for any sign of movement, any disturbance in the snow around the edge of the roof, but there was nothing so I swallowed hard and took my first steps towards the fence.

Nothing.

I crept closer, keeping alert, watching the woods but always returning my gaze to inspect that open window, glance up at the roof.

No movement.

I reached the fence and crouched low, waiting again. I scanned the forest, tried to look into the darkness inside the hut. I was close enough to the building now that any attack from the roof was unlikely.

After a few moments I tested the fence with my weight and, thinking it strong enough, put my foot on the bottom rail and swung my leg over. But I had miscalculated, and the crosspiece snapped under me. My legs were either side when the dry wood gave with a loud crack.

I dropped onto the top rail, my full weight and momentum breaking that one too, bringing down a whole section of the fence. I collapsed and fell to one side, dropping my rifle and revolver into the snow, my legs tangled in the broken wood. I didn't have time to lie and recover my breath; I didn't have time for anything. If the child thief was here, he would know I was here too. All the care I'd taken in my approach was for nothing now.

I rolled to one side, pushed the remnants of the fence away from my legs and scrambled to a pile of cut logs. There I got to my feet and went to the shack, pressing myself against the wall.

I concentrated on bringing my breathing under control, trying to stop the thudding of my heart. All I could hear was the blood in my ears, the rhythm of my body, but I needed all my senses. I stayed low, my head turning, waiting, but nothing came.

No figure rose in the woods. No dark shadow came round the corner. No sounds other than my own. No shots.

I waited a long time, crouched in that corner between the wall and the logs, listening for the child thief. I stayed until my joints began to freeze and my teeth began to chatter. I remained motionless, part of the cabin, part of the woods themselves, and yet I felt exposed. I had no weapon, no means of defence. I stared at the place where my weapons had sunk beneath the snow by the broken fence and, when I finally moved, muscles screaming, my first thought was to retrieve the revolver.

I edged towards the broken fence, allowing myself only the briefest look at the place where I had fallen before I scanned the surroundings once again, my eyes moving constantly as I put a hand to the ground and searched.

I ignored the rifle and satchel and closed my cold fingers around the grip of the revolver before I scuttled back to the place by the cabin wall to check the weapon was still good.

Satisfied it would still work and feeling more secure now I was armed again, I stood and edged behind the pile of logs, pressing my back to the cabin wall as I approached the open window.

I raised the revolver so it was out in front of me, and from that angle I could see a tiny dark slice of the inside of the hut. Just a shadow. And I knew that to see anything more I would have to put my head close to the window – a perfect moment for the child thief to strike. But I saw no other option. If I tried the door, my enemy might be waiting for me just the same as he might be watching the window.

I prepared myself for the worst. I froze everything from my thoughts except for this moment, this *second*. I visualised what I was going to do. I was going to move quickly, turn and point the revolver into the cabin. I was going to shoot at anything that might be a man. If there was anything other than a child inside that cabin, I was going to kill it. I saw it in my mind. It was as good as done.

I took a deep breath and moved, standing, turning, pointing the revolver through the window.

A shard of sunlight cut through the trees, falling directly into the room. It slipped across the floor as an illuminated marker, pointing to the figure lying there. A dark shape, too big and bulky to be a child. And in that tiny slice of time I wondered if the child thief had grown tired of waiting; if he had fallen asleep at his post.

And then I fired. The revolver shots were loud, constrained inside the room. They merged into one as I thumbed the hammer and squeezed the trigger three times, certain that each one hit the target prone on the floor. The muzzle flashes lit up the room, smoke plumed around my face and the revolver kicked in my hand.

When I stopped firing, my ears were ringing and my nostrils were full of the smell of gunpowder. Steam rose from the heated barrel of the weapon, and I kept the revolver pointed into the room and scanned the space, my eyes adjusting to its darkness.

No sound from the figure on the floor. No movement.

'Dariya?' I spoke into the silence. 'Dariya?'

I waited. Listened.

Nothing.

'Dariya?'

I stepped back from the window, keeping the revolver ready, and made my way round to the front of the hut, where the faint remnants of footprints lay in the shelter of the overhanging roof. Just a trace remaining after the last fall of snow. There were no other marks. Someone had come here, but they had not left. I felt a moment of relief. A moment of belief that I had caught him;

that I had killed him; that Dariya would be inside, waiting for me to find her and take her home.

I reached out with my left hand and pushed on the door. I followed the revolver into the room and looked around. Wisps of gunsmoke hung in the air, broken by the shafts of light from the window. It floated and curled and twisted, becoming nothing when it touched the shadow.

'Dariya?'

The room was empty apart from the body, but there was a second door in the far wall, slightly ajar, leading to another part of the hut, and I wondered if that's where Dariya would be waiting. Hiding. Afraid.

I took another step into the cabin and glanced down at the corpse on the floor.

20

There was no furniture in the room except for a single wooden table and one chair. The table was rough, built from uplaned planks of wood, their edges uneven, the surface of it scratched and marked. The solitary chair lay on its back. Again it was basic in design, its square seat primitive, its legs uneven. In the centre of the far wall there was a small brick-lined fireplace. There were two or three half-barrels stacked on top of each other close to the fireplace and, beside them, a round board attached to the end of a wooden pole. From a beam in the ceiling hung a heavy chain, almost long enough to touch the floor.

On the table there was a bottle of clear liquid with a small amount missing, a cork pushed tight in its mouth. Beside that lay an aluminium water bottle like the one I carried. A soldier's water bottle. There was also a sheath for a knife, but the weapon was missing. A row of rifle cartridges stood upright, arranged in a line beside a small parcel of waxed paper, a packet of cigarettes, a box of matches, some other bits and pieces. There was also a satchel and a pack the man would have carried on his back. Leaning in the corner, to the right of the window at the front of the cabin, a German Mauser rifle with a mounted scope. It was almost exactly like my own.

I stood as I was and took everything in, inspecting the table, turning to look out the window cut into the front wall of the cabin. I could see right across the open stretch of land to the place where we had stopped and looked up at this hut. From here the forest looked dense, and there was no sign of Viktor and

Petro, but I knew they'd be watching. They would have heard the gunshots and would be wondering what was going on.

I looked down at the body on the rough wooden boards of the floor.

The man was dressed, and partially covered by a blanket over his legs. He looked to have slipped from a position where he might have had his back against the wall, his legs stretched out on the floor, as if he'd been taking a moment of rest from looking out the window. He had taken off his boots, which lay beside him on the floor, and I thought perhaps he'd grown tired of watching and waiting and risked a few moments of sleep during the night.

I picked up the right boot and turned it over to look at the sole, taking note of the split near the toe, a piece missing. This was the defect I'd seen in the prints we'd been following. These were the child thief's boots.

I put the boot down and glanced around again, settling on the scoped rifle leaning in the corner of the room, just out of arm's reach. It was in good condition, the wood well cared for, the metal well oiled. It was the weapon of a man who knew how to shoot. The kind of man who could have taken the near-impossible shot that killed Dimitri.

'So why is it out of reach?' I spoke aloud, turning back to the dead man. 'Why not have it right here, in your hand?' He must have been tired. He'd come a long way, dragging a reluctant child. He'd made a mistake and paid for it.

Like me, the man was bearded, but his was matted with frozen blood. His dark eyes were wide, caught in a moment of surprise. The knife that was missing from the sheath on the table was lodged in his throat, the blade pushed right in so all I could see was the worn wooden handle. The front of his coat and much of the blanket were dark with his blood, and the area where he was sitting was thick with it.

I crouched beside him and stared into his open eyes. I lifted my hand and touched a finger to the handle of the knife, feeling not revulsion or fear, but dissatisfaction. There were holes in the coat, places where my bullets had pierced him, but no blood had leaked from those wounds. My bullets had not killed this man. This man was dead before I shot him. I had not killed the child thief, and yet here he was with his head back, his mouth wide, his teeth stained red, and his tongue far back in his throat. I even thought I could see the steel of the blade where the tip had pierced the soft flesh at the hollow of his throat and slipped through. It looked as if it had been pushed hard, and he had died with one hand on his chest as if raised to the handle of the knife. I imagined him gripping at its slippery surface, trying to remove it from his body.

I saw every line in his contorted face, every dirt-filled crease in his skin, and while I was glad to see him dead, I felt disappointment it wasn't me who had finished him. I had come so far, risked so much, and my sense of justice had been stolen. I grabbed the fur of the man's hat in my fist and dragged it from his head, disturbing his position, pulling his head forward. His muscles were frozen into stiffness and his head came up a little then sprang back, banging against the wooden wall of the cabin. It was an empty sound in an otherwise silent room. I dropped the hat on the bare floorboards and stared at the face of the man I had vowed to kill.

I stood, feeling pain in my joints, calling, 'Dariya?'

I went to the far side of the room and put my hand on the door, readying my revolver. The child thief might be dead, but I didn't know who had done it or what had become of my niece.

'Dariya? Are you here? It's Luka. Your uncle. It's all right. I've come to take you home. Don't be afraid.'

I pushed the door, wincing at the way the hinges creaked, and looked into the room beyond.

'Anybody?'

This room, like the last, was almost empty but for a few half-barrels and some tools. The smell here was strong, but it was not a smell of death. It was pungent and mouldy, and I guessed this was where the shepherds would have stored the cheese they made.

There were no windows here, but another door, at the opposite corner, was open a fraction, and the sharp white of the snow outside was visible. I kept the revolver ready and crossed the room, stepping out into the cold air, seeing the fresh, familiar child's tracks which led away from the cabin. I knew these prints were recent, made within the last hour, and I felt my mood quicken. Whatever had happened to Dariya, she was still alive and she was moving. Perhaps the scalp we'd seen had been a trick, another of the child thief's games.

'Dariya!' With renewed hope, I called her name again and again as I followed her trail away from the cabin, but there was no reply. I stayed with the tracks for a few minutes until I reached the crest of the rise and looked down the other side towards the forest, but I saw no sign of her other than the trail, which continued away into the distance.

I tried to make sense of what I'd seen and what must have happened. The child thief was dead, and the only trail leading away from the hut looked as if it belonged to Dariya. There was only one conclusion to make. Whatever condition she was in, Dariya was still alive and I needed to follow her, but I had to let the others know I was safe, so I turned and hurried back to the hut.

Once inside, I went into the main room and something caught my eye close to where the half-barrels were stacked and the chain hung from the ceiling. Here, another blanket lay beside the fireplace, thrust into the shadows, and I went over, bending to pick it up, lifting it and shaking it. Something fell from among its folds, a metallic sound as it hit the floor. I crouched to inspect the floor, putting out a hand to run it over the boards. As I groped for whatever had fallen, I saw that a thin rope was tied around the last link in the heavy chain. The knot which held it in place was good and tight, but the other end was frayed. And when my grasping fingers found what had fallen from the blanket, I thought I understood what had happened. I looked at the nail for a moment, then put it in my pocket and left the hut.

*

I stood at the front of the cabin and waved my arms until one of my sons emerged from the trees, then I went to the place where I had broken the fence and fallen. I collected my rifle and satchel, and returned to the front door, seeing three figures making their way up towards me.

Inside, I took the cartridges from the table and scooped them into my satchel. I packed the waxed paper parcel and the bottle, and I put the child thief's rifle on the table along with his pack and the other things, sure that my sons would have the sense to collect them. Coming straight up the hillside they would reach the cabin within fifteen minutes but I didn't want to take any longer than I had to. The tracks leading away from the back of the cabin were Dariya's, I had no doubt about that, and I estimated they'd been there for only a short while. The snow had stopped now, but for some time it had been heavy and would have covered these tracks if they had been made much earlier. Dariya was out there somewhere, close, and she was alone now. I needed to find her as quickly as possible, and I would now be able to move without the fear of her kidnapper lying hidden, with his rifle scope trained on my heart.

21

Leaving the cabin from the back door, I followed the single line of prints, feeling some comfort that I was no longer tracking the familiar large tread with the piece missing from the tip of the right toe; that the only footprints ahead were those of a young girl. But now she was alone, and alone she wouldn't last long exposed to the Ukrainian winter.

It was a strange contradiction that the man who had taken her had kept her alive, made her dependent upon him, and that now she was free of him, she was at equal risk. Dariya wouldn't have been able to survive for as long as she had in the wilderness if it hadn't been for the child thief keeping her safe. But his aim had not been her long-term survival.

Halfway down the hill, I turned to look back at the cabin. The sun was lying across the hill, a hazy orange disc diffused by low dark clouds, its outer rim just visible over the roof of the hut. I raised a hand to shield my eyes, hoping to see a figure standing close to the crest of the hill, but there was no one there. The others hadn't reached the cabin yet, but they'd be there soon and they would catch me up. They were young and strong; they'd keep up a quicker pace than me, and I calculated they'd be with me in half an hour or so, as long as they didn't take too long in the hut. They would find the body and try to piece together what had happened, just as I had, but they would follow soon.

As I walked, I took off my glove and put a hand in my pocket to take out the object I'd found on the cabin floor close to the chain and the rope. I held it out on my palm: a single nail, rusted and old, as long as my index finger. The point was still keen but it was bent at the top as if it had been hammered in at an awkward angle. The flat area at the head was bloody and I was certain the blood was Dariya's.

I pieced together what I thought had happened inside the cabin. The child thief had restrained Dariya while he waited for me and my sons to appear at the base of the hill, where he planned to shoot and kill at least one of us – I suspected he planned to kill only one, as he had done when he murdered Dimitri, because I believed that for him the thrill was in the chase and in the kill. If he killed us all at once, he'd have nothing but a child, and she was only part of his game.

The child thief knew he had to restrain her well, because she had tried to escape once before – I'd seen evidence of it in their tracks – but he'd made a mistake. Whether it was because he was tired or overconfident, I couldn't know, but he had under-estimated Dariya. Sitting on the cold floor of the cabin, she had found something to pinch in her fingertips. The blood on the head of the nail made me think Dariya had prised it out of the old wood with her fingernails while the child thief looked out the window. And when she had loosened it, she pulled it from the wood and used it to fray the rope which secured her.

Dariya must have been terrified, quietly working at the rope while the man waited, just a few feet away with his back to her. I could almost picture him hearing a noise, turning to look at her, seeing her stare back with hatred in her eyes, hiding the nail from view. But she had been more patient than I could believe. And even when she had freed herself from the rope, she had waited longer still, knowing he would sleep. She had been with him long enough to know he needed to close his eyes, at least for a few minutes. And then she had struck.

I saw Dariya in the semi-darkness of the room, crouching behind the table, creeping closer, reaching up and taking the handle of the knife, slipping the blade from its sheath. I saw her approaching the sleeping man, her small foot putting pressure on a floorboard which creaked, the man's eyes opening in surprise, the knife coming forward with all the strength a small girl could muster. And then the point pierced the soft flesh in the hollow of his throat, slicing through skin and meat, the keen point grating against the vertebrae in his neck, his breath leaving him. I imagined the child thief's surprise at seeing her standing over him, pushing the knife deeper, forcing it into him until only the handle was visible. He would have reached up to grab it, to pull it out, but he was already dying, his life bleeding away, soaking into his coat, slipping away to pool around him on the floor, seep between the boards.

Then she had fled that place. A child who had murdered the man upon whom she had become dependent. And if that was really what had happened, I also had to believe that Dariya was all right – strong enough, at least, to kill a man in his sleep.

Deep in thought, I followed Dariya's tracks to the forest almost without thinking, but now I glanced back to see the others at the crest of the rise, and nodded to myself before slipping among the trees.

The pocket of forest was narrow and dense and the snow was shallow. I crossed it quickly, reaching the far side, breaking back out into the open. Beyond, the land was flat, and I could see a road curving round from the right. It was the same road Aleksandra and the old man had been travelling, and I was eager to keep away from it, but Dariya hadn't been so cautious. Her tracks led right to it and veered left to follow it.

Standing in the shadow of the trees, I watched the road. It lay silent across the country. Not a cart, nor a horse, nor a single traveller. The only marks upon it were those created by Dariya's feet. I looked both ways, scanning as far as I could, knowing I'd have to go after her but reluctant to move out into the open. Something wanted to hold me from rushing out. But Dariya was close, perhaps just a short way along the road, and I had to go to her. I was so close. I had to find her and bring her back. I had made a promise and I was going to keep it.

I stepped out from the cover of the trees and crossed the open ground to the road, still watching both ways, and turned in the direction Dariya had taken. But I had travelled no more than a short distance on the road before there came a heavy, muted thumping from behind.

My first reaction was to get off the road, but the land was flat and open on either side. It was close to fifty metres back to the line of the trees.

The thumping grew louder.

I froze, calculating the possibilities, considering options, trying to identify the sound, all at the same time. Rhythmic. Steady. As it grew louder, closer, the sound faltered, became irregular, as if there were two sounds competing, crossing over one another, falling in and out of step with each other, and I knew what it was. And with that realisation came the knowledge that I was trapped. There was nowhere for me to go. The road was too open at either side, the forest too far for me to reach. I cursed my luck. If I'd stayed just a few minutes longer in the trees, I would have been safe.

Behind, the sound stopped and I turned to see two riders in the road, both of them with rifles raised. For a second I wondered if I could unsling my rifle and kill those two men, shoot them right off their horses before they could react. They wouldn't expect it. They would expect me to stand down.

From where I was, I could see they were young, probably inexperienced. They wouldn't have seen much action and they would be nervous – as surprised to see me as I was to see them. But their youth would give them quick reactions. And they would not be tired and hungry like I was.

'Stay where you are,' one of them called out. 'Stand still. If you move, I'll shoot you.' The words he used were spoken in Russian.

I put my hands out to the sides and glanced at the place where

I'd emerged from the forest, trying to guess where Viktor and Petro might be. When I'd entered the woods, they'd been at the crest of the hill, which meant they hadn't been too far behind. If they'd moved more quickly than I had, perhaps they were already through the forest. They might even be there now, watching, wondering what to do, crouched in the shadow with their sights trained on the two men.

The soldier who had called out, spoke to his comrade without taking his eyes off me. His comrade nodded and shifted in his saddle as if to find a more comfortable shooting position, then the other one took the reins of his horse with one hand, keeping his heavy rifle held at waist height. He nudged his ride forwards and came closer.

'Put the rifle on the ground,' he said, pointing his weapon down at me.

I stepped back and took the rifle from my shoulder. I bent to lay it on the ground, then straightened and looked the soldier in the eye. A young man in his early twenties, he was wearing the uniform of a Red Army soldier – tunic and trousers, a heavy long coat. His leather boots almost reaching his knees, the earflaps of his *budenovka* broadcloth helmet unfurled and fastened together under his chin. The red star sewn onto the front was clean. He had the beginnings of a moustache on his upper lip, but it was soft and boyish.

'Please,' I said. 'I'm looking for my—'

'Speak Russian.'

I hadn't used my own language for a long time. I barely even used it in my thoughts any more. 'I'm looking for my daughter,' I said, thinking the man would be more sympathetic if he thought I had lost my own child.

'Where did you get that?' The soldier shifted his eyes to glance at my rifle. 'You steal it?'

'No. I'm looking for a little—'

'Answer my question. Where did you get the rifle?'

'I took it from a German soldier.'

'When?'

'*When?*'

'It's not an unreasonable question. Where are these German soldiers?'

'No. It was a long time ago. In Galicia. But please, I'm looking for a little girl. My daughter.'

The young man paused, looking me up and down. 'You're a soldier?'

'I was.'

'Ownership is restricted.'

I nodded, biting my lip.

'It's a crime to own a rifle.'

'I'm a soldier. It's unnatural for me not to have a weapon.'

'Which army?'

'Which army was I in?'

'Yes.'

'I've been in many armies. The Imperial Army . . .'

The young soldier made a tutting sound, sucking his tongue against his teeth. 'Tsarist.'

'. . . and the Red Army,' I continued. 'I fought against the central powers for your safety and then I fought a civil war for our revolution. I am a communist, not a tsarist.'

'Don't be petulant.' He took a deep breath. Beneath him the horse shifted impatiently, shaking its head and blowing out into the cold. 'So you're Russian?'

'I am.'

'Then what are you doing in this shit hole?'

I looked around, wondering what would make a man describe this beautiful land as a shit hole. But of course the soldier saw nothing of the land. He was blind to the forests and the steppe and the mountains and the fields. He saw only the villages that he moved into. He saw only the squalor and desperation of people whose belongings are taken from them; whose families are ripped apart; whose lives are invaded by greed and malice and poison. He saw men begging for their livelihood, women crying for their lost sons, streets filled with the walking dead.

I held on to my anger, fought the desire to reach out for the barrel of his rifle and pull him from his horse. 'This is my home now,' I said. 'I live here. And I'm looking for my daughter. Please, I need to—'

'Take off your satchel and put it beside the rifle.'

I hesitated, once more allowing myself a quick glance to the treeline, before doing as he instructed. The young man shifted as his horse moved and he spoke soothing words to calm it. Then he hardened his look. 'You're not from Sushne. I would know you. I'd remember. Not from Uroz either. What village are you from?'

'I don't live in any village,' I said.

'You have to live somewhere.'

'In the hills.' I inclined my head towards the line of trees, the hills beyond. 'I have a small hut.' It was a risk. If they made me show them, they'd find the body of the child thief, but I couldn't betray my own village; my own wife and daughter. They'd find it eventually, but not yet. And not by my word.

'What do you grow?'

'Grow?' I forced a smile. 'I don't grow anything. I sometimes work, but I don't grow anything. I'm not a farmer. I have nothing.'

'But you have a rifle.'

'For hunting. I shoot rabbits, sometimes deer or wolf. You're a soldier; you understand I need a rifle.'

'Take off your coat.'

'What?'

'Take off your coat.'

'In this cold? I'll freeze.'

The soldier lifted his rifle so it was pointed directly at my face. 'I could shoot you right here. Your choice.'

I nodded and started to unbutton my coat.

Without taking his eyes off me, the soldier raised his voice and called to the second man. 'Andrei, get over here and take this man's coat.'

Andrei lowered his weapon and trotted his horse over. When

he reached us, he swung his leg over and dismounted, coming close, waiting for me to remove the coat and hold it out. Without looking me in the eye, without speaking, Andrei took it and put his hands into the pockets. He pulled out the revolver and held it up for the other man to see.

'You're well armed.' The first soldier kept his rifle pointed at me.

I shrugged, feeling the cold circling.

'What are you doing out here?'

'That's what I've been trying to tell you. I'm looking for my daughter. I need to go after her, she's very young and she . . . Look.' I pointed at the tracks. 'You can see where she's gone. I have to follow her.'

The mounted soldier leaned down to take the revolver from Andrei, sitting straight in the saddle again, inspecting it. 'Search him.'

Andrei ran his hands over my shirt and trousers, turning to shake his head when he found nothing.

'Have you seen a young woman and an old man?' The first soldier asked.

'I've seen no one.'

The young man stuck the revolver into his belt and sniffed. He put his fingers under the peak of his *budenovka* to scratch his head and stared down at me. 'They were supposed to be coming this way; coming to report to the commander in Sushne. We were following their tracks along the road and then . . . and then no tracks.' He reached into a pocket and took out a packet of *papirosa* cigarettes, his rifle waving in my face as he steadied it with one hand. He pinched the tube and put it into his mouth. 'What do you make of that?'

I shook my head.

'But what would *you* think? If their tracks just stopped?'

'I wouldn't know what to think.' I could feel the cold air around me. I'd been warm under the coat, had even sweated a little from the exertion of trying to move quickly, the adrenalin from confronting the child thief, and now the sweat was cooling in the wind that blew along the road.

'It was like they just vanished,' the soldier said.

I glanced over to the trees again, wondering if my sons were there yet.

The young soldier followed my gaze. 'Something there?' he asked. 'Or are you thinking you can make it to the trees?'

'What? No. I told you, I'm looking for my daughter.'

The second soldier, Andrei, glanced out towards the trees. 'How old is she?'

'Eight years old,' I said, trying to catch his eye. 'Her name is Dariya. Let me go after her.'

'How long has she been missing?'

'A few hours. Please. She's just a little girl and she's lost out here in the cold.'

'Only eight years old?' He studied me, pursing his lips, as if considering my plea.

'What does it matter?' said the first soldier, making his comrade look up at him. 'One less kulak.'

'No, we're not kulaks, we're—'

'You're all kulaks,' he said. 'All trying to keep your wealth to yourselves. Hide it from those that have nothing; people who are willing to work.'

'*We* have nothing.' I spoke to the man standing beside me. I could feel he was more sympathetic. Perhaps he might be able to influence his comrade. 'Please, I need to find her. Look.' I pointed again. 'You can see her tracks. She went along the road. Please. Just let me follow her. Come with me.'

The mounted soldier shook his head. 'All you ever do is lie. You're all enemies of the people.'

'I'm telling the truth.'

'Maybe we should follow these tracks now,' Andrei said. 'We're going that way anyway.'

'He's trying to trick us. Trick us so he can run.' The mounted soldier stared down at me. 'You think you can run?'

'No. No, I'm just looking for—'

'Take off your boots.'

'My boots?'

'There *are* tracks, Yakov.' Andrei said. 'And they *are* small. Maybe he's telling the truth.'

'Shut up.'

'We could follow them.' He turned to look along the road. 'If he's lying, we'll arrest him – it doesn't make any difference.'

Yakov turned to look down at his comrade, contempt in his eyes and on his lips. 'You're right about *that* – it makes no difference. Lying or not, we're going to arrest him.' He turned back to me. 'Take off your boots.'

'Let him keep them,' said Andrei. 'He's done nothing wrong.'

'He's a kulak. Take them off.'

I hesitated, looking first at Andrei, then up at Yakov. I wondered if I was quick enough to overpower these two young men, but my question was answered by a vicious and powerful blow. The man on horseback thrust the barrel of his rifle hard into the place where my neck met my collarbone, a sharp and sudden pain which took me by surprise and dropped me to my knees, gasping for breath.

'Take off your boots or I'll kill you right here.'

I coughed, putting a hand to the place where Yakov had hit me, and I sucked air into my lungs before looking up at him, wanting to drag him from his horse and beat him for what he'd done.

'Take them off.' Yakov pointed the rifle at my face, and I had no doubt he would use it if I didn't do as he instructed.

I nodded and pulled the boots off, leaving them in the snow.

'All right,' Yakov said. 'Now there's no running away. Now there's only walking.' He motioned ahead of him with the barrel of his rifle. 'Go on, tsarist. Start walking.'

Andrei collected my satchel and rifle, putting them across his back before he picked up my boots. He looked at me, but only caught my eye by accident, and there was something like shame in his expression. He was not comfortable; this was not what he wanted; he was doing his job. Yakov, though, was enjoying himself.

'I'm no tsarist,' I said.

'You're whatever I say you are. Go on. Walk.'

22

It was only a matter of minutes before my feet were numb and I felt nothing of the ground upon which I walked. I might have been walking on a bed of feathers or a field of the sharpest nails, it wouldn't have mattered. And as the sun dropped from the sky, the temperature fell with it and the cold wind plucked at my clothes, finding its way through. I stayed upright, head straight, eyes ahead. I was a soldier. I had marched in the cold before. But I was older and my age punished me as if it were scornful of what I'd become. My steps were laboured. I was exhausted, hungry, and with no feeling in my feet I couldn't help stumbling from time to time. And every time I fell to my knees, the riders stopped behind me and waited for me to stand and begin walking again. If I took too long, Yakov would edge forward and prod me with the barrel of his rifle, digging at my ribs, my spine, the back of my head. He had learned to poke at the places where the bone was close to the skin.

Ignoring the pain, I focused on the footprints ahead. The only prints on the road. Dariya's small feet leading the way; her amazing, resilient little feet that had endured so much walking and so much horror and yet walked on. I stared at those prints and kept my mind away from the cold and the snow and the riders behind. I thought of Natalia at home, sitting with Lara, wondering when I would return with the boys. And I thought about my sons following, wondering when I would hear their first shot, waiting for the moment when they would shoot these two men from their horses and come for me.

But when we rounded the last corner and I saw the village ahead, I knew my sons were not going to rescue me.

Dariya's trail led all the way to the village, where it disappeared in the clutter of a thousand prints crossing and re-crossing the paths between the houses and through the centre of the village. Here the snow was trampled by the feet of many people and horses and carts.

'Over there,' Yakov ordered.

I had been to Sushne before, a few years ago, when times were good. It was much like Vyriv, but larger. There were houses arranged around a central space, with others lying behind them. Families had expanded; new people had come to live here during the good years, and so the village had grown and houses had been built. Far to the left a simple church with a belfry that stood empty. To one side of the church's broken steps, the bell lay on its side, half the height of a man, a great piece smashed from it so it would never ring again. There was evidence of the path it had taken when the soldiers had cast it from the tower, the great weight of a symbol of faith and calling, free-falling to the steps, where it shattered the concrete, powdered the balustrade and fractured.

Two men in uniform, rifles over their shoulders, stood at the base of those damaged steps, leaning against a part of the balustrade that was still intact. They were smoking cigarettes and looking in our direction. I didn't need to see the man behind me to know this was where he wanted me to go. This was where they had made their jail in Sushne.

I walked on, heading towards the church, drawing no looks because there was no one in the street to watch me. There was no one outside but the two soldiers by the steps and the two behind me on horseback.

The sun had almost set now, the sky was dark with cloud, and there were lights on in some of the windows. Weak lights that flickered and melted the frost that had formed on the glass.

When I reached the steps of the church, the two soldiers came forward, flicking their cigarettes away and moving to either side of me, taking my arms.

'Put him with the rest,' said Yakov, and I heard his horse turn and move away.

The soldiers said nothing. They gripped me tight and bustled me up the steps as if I had resisted. One of them put his booted foot against the door and pushed it open.

Inside, the church was dim and smelled of stone and wood. It was a simple building, like the one in Vyriv, perhaps a little larger. From this place of faith, however, all traces of religion had been stripped away. The simple wooden benches, once arranged before the altar, were now swept aside and roughly piled around the edges. Some of them had been broken with boots and axes, kicked and cut for easy firewood. The altar itself had been stripped of its adornment and was now just a sturdy wooden table in the centre of the room. While it had once been pristine and well cared for, it was now functional and basic. Upon it there were no candlesticks, but there were candles, stuck in their own wax to secure them to the uneven surface. One or two of the candles were burning with strong flames that danced in the breeze from the open door, trailing capillaries of black smoke, giving enough light to see the wooden crucifix discarded on the table and dark patches on the walls where icons had been removed. They had been smashed and burned in the centre of the village along with any other symbols of religion.

The soldiers' boots were loud on the stone floor, the pad of my own bare feet inaudible as we went to the far end of the church, where there was a single door in the wall. We stopped a few feet from it, and one of the soldiers released his grip, running his hands over my clothes, squeezing my pockets, feeling for any belongings. The other stepped forward, taking a key from his belt, and when the first soldier had finished searching me, the second unlocked the door and his comrade pushed me into the blackness.

The door shut behind me and the key turned in the lock.

I stood while my eyes grew accustomed to the darkness. The smell was not of wood and stone in there, but of sweat and fear. Of human waste.

The air was thick with it, closing around me.

'Who is that?'

A single voice in the dark. A man speaking Ukrainian. Then a cough.

The blackness became grey as my eyes took in what light was available, but I could still see very little inside that room. I guessed it was the place where the priest would have prepared for mass, and that it had no windows, explaining the minimal light.

'Who is it?' The same voice. Weak. An old man with a dry throat.

'No one,' I answered, putting my hands to the door, running my fingers around its edges, feeling its contours. I could hear the receding footsteps of the soldiers and I put an ear to the wood, listening until they had gone. Then I took the handle and shook the door, barely even rattling it in its frame, it was so solid and well set. I felt the keyhole and crouched to look through into the church, but there was little to see other than the table with the crucifix and the candles burning on it. I felt further, testing the large iron hinges, slipping my fingertips beneath the door and trying to find any way it might open.

'We've all tried it,' said the voice. 'Every one of us.'

I stopped, stood, took a step forward, my feet catching on something that moved and pulled away, accompanied by a sharp intake of breath. A person's leg, outstretched.

'I'm sorry.'

'Sit down,' said a voice, this one different, but with the same dryness, the same weariness. 'Sit down before you hurt some-one.'

I touched the section of wall beside the door and put my back to it, sliding down, grateful for the relief in my legs.

Reaching out, I pulled one foot up, lodging it on the knee

of my other leg and rubbing some life back into it. Already the feeling was coming back and the intensity of the pain was increasing.

'You're from this village?' said the first voice.

'No.'

'What's your name?'

I hesitated. 'Luka Mikhailovich.'

'Ah. Luka. A strong name. You'll do well. You'll survive with a name like Luka. It's the Mishas and the Sashas that find it hard. My name is Konstantin Petrovich. Kostya. That's a good name too.'

By now my eyes had begun to accept the tiniest light which filtered through the keyhole and beneath the door, and I could see the faint shadow of the man who had spoken. He sat opposite, against the other wall, but he shifted when he spoke his name, and I understood he was holding out his hand.

I leaned forward and took it.

'Our fellow prisoners,' he said, 'are my brother Evgeni Petrovich and my neighbours Yuri Grigorovich and Dimitri Markovich.'

I immediately thought of the man whose daughter I had come to find. My own brother-in-law, Dimitri, lying dead in a field with his wife waiting for him at home, but I turned my head, looking for the dark smudges of the other men, reaching out and shaking their hands in a solemn act of mutual understanding.

'But there are no formalities here,' said Yuri Grigorovich. 'We're all friends. Call me Yuri.'

'Where are you from?' Kostya asked. 'What village?'

Even here, among these other prisoners, I wanted to protect my home from the men who might destroy its heart. I didn't know the people with whom I was imprisoned, but I knew of the OGPU and I knew of the activists sent to control our land. Any of these men might be here to gain my trust, find out something that might be of use to them. There were people everywhere, well placed and well trained to turn neighbour against neighbour, husband against wife, father against son. Any one of them might be a spy.

'No village,' I said. 'I live alone with my daughter, close to the forest.'

'No wife?'

'No. The famine was not kind to us.' I hated saying it, denying my own wife.

'I'm sorry to hear it. You farm?'

'Nothing to speak of. I hunt for food and skins.'

'So what brings you here?' asked Kostya, then he chuckled to himself, a low throaty sound that again made me picture him as an old man, his skin beaten by the weather, his hands hardened by years of working on the land. 'I think you probably should've stayed in the forest.'

'I'm looking for my daughter,' I said.

'Your daughter?'

'She's lost.' I took my foot in my hands and began rubbing again.

'How does one lose their daughter?' asked Yuri.

'It's a long story.'

'We have a long time.'

'She wandered off, that's all. I was following her tracks when the soldiers found me on the road.'

'That's unlucky.'

'Do you know anything about her?' I said.

For a while the men were silent. No one spoke.

'Have I said something to offend you?' I asked.

'Tell him why you're here, Dima.'

I waited for Dimitri Markovich to speak. He cleared his throat, shuffled a little, moved against the hard stone floor.

'A girl came into the village this afternoon.' Like the others, his throat was dry, his voice tight in his throat. He sounded as if he had resigned himself to his fate, sitting in that dark room.

'A girl?' I asked, sitting up straight. 'Did you see her? Was she all right?'

'She came and she stood, waiting for someone to see her, to say something, but no one dared go to her.'

'Was she *hurt?*' I asked, feeling my anxiety rise, but it was as if he didn't hear me.

'No one . . . no one dares to even come out of their home for fear of being brought to the church, or their husband being taken away in the night. Or their children. But I saw her from my window, so I went out. My wife tried to stop me, but I went anyway. You see, we had a daughter and—'

'Was she hurt?' I asked him again, wanting to reach over and grab him, shake the answer out of him. 'The girl who came into the village. Was she *hurt?* It's important you remember.'

'When I got to her, she just stood there, saying nothing. She didn't even look at me.'

'I need you to tell me how she was,' I said, trying to stay calm. 'Please.'

When he spoke again, there was a low grumble behind his voice. 'I'm sorry. She had a lot of blood on her. On her face and on her hands and her clothes. In her hair.'

'Her hair?' I tried not to think of the scalp we'd seen hanging from the tree. 'What about her hair?'

'Beautiful,' he said. 'But there was blood.'

'She had her hair?'

'Yes. Yes, of course, but she was . . .' His voice trailed away. He was either remembering or he was reluctant to go on, but my attention had slipped for a moment. All I could think was that the scalp *wasn't* Dariya's. I almost hadn't dared to believe it before. But now, with Dima's words, it seemed even more real. That terrible obscenity had not been hers.

'Tell me what happened,' I said. 'Tell me about Dariya.'

'That's her name? Dariya?'

'Yes.'

'I tried to talk to her, but one of the soldiers came over and shouted at her, asking where the blood was from. She said nothing so he shook her like she was going to fall to pieces. It was like she was switched off. She made no sound at all. No reaction. Nothing. He shook her and shook her, asking who she was, and she stayed silent, her body moving like she was a pile of rags. She just stared ahead of her. Staring and staring like she'd seen something terrible and it was still fixed right in front of her. I wanted to tell him to stop shaking her but I was afraid he would punish me. I was a coward.'

'No,' Kostya said. 'Not a coward.'

'But then he hit her, slapped her so hard he knocked back her head, and when he raised his hand to slap her again, I felt like my blood was going to boil. Before I knew it, I grabbed his hand and when I realised what I'd done, I begged him not to hit her again. I got to my knees and begged him. So he hit me. He hit me over and over, shouting how could I question a soldier of the state, and when I fell, he started kicking me. He kicked me so hard I don't remember them bringing me in here.'

'And Dariya?'

'I don't know,' Dima said. 'I wish I could tell you.'

'I have to get out of here.' I turned back to the door, pulling at the handle, raking my fingernails over its solid surface. 'I have to find her.'

'There's no getting out of here,' said Kostya. 'Not until they come to take us out.'

'I have to,' I said, trying to find purchase on the door, a way of opening it. Then I turned my fists on the wood, beating it as if with two hammers, venting the frustration and rage that had grown these last few days.

The other men left me to my madness as I rattled the door in its secure frame, and when my energy abandoned me, I stopped, putting my forehead against the cold wood. 'I made a promise,' I said. 'I made a promise.'

'Sit down.' Yuri put a hand on my shoulder. 'Save your energy for later.'

'Later?'

And there was a silence in the room. I sensed the men turning to each other in the darkness, something unspoken passing among them. But I knew. I'd seen things that would make these men cry out in their sleep, and I knew what was coming later. I understood at least a part of what was going to happen to me.

I reached up and put my own hand on Yuri's. I patted it and then took it from my shoulder. 'You're right,' I said, turning, sitting once again. 'You're right.'

I sat on the stone floor once more, leaning my head back to rest on the wall, my mouth falling open. I thought about poor Dariya and everything she'd had to endure. She'd seen her father raise a rabble to hang a man from the old tree in the centre of the village. She'd become dependent on the man who had stolen her from her family, and she'd eventually murdered him in a most horrible manner. It was little surprise she was silent when she came into Sushne, thinking she had found safety.

'Thank you, Dima. Thank you for trying to protect Dariya.'

Dimitri Markovich said nothing.

'And is she really your daughter?' Yuri asked.

'Of course. Why would you ask that?'

'It's just . . . you didn't say why you're here. Perhaps the soldiers thought you did something to harm her, make her like that.'

'Harm her? No. I was carrying a rifle; they asked where it came from.'

'You're a soldier?'

'I *was* a soldier. But I have no allegiance other than to our leader.' The words tasted sour but I had to say them. I didn't know these men and I didn't know what they might say or do to try to improve their own situation.

'What kind of soldier were you?' Yuri asked.

'I was on the front against the Austro-Hungarians and the Germans—'

'Which army?'

'What difference does it make?'

'Yuri was there too,' said Evgeni. 'In Galicia. There are people here who think he was a war hero.'

'You were there in June?' I asked. 'For the offensive under General Brusilov?'

'Eighth Army. But it was July as I remember it. Are you testing me, Luka?'

I stayed quiet.

'Many soldiers died,' Yuri said.

'But not you.'

'No. Not me. After the fall of Tarnopol we pulled back, making a stand east of Czernowitz, but we were tired and people began to desert.'

'Did *you*?'

'I waited until the very end, Luka.'

'I waited too.'

'And then?'

'I joined the first revolutionary army,' I said.

'Ah,' Yuri laughed. 'A good communist.' There was sarcasm in his words.

'Yes. A good communist.'

'So they arrest their own now?'

'Probably. But I'm not with them now.' I didn't tell him I abandoned the Red Army during the Crimean mutinies and went to fight with Nestor Makhno.

'Imperialist and revolutionary?' Yuri said. 'One would be forgiven for thinking you don't know your loyalties.'

I had said too much. It was a mistake for me to have told them anything; any one of them might have been a planted informer. My truth was that I had lost my way. I had fought for one army after another because it was what I had in my blood. I had changed my allegiance only for vague ideals. I had believed the communists offered a better life, but it became clear that what they offered was not freedom. I had defected because Makhno offered self-government protected by a people's army, but I saw the truth of it now. They had all wanted the same thing. Whether they were Red or White or Black or Green, they had all fought to gain power over the common man. To take what they had, and to keep on taking until there was nothing left but the brittle bones in their bodies. I saw now that only one thing was important, irrespective of colour or ideal, and that was to protect my family.

'What does it matter?' said Kostya. 'We're all revolutionaries or counter-revolutionaries now. There is nothing else. No more individuals. We're all part of the collective.'

'Or perhaps you liked the fighting?' Yuri ignored him. 'The action? I can understand it. There's fear and horror in fighting, but when you've fought for so long it becomes part of you.'

'I manage without it. I put those things away.'

'Is that what you do with your guilt?'

'There's no guilt,' I said.

'But it's how you live with the things you saw,' Yuri said. 'How you forget the men you killed and the things you did. You put them away.'

'How do *you* forget?'

'Who says I do?'

I looked across at the dark shape that was Yuri Grigorovich.

'So you lock them away in your mind,' he went on. 'You leave them behind a door in the dark. And what happens when that door opens, just a crack?'

'It never does,' I said.

Yuri grunted, making a dismissive sound, and the room fell into silence.

There was no way to measure time in the obscurity of our prison. The only light was that which trickled around and beneath the door. The only sounds were of breathing, of bodies shuffling, throats being cleared. We were left to our thoughts, only drawn back to the present by sporadic snatches of conversation.

'So they arrested you for owning a rifle,' Kostya said into the gloom.

'Maybe for that.' I was glad for the change in subject. Yuri's direction had been unsettling. 'Or maybe for fighting in the Imperial Army? For being a tsarist? I don't know. What reasons do they need? They arrested Dimitri for trying to help a child. And the rest of you? What are you locked in here for?'

'Maybe because there was no one else to arrest,' Evgeni said. 'Because the soldiers were bored.'

'So why are *they* here?' I asked. 'The soldiers. Moscow doesn't send soldiers to every village. Activists, maybe, but soldiers? And this many?'

'We refused to join the *kolkhoz*,' Kostya said. 'It's not our tradition; we're single farmers. We work hard for what little we have, and they tell us to give it away and to move out to one of their farms. They said it would be good for us all, that they would give us tractors and we would grow so much we could feed the revolution. But we said no, and one of their activists came two weeks ago – one of their young men from the city who knows nothing of our lives or the country.'

I waited for him to go on.

'He came with two soldiers, and they wanted to take our land and our animals. So we slaughtered them.'

'The activist?'

'No,' Kostya half-laughed. 'That came later. No, we killed the animals so they couldn't take them for their *kolkhoz*, so they took our belongings instead, burning what they didn't want, and then they began to take the men. There were those in the village who called themselves good communists, people who spied on the rest of us, and they pointed their fingers, and there would be a knock on the door in the middle of the night, and people disappeared and didn't come back. Some of the men, the ones who were left, they protested.'

'Protested how?' I asked.

'By bringing a death sentence on the whole village,' Yuri said.

'They went to the house where the activist and the soldiers were staying, and they burned it to the ground,' Kostya said. 'But it was a small victory. They came back last week in numbers and threw the bell from the tower, rode their horses into the church, and when the priest tried to stop them, they ordered him to strip naked and walk out into the snow. They watched him until he began to cry. A grown man, a *priest*, reduced to tears and begging. So they whipped him across the back with their pistols and left him to bleed while they burned the icons and turned the church into a prison.'

I was surprised at the tone of Kostya's voice – as if he was recounting something that had happened many years ago, and to someone else. There was no anger or indignation or sense of injustice. There was only a weary acceptance, as if he had all but given up.

'And they began their liquidation of kulaks,' he said. 'If anyone even knows what a kulak is.'

'Everyone is a kulak,' Evgeni said. 'If you have a small plot of land, you're a kulak. If you own an animal, you're a kulak. If you've *ever* owned an animal, you're a kulak. And they're terrified of the kulak like they're afraid of the Jew.'

'But they didn't deport any of *you*?'

'You mean we might be spies?' Yuri asked.

'No, I . . .'

'Of course that's what you mean,' said Kostya, 'and why wouldn't you? It's just like it was after the revolution. No one can trust anyone. It's how they want it.'

'And why are they still here?'

'They made this their headquarters,' he said. 'From here they find the other villages and farms and they force them into the *kolkhoz* and they take away *their* belongings and *their* food and *their* kulaks. And then they'll send workers from the cities to farm the land because there'll be none of us left. We'll either be deported or we'll be dead. If not by their hand, then because we have nothing to eat. My wife, she used to be fat. Fat and beautiful, but now I can see her bones through her skin, and she goes into the forest to look for mushrooms or whatever she can. If we could catch the birds from the sky, we would eat them.'

No one spoke. The sound of breathing filled the room and I felt the despair and resignation in these men.

'We are beginning to starve,' Evgeni said. 'All of us. Much more of this, and there'll be no one left. It'll be like it was ten years ago when there was nothing to eat and the Volga refugees brought cholera and typhus.'

'They say people even ate their own children,' Yuri said, and it made me think of the bodies I'd found on the sled just a few days ago. 'You ever hear stories like that, Luka? You ever hear of people eating their own children?'

'Not their own, no.'

'But something like it?'

I didn't answer.

'A soldier like you, you must have seen things,' he persisted.

'As must *you*.'

'They'll let us all die in the streets,' Evgeni said.

I put my hands to my face and rubbed hard. I wondered if it was possible to die from despair. 'And you men?' I asked. 'Why were *you* arrested?'

Kostya laughed, but it was a sad sound, made low in his chest. 'Does there need to be a reason?'

No one answered.

'I made a joke,' he said. 'I made a stupid joke that our great leader must be getting fat with all the bread he has while we're getting thinner. A soldier heard me and now I'm an agitator. An enemy of the state. My brother, Evgeni, he's here because I am, and I will for ever be sorry that I have made it so. If I'm an enemy of the state, then so must he be.'

'They beat me for being a conspirator or an enemy of the state or something,' Evgeni said. 'A counter-revolutionary. They beat me and put me in the bell tower to make me admit it. So I admit it.'

'The bell tower?'

'They left me up there. Naked, in the cold, until my heart felt like it was going to freeze right in my chest. So I admitted to whatever they asked me.'

The men had exhausted themselves and they fell silent for a long time, all of them thinking about what had been said. The room was blank but for the soporific sound of steady breathing, the occasional cough.

Sitting against the wall with my head tipped back, the hardness of the stone was cruel on the places where my bones were closest to the skin. I had no coat to make myself comfortable, to use as a pillow or a mattress, and sitting in the darkness it was impossible to know what time of day it was, but eventually I slept, waking only to the sound of the church door banging and the advance of heavy boots across the floor. There was a scraping of wood on stone, a voice speaking with authority, rapid sentences, and then the footsteps approached the door that was keeping us sealed inside that small room. They stopped. A key in the lock, turning, metal on metal.

The door opened wide, allowing a small amount of light to enter. It was weak and orange, of little real consequence, but to us, deprived of light, it was a connection to whatever was on the other side of the door.

The fragile glow slipped across the floor and reached for the face of the man who owned the voice I knew as Kostya. I saw him for the first time, drawn and thin, and I realised I hadn't asked him how long he had been in this room. His beard was wild and scruffy, clinging to sunken cheeks, with patches of grey and places where it grew in tufts as if it had either been torn out or had fallen out. He reminded me of a starving feral dog with its stomach arched and boned, its hair missing in clumps. His skin was fissured into deep wrinkles across his forehead and around his sunken eyes. He was wearing a shirt and a waistcoat, the standard dress of a peasant, with dirty trousers and worn boots on his feet.

He looked over with watery eyes, but when hands took my shoulders and dragged me to my feet, Kostya looked away.

I was dragged backwards from the room before I even had a chance to stand, then hauled to my feet by one soldier while another kicked the door closed and locked it once again. The sound of the door slamming back into place reverberated from the church walls, filling my ears.

It was colder out there than it had been inside the room, and there was a harsh feeling of being taken out, like a traumatic birth. Inside it had been dark and disorientating, the stench of fear and urine in the air, but it had been warm, and now I was back in the cold, my bare feet on the freezing stone floor. In there it had been terrible – the waiting and the not knowing – but it had been safer than I knew it was out here.

23

The soldiers didn't speak while they took me to the table in the centre of the church. They pushed me down into a chair and stepped away, one on each side, just a few feet away, and there they remained silent. Waiting.

On the table the candles flickered, flames twisting in the air, their light glinting on the surface of a heavy glass tumbler of water that stood by a dented metal jug. I sat straight in the chair, staring at the wooden crucifix lying on the table close to the half-burned candles. Its main upright was as long and thick as my forearm, and I could see where it had once stood in a base. It was not ornate, but a simple representation of the cross. I stared at it and prepared for what was to come. I tried to relax, calm my mind. I tried to close myself off and pretend I wasn't here. I was at home, at the table in the kitchen. The *pich* was alight and warm. The table was laid with fresh bread and *salo* and mushrooms that Natalia had picked from the woods in the summer. There was a full bottle of *horilka*. And my family was there. Natalia beside me, my sons and my daughter around the table.

But I couldn't hold the image in my head. I was cold. I was tired and hungry. And for all my strength – for all the things I had seen and done – I was afraid.

When the main church door opened, I could see it was night. I saw no stars or moon, just the darkness.

Two men entered and closed the door behind them. The first was younger than me, maybe in his early thirties, and he was

239

clean shaven. Light blue eyes as cold as the night outside, and thin lips that were dry and broken by the weather. He wore a heavy coat and a small-peaked wide-crowned cap pulled tight on his head. His knee-length leather boots were polished to a proud shine. In his left hand he carried my satchel, and in his right he held my rifle.

The second man was closer to me in age and was dressed in the same way as Kostya, except that he wore an ill-fitting coat and had a cap on his head. His trousers were bagging around the knees because the bottoms were tucked into his boots. The boots looked new. He was bearded and dark and I thought he might be from the village, perhaps a loyal communist who was now part of a newly formed local soviet. Whether he was a true communist or just someone trying to save his own life and that of his family was irrelevant. He did what was expected of him.

They came along the aisle between the discarded and broken pews, and they stopped in front of the table. The young man looked down at me. He stood for a while, not speaking, then made a satisfied sound, low in his throat. He nodded and placed the satchel and rifle on the table, out of my reach, before removing his hat and laying it down so the red star was facing me. The hat looked as if it might be new; the royal-blue crown was still neat and clean, the red band not yet marked with mud and grime, the Soviet star pristine.

It was cold in the church, but the young man took off his coat and draped it over the back of one of the chairs, standing before me so I could see his uniform. The dark kitel tunic with the red collar tabs and gleaming black buttons. He was showing me who he was, and though I was unfamiliar with his uniform, I guessed the man was OGPU, perhaps the head of a provincial department. We used to call them Chekists, but the name made no difference. Whatever you called them, political police were renowned for their power and their brutality.

The young policeman sat down and folded his hands, resting them on the table. He looked me directly in the eye. The man beside him placed his hands in his lap and looked at the tabletop.

I met the policeman's stare only for a few seconds before I deferred to him, looking down. The policeman responded by taking the glass of water in one hand and drinking its contents in a few long gulps. He refilled it from the jug, then wiped his lips with his fingers before folding his hands again.

'What's your name?' He spoke in Russian.

I opened my mouth to reply but my tongue was dry.

'Name?' He asked a second time without taking his eyes off me.

'Luka Mikhailovich Sidorov.'

He nodded. 'Russian.'

'Yes.'

'Good. Then this should be a civilised conversation. My name is Sergei Artemevich Lermentov and I am the head of the provincial OGPU department.' I remembered the name: Lermentov. The man who'd been in Uroz – the village Aleksandra came from.

He sat back and crossed his arms, still staring. 'Can you tell me what you're doing here, Luka?'

'Your soldiers brought me here.'

'That's not what I meant.'

He removed a packet of *papirosa* cigarettes from his pocket and took one out. He left the packet on the table and crimped the tube of the cigarette before putting it into his mouth. Then he produced a match and scraped it across the surface of the table that had once been an altar and he touched it to the tobacco. He drew in a deep drag and blew it out without leaning away. The smoke came at me in a stream, tinged with the smell of alcohol.

'Why are you in this shit hole? Ukraine, I mean. Why would any Russian want to be here?'

'I fought here,' I said. 'And when we were demobilised I stayed.'

'Red Army?'

'Yes.'

'So you fought the anarchists, you crushed their resistance and then you stayed?'

'Yes.'

'Interesting.' He dragged on the cigarette again, raising his eyes as if he were mulling over what I'd just told him.

'And before that?' Lermentov asked. 'Before the Red Army?'

'Before that I fought for the Imperial Army.'

'A war hero, no doubt.'

'Just a soldier.'

'Is that where you got this?' He reached across and took up my rifle. He drew back the bolt as if to show that it wasn't loaded, then he pulled it to his shoulder and sighted across the church using the scope.

'Yes.'

'Of course, we have better rifles now. Better marksmen.' The policeman held the rifle out for one of the soldiers to take, then he waved him away with one hand. 'Get rid of it.'

Lermentov looked down at his hands and used a fingernail to scrape something from beneath his right thumbnail. Perhaps some oil from the rifle.

'Are you a tsarist?' he asked.

'No. I joined the revolutionary army.'

'But you didn't stay.'

'No.'

'A counter-revolutionary, then.'

'No.'

'You're sure? I can find out. It's easy enough to make you admit to it.'

'I think you can make me admit to almost anything.'

He nodded. 'And now? Where do you live? What village?'

'No village,' I said. 'I live by the hills. I grow a few potatoes, I hunt—'

'With your illegal guns.'

I bowed my head. 'I'm a soldier.'

'I understand,' he said, reaching down and unbuttoning the holster at his side. He drew out his pistol and put it on the table in front of him. 'I feel naked without my weapon. Like you, I'm a soldier.'

'Please,' I said. 'I'm looking for my daughter.'

'We'll get to that. What village are you from?'

'I already told you, I live not far from here, in the hills.'

'Hm.' He took the pistol and sat back again, turning it over in his hand. The cigarette in the corner of his mouth burned with grey smoke that filled the space above us. He lifted a hand to take it between two fingers. 'Something about you isn't right.'

I didn't reply.

'Do you know why I'm here?'

'No.'

'They brought me from my nice life in Moscow to this shit hole because these peasants won't do as they're told. Did you know that the people in this village murdered the party activist who came here? They burned him alive just a few weeks ago.' He shook his head. 'And because these peasants want to keep everything for themselves, because they don't want to be a part of the great plan, people like me – good communists, loyal to their leader – have to come down here and make sure they do what they're told. And it makes me angry. It makes me . . .' Again he shook his head, lips pursed tight. He dropped his cigarette to the floor and ground it with his boot heel before leaning forward again and staring right at me. 'This morning two enemies of the state were sent from Uroz. Agitators. They were – they *are* – withholding vital information for the furtherance of the collective, so they were to walk here for interrogation, but they didn't arrive. Do you know anything about that?'

'No.'

'I think you're lying.'

'No.'

His hand shot out, still holding the pistol, and struck me across the left side of the face. The violence of the blow twisted my neck, knocked me sideways from the chair. It had come with such speed and such ferocity that I had hardly even registered the movement before I found myself on the stone floor of the church, lying on my side, staring under the table at the policeman's boots.

The floor was cold against my cheek, and I put my palms flat on the stone to push myself up, shaking my head, seeing brightness in my eyes.

'Help him up,' the policeman said with a hint of boredom, and there were hands on my clothes, dragging me up and pushing me back into the chair.

I rubbed the side of my face and raised my eyes to look at the man who had struck me. He was staring right back at me, leaning forward, his pistol on the table, one hand placed over it. Beside him, the bearded one refused to meet my eyes.

Lermentov continued to look at me for a while before he smiled. 'I know. You hate me now and you'd like to kill me.'

'No.'

'Liar.' He struck out again, but this time I saw him move and I leaned back, the blow missing me by the breadth of a blade of grass. The muzzle of the pistol hissed past the end of my nose, almost brushing it, and the policeman's hand swung into nothing but air. I saw the strength he had used, because the man unbalanced himself, lurching sideways in his chair.

When he had composed himself, he spoke to the soldier behind me. 'Hold him.'

And then hands were on me again and I was held tight.

The policeman stood and came to me, pulling the table away, making his bearded companion shift quickly.

'Fast,' the younger man said, raising the pistol and pressing it against my eye, pushing hard enough for light to explode in my vision. 'But not fast enough.' He removed the pistol, slipped it back into the holster before taking up the crucifix from the table. He smiled at me again and swung the crucifix against the side of my head, darkening my world.

When I opened my eyes, I was on the floor once more. Hands were on me, dragging me, but I was a deadweight. My face was numb and my feet were numb and everything refused to work. For a moment I wanted to be left alone on the cold stone. I wanted to curl into a ball and close my eyes and not wake up. But then I thought of all the things that were waiting for me and I forced my mind to work; forced my body to work.

I willed resolve into my muscles and I climbed back to the chair, seeing that the table had been straightened and the two men were sitting opposite me once more. I wiped a hand across my face and looked at the blood smeared on my fingers.

'I think now we understand each other,' the man said. 'Am I right?'

'Yes.'

'I'm in charge here and you will accept my authority.'

'Yes.'

'And you will stop lying to me.'

'Yes.'

'Good.' He smiled. 'Now let's talk about my missing agitators. Where are they?'

'I don't know.'

He reached out and slapped me across the cheek, bloodying his hand. 'Where are they?'

'I don't know.'

He slapped me again. 'You killed them.'

'No.'

He struck me again, turning my head, opening the cut on my cheek, spraying blood onto the table.

'Admit to it.'

'No.'

He hit me once more and the bearded man opposite flinched, looking away, pushing back his chair to avoid the blood.

The policeman turned to look at him with distaste. 'If this is too much for you, Anatoly Ivanovich, then maybe you should leave.'

Anatoly Ivanovich swallowed and nodded. 'There are things I should do. I—'

'Just go.'

The peasant nodded and stood, scraping his chair on the stone as he pushed it back. He glanced at Lermentov before turning and walking away. He had almost reached the door when the OGPU man called out to him, his eyes still on mine.

Anatoly Ivanovich stopped and waited for Lermentov to leave

the table and go to him. They spoke for a moment in the darkness at the far end of the church and then the bearded man left and the policeman returned to the table.

'So, you were just saying that you killed my agitators.'

'No.'

Lermentov rolled his eyes and sighed. 'Am I going to have to keep hitting you, Luka? You're a soldier; you know how this works. It's my job. It's what I was sent here to do, whether I like it or not, and I'll do it properly. So I'll keep hitting you and then I'll put you back in that room to bleed. And before you can get any sleep, I'll bring you back out here and I'll hit you again. And it will go on and on. And when I finally get bored, I'll have you shot.'

I stared at him.

'Unless I get a confession.'

I looked away.

'Where did you leave their bodies? It doesn't matter that you killed them, they were enemies of the state, but I want to know where the bodies are.'

'I didn't—'

Lermentov picked up the crucifix and poked it at the hollow of my throat, the same place where Dariya had stabbed the child thief. I coughed loudly, doubling over.

'All right,' I said, straightening up, rubbing my neck. 'All right. I saw tracks in the forest, but I didn't see anybody. I was following other tracks, trying to find my daughter.'

'Why didn't you say so before?'

'All I want is to find my daughter.'

'Maybe we should talk about her for a moment. Your daughter. What did you say her name was?'

'Dariya.'

'And you lost her in the woods, is that right?'

'Yes. She came here. To this village.'

'And she was well?'

'What?'

'She was well when you last saw her?'

246

'Yes.'

Behind Lermentov the church door opened and he turned to look.

'Ah,' he said. 'How convenient. We speak about her and she arrives. As if by magic.' He smiled a wide grin, but his eyes held something other than laughter, something other than the bored look of an official performing yet another interrogation. Now there was dark hatred in his eyes. 'Bring her in, Anatoly.' I noticed he had dropped the formal usage of his comrade's name.

Anatoly came forward with Dariya at his side.

She looked pale and small, but she was alive. And she was, more or less, unharmed from what I could see. My deductions from the scene at the hut and my fellow prisoner Dimitri's account had been accurate – the scalp that the child thief had left for us had not belonged to Dariya – and seeing her standing there was overwhelming both because I was relieved and pleased but also because I had wished to find her under different circumstances. I'd hoped to rescue her and take her home, but that outcome now looked unlikely. My chest heaved at seeing her, and I had to control my emotions. I had been searching only for two days but it felt as if I had been on Dariya's trail for weeks. All the time I had been looking for her I had closed everything away, locked my feelings behind the strong door I kept in my mind and in my heart. I had kept those feelings so well contained that I hadn't known how afraid I was for her, but now that door threatened to burst open. I took a deep breath and hardened myself. Now was not the time for weakness.

Dariya's eyes were ringed red and her hair was tangled about her small face. Her sheepskin coat hung open, and beneath it she wore the same dress she had been wearing when I last saw her, but now it was dirty and torn in more than one place. There were rusty patches where the child thief's blood had dried on the material, and when the snow fell away from her woollen boots, I could see dark stains there too. She stared ahead of her as if she saw nothing. Like a blind child being led into the room.

Anatoly did not hold her hand; instead he had one hand on the top of her head as if to make her move in the right direction, but that was all. He brought her close to the table and I started to stand, but Lermentov prodded me with the crucifix once more and I stayed where I was.

'So this is your daughter?'

'Yes. Let me go to her.'

Lermentov turned to Dariya standing at his side. She looked so small and empty, and it filled me with despair. 'Is this your father?'

Dariya offered no response. Nothing. She didn't move her lips. She only blinked, but it was not in response to his question.

The policeman shook his head. 'She doesn't recognise you.'

'What have you done to her?'

'What have *we* done to her? We don't harm people, we protect them. She was like this when she arrived. Well. Not quite like this. She had blood on her hands and face, but one of the women has washed it away. At first I thought maybe it was her blood, but she seemed unharmed.'

'Thank God.'

'There is no God.'

'Of course. I just meant . . . I'm glad she's unharmed.'

'She isn't. I thought she was, but when we looked further . . .'

He leaned to one side and lifted the hem of Dariya's dress.

She remained still as he drew it up her leg so I could see a rough bandage wrapped around her right thigh. Lermentov took one end of it between his fingers and pulled it away to reveal the wound where a piece of flesh had been cut away from her leg. It was an area about the size of a cigarette packet, dry and well tended. It looked as if it had been treated as soon as it had been done. Cauterised, perhaps, with something hot, but done so perfectly and so completely that in only a few places did it look raw, and there was almost no weeping of blood or fluid from the wound.

I turned away, remembering the screams I'd heard in the night. I didn't know if the child thief had mutilated Dariya like this for his amusement, his hunger or just to frighten his pursuers with her terrible screams. I was sorry for her in ways I could barely understand.

When the policeman spoke again, his words were slow and considered, and with those words came an awful understanding.

'Why did you do this to her?' he asked.

I turned to meet his stare. Thoughts and feelings confused themselves into a terrible jumble as I realised what Lermentov was saying. 'What? No. I . . .' But I didn't know what to say. Nothing would convince the policeman.

'She's not your daughter, is she?' Lermentov almost curled his lip. The interrogation about the missing prisoners was just a lead into this. Before it had been routine, mundane, but something in Lermentov's expression and intonation felt personal. As if Dariya's condition meant something to him.

I looked at the man across the table and wondered what I could tell him. I had lied about Dariya being my daughter because I thought it would make them more sympathetic, make them hand her over. But now they thought I'd done something to harm her. The only people who could confirm who I was were the people from Vyriv, but I couldn't risk exposing them. Perhaps it was time to change my story. Give them more of the truth. Let them think they had beaten it out of me.

'She wasn't lost.' I hung my head. 'She was taken from me. That's why I had my rifle. I was hunting for the man who took her.'

'Why didn't you tell me this before?'

'Would you have believed me?'

'No.' Lermentov carefully reset the bandage and dropped the hem of Dariya's dress, letting the cloth fall over the wound. 'And I don't believe you now, either. You're lying.'

'No.'

'You're lying to me again. This girl isn't your daughter any more than she's mine. You did this to her. You hurt her like this. You're an animal.'

'No. Please. She *is* my daughter.' I looked at Dariya, my eyes filling with tears, my nose streaming. 'Tell him, Dariya. Tell him who I am.'

But Dariya just stood and stared ahead of her as if none of us was even there. The man standing beside her, with the farmer's clothes and the hands of a man who worked the fields, looked away at the far wall of the church.

The policeman pulled my satchel towards him, dragging it across the surface of the table. I had forgotten about it. I had barely even looked at it since my interrogation had begun, but now I stared at it as Lermentov opened the fastening and put his hand inside.

A couple of cartridges rolled out when he removed the aluminium water bottle, and he took out the bottle I had brought from the cabin where Dariya had killed the child thief.

'This yours?' Lermentov asked, placing the bottle upright on the table.

'Yes.'

He considered the clear, unlabelled bottle for a moment, then looked across at one of the soldiers. 'Open it.'

The soldier came round to Lermentov's side of the table and took the bottle, biting on the cork and pulling hard. After a few seconds the cork eased from the bottle with a quiet pop and the soldier put it on the table, pushing it towards the policeman, who nodded once. The soldier returned to his post behind me.

The OGPU man sniffed at the open bottle and looked at me. 'Vodka?'

'*Horilka.*'

He nodded and raised the bottle, saying, 'Your health.' He took a sip, tasting, before smiling and taking a deeper drink. He wiped his mouth with the back of his sleeve. 'It's good.' He took another drink and put the bottle aside.

'She is not your daughter, is she?'

'She is.' I turned to Dariya once again. 'Please. Tell him. Tell him who I am.' I looked at the OGPU man again. 'I swear it. She *is* my—'

'Then explain this.'

Lermentov reached into my satchel once more and removed the waxed paper parcel I had taken from the shepherd's hut. He put it on the table, pushing the satchel away.

And I knew. Before Lermentov unwrapped it, I knew what it would contain. Even in death the child thief had won his game. From his grave he had found a way of killing me.

The OGPU officer took the edges of the paper in his fingers and pulled them apart, opening them out and smoothing them against the surface of the table. Then he turned the open package around and pushed it a little closer so I could see the piece of meat it contained.

When I had first taken it from the cabin, I had expected *salo*. Salted pork fat that I had intended to share with my sons to stave off the hunger. But this was not pork fat. This flesh was from a different animal altogether.

My world stopped. Nothing was real any more.

Dariya was not my daughter, but I had said it so many times, tried hard to believe my own story, that now I felt as if I truly were her father. After all, she had no other father to protect her, for her own lay dead beneath the snow. Somehow she had managed to do what I – and who knew how many men before me – had failed to do. She had killed the child thief. She had pierced his throat with steel and taken his life, and now she had stumbled from one nightmare into another and her child's mind was unable to cope with it. She had receded into her own head and I found myself envying her. Right now I wanted to do the same thing, but my mind was stronger and I was conditioned to withstand atrocity. I was hardened to the things around me, just like all those who had grown to maturity in those godless times. From the Great War to the revolution and the civil war and the following hardships, we were all conditioned to a life of struggle. But this child before me, not even nine years old, she knew none of those things. She had lived apart from those things, but now they had entered her life, and they had turned her inwards and broken her.

I wanted to reach out to her. I wanted to hold her. This poor girl with no one to help her. No one to protect her.

I stood and took a step towards her, wanting to pull her close and let her bury her face in the folds of my shirt. I wanted her to know that she wasn't alone, to whisper in her ear and tell her I would keep her safe. And for a moment she was Lara, standing there on the cold stones, looking at me, asking me to bring back her friend.

'I promised,' I said. 'I promised.'

'You child-hating bastard.' Lermentov spat his words into the cold church and the blow from the crucifix was like none that had come before it. The old wood cracked into the side of my head hard enough to knock me off my feet. I fell against the chair, forcing it away from me, my face smashing against the seat before I was on the floor.

From my prone position I looked up at the policeman standing over me, the crucifix in his hands. The bearded man from the village was looking at me now, his lips pursed, a slight shake in his head. Beside him Dariya continued to stare ahead.

Then I closed my eyes.

24

When I woke, I was in darkness. For a second I thought I was blind and there was a brief moment of panic before I saw the faint light sliding beneath the door. There were voices too, quiet but insistent, and someone's hands were on me, but they weren't there to inflict pain.

'He's waking up, I think.' It sounded like Kostya, the man who was imprisoned for making a joke about our great leader.

'I'm fine,' I said, pushing the hand away, sitting up and moving back to lean against the wall. 'Leave me.'

'You've been asleep for a while.'

'How long?'

'It's hard to say.'

'Hours? A day?'

'Much of the day. At least I think it's day. They brought food a while ago, and I think that usually comes in the morning.'

I touched the side of my face, feeling the split in the skin, the hardened crust of blood. There was a graze across my forehead that was rough and dry, and my head was pounding like I'd drunk a whole bottle of *horilka* myself.

'Here.' I felt a hand on my own and I tried to pull away, but the grip tightened.

'Please,' Kostya said. 'Take this.'

I remained tense for a second, untrusting, then relaxed and allowed Kostya to take my hand, open my fingers and touch something to them. Something metallic.

'Drink it,' he said.

I took hold of the cup and lifted it to my nose to sniff it.

'Water,' Kostya said. 'It's a little stale, but it's water.'

'Where . . .' I began to ask, but my mouth was dry and my tongue was swollen. My lips were thick and fat from where the policeman had hit me.

'They give us water once a day,' said Dimitri Markovich. 'We all save a mouthful to make it last. There's a little bread too. Take it.'

'This is all of it,' Kostya said.

'I can't—'

'Drink,' he said, and I felt his hands touching me again, finding the cup and pushing it towards my mouth. 'You need it.'

I put the metal cup to my lips and tipped it, the warm liquid moistening my mouth. I kept it there, savouring the feeling, then took it away, not wanting to drink it all at once. There wasn't much more than a drop left.

I fumbled the crust of bread that Kostya pressed into my hand, feeling its hard edges, the softer interior, and I remembered I hadn't eaten for a long time. I'd taken the child thief's parcel, thinking it would be my next meal, but the thought of it now filled me with revulsion. That small piece of meat wrapped in paper.

'Eat,' Kostya said, touching my hand. 'Eat.'

I pushed aside the image that dirtied my thoughts. I pictured not the flesh nor the wound, but the girl. Dariya was safe and she was alive; that's what was important. And if I was to have any chance of helping her I needed to be strong. I needed to eat.

I bit off a small piece of bread with my front teeth and tried not to feel the guilt of taking the last of the food and water.

I wanted to see the faces of the men who had given me everything they had. Men who knew nothing about me and yet offered everything. And it struck me that in these hard times there were small moments of kindness which lifted us above the filth and the death. With these tiny acts, we were still human, still able to have faith in one another. There was still something good left in the world.

'Thank you,' I said to the darkness. I drank again and somewhere outside I heard a *garmoshka* begin to play. The music went on for a few bars, a melancholy tune, and then someone began to sing. A deep voice, the words sung in Russian.

'Always this song,' said Dimitri. 'He always plays this song.'

'To stop us from sleeping,' said Kostya.

'His awful Russian songs.'

'Russians. They're all drunkards and thieves,' said Yuri.

I let the water slip down my throat and I leaned my head back on the wall and listened to the song. A Russian folk song, about a man imprisoned for telling the truth. He escapes his prison one dark night and comes to Lake Baikal, where he takes a fisherman's boat and sings a sad song as he crosses the lake to his mother. When he reaches the furthest shore he embraces his mother and asks for his father and his brother. But his father is long dead and buried beneath the damp earth, and his brother is in chains in Siberia.

When it was finished there was silence for just a few moments, probably for someone to take a drink of vodka, and then the music began again, this time a faster tune, someone clapping along.

Inside our prison a quiet voice began to sing 'Ukraine Has Not Yet Perished' – the anthem of what was, for a short time after the revolution, the Ukrainian People's Republic. The song had been banned ten years before by the Soviet regime, but many still knew it by heart. Evgeni's voice was weak and hoarse and almost drowned by the Russian song outside, but I heard the words: 'Ukraine has not yet perished. The glory and the freedom.'

Kostya joined his brother, mumbling the words. There was no hearty bellowing of the song, just a jumbled pride and defiance, no one daring to sing too loudly.

'Still upon us, brave brother, fate shall smile.'

I had heard it sung during the war and even afterwards, more recently, around the oak that stood in the centre of Vyriv. The oak that had seen too few good summers and too many bad winters.

'Our enemies will vanish like dew in the sun.'

The oak which had borne the awful fruit of Dimitri's mob.

'We too shall rule in our country.'

Their singing was quiet – barely more than a whisper – but outside the *garmoshka* had stopped.

'Soul and body we will lay down for our freedom.'

Then a loud banging on the door. 'Do the counter-revolutionaries want to stand naked in the snow?' It was the slurred voice of Sergei Artemevich Lermentov.

The singing stopped and there was silence.

'That's what I thought,' Lermentov said to the dead wood. 'That's exactly what I thought.'

'I don't know what he wants me to tell him,' I said to Kostya.

'What does it matter what you tell him? He isn't investigating anything; he's humiliating you, making you something less than human. The OGPU, their job is not to discover crimes but to arrest people.'

'The one with the beard,' I said. 'He's not OGPU. He's more like a farmer. Is he from your village?'

'Anatoly Ivanovich,' Kostya said, and it occurred to me that it was Kostya who spoke more than the others. It was he who had given me the water. Either he was a planted informant or he had earned these men's respect in some other way.

'You know him?' I asked.

'Of course. We all know each other – those of us that are left here, anyway. Anatoly is a lazy man. He didn't have any land of his own, he just worked for those who did. They paid him money when they had it, or sometimes in food.'

'And now he sits at the table with the OGPU.'

'Yes.'

'But he doesn't like it,' I said. 'I can see the shame in his eyes.'

'He protects himself,' Evgeni said.

'He says the right things,' Kostya added. 'He uses the language

256

they like. He talks of "workers" and "proletariat" and "kulaks". He denounces those who ever employed him and sees them arrested for being wealthy farmers.'

'And you?' I asked. 'You never employed him?'

Kostya laughed. 'We never had enough land to need him. And the others, they had almost nothing either. A pig maybe, a few acres of land, and now they're on their way to labour camps or lying in a trench in the forest. Who knows.'

'The trench would be better,' said Yuri. He was sitting close to me but hadn't spoken for some time and I'd almost forgotten he was even there. There was something about him I didn't like, something to do with the way he had questioned me about my past.

'Better?' I asked. 'It's better to be dead?'

'Of course. Taken away in cattle trucks like animals, fed only salted fish and given nothing to drink, then dropped in some godless place where the cold is deeper and hungrier than it is here. Siberia maybe, the White Sea. There are places where people are made to work so hard and for so long that they cut off their own hands and feet just to get some rest.'

'Who told you that?'

'Lermentov.'

'Why are they doing this to us?' Evgeni asked. 'Why must they beat us and humiliate us?'

'For a confession,' said Yuri.

'All they have to do is arrest us and send us away and be done with it. Why waste time with confessions?'

'Maybe it makes this man Lermentov feel better,' I said.

'Feel better?'

'He's just doing his job. If he gets a confession, it probably makes it more legal for him. More *right*. Like he's punishing a criminal instead of a man who was in the wrong place at the wrong time.'

'It makes no difference,' Evgeni said. 'Enough beating and we'll tell them anything. Admit to anything. Denounce our own neighbours. And all we do is sit here and let them treat us like this.'

'What else can we do?' said Kostya.

'We can tell them to fuck themselves,' Dimitri shouted. 'What have we done? I tried to help a little girl. *A little girl.* And now I'm what? A counter-revolutionary? An enemy of the state?'

'Shouting does no good,' Kostya said

'At least it means they know what we think.'

'They already know what we think,' I said. 'And that man out there – Lermentov – he's probably just as afraid as we are. You think he's exempt? They can put him on a train to Siberia just like they can put us on one. He does what he has to.'

'You want us to feel sorry for him, Luka?'

'No. I'm just telling you how it is.'

'So we do nothing?' Yuri asked. 'We just wait to be deported?'

'Put a gun in my hand and I'll shoot him, but other than that . . .' I let the words trail away and thought back to the moment on the road when the soldiers had approached me. I wished now that I had tried to do something – shot them from their horses and dragged their bodies away from the track. 'I have to get out of here,' I said. 'I can't believe it's come to this. I shouldn't be here. It's not where I'm supposed to be.'

'Where *are* you supposed to be?' asked Yuri. 'Out there with your sons?'

'Yes. There must be a way to get out.'

'There's nothing,' Kostya said. 'No escape.'

I shook my head in the darkness and thought about my sons out there in the cold, wondering if they had followed my tracks to the village. There was a small part of me that hoped they would bring their rifles and shoot every one of the soldiers in this village; that they would hand me a pistol so I could put it against the head of this man Lermentov and spill his brains all over the snow and the dirt. But my sons were not soldiers, and I prayed they had turned around when they realised my fate. I prayed they had returned home to Natalia and Lara. I even allowed myself a vague smile as I imagined them arguing about what they were going to do. I pictured them outside the village, hidden among the trees, watching, discussing.

Viktor would want to fight while Petro would pull him back, try to make him see sense.

I closed my eyes and wished I could remember my last words to them. I tried to see their faces.

Still the music played outside in the church. Lermentov's repertoire was a mixture of old folk songs and songs of the revolution and labour and the motherland, but it wasn't long before he was playing the same tunes again. Every now and then there was a lull in the music and I could hear the murmur of voices talking, sometimes loud laughter, and I guessed the policeman had drunk most or all of the *horilka* I had taken from the cabin where the child thief lay dead. At least I had *that* satisfaction. The child thief would take no more children.

It was warm and close in the room and I felt sleep beginning to take me. I didn't know how long I slept for, perhaps until night, perhaps not, it was impossible to tell, but I was roused by the sound of the door being unlocked.

The dim light crept in, and I braced myself for the hands that would drag me from this cell. I waited for the soldiers to grab me and pull me to my feet, but they came past me and went to Kostya.

They stooped to grip his thin shoulders, and when they lifted him, I saw how light my new friend was. The soldiers pulled him up with little effort and took him from the room, slamming the door closed behind them.

'God help my brother,' Evgeni said, the only words any of us spoke for some time.

Through the solid door I heard the muffled voices as they interrogated Kostya. I couldn't make out any of the words, so it was still possible that he'd been put inside the cell to trick me, but any doubt was dismissed by the sound of Kostya's beating.

When the interrogation was over and the church finally became quiet, I let out my breath as if I'd been holding it for the duration and waited for Kostya to be returned to us. But the door didn't open again.

'He was a good man,' Evgeni said into the silence. 'My brother was a good man.'

And when Lermentov began playing the *garmoshka* again, we knew Kostya would not be coming back.

25

When Kostya was taken, he took with him the hope of the other incarcerated men. Before, they had hardly spoken, but now they said nothing at all.

I tried to move about, find a comfortable position. If I stayed as I was for too long, pains developed. I tried sitting with my legs crossed, stretched out, with my back against the wall, or leaning forward. I tried standing, but my bare feet hurt, and I tried lying, but the floor was too hard. There was no comfort to be found in that room, and I understood it had been well chosen as a prison.

After some time Dimitri Markovich offered his lap as a pillow, and I realised that in their silence the men had been following an order of lying on each other, taking turns, looking for the briefest moment of sleep. So I accepted, and I put my head on Dimitri, snatching the slightest respite before he tapped me on the head and told me it was his turn.

But Dimitri was denied his sleep because once again the door opened and the soldiers came in. This time they had come for me.

They dragged me to the table and pushed me down into the chair. The crucifix was still there, but my satchel and the parcel of flesh were gone. Instead, there was a *garmoshka* and the bottle of *horilka*, now almost empty.

Sergei Artemevich Lermentov sat opposite, his eyes red and tired.

'Where's Dariya?' I asked.

Lermentov didn't reply.

'Where is she? And where's Kostya? How long have I been here?'

'I ask the questions.' His words were lazy and much of his officious manner had relaxed.

'Of course, comrade.'

Lermentov looked over my shoulder and watched the guards standing behind me. 'You're not my comrade. You're my prisoner. An enemy of the state. You have no comrades. You have no *right* to call anyone comrade.'

'I'm not an enemy of the state.'

'Conspirator, counter-revolutionary, criminal – what does it matter? You belong to the state now. You're white coal. That's what the guards will call you.'

'And Dariya? My daughter?'

'She's got work in her,' he said, looking away with a regretful expression. 'Not much, I don't think, but some. She'll be sent to work.'

'I thought you people call it re-education.'

'No one talks about that any more.' Lermentov continued to stare at nothing, as if his mind was elsewhere. 'Now it's just labour.'

I bit my lip, trying to compose myself. 'Please,' I said. 'You have to believe I didn't harm her.'

'Who knows what to believe?' Lermentov said quietly so that only I could hear it. He had seen my face when he showed me what had happened to Dariya. He had seen the shock in my eyes, and I hoped it was a look that was plaguing him. He'd been sure that I was responsible for what had happened to Dariya but now, perhaps, there was doubt.

'If you have to send me away, then do it, but keep her here. Someone must be able to look after her.'

'Nothing I can do for her.' Lermentov sniffed hard and shook his head. 'She can work so that's what she has to do.' He reached out for the bottle and pulled it towards him. 'There's enough for everybody.' His words were slurred, his eyes distant. 'We're all workers now, and there are quotas to fill. "We need more workers," they say, and in the north they dig and they cut and they build.' He took a long drink from the bottle and banged it down on the table. 'And when they say they need more workers, we send them more workers. This great country will be even greater because we have so many workers. Endless workers.'

'But not children.' I watched the inebriated policeman, seeing something other than hard coldness in him.

'Everyone,' Lermentov said. 'We're lucky to have so many people who will give their hands and feet to the glory of the revolution.' He leaned back. 'And even children must work.' He took another drink and slouched in his chair, waving a hand as if nothing mattered.

'But Dariya is so young.'

Lermentov looked up again and saw the guards watching him. Everyone was always watching each other. He sat upright, as if remembering what he was here for, the role he had to play. There was no crime other than against the state. The fate of one small girl meant nothing in the great scheme of things. 'Have you remembered what happened to my prisoners yet?'

'Please,' I said again. 'She's just a girl.'

He faltered, looking at the guards once more before speaking. 'Where are my prisoners?'

'She's only eight years old.'

He hardened his gaze, remembering his purpose and position. '*Where are my prisoners?*'

I sighed and shook my head and spoke as an automaton. 'I saw tracks in the forest. I didn't follow them. I was following my daughter. She came here and—'

'Enough.' Lermentov waved a hand.

I didn't know what this man wanted from me. Even *Lermentov* didn't know what he wanted from me. I was there simply because I'd been in the wrong place and because I owned a weapon. And Lermentov was there because he'd been sent. Neither of us wanted to be there. We were just two men who had lost control of their own circumstances, their own lives. Men who had been sucked into a great machine which pushed and pulled them in random directions that meant nothing to either of them.

'Let me go,' I said. 'Let me take my daughter and go.'

'I couldn't do that even if I wanted to,' he said. 'It's too late for that. Too late for all of us.' Lermentov had probably never released a prisoner. He would never have been able to show any weakness or disobedience; never given anyone a reason to report him as a conspirator or an enemy of the state. 'Anyway, you're lying – trying to fool me into letting you take her away. She's not your daughter, is she? I mean, what kind of man would cut his own child into pieces?'

'I didn't do that to her, and you know it. If you really think I did, I wouldn't be here now. You'd have taken me into the forest and shot me.'

'We don't shoot workers.'

'That's not true.'

'And if you didn't do it, then who did?'

'Someone else.'

'Who?'

'Another man. He stole her and he cut her. Please. Go to my hut and you'll see. It's close to where your soldiers found me. The man who did that to her is dead.'

Lermentov put his elbows on the surface of the table and looked me right in the eye. 'You killed a man?'

'No. I didn't kill him.'

'Then who?'

'I . . .' I dropped my gaze and thought about what Dariya had done. 'Yes. I killed him.'

'So you're a murderer *and* a mutilator?'

'No. I—'

'It doesn't matter.' He leaned back again, drinking the last of the *horilka* but keeping the bottle in his hands, looking at it for a moment as if lamenting its emptiness. 'You could be the Devil and it would be none of my concern. I'm not here to investigate your crimes. I'm here to make sure the peasants join the *kolkhoz* and that the kulaks are dealt with. As an officer of the OGPU, I don't care what you've done; I'm not *that* kind of policeman. You could have cut a hundred children and it would be none of my business. My job is to feed the camps and to make you damn Ukrainians do as you're told.'

'I'm Russian. Like you.'

'I don't care. As a policeman, I don't care. But as a man . . .' Now he stared right into me. 'As a *man*, I care what you've done. If there's even the slightest chance you did that to that little girl—'

'So how do you justify how many children you've deported?'

Lermentov stared at me for a second, then told me the lie he must have told himself every night. 'They're all in good health when they leave me.'

'And their fathers?'

'This is different.'

'Different how? You destroy their lives. Don't try to justify it by saying it's your job; that you send them away in good health. You know what's going to happen to them. Their families too.'

'Yes.' Lermentov clenched his hands into fists. He glanced at the guards before leaning forward and lowering his voice. 'And I barely sleep at night. I do my job and I drink and I try to sleep and I hope that when this is finished I can go home to my—' He stopped and glanced away.

'Family,' I said. 'That's what you were going to say. Family. You have a wife. And a child?'

The policeman snapped his head round, setting his jaw tight.

It had been a guess, but I knew from Lermentov's reaction that I was right. And with that turn of the head – that telling change in the policeman's expression – came a strengthening of my resolve. Lermentov had a weakness that I could exploit. He was drunk and he had an Achilles heel. There was something that made this man human.

The policeman stared.

'You do, don't you? A son? A daughter?'

He looked away.

'A daughter. What's her name? How old is she?'

'That's none of your business.'

'No, but it's why you want to punish me. Because you think there's a *chance* I hurt Dariya. It gives you an excuse. But I didn't hurt her. *You're* punishing her by taking her away, don't you see that? By separating us, *you're* making her suffer.'

'I do my job.' Lermentov held the bottle by its neck, his fist so tight his knuckles were white.

'And you're punishing me because you hate that your job demands you send children to labour camps.'

'I'm punishing you for what you did to her.'

'And Dariya? Why punish her? Let her stay here. You know what happens to people on those trains. In those camps. Don't send her away. She'll die and you know it.'

'Shut up.'

'Please,' I said. 'If you must punish me, then do it, but not Dariya. You have a daughter; I can see it in your eyes.'

'*Shut up.*'

'You know this is wrong.' I leaned forward, putting my fingers together as if in prayer. 'You know that what you're doing is wrong. Would you do it to your own child?'

'You know nothing of my own child. You, a man who cuts the flesh from little girls.'

'I would never do that.'

'Lies.' Lermentov spoke through his teeth. 'No one tells the truth any more.'

'Please,' I said. 'Let her stay here. Think of your own daughter.' I stood, raising my hands, almost unable to control myself.

'Sit down.'

I tried to reach out to Lermentov, not to hurt him but to plead with him. I wanted to put my hands on his tunic and pull him towards me, and for a moment I almost managed it. 'Let her stay here. Let someone take care of her. Think of your own—'

But my words were cut short as Lermentov struck out with the bottle he was holding. He swung it hard against my head, the same place where he had hit me with the crucifix, and for a while I saw nothing. I heard nothing. My world was nothing.

The cold bit so hard that it hurt. There was a throbbing ache in my back that lived at the base of my spine and pulsated along its length. My fingers and toes were numb, and I couldn't feel my face. I opened my eyes and discovered a harsh pain in my head.

'Luka?'

I took a deep breath of cold air that gripped my lungs and made me cough hard.

'Luka?'

I tried to sit up, but my arms and legs wouldn't move and I felt a slow ease of panic creep into my consciousness. I fought to keep it away and concentrated on moving.

'Luka?'

I ignored the voice and focused on my arms, but they refused to do as I wanted.

'Luka, they tied you.'

That explained why I couldn't move. I wasn't paralysed, I was bound. My hands were tied together behind my back, and my feet were fastened with the same binding. I was roped like a pig that's to be slaughtered. I was also naked. Dehumanised. Made less than nothing.

I moved my head, hardly feeling my cheek scraping across the cold wooden floor, but the voice was coming from behind me, so I couldn't see who was speaking. I took another deep breath and rolled over. The hard wood was cruel against my spine, my shoulders, my elbows. Arms and legs pulled against each other in their bindings and it was a struggle to turn so that I flopped without grace onto my other side and found myself staring at Konstantin Petrovich. Both of us naked but for our beards.

'Are you all right?' I asked him.

'Cold.'

'Where are we?' I tried to look around, but my vision was restricted. By my head there was a wall and by my feet a construction that had once supported a bell. We were in the belfry. I had seen the bell when I first came to the village, broken and abandoned by the church steps, a symbol of the casting out of religion. The wall that ran around this part of the bell tower was low, probably waist height if I were to stand, and I could just about see over it to the sky beyond. It was night. There was a pitched roof over us, and in its beams old cobwebs shifted in the wind.

'How long have I been here?'

'A few minutes.' Kostya's voice was weak.

I tried to remember how long it had been between Kostya leaving the prison room and Lermentov coming to interrogate me. It wasn't long, but it was long enough for a man to be close to death. Beaten and left to freeze in the bell tower.

'You married?' I asked Kostya.

'No.'

'My wife . . . she doesn't know where I am.' I looked at Kostya and saw he was crying. There were tears on his cheeks and frozen patches in his beard. There was blood on his face too, places on his body where he had been beaten. Some of the bruises were old – they had spread the width of his thighs, covered his upper arms and shoulders. There were other marks on his chest, almost a perfect match for the base of the same crucifix Lermentov had used to beat me.

'I don't want to die,' Kostya said.

'You won't,' I told him.

'It's so cold.'

'But we're sheltered.' It was difficult to speak, my teeth chattered so much. My whole body shook with the cold, and I still couldn't feel my fingers and toes. 'And they'll come for us. We're precious workers; they won't let us die.'

'It'll be too late.'

'No,' I said. 'We'll be fine.'

Kostya closed his eyes, squeezing them tight. This close to him, and with just enough light from the stars and the moon, I saw how his wrinkles were exaggerated by the expression, lines spreading from the corners of his eyes and reaching into his hairline. They were not lines that had grown from years of laughter; they were the marks of a hard life. A man who had aged before his time.

'Kostya.'

'Hm?'

'Stay awake.'

'Mm.'

'Stay awake. They'll come for us soon. Take us back to the warm room. We're no good to them dead. If we're dead we can't work.'

The look in Kostya's eyes was distant, as if he wasn't seeing anything at all. His face contorted now into something that looked like a smile.

'What?' I asked. 'What is it?' My teeth hammered together as he spoke.

'I don't want them to come for me,' he said, closing his eyes. 'Not now. Don't let them take me.' His voice was slow and thick.

'What are you talking about?' Speaking aloud brought pain to my head. The place where Lermentov had struck me with the bottle. I could feel where the blood had dried or frozen on my skin.

'I think I'll go now. Find somewhere warm. In the field in summertime.'

'What?'

'Summertime. It's so beautiful. I'll go into the field.'

'Kostya, stay here. Look at me and stay here.'

He had stopped shivering. His breathing was slow and heavy.

'Kostya, you need to focus.' I shuffled close so our bodies were touching. Kostya still had some warmth left in him, but his skin was as cold as the floor we were lying on. 'We need to keep warm.' For some men hypothermia took longer than for others, but once the cold found its way in, it was almost impossible to get warm again.

'I am warm.'

'What? Please,' I said. 'Look at me.'

Kostya opened his eyes again, our faces so close that I could feel his weak and sporadic breaths.

'Tell me about your family,' I said.

'This is easier.'

'What about your brother?'

'Hm?'

'Evgeni. Your brother.'

'He'll be fine. The harvest will be fine.'

'Kostya.'

'Let me sleep now. It's easier. So easy.' His eyelids drifted down and his eyes rolled as if he were falling into a drunken sleep.

I nudged against him, trying to wake him, saying his name. 'Kostya. Wake up. Kostya.'

But Kostya did not open his eyes again.

I continued to say his name, feeling the weakness in my own voice, sensing the drowsiness descending over my own mind. I pulled myself as close to Kostya as possible, taking the last of his warmth, listening for his breathing as my own eyes began to close and I struggled to remember where I was and how I had come to be here. So I told Kostya about my family. About my sons and my daughter. About my wife Natalia, waiting at home, baking fresh bread, preparing hot soup. It was warm in the kitchen and our children were sitting at the table. Outside, spring had come and the steppe was green and lush.

And when the soldiers came to get me, just a few minutes later, Kostya was no longer breathing.

26

Without making eye contact they dragged me back into the cell, throwing my trousers and shirt behind me. Lermentov wasn't anywhere in sight, nor did I see them take Kostya's body away.

I could barely move to get my clothes, let alone put them on, but the others knew what to do. They had been in there long enough to run through the motions. They helped me dress, and they rubbed my skin with their grubby hands, trying to encourage the circulation of my blood. They pressed about me, like a nightmare in the dark, their filthy bodies washing around me like the undead stinking of the grave, but I was grateful for their care and their kindness. They were keeping me alive. Evgeni, Yuri, Dimitri. These good men were doing what they could to save my life, just as they had kept each other alive and sane while incarcerated, not knowing what their fate might be. It was a touching and human gesture, given without thought.

After the freezing cold of the bell tower the room felt like a furnace, and I knew I'd been lucky when I felt life returning to my body and the feeling returning to my fingers and toes. And when I was able to move, I pushed up against the wall and felt two of the others press on either side of me, lending me the only thing they had left. Their warmth.

Later, when the soldiers threw in a few pieces of bread and a tin bowl with a few mouthfuls of water, Evgeni collected it and tore the bread, passing a piece to each man, saying in a quiet voice that he'd save a piece, put it in the corner of the room in case any of us needed it later. It was incredible how those men had managed to remain sane in the obscurity of that room, feeling their way in the dark, and still have the capacity to make provision for later. All instinct was to devour whatever was put through the door, not to save it. And how easy it would be for one man to creep over in the darkness and steal the last piece of bread.

I ate the scraps like a rat, crouched against the wall, gnawing at it to make it last. Tasting every tiny bite, I kept the bread in my mouth until my saliva melted it to a paste, and even then I held it behind my lips until it dissolved to nothing. I ran my tongue about my teeth, savouring every last crumb. And when we had eaten, we passed the bowl around, taking tiny sips until there was almost no water left and Evgeni poured it into the cup he'd handed to me last night.

'I saw Kostya,' I said.

'You spoke to him?' Evgeni asked after some time.

'Yes.'

'What did he say?'

'He was happy,' I told him. 'He said it was easy. That everything would be easier.'

'How did he look?'

'Cold and tired.'

'Beaten?'

'I didn't notice anything.'

'Good. That's good. Thank you for being with him.'

I drew my knees close and wrapped my shaking arms around them, burying my face and staring at the blackness, trying not to think about what would happen now, about Kostya lying cold and dead in the bell tower. I thought instead about Dariya, and hoped someone was looking after her.

And with those thoughts I tried to keep awake. I didn't want to talk to the other men right now, and they didn't attempt to speak to me, but I was afraid to sleep. I didn't even want to close my eyes for fear that I might not care what happened to me. Like Kostya, I might decide that to die would be easier than to keep fighting and fulfil my promise to Lara. But however hard I tried, my mind kept going back to the bell tower and to Kostya's freezing body. Something about it made me think of what I had found in the hut. The child thief stiffened by the cold. And somewhere at the back of my mind there was a faint notion that something was wrong.

But whatever it was, it was beyond my grasp, lost when exhaustion finally claimed me into an easier world.

The next time the soldiers came to the room, they took Dimitri. He protested, shouting and struggling, but they held him tight and forced him to do as they demanded.

The rest of us remained quiet in our prison, listening to the voices behind the heavy wooden door but making out none of the words other than an occasional shout from Dimitri. The interview was brief, followed by footsteps and a short moment of stillness before they came back for Evgeni, who complied without any fight. His resistance was all gone.

Again the voices. The footsteps. The respite.

'What's going on?' asked Yuri.

'I don't know, but they're not being beaten. It's something else.' I stood and shuffled to the door, putting my eye to the keyhole. In the main hall of the church three men were sitting behind the table where I had been beaten. Lermentov was in the middle, in full uniform, the tunic clean as if new. Anatoly Ivanovich was on his right, holding his cap in his hands, his demeanour apologetic. To Lermentov's left, another man. Like Anatoly, this third man was in civilian clothes, but his were in better condition and he sat upright and officious.

'It's a *troika*,' I said. 'We're being tried.'

'Tried? For what?'

'Our crimes, Yuri. It looks like we're leaving. Perhaps now there'll be a chance.'

'A chance for what?'

'To get away, of course.' I was thinking that trapped inside this room I was powerless, but outside, without the walls to contain me, there might be a moment, just a *moment*, for me to use to my advantage.

'Have you seen how many soldiers are in this village?' Yuri said.

'It doesn't matter. If there's the slightest chance—'

'You're no good to that little girl if you're dead.'

'And I'm no good to her in here, either.' I kept an eye to the keyhole, watching the men take Evgeni from the church. 'You know, you never said why they put you in here, Yuri.'

'Didn't I?'

But already the soldiers were approaching the door, and I took my eye from the keyhole, moving back to where I had been sitting. And when they took Yuri, bringing light into the room, he turned to look me in the eye. 'I'll tell you another time,' he said. And then I was left alone in the room.

I went back to the keyhole, seeing Yuri sitting with his back to me, a soldier on either side. His shoulders were slumped and his head hanging so his chin was almost on his chest. He would be feeling some relief at his release from the room, but at the same time it may have become a refuge for him. Inside the room he was safe; it was only when removed from it that he was threatened. But at least he was outside, and at least something was happening. Sometimes waiting is the worst thing.

It was only a few moments before the soldiers pulled Yuri from the seat and he began walking towards the main door of the church. Still hanging his head, his feet shuffling, he waited for them to open it and usher him out into the daylight. They all disappeared and the door closed, only to reopen a few moments later.

They would come for me next.

I went to the corner of the room, feeling for the piece of bread and the cup of water the men had saved. I swallowed the dry bread and drank the last of the water, putting the empty metal cup on the floor and stepping on it with as much force as I could muster in my bare feet. I crushed the cup flat and picked it up, feeling the sharp point where the edges had come together. I slipped it into my trouser pocket and sat with my back to the wall, waiting for them to come.

The blood was gone from the tabletop. The crucifix was pushed to one side. There was no bottle of *horilka*, no satchel, no parcel of flesh.

Instead there was a book, the left page filled with handwritten names and information. The page on the right was half full.

Sergei Artemevich Lermentov held a pen in his hand. He barely looked up as the guards ushered me to the chair.

'How long have I been here?' I asked.

'Name?'

I waited for a moment, watching the other men sitting either side of the policeman. Anatoly Ivanovich, the farm labourer turned party faithful, sat on Lermentov's right-hand side. On his left sat another man, short and stocky, bearded. He was wearing a cloth cap and a woollen jacket. He would be another member of the local council. I studied them, wondering what kind of men they were. Hungry for power maybe, or just frightened like everybody else was.

'Please. How long have I been here?'

'Name?' Lermentov repeated.

I rubbed my face. 'Luka Mikhailovich Sidorov. But you know that. How long have I been here?'

Lermentov wrote in his book and looked up. 'You are accused of crimes against the people.'

'What crimes?'

'Assaulting an OGPU officer—'

'I didn't touch you.'

'—and owning a rifle.' Lermentov leaned forward and spoke quietly, voicing the charge that was of no consequence to the regime: 'And assaulting a child.'

'No.' I felt immense frustration at this charge. I owned a rifle, that much was true, and although I hadn't laid a hand on Lermentov, I didn't care about that lie because all three of these men knew I was not an enemy of the people. They knew I was not a counter-revolutionary but they really did think I had harmed Dariya, and the injustice of that accusation swelled my anger at the world immeasurably. The stranger who had come to Vyriv, pulling his own dead children on a sled, had been accused of the same thing by Dimitri. The child thief had managed to orchestrate *that* man's guilt just as he had orchestrated mine. Whether it had been intentional or not, he had consigned us to similar fates: to be thought of as men who butchered children. And that fate was almost too much for me to bear.

In Vyriv they had hanged such a man from the tree in the centre of their village. I would be sentenced to a slower, harder death. Perhaps cutting forests in the frozen wastes of Siberia with a few grams of bread each day until either my mind or body gave up the will to continue. But either fate carried the same ultimate penalty, and even though the child thief was long gone, a frozen corpse in a deserted cabin, his game was won.

'Where is she?' I asked. 'Is she safe?'

Lermentov looked to Anatoly Ivanovich. 'Guilty?'

'Guilty,' Anatoly agreed.

'Guilty,' said the other man.

Lermentov wrote in his book, his penmanship slow and deliberate. The nib scratched on the paper as he wrote, and when he was finished he put down his pen and folded his hands. 'You will go for correctional labour,' he said. 'Fifteen years.'

'You always need more workers,' I said.

'Always.'

27

Outside the church, in the centre of Sushne, there were close to twenty people huddled together surrounded by guards. Men, women and children, some without coats, none of them carrying any belongings. Evgeni, Dimitri and Yuri were among them, stamping their feet, their arms crossed in front of them. Others were being brought from their homes to join them. One woman hurried to the prisoners and bundled into Dimitri's arms, sobbing for everything they'd lose but grateful at least to be with her husband.

The soldiers pushed me out of the church and down the steps, so I was standing barefoot in the snow. I shifted from one foot to the other, trying to avoid the pain, but there was no use in it. Soon they were numb.

Lermentov came to stand beside me, capped and coated, looking down at my feet. 'It's a long walk to the train,' he said. 'You may not last without shoes.'

I pretended not to hear, but Lermentov was already walking away as the guards herded me among the others. Lermentov was heading past the other prisoners to the village entrance, where a lone man was approaching on horseback. The soldier's heavy coat and his *budenovka* were dusted with snow, and as he came close to where the people were huddled, pushing together for warmth, I recognised him as one of the men who had arrested me on the road into Sushne. He was the young man who had been uncomfortable with his comrade's brutality. Andrei.

Andrei recognised me too, the expression in his face betrayed him, but he looked away as he dismounted and came close to speak to Lermentov.

The guards began to arrange the *zeks* into pairs, shoving us together, and I went where directed, keeping my eyes on Lermentov, wondering if I would be able to reach him before one of the guards shot me down. Compliant and malleable, I would surprise them, breaking ranks and heading straight for him. I put a hand into my pocket and felt the crushed metal cup, touching the sharp corner with one fingertip. There was so little for me to lose now. Perhaps I could reach the policeman and put the pointed edge to the soft hollow of his throat, force it into his flesh then take the pistol from his belt. Perhaps there was still a chance for me.

I felt adrenalin begin to surge, a vibrancy in my muscles as my body prepared itself, but it was as if Lermentov sensed it, and he turned his head to meet my gaze. The soldier who had ridden in on horseback was still taking to him, Lermentov nodding his head slightly as he listened, but his stare never left me. It was as if Lermentov and I were connected. He even continued to watch as he called over another soldier and gave instructions, the man hurrying away to carry out his orders.

And when the conversation with Andrei was complete, only then did Lermentov look to the ground, his lips pursed. His shoulders rose as he drew in a deep breath, then he walked in my direction.

'Come.' Lermentov took my arm and pulled me away from the others. 'I have a surprise for you.' He turned me round and gestured to the soldier he had instructed just a few moments ago. The young man was now returning along the frozen street with Dariya at his side.

'Your daughter,' Lermentov said. 'Or should I say, your niece? Go on.' He released his grip and I went straight to Dariya, crouching to her level, ignoring the pain in my feet. I fastened her sheepskin coat around her and took her head in my hands, turning it so we were looking at each other.

'It's me. Everything's going to be all right.'

For a moment there was no response from her at all. She didn't even blink.

I moved close to her, leaning in to whisper into her ear. 'I've come to take you home. I promised Lara. I promised her I'd bring you home. Remember Lara. Remember her.'

And Dariya pressed her head against my face. Her cold ear against my lips. The side of her head against my forehead. And when she put her arm around me, I knew she remembered. Beneath everything that had happened to her, she remembered who I was.

I held her tight, pulling her right into me and holding her for a long time. Only when the guards began to move, shouting for us to make a line, did I finally release her.

I stood, and even then Dariya put her arms around my legs as if she would never let me go.

'I don't know if you're a brave man or a stupid man,' Lermentov said. 'The soldier I was talking to told me they found another village. Vyriv, it's called. It's small, well hidden, and there wasn't much there. Some food supplies which have been taken.'

I said nothing.

'And he told me something else. Something that's of no consequence to me but might interest you. Apparently a girl was taken from the village.' He looked down at Dariya. 'She was taken from the village and some of the men went to bring her back. A soldier and his two sons. So which are you, Luka Mikhailovich Sidorov? The child taker or the one who went to bring her back?'

Tears came to my eyes, a heavy sadness to my heart. They had found Vyriv. 'My wife?' I said. 'What about my wife? My sons?'

'Don't ask me what I can't tell you. Maybe you'll see them again when you get to the train, maybe you won't.' He shook his head. 'You let us think you had harmed this girl, and you did it to protect a tiny piece of land and a few peasants in this frozen shit hole. Like I said, I don't know if you're brave or stupid. But either way it doesn't make any difference.'

'But you know I've done nothing wrong. You *know*.'

Lermentov shrugged. 'You lied. You had a weapon. It's enough.'

'Take Dariya home. Please.'

'There's no going home now. Not for you, not for me, not for any of us. Work is all there is now. Everyone is a worker.'

'She's just a child.'

'It doesn't make any difference.' He looked away, watching the other prisoners. 'She has fingers, she can work. It's just the way it is now. There's nothing I can do.'

'Would you do it to your own daughter?'

Still he wouldn't look at us. Instead he waved his hands at the guards. 'Go,' he said. 'Get these prisoners to the train.'

'Where are we to go? Where are you sending us?'

'Work. You're being marched to the transit prison at the station and then you'll be taken for work.'

'Where?'

'What does it matter? It's all there is, but at least you'll be together.' He looked at me. 'You asked how long you have been here.'

'Yes.'

'Two days. You've been here two days.'

'It feels like longer.'

'It always does.' He turned and began to walk away, one of the soldiers coming to push me and Dariya into line with the others.

As he ascended the church steps, Lermentov stopped and looked back. 'Someone give that man some socks and boots,' he said.

Then he went into the church and closed the heavy door behind him.

28

They marched us out of the village in pairs, two lines of shuffling, bowed prisoners. Dariya held on to my hand as if she would never let it go, and we fell in at the rear of the pathetic column. Ahead of us Yuri and Evgeni and Dimitri were lost among the other *zeks*, who shambled like the walking wounded returning from battle. Men and women whose hope had deserted them. Twenty, twenty-five people, some of whom had already been marched from other villages, their own homes left far behind.

No one spoke. Four guards went with us, two at the head of the column, Yakov and Andrei on horseback – the two men who had arrested me on that very road – and two at the rear, dressed in good winter coats and warm boots.

I looked down at my own feet, almost to check they were still on the end of my legs, for there was barely any feeling in them at all now. Even with boots and thin socks, the cold had set so firmly into my flesh that I felt I would never be free of it. On my back I wore only a shirt, and the wind plucked at it as I crossed one arm over my chest to protect myself, but I was thankful that Dariya was better dressed than I was. She had suffered more than enough. With my other hand I grasped her small fingers, determined not to let go of them. I would keep her with me now, whatever was going to happen. She would not be alone again. But my body was reluctant to keep going. I had been beaten and left in the cold, and now my mind was closing and I fought to keep it open. My whole body was trembling, the shaking growing worse so that I could hardly put one foot in front of the other. I had to focus all my strength to stop from falling to my knees and giving up. Kostya had said it was easier to close his eyes and imagine a better place, and I had to concentrate hard not to do the same thing. I looked down at Dariya beside me and reminded myself she had endured as much as I had and more. She was only a child and yet here she was, still walking, still strong. If she could survive so much, then so could I. And as long as we were together, I had to make myself believe there was a chance for us. I couldn't afford to think, even for one second, that our fate was now decided. But in the face of the crippling cold, the warmth of Kostya's peace was inviting, almost overwhelming, and my eyes began to close and my legs ceased their walking.

The guards noticed straight away that one of their *zeks* had stopped. They shouted at me to get back in line, startling my eyes open in time to see one of them raising his rifle, coming towards me. But I was too tired even to move. All I wanted to do was to lie down in the snow and go to sleep.

Up ahead, the rest of the column was faltering. Some had turned to see what was happening, look for the source of the disturbance, while others continued in their bewilderment. Bodies bumped together; prisoners stumbled.

'Keep walking.'

I raised one hand and looked at the guard. 'I'm so tired. So cold.'

He sighed and I saw a look of sorrow in his face before the soldier shook himself back into character and spoke to me. 'Walk.'

I nodded.

'Walk.'

Dariya squeezed my hand and looked up at me, pulling me on, encouraging me to quicken my pace and catch up with the others. I caught sight of Evgeni leaning out of the line and looking back, and I nodded to him, showed him a forced smile and mouthed to him that I was all right.

The walk was slow and painful, and I was not the only one to hinder the column. Ahead there were old men, women, people who were sicker from hunger than I was, more infused with the cold than I was. Some of these people had been walking for many hours already, and their stop in Sushne had been their only rest. And I had seen no sign of food.

As we came to the spot where I had been arrested by the two soldiers, I watched the trees, hoping my sons had made it home.

At times the line lagged, someone would fall to their knees, be dragged up by the guards, supported by their friends or walking partners. And from one of those occasions, from the misfortune of another, a little luck came to me.

We had been walking for less than half an hour when one of the prisoners in the middle of the line collapsed and was unable to get up. The guards called for us to stop and Andrei came from the head of the column. I shuffled to one side so I could see along the line of bodies, watching as the guard dismounted and tried to drag the man to his feet, but he was a deadweight.

Andrei called to one of the soldiers from the rear, the young man who had told me to keep walking, and together they tried to pull the old man to his feet, but each time he collapsed back into the snow.

The horses snickered, stepping back and forth on the road, their bridles clinking. Yakov, who was still mounted, controlled his own ride and came to take the reins of the other while the guards struggled with the prisoner. I glanced behind at the single soldier at the rear of the column, and then ahead at the other three, all of them watching the old man. I considered if I would be able to overpower the guard behind me. I was old and the guard was young. I was tired and weak and slow with cold, but perhaps I could take him by surprise.

I looked back at him again, seeing that he was focused on what was happening up ahead. He was distracted. But when I glanced along the line for a last check, Yakov had turned, pulling his horse's head round, trotting the length of the line, shouting at us to get back into pairs and reform the column.

I moved back into the line, any hope of surprise now gone, and watched the soldiers struggle with the old man's weight. He looked close to death. His bony frame was malnourished, and every time they pulled him to his feet, his knees buckled, his ankles twisted and he collapsed back onto the road. I wondered how long I could go on before I was the same.

The guards made the same assessment of the old man as I did, and Andrei squatted beside him and removed a glove. He put his naked fingers to the man's neck and looked away while he felt for a pulse. After a moment or two he stood and replaced his glove. Then he and the other soldier each took an arm and dragged the old man to the side of the road, laying him in the snow. He was dead, or dying, and they were going to leave him behind.

When the order went out to continue walking, we began shuffling again. Andrei had remounted his horse, but instead of returning to the head of the pitiful column, he trotted back and turned his horse so he was alongside me.

'I'm sorry for what happened to you,' he said.

I looked up at him.

'You found your daughter.'

'Yes.'

'Only she isn't your daughter, she's your niece.'

I gripped Dariya's hand tighter. 'Lermentov told me you were in Vyriv.' I was almost afraid to ask, afraid to know what had happened in my village.

Andrei nodded. 'I spoke to your wife. Natalia Ivanovna.'

For a moment it was as if there was no cold. The crippling temperature that clouded my thoughts was pushed aside and everything was clear. The mention of her was enough to remind me what I had to get home for, and I was encouraged that I was not too exhausted and too numb to feel uplifted by the sound of my wife's name.

'Is she all right?' I asked.

Andrei's face softened. 'She was when I saw her. And your daughter. Larissa.'

'My beautiful Lara.' I had made her a promise. I had told her I would bring Dariya home. And now my heart was filled with both relief and fear. They were safe, but for how long I had no idea. 'What will happen to them?'

Andrei glanced away. 'I don't know.' Then he looked down at the girl beside me. 'It's good you found her.'

'Thank you.'

'I'm sorry this happened to you,' he said again, and as we came to the place where the old man had collapsed, I looked over at the body lying at the side of the road. Andrei halted his horse, making me turn to look up at him again, and when our eyes met, the young soldier nodded once.

At first I was confused, but then I understood what he wanted me to do.

I took a tentative step out of line, and the guard tightened his reins, pulling back the horse's head, a slight turn. I could smell its sweet breath, the faint odour of its sweat.

'Be quick,' Andrei said.

Dariya refused to let go of my hand when I left the line of prisoners, and I had to yank it from her grip in order to get to the side of the road.

The old man's skin was cold and lifeless, his glazed eyes staring, unseeing, at the clear sky. I pulled his arms from the sleeves of the coat, heaving his body to roll it over and slip the garment away. I dusted the snow from it and drew it around me, feeling the last of the old man's warmth. I fastened it tight and looked down at the corpse.

'Go,' the soldier told me. 'Get back in line.'

Ignoring the order, I bent down to roll the old man onto his back again, turning his face to the sky, thinking no man should be left face down at the side of the road. There was something like a smile on his lips. In the bell tower Kostya had been pleased to be leaving this place, and perhaps this old man too had found some peace in his last moments. A single, clear and pleasant thought to send him from this world to whatever might be waiting beyond. I thought about my own feelings not long ago when I had considered the peace of giving up. But I had something to live for. Natalia and Lara were safe for now, and Dariya needed me. I had promised to take her home, but if that was not to be, then at least I could stay with her, protect her. And seeing the old man with his dead blue eyes turned to the sky, the pupils widened in the relief of death, I knew there was no easy way out for me. My own relief would not yet come.

I closed the man's eyes with my fingertips and thanked him for his coat.

Behind me Dariya stood silent, her hand outstretched for mine. I showed her a smile and took her hand, joining the back of the line with a new-found strength. I had boots on my feet and a coat on my back. I was better off now than I had been this morning. Today would not be a bad day. Something was watching over me.

I walked now with my head up and my eyes facing forward. Beside me Dariya continued without speaking, but from time to time her small hand squeezed mine as if to reassure herself of my presence. I no longer watched my feet and considered falling to my knees. I was still tired and I was still hungry, but my resolve had hardened like iron in the cold, and I was determined not to fall by the side of the road as the previous owner of my coat had done. We were at the back of the line, two soldiers on foot behind us. We were best placed and I was waiting for the right moment. And then we would make our escape.

Ahead of us the column continued to shuffle. Stopping and starting. The aggressive Yakov reined his horse back from time to time, shouting an order, waiting for the line to pass him so he could watch each prisoner. I didn't look up to meet his eye, but I could feel his stare every time he was close.

We were on a straight stretch of the road now, the forest closing in on either side as if it intended to swallow us. The trees reaching out in places, stretching across the track like the dark fingers of forest spirits. There had been a fresh fall during the night, and the snow had piled in ridges along each branch. The sky was clear, brightening, with a tinge of orange just above the trees, only a few wisps of cloud. Yakov had halted his horse at the roadside so he could watch us shamble past, the animal stamping its hooves, moving from side to side. Its eyes rolled white and pale air blew from its flared nostrils.

And then a shout went up at the front of the line. Immediately we stopped, some of the prisoners bumping into those in front, their bodies closing together so there was almost no space between them. There was a moment of stillness before people began to move, leaning out to each side to see why we had come to a stop. Others leaned further to see past those in front, then Evgeni took a step to one side, a cue for others to do the same until everybody was shuffling out of line.

'Get back!' Yakov shouted, pulling his horse around and moving up the length of the column. 'Get back in line!' He slipped his foot from the stirrup and kicked one man in the shoulder, pushing him into his partner, the two of them stumbling but managing to stay on their feet.

'What's going on?' Yakov said, nudging the horse into a trot, moving to the front of the column.

When he was past, I glanced back at the two guards behind, seeing they had stepped wide on either side, moving off the road and looking in the direction Yakov had ridden. They shared a glance, not noticing me watching them, then went back to looking along the broken line of *zeks*, moving wider still, taking a few steps forward to better see what was happening.

Keeping my hand clasped around Dariya's small fingers, I began to edge out from the line. The perimeter of the forest was close. The trees were just a few metres from where I was standing. I scanned the dark sentinels, looking for a dense patch, searching for an escape route, trying to identify a place where the horses would find it hard to penetrate. But the trees were spaced too evenly, and I wouldn't be able to outrun the mounted soldiers. Not with Dariya. Not without a weapon.

Behind me both soldiers still had their rifles over their shoulders. They had made no attempt to make their weapons ready; they saw no threat from whatever had stopped the column of prisoners. I took another step out from the line, moving back just a touch, thinking I would overpower the one closest to me. If I could get to him before he could react, there was a chance I'd be able to take his weapon from him. In the forest, armed, the three remaining soldiers would be no threat to me. Horses or not.

I moved out further until I could see the two mounted soldiers at the head of the line. They were inching forward, the flanks of their horses almost touching, their bodies alert, leaning forward in the saddle. Yakov had kept his rifle over his shoulder, but he had drawn and cocked his revolver.

A few metres in front of the column a muddled shape lay in the centre of the road. From where I was standing, I was sure the shape was a body. Dark and out of place, a light dusting of snow across it as if it had been there for some time.

Yakov spoke to Andrei. There was a pause and then Andrei nodded and dismounted. He took the rifle from his shoulder, but there was inexperience in the way he held it, muzzle to the ground, as he approached the body. The line of prisoners was silent. Watching. Even from the back, I could hear the squeak of the soldier's boots in the snow.

When he was close to the shape, Andrei stopped. 'Who is it?' he asked. His voice was alien in this place. Muffled, as if the land wanted to quieten it, smother it. As if this place of calm and peace was not meant for humans.

'Are you all right?' he asked, but still there was no reply. No movement.

I felt a surge of concern for Andrei but I knew this was my chance. There might not be another opportunity to escape. And yet I was transfixed by what was happening. I couldn't tear my eyes away as Andrei stepped closer and put out his foot, touching the toe of his boot to the bundle and nudging it. I couldn't help but watch as I saw a slight resistance in the shape, as if it were not completely frozen.

I saw Andrei turn to Yakov, lifting his arms in question, in anticipation of his next order, but as he did, the shape moved. Like a forest wraith, rising from a pile of clothes, materialising and making itself whole, the shape shifted and grew. It moved with speed, the dusting of snow showering and falling from it as it stood tall and wrapped itself around the young soldier.

But this was no wraith, this dark shape that now rose from the road. This was a man, wrapped well against the cold. He wore a full coat and a fur hat, his face covered with scarves that were bound tight. Only his hands were not gloved. He rose up and grabbed the soldier, pinning his rifle arm to his side as he embraced him from behind, making the cumbersome weapon useless and using Andrei's body as a shield. The attacker's other hand rose up to point at Yakov, still astride his horse, and extending from that fist I could see the slim barrel of a pistol.

But it was Yakov who discharged his weapon first. Whether he did so because he was inexperienced and taken by surprise, or whether his actions were calculated, I don't know, but Yakov's revolver kicked hard in his hand, the first shot hitting the human shield. Before he could thumb back the hammer to fire again, his horse reared, lifting its front hooves from the ground, twisting to the left. Yakov pulled tight on the reins, but he was forced to lean hard to counter the movement of his ride. His aim was disturbed and his second shot went wide, thumping into the trees beyond. The man who had materialised from the dark shape on the road released his grip on Andrei and, as the body collapsed at his feet, he took aim and fired three quick shots, knocking Yakov from his horse.

And then the attacker was moving. Hurrying through the snow, the hem of his coat thumping against his boots, until he was standing over Yakov, his pistol pointing down at him. He fired again.

The attack had come with such speed and ferocity that I barely had time to react, and I suspected the same was true of the two guards behind me. When I turned to look at them, neither had even had time to unsling his rifle. Both soldiers were standing with their hands out in front of them, each with a gun barrel to his back. And behind them were tracks on either side of the road where two more men had come from the forest. But when they gripped their scarves and pulled them down to reveal their faces, I could see they weren't two men at all. One of them was my son Petro, and the other was Aleksandra, the girl from Uroz.

29

I didn't go to my sons straight away. Instead, I went to Andrei, the soldier who had waited for me to take the old man's coat. When I'd looked at him earlier, I had seen something of my own sons in him. He was young like them, inexperienced like them. Out of his depth like them. And now he was lying in the snow, shot by his own comrade.

He was still alive, but the life was leaving him quickly, spilling inside him somewhere; there was little sign of it in the snow. His chest barely moved, nothing more than a slight rise and fall. Erratic and laboured. His eyes were glazed and unseeing. His mouth open, his lips dry, his tongue just visible.

I pulled my hand from Dariya's and crouched beside him, putting it to his face. 'I'm sorry,' I told him.

A blink was the only acknowledgement he could make. His chest continued to hitch with each failing breath.

'It's Andrei?'

Again just a blink.

I removed the boy's glove so that my skin could touch his, and I watched him. I looked into his eyes as his life left him, so that he was not alone and he was not any more afraid than he had to be. And when he was gone I felt a hand on my shoulder, and I turned to see Dariya beside me, looking down at the dead man.

I stood, taking her hand again, and turned to my sons and the *zeks* gathered there.

The huddle of prisoners remained silent. They didn't know what to say. They didn't know what sound to make. The women didn't gasp, the men didn't cheer, the children didn't cry. They just stood and watched. No one knew if this was a good thing or a bad thing. For now they had been spared the Stolypin cars, the endless journey in crowded wagons without food or water. They had escaped, for now, the prospect of a short life of forced labour in a distant forest or mine. But they couldn't see a future in which they all walked away from this. From the shooting of a Red Army soldier. They couldn't see a future at all.

But I saw one. In the eyes of my son I saw myself returning home. I saw myself with my family once again, and I pushed movement into my legs, forcing one step after another, going to where my son stood.

'You came,' I said.

Petro nodded. He managed something close to a smile and looked down at Dariya. 'You found her.'

'Yes.'

And then Petro seemed to shake himself, remind himself what he was doing here, what his plan was. He prodded the soldier and told him to move to the front of the column. The prisoners were beginning to mutter a few words now. There was an increase in the volume of their voices. Above all of them I heard a man say, 'Bless you.'

I went with Petro and Aleksandra, going to where Yakov's body lay. And there, at the head of the column, Viktor stood holding the reins of the two horses in one hand. In his other hand he held the pistol which I had taken from the sled of the man who had come to Vyriv just a few days ago.

'Papa.'

'Viktor.'

He passed the reins to Aleksandra, and we stripped the soldiers of their rifles, laying them across Yakov's body to keep them out of the snow. When that was done, Viktor pushed the first of the soldiers away from him, then the other. 'Go on,' he ordered them. 'Into the trees.'

I felt Petro tense. 'No, wait.'

Viktor turned to his brother. 'It's the only way.'

I glanced at the small group of *zeks*. Evgeni and Dimitri had stepped away from them, coming closer to where we stood. I could see in their faces what I knew I would see in my own if I were to look in a mirror.

'Viktor is right,' I said to Petro. 'It's the only way.'

'We can tie them,' he said. 'Leave them here for—'

'They'd die from the cold,' I told him.

'Then let them walk back to the village.'

'For them to send help?'

'They'll send people to search for them anyway. As soon as they don't reach wherever they're supposed to be.'

'Not until tomorrow.' I went to my son and put a hand on his shoulder. 'But you already know this, Petro. You knew it would have to be this way.'

Petro looked at the ground and I put both arms around him.

'Please, Papa,' Petro said, his voice muffled against my cheek. 'We're not barbarians.'

I released him and put my hands on either side of his face, looking into his eyes, seeing something that reminded me who I was. I wasn't just the man who had been arrested for no reason and thrown into a dark room. I wasn't just the man beaten by a policeman who had lost his soul somewhere in the darkness of our times. I was the soldier who had deserted his army because he refused to force young men to dig their own graves, and because he turned his back on shooting uniformed boys who ran scared in the face of a fierce and experienced enemy. I was a husband and a father, and I was the man who had made a promise to find a stolen child. I had killed in the name of freedom and defence and protection and what I believed to be right, but I was not a murderer. I had never been a murderer.

I took a deep breath and nodded. 'You're right. This isn't even a war.' I turned to Viktor. 'Not any more.'

'So what do we do?' asked Viktor. 'We let them run for help?'

I stepped back from Petro and looked around. The *zeks* were watching. Expecting.

'I think he's right,' Evgeni said. 'You should shoot them. It's too much of a risk. What if they come after us?'

'They're just boys,' I said. 'You think they'll come after us without rifles?'

'They'll get help.' Evgeni came close and lowered his voice. 'These people are angry. After everything that's been done to them, they want to see some justice.'

'I'm not sure shooting these boys would be any kind of justice.'

'They killed my brother.' He spoke through gritted teeth.

'And you think killing these boys will avenge that? It will make you feel better?'

'Yes.'

'You really think so?' I bent at the knees and put a hand in the snow to retrieve the pistol Yakov had dropped. The steel was icy cold, but I gripped it hard and took it to Evgeni, putting it into his hand and curling his fingers around the handle. 'Then you should kill them. It'll make the revenge even better.'

Evgeni looked at the weapon in his hand.

'Shoot,' I said. 'Why not shoot?' I held Evgeni's hand in my own and lifted it to point at the two soldiers, making Viktor step aside, moving away from us.

'Into the trees,' Evgeni said.

The soldiers both raised their hands in useless defence, shaking their heads. 'No.'

'Why not right here?' I said. 'Where everyone can see.'

I thumbed back the hammer for Evgeni, pulled it back until it clicked and forced the cylinder forwards to create the gas seal. 'Shoot them.'

I felt Evgeni take the weight of the pistol. I sensed the contraction in the muscles of Evgeni's arm as he steadied the gun himself.

'But before you do,' I said, 'let me ask them something.'

I went to stand beside the guards, feeling the panic coming off them. Their faces set tight, their eyes wide, the almost imperceptible shaking of their heads. Their throats contracted, tightening in anticipation.

'What's your name?' I asked the first of them.

'Sasha.' His words were laboured, his tongue lazy with fear.

'How old are you, Sasha?'

'Nineteen.'

'Where are you from?'

'Kharkiv.'

'And why did you join the army?'

He looked at me as if I'd said something that didn't make sense.

'Why did you join?' I asked again.

'I had to.'

'No choice?'

'No choice.'

'And you?' I asked the second of them. 'Your name?'

'Anatoly.'

'And your age?'

'Twenty-one.'

'You had to join too?'

'Yes.'

'And you have a family?'

'A wife. Irina.'

'Children?'

He shook his head.

'Good. That should make it easier for Evgeni.'

'Please. We had only a short time together before I had to join the army,' Anatoly said. 'I don't even have a photograph. I can hardly remember what she looks like.'

I stayed with them a moment, looking at them, studying their faces, then I walked back to Evgeni and stood beside him. 'OK, now you can shoot them. Shoot Sasha and Anatoly.'

Evgeni remained as he was, arm outstretched, weapon cocked.

'What's the matter?' I asked him.

Evgeni released his breath and looked to one side as he lowered the pistol until it was hanging by his side.

'That's right,' I said. 'You can't.' I took the pistol from him and eased down the hammer. 'Because you know it's wrong. When it's right, you know it's right. But when it's wrong, Evgeni, the trigger is a heavy thing to pull. These men don't need to die. My son Petro is right. We're not barbarians.'

'Then what *do* we do with them?' Viktor asked.

'We let them go,' I said, looking down at Yakov lying close to my feet. He was on his back, one arm outstretched, the other twisted under his body as if it had broken when he fell. There was blood across one side of his face where one of Viktor's bullets had caught him in the neck. He had leaked into the snow, and already the blood had started to thicken and freeze. His eyes were wide open, staring at the few wisps of cloud.

'Let them go?' said Viktor. 'We can't just let them go. They'll come after us before we—'

'It's the only way,' I said.

'So what do *we* do now?' Evgeni asked. He was standing with his shoulders hunched, the weight of his situation weighing him down. He glanced back at the group of prisoners huddled behind him. 'What do any of us do now?'

'My sons and I are going to take these horses and we're going to go to my village. My wife is there. My home too, but that is lost. I think, perhaps, your homes are lost too.'

None of them spoke.

'I know they've found my village. They've stripped the food, taken anything of any value, arrested or shot the men. I'm going to find my wife and then I'm going to head for Poland.'

'You think you'd make it?' Evgeni asked. 'In the winter? With the borders closed and the villages occupied? Even if you can take your wife from the village, you really think you can make it to Poland? On a horse?'

'I'm going to try,' I said. 'There are many ways to get into Poland, and I know how to live when the weather is bad. It'll be hard, but I have to try. You people are free to do whatever you like. You can risk returning to your homes, or you can go somewhere else; it's up to you.'

'Just like that?'

'What else can I do?'

'What about them?' He gestured at the soldiers.

'What about them?' I asked. 'They're in the same position as we are. You really think they can go back? Do you know what the Red Army does to men who retreat? Men who lose their rifles and their prisoners? If these men go back to Sushne, they'll be shot. They can't go back there any more than you can.'

Evgeni looked at me for a long while. Beside him Dimitri was silent. The scene was like a photograph, no one moving, no one making a sound.

After a moment, Evgeni nodded and that simple gesture broke the scene. Dimitri spoke quietly to him before they went to the group of prisoners.

'Strip him,' I said to Viktor, pointing to Yakov's body.

While Viktor did as I instructed, I removed Andrei's coat and gloves. I took his shirt and his boots and swapped everything for my own. I pulled on Andrei's *budenovka* hat, dropping the flaps over my ears, and dragged the young soldier from the road into the trees. Viktor pulled Yakov in beside him, and while Aleksandra and Petro watched the soldiers and the horses, we threw snow over the bodies.

'You should have gone home,' I told Viktor as we worked.

'Maybe.'

'But I'm glad you didn't. And it's good to see you looking strong. You did well.'

Viktor nodded.

'You have the things I left in the cabin?' I asked.

'In the woods.'

'Everything? You have the rifle?'

'Yes.'

'Good.'

When we were done, we piled Yakov's clothes together with the soldiers' rifles by the roadside. I could see Evgeni and the others in conversation. They were still in a huddle, and they reminded me of sheep, the way they'd come together for mutual protection. Even Yuri had lost himself among the others. It surprised me he hadn't stepped forward, a soldier with his experience. It had never seemed as if his spirit had been broken, yet he remained huddled among the others, looking to Evgeni and Dimitri for leadership.

As Viktor and I approached the place where Petro stood with the horses, so the huddle became silent and Evgeni and Dimitri came to join us.

'None of us has anything to return to,' Evgeni said. 'Nowhere to go.'

I waited. Beside me one of the horses began scraping the ground with its hoof, nuzzling the area, looking for something edible.

'They want to follow you to Poland.'

I almost laughed at the thought of leading this rabble to Poland. 'We'll be on horseback,' I said. 'They'd never keep up. And I can't be responsible for these people. I already have enough.'

Evgeni looked down. 'They're afraid. Cold. They have nothing to eat.'

'What about you?' I asked. '*You* can take them.'

'I'm not skilled enough.'

'You'll have Yuri with you. He has enough experience. He said he was a soldier; he'll know how to survive. Let him help lead you to Poland.'

'We've spoken to him; he's not coming.'

'What?' I looked back at the huddle of prisoners but couldn't see Yuri.

'He said he'll be safer alone, that he's going east.'

'East to where?'

'He wouldn't say.' Evgeni shook his head. 'He's afraid of informers.'

'*Everyone's* afraid,' Dimitri said to me. 'That's why we're looking to you.'

'You know how to use a rifle?'

'Yes.'

'Good. There are rifles there for you.' I pointed to the small pile of belongings. 'Take them and whatever you need of the clothes; it's all I can do. You can make it. Yuri will see sense if you talk to him. He'll go with you.'

'I'm not so sure.'

'Then you'll have to manage. I haven't time to stand here talking, and you won't be able to follow us when we're gone. We'll move too quickly on the horses.'

Evgeni nodded once to Dimitri, then took my arm and walked me away from the others.

'You must be very proud of your sons.'

'There's no time for pride,' I told him. 'There's only time for doing what we can.'

'And what about these people here?'

'I've no time for them either – I told you that. I have enough responsibility already.'

'These people have seen what you can do,' Evgeni said. 'You and your sons. They see what kind of men you are, and now they want to follow you. They won't follow me like that.'

'And what do *you* think?'

He shrugged. 'I think if I want to stay alive, I need to be with you.'

I looked Evgeni in the eye and ran a gloved hand across my face. I had watched his brother die in the belfry, and he had given me warmth and the last scraps of bread and water. 'You know Vyriv?' I asked.

'I've heard of it.'

'You know how to get there?'

'I think so.'

'That's where I'm going. On horseback I think we can make it by tomorrow morning, but I don't know how long I'll be there. There's a ridge to the north-west that overlooks the village. Head there and I'll try to meet you, and we'll travel together. But I won't wait. As soon as I have my wife and daughter, I'll move on and I'll try to leave no tracks.'

Evgeni nodded and turned as if to go back to the others, but I stopped him.

'There are enough rifles, so you should split into two groups.

You take some of the people; Yuri and Dimitri take the others. Try to cover your tracks, but if someone finds them, you'll be harder to follow if there are two trails.' I glanced up at the sky. 'And it looks like someone is finally looking out for us.'

'What do you mean?'

'It's starting to snow again.' I smiled. 'With a bit of luck it'll cover our tracks anyway. It's about time we had some help from up there, don't you think? Maybe we haven't been abandoned after all.'

Evgeni stared for a moment. Thick flakes were beginning to drift around us, not many, but the sky was turning grey, and somewhere far away there was the long rolling sound of thunder.

'How can you smile?' he asked.

'Last night I was freezing to death in a bell tower. Today I have a good coat and boots; I've found Dariya; I'm with my sons, and the snow is falling to cover our escape. I have a lot to smile about. We need to look for the good in what we have, Evgeni; it's the only way to survive.'

'I'm not sure I can find good in anything any more.'

'You're free, aren't you? You're no longer on your way to a labour camp. You could've been mining coal, building a railway, but now you have your freedom.'

'For now.'

'Then we must keep it that way.' Evgeni and his friends had given me bread and water when I needed it. They had offered me warmth and solidarity. I could see that Evgeni was afraid, just as I had been before, but now for different reasons. Now Evgeni had the responsibility of the others and he faced the possibility of being followed by soldiers. I wanted to do more to help, but there was nothing left for me to do other than reassure him.

'The way it's falling now, the snow will be your friend. It will cover those bodies and maybe no one will even come looking for you,' I told him. 'They won't care that much about a few old men and women going missing. I've met people like Lermentov, and I'm sure he wouldn't follow us even if he knew we'd gone; he can't spare men to the wilderness. He has other things to keep him occupied. No, he'll just hope the weather kills us.'

'You think we can survive out here?'

'All you have to do is survive long enough to get to Vyriv. Keep moving, keep warm, keep to the trees and you'll be fine. We'll meet you and cross to Poland together.'

'You really mean that? You'll wait for us?'

'For a while. But don't tell any of the people where you're going. Only Yuri and Dimitri.'

'Why?'

'Any one of them could be an informer,' I said. 'Any one of them could try to pass on the information.'

'Out here?' He looked around him.

'Anywhere,' I said.

'So what do I say?'

'Tell them you're going to meet us – that's enough.'

'So what about me? What about Yuri and Dimitri? You trust us?'

'I suppose I have to.'

30

While Evgeni and the others gathered the rifles and clothing, I prepared the horses to leave. I mounted, taking Aleksandra and Dariya, while Petro and Viktor took the second horse. We would be a heavy load for the animals, but the horses were strong and they would cope. When they grew tired we would walk for a while, give them a chance to rest.

'What about us?' Anatoly asked. The two soldiers were standing like abandoned children, not knowing what to do. 'Where do we go?'

'You can do as you please,' I said, looking down at them. 'But if I were you, I wouldn't go back to Sushne. If you're lucky, Lermentov will shoot you; maybe watch you dig your own grave first. If you're not so lucky, maybe he'll put you up in that bell tower for a while.'

The two soldiers looked across at Evgeni and the others preparing to leave.

'*They'll* never trust you,' I said. 'After what's happened to them, they may even kill you.' I watched them, feeling a weight in my chest. They probably had no idea how to survive alone in good weather, never mind in these conditions.

'Please,' Sasha said. 'You can't just leave us here.' The snow was falling faster now, the flakes smaller but filling the air, covering our hats and settling on our shoulders.

'What do you want me to do?' I asked them.

'Take us with you.'

'I can't do that.' But I couldn't leave them out here to die either. I closed my eyes for a moment and turned my face to the sky, feeling the cold spots on my eyelashes and lips. I had come out here to take responsibility for one small child, but now it seemed I'd collected far more along the way. Aleksandra, the refugees, and now two young soldiers who were out of their depth and afraid.

The horse was becoming restless and it shifted beneath me. I opened my eyes and leaned forward to reassure it, speaking to it, stroking the side of its neck.

'In your shoes,' I said to the soldiers, 'I'd go on. Wherever you were supposed to take us, go there and hope that whoever is in charge is more forgiving than Lermentov. Maybe you can even lose yourselves at the transit prison – God knows there'll be other prisoners and soldiers. Disappear among them. Take a train back into Russia and go home. Find your wife.' I looked at Anatoly. 'Go to her so that you can remember her face. It's what I would do.'

'And then?

I shrugged. 'And then find somewhere to hide. For now it's kulaks, but soon I think there'll be enemies of the state everywhere. Russia will suddenly be full of them, and there will be plenty of work for them all. All I can do is wish you luck.'

I turned the horse and called over to Evgeni, raising a hand to him. Evgeni nodded, lifted a hand to head height and held it there. He was still standing that way when I nudged the horse and left the road, making for the trees and the place where Viktor and Petro had left our belongings.

The horses were well-trained rugged beasts that moved without complaint. Mine worked hard beneath the extra weight, but Aleksandra and Dariya were not heavy and it walked on with little encouragement. I swayed with its movement, keeping balanced in the saddle, wedged between Dariya in front and Aleksandra behind.

There was great respite in not being on my feet, and I could feel the ache in my legs from the walking and the sting in my toes from the cold. I wanted to hurry back to Vyriv, knowing what might be happening there, but now I was back with my sons and I had found Dariya, there was a sense of relief that melted with the tiredness and the hunger and slipped around me.

'How far?' I asked, shaking my head and forcing myself to concentrate on following my sons. In front, the rear of the other horse moved on.

'Not far.' Petro turned so he could look back. I saw the profile of his head, only his nose poking between the covering of his scarves and his hat pulled low to his eyes.

'A few minutes,' I heard Viktor agree. 'And we have some meat. We can make a fire, boil water, have some tea—'

'We haven't time for that,' I told him. 'We have to get home.'

'I want to get home too,' he said. 'But when was the last time you ate?'

I thought back to the rabbit we'd shared and tried to remember if I had eaten since then. I could almost taste the meat now; feel something in my belly cry out for it. 'I had some bread. Just before I left.'

'Enough?'

'Of course not. But we haven't time to stop.'

'What difference is a few minutes going to make? You need food and something hot.'

'We need to go on,' I said.

'And Dariya. She needs to eat too.'

'She can eat while we ride.'

'She needs something warm. We all do.'

I started to protest again, but this time Aleksandra spoke from behind me. Her arms were tight around my waist, her mouth close to my ear so it sounded as if her voice was in my head.

'You're falling asleep,' she said. 'I can feel you relaxing. You're hungry and you're tired. And the way your face looks . . . Something to eat and drink will make you feel better.'

'I feel fine.' The blood was dried and crusted over the wounds that Lermentov had given me. My jaw hurt when I spoke, and the bruises ached when I moved.

'Papa, you look like shit,' Viktor said.

'Don't be a stubborn old man,' Aleksandra spoke in my ear again. Then she lowered her voice. 'Think about us. We're depending on you. All three of us need you to be strong and fit. You're no good to us if you're weak and tired. Eat something. Drink something. It'll take a few minutes, and then we'll move on. You'll be stronger and less likely to let us down.'

I turned to see her, look at her eyes, our faces inches apart.

'We need you,' she said.

I sighed and looked away. 'All right, we'll stop. But no more than a few minutes.'

Further into the forest we came to a place where a rotten tree had fallen, snapping low on its trunk. It lay across the ground, snow drifted against it so it formed a low wall, the perfect shelter from the wind. Viktor stopped, so I tightened my grip on the reins and halted behind him. Aleksandra slipped down as Viktor and Petro dismounted.

Petro came to me while Viktor gathered wood, breaking dry twigs from the dead tree, piling them in a pit they'd lined with stones and protected with a low wall of snow.

The way they had organised themselves was impressive. 'You've done well,' I said as Petro reached up to help Dariya from the horse.

'We've only done what you taught us,' he said, taking Dariya's hand. 'This is Aleksandra,' he said to her, squatting so he was at her level. 'I want you to stay with her for a while; can you do that?'

Dariya didn't respond, and there was a look of sadness in Petro's eyes.

Petro forced a smile and turned to go, but Dariya clung tight to his hand.

'Don't be afraid,' he said. 'Aleksandra is our friend. She'll look after you.'

'Of course I will,' Aleksandra squatted too. 'We'll be like sisters.' She reached out and took Dariya's other hand, encouraging her towards her. 'Come.'

Petro pulled his hand away and Aleksandra drew Dariya close to her saying, 'We're going to be all right now. Everything will be all right.' But she lifted her eyes so she could look at me. 'Luka is going to take us home. Isn't that right?'

'Yes,' I said. 'We're all going home.'

Petro went to the fallen tree and dusted away a covering of snow, reaching in to pull at a bundle of wood they'd leaned against it. Drawing it back, he revealed a clear area behind where they'd left the belongings they didn't want to carry to their ambush. He removed our packs and the rifle they'd taken from the hut where the child thief lay dead.

Petro brought the rifle and handed it to me as I dismounted.

'And the rest of his things? I asked. 'There was a pack.'

'We looked through it.'

'And? What was in it?'

Petro glanced at Dariya and came closer to me, lowering his voice. 'Old clothes, furs, a groundsheet, some dried meat—'

'What kind?' I was almost afraid to ask.

'I don't know.'

'You didn't eat any of it?'

'No.'

'Thank God.'

'We buried everything but the rifle. There was another scalp in the pack, wrapped in cloth. Like the one we found in the tree. And there was a bottle of something that looked like blood.'

'It explains what he left behind for us,' I said. 'Trophies from previous victims used as bait for new ones.' Just like a sharpshooter wounding a man and leaving him to draw out others.

'You think he was going to do that to the two we found?' Petro asked.

'Probably, but I think their father stopped him. Somehow he got them back before he could do anything more.'

'But they were already dead.' Petro glanced back at Dariya.

'Maybe it was part of the game,' I said. 'Who knows how such a man might think. Perhaps it was another way to taunt the father. Let him see his dead children before finishing him off. Except we found him before that happened.'

'I hope the bastard's burning in hell.'

'He will be,' I said. 'You've done well. I'm proud of you both, Petro.'

Petro forced a smile and took the reins, hitching them to a low branch while I checked the weapon. I inspected the magazine, drew back the bolt, saw the brass casing in the breech, turned and pulled the stock firm against my shoulder. I sighted through the scope at the forest beyond. The rifle was much like the one taken by Lermentov, but this one had fired the bullet that killed Dariya's father, and she had meted out her own punishment, taken her own revenge without knowing it. She had killed the man who murdered her father, and now she was only a shell of the little girl I had known. I was afraid she would never speak again, never see anything with the same eyes.

'Has she said anything?' Petro asked.

'Not a word. She just stares.'

'You think she'll be all right?'

'I don't know. Maybe she needs her mother.'

Petro left me, going to the others, and I lowered the rifle to watch them. Aleksandra and Dariya had joined Viktor by the fire. There was a low flame among the twigs, and Viktor was laying larger pieces on it while Petro scooped snow into a tin. Aleksandra stood by, unspeaking, and Dariya clung to her hand.

'Come and sit by the fire,' Petro said to me as he placed the tin over the flames. 'You look cold.'

'I'm not cold any more.' Feeling had returned to my feet, but the only sensation it brought was pain. My muscles ached from the hunger and the cold, and my face was sore from Lermentov's beating.

'Well, come and sit down anyway,' he said. 'Rest a moment.'

I hesitated, looking at my sons and then back out at the forest.

'Just a short while,' Petro said.

I was afraid to rest. I was afraid because I didn't want to go back to that small room, or any room like it, and I didn't want any of us to be dragged away to a Stolypin car. I wanted to keep moving, put as much distance between us and Lermentov as was possible. I had told the others that Lermentov wouldn't come after us, that he would leave us to the weather and the wild animals, but a part of me believed that if he knew we had escaped, that two of his soldiers lay dead beneath the snow, he would send his men to find us and bring us back. He would sentence us to a life of labour so hard we would waste away in less than a year. We would be worked to death.

And there was something else I was afraid of. Something which scared me more than Lermentov and his promise of distant Gulags. I was afraid that if I stopped to rest I would lack the energy to move again.

'We need to move on, keep watching in case they follow.'

'You said they wouldn't.'

'If they do, though . . .'

'*We'll* watch for anyone following.' Viktor came over to me and stood close. 'You relax. We're here now. Petro is warming some water; you can drink tea, wash your face.'

I put a hand to my beard and felt the places where it was matted with blood. 'Do I look bad?'

'You look fine, Papa.'

'I look like a man who has been beaten,' I said.

'Why did they do that to you? Why did they . . .' Viktor squeezed his eyes closed and shook his head. When he looked at me again, there was anger and pain and sadness in them. All of those things mixed together in a violent and poisonous brew. 'We could go back,' he said. 'Go back and find the—'

'There's no going back,' I told him. 'There's nothing good to come from that. We have to go forward. Find your mother, Lara, and then move on; get away. We can't fight what is happening here.'

'Maybe we *should* fight it. Maybe that's what we have to do. We have to fight and show these people we won't let them do this to us. If we just sit back and let them walk over us, we're as good as dead. We have to stand up and show them we can't be beaten like that.'

'They've already done it, Viktor. They've already won.'

'No. They've only won when the last of us gives up fighting them. I killed one bastard soldier today; put another ten in front of me and I'll kill all of them too.'

'The fighting is over. Now it's up to us to survive. That's all we must do. Survive.'

'After what they've done to us? They take everything we own. They beat us, kill us, deport us.'

'People are tired now, Viktor. Weak and tired.'

'And you? You're too tired to fight?'

'I'm tired, yes, but too tired?' I shook my head. 'I don't know. Maybe. But I've seen enough to know when to fight and when to get away. Now I just want to find some peace.'

'Then we have to fight for it.'

'No. I told you, there's no fight we can win. What we have to do now is take care of your mother and your sister. Of Dariya over there. We have to find somewhere safe for us.'

Viktor turned to look at Dariya. 'Why won't she speak? She just stares and says nothing. If I have to look at her too long, I think it might drive me mad.'

'Have some sympathy,' I said. 'We can't imagine how she feels . . . what he must've done to her.'

'I wish *I'd* killed him. Doing something like that to children. Cutting them and . . . He was a monster. I would've—'

'I've had enough talk of killing. He's gone now. Let's concentrate on living.'

Viktor took a deep breath and nodded. He clenched his teeth hard, the muscles of his jaw working, and I could feel the tension in him. All the hatred.

I put my hand on him but said nothing. There are times when no words can convey feelings. Sometimes a gesture is all that can be made, a gesture that overpowers the weakness of empty words.

Viktor sniffed hard and turned away, pressing the palm of his hand against his right eye. 'I'm sorry, Papa. I'm sorry for not coming sooner. For letting them hurt you.'

'You didn't let them do anything, Viktor. You did exactly what you had to do. What I would have done. You waited until you could win your battle, then you struck. And now I'm free, and Dariya is safe.' I looked back at the forest. 'All those others too. They owe you their lives.'

Viktor wiped his hand across his nose and tipped his head back to look at the treetops. He stayed like that for a while before he spoke again. 'There's some meat,' he said. 'I shot a deer yesterday and we ate well. You should have some before we leave.'

I watched him, standing silent beside me, and I wished there was something I could say to make my son feel better.

When I went to sit with them, Petro handed me a tin mug of tea, black and steaming. It was without sugar and tasted bitter, but it was good to feel its heat. It burned its way into my stomach when I swallowed and my throat stung, but it was a good sensation.

There was venison too, the thin strips of meat smoked over the fire until they were almost black. They were hard to bite into, but the flavour was unlike anything I had tasted in a long time, and I immediately felt the benefit of something good to eat. My worries about not being able to continue once I had allowed myself to rest began to subside, and I stretched my feet close to the stones surrounding the fire so the heat could dry my boots. With the hot food and the tea and the warmth, my pains were all but forgotten, and I was glad to have my sons. They had relieved some of my burden of responsibility.

'Viktor shot the deer yesterday morning,' Petro said. 'He saw it through the trees and I told him to leave it, that someone in the village might hear the shot, but he was right to ignore me. He tracked it for most of the morning; let it move away before he killed it. Took what meat he could carry and brought it back.

Aleksandra and I prepared it while Viktor went back to watch the village.'

Dariya sat between Aleksandra's legs, chewing on a strip of venison, her eyes still distant. I looked at the piece of meat she held in her small fingers and tried not to see the flesh Lermentov had unwrapped on the altar table in the church. I'd hardly even had the chance to think about the wound on her leg, I was so caught up in having found her, in keeping her with me during the march, in looking for an escape and in the arrival of my sons.

Now I came forward and lifted the hem of her dress, Aleksandra and Petro watching me with concern.

Dariya's thin legs were pale and dirty, her boots oversized and out of place. Her right thigh was still bandaged, and the bindings were clean.

'What's that?' Petro asked, coming closer.

'He cut her,' I said, almost a whisper. Dariya continued to stare ahead as if none of us was there. She took another bite of the venison and chewed slowly. 'The one who took her. The child thief.'

Petro was staring at the bandages, his eyes wide.

I pulled Dariya's dress down, straightening it.

'Like we saw on the other?' Petro continued to look at the place where Dariya had been cut. 'Is she going to be all right?'

I didn't know how to answer that question. Although the child thief had left her alive, it was as if he had reached into her and torn out her soul. He had removed everything that made her the little girl she had been, the child who was my daughter's best friend and cousin. Now, she was nothing more than a shell. Staring and eating, not speaking. Just the movement of her jaws, the blinking of her eyes. She was all instinctive function, and nothing else. I wondered what could bring her back. What could reunite her body with her soul.

I sat back against the fallen tree and said nothing. I loosened one of the buttons on my coat and slipped a hand inside to take out the young soldier's cigarettes. I lit one with a match and drew the smoke into my lungs as if it would give me the strength to overcome what lay ahead and what lay behind.

'How did you know where I was?' I asked.

'By the time we got to the road, you were gone,' Viktor said. 'We looked at your tracks, seeing there'd been horses, and we followed the road until we saw the village. There were soldiers close to the entrance, so we moved back into the trees and found a place to watch.'

'We saw you go into the church,' Aleksandra added, 'and we knew there was nothing we could do. We were beginning to think we should go back to Vyriv.'

'No,' Petro said. 'We would never have left you.'

'You should have,' I told them. 'You should've left me, but I'm glad you didn't.'

Dariya raised her head and looked at me. She didn't speak and her expression barely changed, but there was something in her eyes. Something new.

'We were waiting for the right moment,' Petro said. 'We trekked all around the village, looking for the best way to come in, but there were too many soldiers. There was just no way, so we had to wait.'

Aleksandra ran a hand over Dariya's head, brushing back her hair and putting her fingers through it. 'I told them they should go. But neither of them would listen. I made them promise they would stay only one more day, but I don't think they'd have kept their promise.'

I passed the cigarette to Viktor and lifted the tin cup to my mouth, the tea steaming in the cold, and I saw my hands were still shaking. The dark liquid swelled and threatened to spill from the cup, so I bit the rim to keep it steady and let the steam roll around my cheeks.

'We should go now,' I said after a moment.

'Another minute,' Petro said, coming forward with another cup of water. He held a rag in his other hand, and he dipped it into the water and crouched to wipe the blood from my face.

I took his wrist and stayed his hand.

'Let me,' he said.

'I can do it.'

'Let me.' He pulled his hand away and scrubbed at the dried blood.

31

The horses were sure-footed, picking their way through the forest as if they'd done it many times before. Once again I rode with Aleksandra and Dariya, the dream-like sway of the animal beneath me, the jostle of the bodies in front and behind. I soaked up their warmth just as I gave them mine, but now I felt stronger, less likely to slip from the saddle. I was still tired, but there was satisfaction in the fatigue rather than desperation. I was clean and warm and my belly was full. I was in better condition than I'd been in for days, and because my sons were with me, because Dariya was safe, I was lifted above the previous wretchedness. I wanted to be home in Vyriv, but there was nothing I could do other than what I was doing right now. I was making my way home, and I was as strong as I needed to be. All I could do now was hope that Natalia and Lara were safe.

We moved slowly through the trees, but I estimated that if we continued at a good pace we'd be close to Vyriv by nightfall. We could make a camp for the night, leave at first light and be home by late morning. Fortune had turned in our favour. We had transport, food, and now the temperature had even begun to rise as the sky clouded.

With the other prisoners I'd walked close to two kilometres from Sushne so we were well away from the area where the child thief's body lay frozen, but as we came to the edge of the trees to look out on an open area of perfect snow, I pulled the horse to a stop and waited in the treeline.

'What is it?' Aleksandra asked.

'You see something?' Viktor came alongside.

'No.' But the feeling was there: a touch of fear crawling across my scalp, tightening my skin. 'Nothing.' I took the child thief's rifle and scoped the area, looking for anything out of place.

'We should press on.' Viktor started to move off, but I put out a hand to stop him.

'What's the matter? He's gone.'

'Wait a moment,' I said. 'Let me be sure.'

I shouldered the rifle and scoped the area once more, seeing nothing, then sat with the butt plate of the rifle on my thigh, the barrel pointing to the sky, and turned my head in the direction of the shepherd's hut. It was a few kilometres away now, hidden by the trees and the rise and fall of the land, but I could feel him out there, cold and frozen and dead. And there was something about it that gnawed at me. Something that had come to mind when I was locked away in the dark after being dragged back from the bell tower. But even now the thought eluded me.

'There's no one there, Papa,' Petro said.

'I know.' But I had to be sure. Dimitri had stepped out into the open and been caught by the child thief's bullet. I had stepped out into the open and been caught by Lermentov's soldiers. I didn't want to step out into the open here and be caught by something else.

I looked across to the far side where the trees resumed, and I estimated the distance and how long it would take to cross.

'OK,' I said. 'We'll go now. But keep watching and move quickly.' I turned and looked behind, feeling something nagging, as if Lermentov was following, bringing his soldiers. But I saw nothing in the trees and told myself Lermentov would be in Sushne, warming himself by a stove or forcing a confession from a new prisoner.

I nudged the horse and we moved on, coming out into the open, and even though I knew the child thief was dead and Lermentov was unaware of our escape, I braced myself for what might come.

Halfway across the untouched snow, the first crack split the silent air.

For a while all that could be heard was the crunch of hooves in the snow, the heavy breathing of the animals and the chatter of the bridles. In the trees a solitary crow called out. The snow deadened everything. It was as if its presence slowed the world until it was close to a standstill.

When the crack cut through the near silence, I leaned low in the saddle, hunching my shoulders, trying to wrap myself around Dariya as if I could spread myself thin and wide and envelop her completely. I felt Aleksandra stiffen behind me, a shock jolt through her body. Beside us Viktor's horse stopped as if it had collided with an invisible wall, its head rearing back, its hind legs retreating. Viktor gripped the reins tight in his fists and Petro wrapped his arms harder around his brother so as not to slip backwards from the horse.

My horse shifted to the left, its instinct to panic, to run away from the sound. I held it tight, brought it under control, looking around to see what had made the sound.

'What the hell was that?' Petro said.

'Just move,' I shouted. 'Get to the trees.'

And the sound came again, a loud crack, but this time I knew what it was. The first time it had caught me off guard. I had been expecting a gunshot, so that's what I thought it was, but now I heard it in a different way. I heard it for what it was.

'It's ice,' Aleksandra said. 'Underneath us. We're on a lake.'

'A lake?' Viktor kicked his horse, and we drove the animals forward, knowing we had to make it to hard ground.

Side by side, we spurred the horses on, the ice groaning and cracking beneath us. I could hear it split as we passed over it, breaking up behind us, and when I glanced back, I saw the snow parting, dropping and melting into the water beneath the broken surface. The chunks of frozen lake separated, twisted, sank and resurfaced. I kicked the horse hard, driving it on, willing it to move faster, to outrun the weakening ice.

As I turned to face forward again, to concentrate on controlling the animal carrying us, I caught sight of my sons. Viktor was leaning low in the saddle, his teeth gritted, his lips pulled back in a bizarre replication of his horse's expression. Behind him Petro clung to his brother, his eyes wide, but the expression was not one of fear. He almost seemed to be enjoying the thrill, and I found myself smiling. After everything that had happened, the exhilaration of the speed and the fear drew together into a powerful mix and I understood my son's expression. He was alive. He felt alive.

And then the ice broke below them and they were gone.

There was barely time to register it had happened; it was as if someone had stolen the ground from beneath them. My first instinct was to stop, but I fought the temptation, driving the horse on towards the trees, where the ground was solid.

The lake continued to tear and crack as we fled and, without realising it, I was making an inventory of what we had, looking ahead at the trees to see what I could use to rescue my sons from the freezing water. They would struggle to pull themselves onto the cracking ice, there was a chance they might slip beneath it, not be able to surface.

As soon as the ground was hard and firm beneath us, I stopped the horse, dragging hard on the reins so its head pulled right back. I turned the animal, looking out to take stock of the situation, decide on a strategy, but what I saw made me stop dead. Initially I didn't understand what I was seeing. I had expected the horse to be floundering in the icy water, my sons struggling to pull themselves onto the ice. But Viktor and Petro were still on the horse, the icy water ebbing around their calves, their faces alight with laughter. The water was shallow and held no danger for them.

I felt panic fall away, and I dismounted, going to what I thought to be the edge of the lake. 'Can you get to me?' I called.

The boys came closer, the horse finding its footing on the bed of the lake, lifting its forelegs onto the ice, breaking through every time it tried to bring up its weight.

'I thought that was it,' Viktor said with a smile on his face, riding with the movement of the animal. 'I thought we were gone for sure.' He was swaying from side to side, letting the horse take its time to break through the ice.

'So did I,' I called out. 'I thought I was going to have to come in to get you. I didn't even know we were on water.' There was a kind of euphoria in the release of my tension. I could feel it in my throat, and I couldn't help smiling as the horse approached the bank, wading out of the shallow lake, rising up so the water only just covered its hooves.

'How did we not notice?'

'Too much snow,' I said. 'You really scared me there.'

'*You* were scared?' Petro laughed. 'I think I might have soiled my trousers.'

And then two things happened in quick succession. The horse Viktor and Petro were riding stiffened and stumbled to one side. And a fraction of a second later, a rifle shot split the air.

'Into the trees,' I shouted at Aleksandra. 'Fast. Leave the horse.' I struggled with the rifle sling, caught in the folds of my coat, pulling at it, dragging it over my head. 'Run.'

In the water the other horse's right hind leg buckled and the animal's rear dropped back into the water as if its hoof had slipped on the lake bed, but when it tried to regain its footing, it was clear it had been shot. The leg refused to obey and I saw the panic in the horse's face. Its head reared back and up, its mouth open, its eyes wide and rolling in fear. Viktor clung to the reins, trying to control the animal, Petro hugging him tight, gripping hard with his thighs to remain in the saddle.

'They came after us,' I shouted as a second shot hit the horse's rear. I heard the lead smacking into its solid flesh.

This time the horse's legs were taken from beneath it, and it sat back into the lake. The sudden jolt loosened Petro's grip on his brother and he slipped backwards, tipping into the water among the pieces of broken ice. Viktor managed to stay on, but the horse could barely contain its own weight, so he swung his leg over and slipped from the saddle, landing in shallow water that failed to cover the top of his boots.

Behind, I heard Aleksandra and Dariya moving up the gentle slope towards the trees, crunching the snow. Beside me the metallic clinking of my horse's bridle, the confused tempo of its breathing.

'Get out of the water,' I said, turning to take hold of my horse's reins. I moved behind the animal and raised the child thief's rifle. I rested the barrel across the saddle, keeping hidden behind the animal as I scoped the far shore, looking for the place from where the shot had been fired.

Viktor's first instinct was not to come ashore; instead he turned back and reached into the water, dragging his brother to his feet. Petro's coat and clothes were heavy with water and he was coughing the lake from his lungs.

'Get behind your horse,' I shouted at them. 'Use it for cover.'

Viktor pulled at his brother's coat, dragging him in the direction of the shore, releasing him only when he was sure Petro had regained his bearings. Viktor waved his arms at me. 'Get into the trees. They're coming.'

The horse they had been riding was now sitting back in the water, the use of both rear legs gone. Its body was almost upright as if it were sitting on the bed of the lake, its front legs beating the water into a froth before it, and its head moving wildly from side to side. The noises that came from its contorted mouth were like nothing I had ever heard before. The sound of bestial pain and panic and fear.

Viktor and Petro came through the water, giving the beating hooves a wide berth, ensuring their horse was between them and the far bank, giving at least a little protection.

And then a third shot struck the horse's head, putting an end to its agonised cries. It was as if the animal had simply been turned off. One moment it was shaking its head, its wet mane flicking water into the air, its front legs thrashing, and then its cranium erupted in a spray of blood and bone and it fell to one side, weighing on the pieces of broken ice and sinking just below the surface of the water.

'Get out,' I called. 'Get out.' I looked through the scope once again, thinking I could see a vague plume of smoke or breath from behind one of the trees on the other side of the lake. I fired the child thief's rifle for the first time, seeing the bark of the tree erupt, but there was no other movement. I could see no one in the forest beyond, and something unpleasant settled in the base of my spine. A dark and ugly thought.

If Lermentov had sent his soldiers after us, they wouldn't have remained so well hidden. A rabble of young soldiers without experience, they would be hurrying across the open ground, rifles firing, gunsmoke washing the air. It would have surprised me if they were even capable of careful and well-placed shots like the ones that had just been fired.

The thought gripped me like a cold fist. I had seen shooting like this before.

'Get out,' I shouted again, feeling the panic rising. 'Get out, get out, get out.' I glanced away from the scope to see Viktor coming out of the water.

'Get behind the horse,' I said as Viktor turned to encourage his brother.

Both of them were weighed down by the water in their clothes and they stumbled onto the shore, Viktor falling to his knees before pushing himself up again, Petro helping to pull him up. Together, they struggled towards me.

'Faster,' I shouted, putting an eye back to the scope. 'Faster.'

I scanned the place where I thought I'd seen the breath, but there was nothing. I listened to my sons coming closer as I swept the scope across the trees. There.

Something.

Movement.

I brought the scope back and saw the shape. Half the profile of a man, barely visible, as if he were part of the forest. He had settled himself behind a thick tree with low boughs where a number of limbs came out almost at right angles from the trunk.

They cut his profile, disguised how he looked, and the branches provided the perfect spot to rest his rifle barrel.

I stopped. Settled my own rifle, moved the cross hairs of the scope over the silhouette and held my breath. All these things occupied just a fraction of a second, but they felt as if they took so much longer. As if each action took minutes. But I had to get it right.

When the figure fired, I saw the smoke and flash from his rifle. I heard the impact of the shot and I heard the crack of the powder. Then I returned fire, and I saw the dark shape wrench back, drop and disappear from sight.

In front of me the horse jerked, disturbed by the rifle shot, but I paid it no mind.

'Got him,' I said, taking my eye from the scope to draw the bolt. I pulled it back with practised ease and speed. I heard Viktor shouting, but I had slipped into doing what I knew how to do best now. I had found my target and nothing was going to stop me. The brass ejected to my right, flicking out and tumbling as it flipped past my shoulder. I returned the bolt, watching the fresh brass slipping into place, and I let the horse move away as I pulled the rifle to my shoulder, going to one knee to better steady my aim. If I saw any more movement I would fire on it.

I found the spot where the figure had been, my head filled with the sound of my own blood, my own breathing, and I searched for any more sign, but now Viktor's shouts began to break into my concentration and I wondered why my son wasn't further away. He and Petro should have reached the trees by now.

I took my eye from the scope without lowering the rifle and saw Viktor on his knees.

He was looking in my direction, his face contorted with anguish and pain.

Beside him Petro lay face down in the snow.

With the rifle in one hand, I ran out to where my son lay. I couldn't get to him fast enough, my legs stumbling in the deep snow, my arms going out for balance. But even as I came close to where Viktor was sitting over his brother, another shot came from the other side of the lake, and thumped into the ground close to us.

The horse startled and turned, moving out to the edge of the water then veering to trot along the shoreline before turning and heading back towards the trees where Dariya and Aleksandra had run.

Another shot hit wide of its mark, the shooter struggling with his aim perhaps because I had hit him. But no other rifles fired in our direction. No soldiers advanced from the trees. There was only a single shooter out there – a thought that was held in my mind only for a fleeting second, because all else was lost to what I could see right in front of me.

I dropped to my knees as another shot whistled overhead and ploughed into the trees.

There was a hole in the back of Petro's coat, the fabric pushed in to meld with his shirt and to trail its fibres into my son's flesh. He was still breathing, but the breaths were shallow and barely detectable.

'Take his legs,' I told Viktor as I put my hands beneath Petro's shoulders, and together we lifted him, stumbling as we moved back towards the trees, the shooter on the other side of the lake firing two more shots before we were into the shadow of the forest and out of sight.

We carried Petro to a place where oak and maple rose close and tight, as if they'd grown here just for our protection, and we placed him on his back.

His face was pale and the look in his eyes was dull.

'Did they find us, Papa?' Petro asked.

'Shh.' I took off his hat and told Viktor to help sit Petro forward so I could lift his coat and press my hat against the wound. I held it there to stem the flow of his blood, but I already knew it would do no good. I could see no place where the bullet might have escaped his body, so the lead would still be inside him, perhaps lodged in his spine. Already he had lost a lot of blood and life was leaving him.

'Is everybody else all right?' Petro asked. His eyes were wandering as if looking for something to focus on.

'Everyone's fine,' I told him.

'Good.' Something like a smile came to his mouth, but the effort was too great and it faded before it was properly formed.

I looked away, pursing my lips between my teeth and catching sight of Aleksandra standing against a tree, her focus intent upon Petro. Dariya stood in front of her, hands clinging to Aleksandra's, wrapping them around her as if she hoped they would take her from the world. Close to them, the horse stood silent as if it understood what was happening. And, beside Petro, Viktor bore the expression of the helpless.

'What can we do?' Viktor asked, and I could see in his eyes that he wanted me to know just the right thing. He wanted me to take control and tell him Petro was going to be all right. But the truth was I couldn't. There was nothing I could do.

Petro was going to die.

It didn't take long. I held my son's head while the others stood by, and a few minutes was all it took for Petro to leave us. And when his breathing stopped; when his chest failed to rise and fall; when his eyes glazed and emptied, I hung my head and wept. I wept for the darkness that had come into this life and for the light that had gone out of it. I wept for the space that would never be filled.

32

It took only a few minutes for Petro's life to be gone, but I sat for a long time holding his head before Aleksandra spoke my name.

'Luka.'

It seemed as if she were standing a long way from where I sat.

'Luka.'

Her voice coming to me as if from another place.

'Luka.'

I opened my eyes and looked up at her.

'What are we going to do now?' she asked. 'We can't fight the army.'

She was standing closer now, her feet just an arm's length from Petro's still body.

'That wasn't the army,' I said. 'There was only one.'

Dariya was beside her, the two of them still holding hands. 'Is she coming for us now?' she asked. It was the first time she had spoken since I had seen her in Sushne but there seemed to be nothing remarkable about it. Too much had happened for it to have any significance. But I thought about what she said and saw the strangeness in it.

'She?'

'Baba Yaga,' she said. 'Don't let her take me again.'

I stared at her, not sure what to say. I was still trying to process Petro's death. My son was lying dead in my arms and now Dariya was saying something I didn't understand.

'What are you talking about?' I could feel anger rising, and it confused me, fuelling itself further.

Dariya swallowed. 'Please.'

'What the hell are you talking about?' I pushed to my feet, Petro's head slumping back into the snow. 'What do you mean, the Baba Yaga?' I drew up to my full height and Dariya pulled closer to Aleksandra, moving so that she was almost behind her.

'Luka,' Aleksandra said quietly, 'you're scaring her.'

'What's she talking about – the Baba Yaga? It wasn't the Baba Yaga who took her. It was a man. A man took her.'

Dariya shook her head and drew even closer to Aleksandra. 'He looked like a man,' she said, 'but it was the Baba Yaga.'

I stared at her.

'He said he was going to eat me.'

Her words made my breath catch in my throat.

'He said he was going to kill you and that he was going to eat me.'

I put my hands to my face and pressed my fingers hard against my eyes. The imprint of my fingertips on my eyelids darkened and then brightened into a burst of white spots, and when I took them away the brightness smeared my tears and almost blinded me.

I crouched and held out my hands to Dariya, but she shook her head and clung to Aleksandra, drawing away from me.

'I'm sorry,' I said, lowering my voice. 'Please.'

Aleksandra encouraged Dariya away from her, and she reluctantly held out her hands for me to take. I pulled her to me and held her, so that her face was buried against my neck and my face was pressed to the side of her head. For a moment I imagined I was hugging my own daughter.

When I released the embrace I told Dariya not to be scared.

She bit her lip and nodded.

'I need to ask you something and I need you to remember everything you can. Is that all right?'

She nodded again.

'How many men were there?'

She furrowed her brow as if she didn't understand the question.

'How many men took you?'

'There was only the Baba Yaga,' she said.

'Just one person?'

She nodded.

'But you hurt him?'

Again she looked confused.

'With a knife,' I said. 'In the hut where he took you.'

And, slowly, it seemed to sink in. I saw her eyebrows rise as if she was beginning to understand what I was asking. 'In the hut?'

'Yes,' I said. 'In the hut.'

'The dead man?'

'Yes. That was him. The man who took you.'

'No,' she shook her head. 'That wasn't him.'

Leaving Dariya with Aleksandra and Viktor, I went to sit with Petro. I took his head and laid it on my lap and sat looking out through the gaps in the trees, glimpsing shards of the lake. I took a cigarette and bent the tube without thinking about it. For a long time I held the match in my fingers before popping it alight with my thumbnail and touching it to the tobacco.

So many things had led to this exact spot, this unknown place that was marked by nothing until my son's death. We believed we had come close to making our way home without knowing how far we really were. I had made many mistakes, from the moment I had agreed to bring my sons, and now I intended to make no more. I had believed the child thief to be dead, but I had been wrong. Now it was my duty to make sure he would never fire another shot. That he would never terrify another child.

'I made a mistake,' I said when Viktor came to sit with me. 'A stupid mistake. I'm old and foolish and careless.'

'How could you have known?'

'How could I have known? I *should* have known. I thought Dariya killed him; freed herself and killed him in his sleep.'

'It's what we all thought.'

'But I should have known she couldn't do that.'

'Why not? Anyone can use a knife.'

'Because the body was frozen,' I said, finally grasping the dark thought that Kostya's death had brought to my mind. 'Dariya had only just left the hut, but the body was frozen. It must have been there for hours. If she had killed him, she would have escaped right away. Her tracks were fresh – the body would have been too.'

I pictured it now, just as Dariya had told it. I saw the child thief dragging her into the hut, tying her and waiting for me to follow, watching through the window, disturbed by the footsteps outside. I saw the child thief open the door, a friendly face, then take his knife and drive it through the man's throat. The owner of the hut perhaps, or maybe just a farmer from Sushne trying to escape the occupiers of his village, it didn't matter. The child thief had killed him as surely as he had killed Dimitri and as surely as he had killed Petro. And then he had stripped off the man's boots, better than his own, and gone out, leaving Dariya alone with the corpse of a stranger.

'She must have been alone with the body for a while,' I said. 'That's why hers were the only tracks. There was a fresh fall that day. His tracks must've been covered.'

'Or maybe *he* covered them.'

'Why would he do that?'

'So we wouldn't know where he'd gone. If we found the hut before he came back.'

I looked at Viktor and thought about what he'd said. For a moment events had been clear in my head, but now they were muddied again. 'Maybe. However it was, she was lucky to get away,' I said. 'Lucky she wasn't there when he came back.' I shook my head and dragged on the *papirosa*. 'I was so sure he was dead. I'm an old fool.'

'No.'

'I wonder why he left his rifle, though.'

'What?'

'His rifle. He left it in the hut.' I tapped the rifle beside me. 'That means he thought he was coming back soon. So why didn't he?'

Viktor looked down at the weapon, his face blank. Neither of us had an answer.

I passed him the cigarette and breathed out a lungful of smoke. 'You have to go on,' I said. 'Wait for me on the ridge behind Vyriv, just as I agreed with the others.'

'I'm not leaving you alone.'

'It's the only way to finish this.'

'You're going after him?'

'I have to.'

'Let me help.'

'No. Your job is to take Dariya and Aleksandra. Keep them safe.'

'But—'

Turning to look at him, I let Viktor see the intent in my eyes, and Viktor nodded, knowing he wouldn't change my mind. I would be alone for this. Alone and focused on only one thing.

'We'll take Petro home.'

'We have no home any more,' I said. 'You can't take him.'

'But we can't just leave him here. We can't leave him out here for—'

'Petro's gone,' I said. 'This isn't him any more. There's nothing left that was your brother. I'll bury him here.'

We both knew I couldn't bury him deep. The ground would be hard and almost impossible to break.

'We have to think about Dariya now,' I said. 'We have to think about your mother and Lara. Petro's gone; there's nothing more we can do about that.'

I looked down at Petro's face. His eyes were closed now, almost as if he were asleep if not for the paleness of his skin and the smear of dried blood across one cheek.

'It's time for you to go,' I said to Viktor.

They gathered their things, and Viktor mounted the horse, reaching down to help lift Dariya. Aleksandra put her hands on Dariya's waist as if to lift her, but Dariya moved away and came to where I was sitting.

Aleksandra and Viktor watched as the child came and stood by me. She looked smaller than her years now. I had seen this girl grow just as I had watched my own daughter grow and I knew her almost as well. She had spent much of her life in and out of my home, and Natalia had always remarked on how she'd seemed older than Lara. But now she looked smaller. More vulnerable.

She looked at me, long and hard. Unblinking.

'Are you going to kill the Baba Yaga?' she asked.

'Yes,' I said. 'Yes, I am.'

33

Grief expands. If allowed, it can push out all other thought, consuming all other emotion until nothing else exists. Uncontrolled, it smothers clear thinking, can take a man close to madness. I had no time for it, so I pushed the grief into a corner of my mind and closed a door on it. If the child thief was coming, he might be on his way now, perhaps skirting the edge of the lake, staying within the forest, advancing on the place where I now sat holding my son. I had to act now.

There was no way of knowing if the child thief was going to follow me, or if he was too badly wounded to do so, but I had to make a decision, so I chose to wait for him. I would wait a while and, if he did not appear, I would make my way to the place where I'd last seen him. I tried to detach myself from what the child thief had done – the people he'd murdered and the fear with which he'd infected Dariya. I tried to take myself back to the days when it had been my job to stalk men, or lie in wait for them. I would do the same thing for this man. He was no different. He was just a man.

I had no time to bury Petro; that would have to wait until my job was done. Instead, I dragged my son's body to a place where the trees grew closest, not looking at him as I did it. I didn't want to see him. I didn't want anything to distract me from what I had to do.

I dug away some of the snow at the base of a tree and put Petro into the dip, rolling him onto his front, with his chest on the higher section, so it looked as if he were using his elbows to raise his torso from the ground. I covered the rest of his body over with snow and found a straight branch to tuck in beside him, protruding as if it were the barrel of a rifle.

'It's just a body,' I said, speaking in a whisper. 'Not Petro. Just a body . . .'

When I was finished, I walked a few metres away into the forest and turned to see what I had done. From this distance it looked as if a hunter had concealed himself in the snow.

I took a branch from a tree close to me and used it to sweep across the surface of the snow as I returned to where Petro lay. It was intended to be a poor effort to disguise my tracks so the child thief would think I was tired and had become sloppy, that I was not a threat to him. My only advantage was that I knew what the child thief was capable of, but he knew nothing about me.

With that done, I climbed onto a low branch of the tree closest to Petro, first testing my weight on it to be sure it would support me. I looked down at my son, seeing only the top of his head and the stick which I had laid beside him. I raised my eyes and looked out into the forest for a moment, then turned and stretched to the next tree, climbing across to it, making my way through four or five trees without touching the ground, without leaving any trace of myself in the snow.

My intention was to drop down now that I was away from the place where Petro was concealed. I would cover myself in a similar way and wait for the child thief to come to where Petro lay, led there by my failed attempt to cover my tracks. But when I looked up, I saw that the oak whose branches now offered me support was tall enough and thick enough to give me a different kind of cover. Something better.

Two metres above the branch I was standing on, the tree split into three separate trunks, each with its own tangle of smaller branches, and the place where it split would give me the perfect place to conceal myself. My dark clothing would be well camouflaged against the bark and I would have a good view of the surrounding area. If the child thief came within a few metres of the place where Petro lay, I would see him.

I checked the rifle was secure on my shoulder and began to climb.

The sky was clouded grey, glimpsed through the branches above, and the sun was diffused behind it, giving away nothing, but I didn't spend long looking up; my eyes were constantly moving, scanning the trees, expecting the slightest change in the forest; my ears tuned to the weakest sound, ignoring the faint wind that moved through the naked, tangled branches with the sound of rushing water. The occasional disturbance as a broken twig fell to the ground, bustling through the branches.

Somewhere to the right, the dark shapes of nests filled the trees, but they were silent except for the call of a single crow, either unaware of my presence or so used to me now that it bore no fear.

I sniffed quietly behind my scarf, breath moist against the wool preventing it from rolling out into the cold air and betraying me. I had barely moved since settling. Both legs were drawn close to my chest so I was in a semi-foetal position, leaning back against the thickest trunk, the rifle resting between the V-shape of the other two. If I turned my head, I could almost see all around, and that was the only movement I allowed myself. My legs were stiff with cramp, my back was aching from the base of my spine and the muscles were frozen stiff in my shoulders, but I didn't need any of those parts of my body. All I needed was one good eye, something to steady the rifle and a finger with which to pull the trigger. And when I glanced at my hands, I saw they no longer shook.

But as time wore on and the sky greyed further, the temperature began to drop and I felt an easy numbness trying to overcome me. There was a heaviness in my eyelids and weariness lowered itself over me. I shook my head to stay awake, raised my eyebrows and stared so hard the cold air hurt my eyes and made them stream with cleansing tears. But none of those things made any difference now. My body and my mind needed rest. They needed to stop and they were threatening to do it right now.

My aches dulled to numbness. My thoughts began to empty. My muscles felt heavy. The crow's incessant call faded to something barely noticed.

And then it stopped. The bird became silent. And in that silence I heard a single footfall in the snow.

The stillness that followed that first single footstep stretched for a long time. The child thief was close. I could feel him. As if he were something more than human. As if he were just breath that moved through the trees, a feral part of the forest that would always be there.

I pressed back against the trunk of the tree as if I might melt into it to find the perfect camouflage. My steady finger poised over the trigger of the rifle.

And then another footstep. Tentative. Slow. The gentle crush of snow beneath a boot. The crow called once more, a disturbed and irritable cry as it jumped from its perch, flitting out across the forest, a jitter of movement in my peripheral vision. I turned my head. Another footfall.

The grey sky was darkening further, an ethereal gloom descending over the forest, the faint shadows falling long across the forest floor. A breeze stirred the branches, wrapped itself around me before moving on, taking my warmth. And then there was movement. Not the natural movement of the shadows touched by the wind, but the lengthening and shortening of a shadow. The movement of a human being coming into my line of sight, just a few metres away.

The child thief, just below me, had skirted the lake as I had expected. He had made his way to this side, stalking deeper into the forest so he could come at me from behind the spot where we had been. He'd tried to outflank me, expecting me to be waiting for him, rifle trained on the open expanse of the lake.

I wanted to see his face. I wanted to know the face of the man who would steal a child and make a game of it, but the child thief's body was turned away from me, only the back and side of his head were visible. A large hat of good fur was pulled low on his brow, but the flaps remained unrolled so his hearing would be unimpaired. His coat was long and dark.

I swivelled my rifle on its resting place so it was pointing in the child thief's direction, and I leaned forward to sight through the scope. Closing my left eye, I watched the magnified form moving away, towards the spot where Petro lay. I willed him to turn around. I wanted to see his eyes when I took the shot. But the child thief continued forward.

I fixed the cross hairs on the back of his head.

My heart quickened, but I concentrated to control it. I inhaled through my nose, halting to keep the breath in my lungs so my whole body was still.

I tracked his movement with a gentle turn of the rifle.

I tightened my finger on the trigger and began to squeeze, waiting for the moment between heartbeats when my body would be most still.

The rifle kicked back against my shoulder and the child thief's head jerked forward as the bullet pierced his skull and exited somewhere through his face, taking with it bone and tissue, spraying it across the snow in front of him. He dropped to his knees, his body falling forward so he went down face first with his hands by his side.

The sound of the gunshot evaporated leaving only a ringing in my ears. The smoke clung around my head, the smell of it strong in my nose, and then it too vanished and became nothing.

Immediately I drew back the bolt of the rifle, ejecting the cartridge. I drove another into place without pointing the barrel away from where the body lay. I wouldn't take any chances with this man. I knew he was human, just a man, but Dariya's talk of the Baba Yaga had stirred something primal in me.

I let my lungs empty in a rush and took in another great breath, my body hungry for the oxygen. And then I stopped. Something wasn't right.

I had missed something important.

I stared at the body below, the stain of blood sprayed out in a fan, and tried to see what was missing.

And then I realised. There was no weapon.

The man I had shot was not armed.

I sat up, drawing the rifle away from the place where I'd supported it, and began to turn, knowing I'd been tricked.

The second shot that broke the peace of the forest was fired by the child thief. I saw him too late, propped against the trunk of a tree, resting the barrel of his weapon in the nook of a branch. He fired before I had time to sight on him, and my natural reaction was to flinch, to make myself small.

The bullet struck the bark beside me, showering it into tiny pieces, spitting into my eyes, stinging the exposed skin of my face. I turned my head in a sudden movement, shifting my body weight, one hand rising for protection. Beneath me, my feet slipped on the damp bark and I toppled backwards from the tree, a moment in space before I thumped to the ground, pain shooting along my spine. My own rifle, once the child thief's, slipped, caught on a branch, then broke through and fell towards me, the butt plate of the stock smashing into my cheekbone in the place that Lermentov had struck me with the altar cross.

I felt a wave of nausea and a rolling blackness that wanted to take me into its arms, but I opened my mouth and shouted away the pain. I yelled at the forest and let the child thief hear my rage. I was not going to be taken. *Nothing* was going to take me. *Nothing* was going to stop me.

I forced myself to move, turning onto my side to push to a sitting position. Intense pain fired through my lower back as if a glowing bayonet had been forced between the vertebrae and stole my breath, but I had no time to rest, no time to recover. The child thief would be moving in on me now, coming to finish his game.

I struggled to a kneeling position and took up the rifle lying in the snow. My face throbbed where the weapon had struck me; flakes of bark gritted my eyes; my muscles and bones were battered and painful, but I pushed on, crawling to the base of the tree, edging my way around to look out at the place where I had seen the man. And there he was.

The child thief.

A movement in the forest. A dark shape coming slowly, advancing on my position. In his situation I would have been tempted to rush this spot; to get in close before my enemy had time to recover from his fall. But the child thief was calm and self-controlled, taking his time, looking for his moment, stepping from shadow to shadow, tree to tree.

I edged back, slipping onto my stomach and resting the rifle barrel across some fallen dead wood, pulling the stock into my shoulder. I put my right eye to the scope, leaving my left open to keep watching him. I pressed a painful cheek to the cold wooden stock and waited.

For a while I saw nothing. Everything was still. Somewhere behind me the crow cawed loud and raw as if it were angry with the day. Then something moved to the right of the place where I had seen my hunter. Only the slightest twitch, but it was enough to catch my eye. I turned the barrel of the rifle to point in that direction and waited for another sign.

And then the darkness moved. The shadowy edge of a large tree peeled away and stepped out into the clear for just one moment.

I closed my left eye and saw him through the scope. I stopped breathing. I stopped thinking. Now there was only the small circle of the world I could see through the lens, and there he was, captured in that single moment, stepping out from the shadow. Not the Baba Yaga that had clawed into my mind when the screams came on that first night of the hunt. For the first time he was not a ghost that could come and go in the darkness without leaving a trace. But a man. The man who had murdered my son.

The cross hairs were fixed squarely on the child thief's chest, as if it had been his intention to step into my sights. I had no time to shift it. No time to aim anywhere else. And as the child thief stepped into the light, he stopped as if he sensed my aim was on him. As if the cold had frozen him right there where he stood.

He held a rifle in his right hand, resting it across the crook of his left as if he was incapable of holding it properly, and I knew I must have injured him when I fired at him across the lake. He stood hunched, his head jutting forward, and he turned to look in my direction, his face clear in the magnification of the scope.

And I knew him.

My finger froze on the trigger.

Thoughts rushed into my empty mind, jostling for space, crying out for attention. Images and words stumbled over one another and I grabbed at them as they passed, trying to fix on just one. This man was not the child thief. He couldn't be. I knew this man. We had spent time as comrades in hardship, locked up together in the church in Sushne. I had not warmed to his insistent questioning about the war, but I had shared some of my darkest moments with the man who now turned to look at me in the magnification of the scope. But at the same time I knew he was the one. I saw it in his eyes. An instant of realisation and then indecision. The wide expression of a man who has been caught, followed by a sudden change as if he were torn between facing up to it or pretending once again to be something other than he was. And now I understood why this man had hidden among the other prisoners when Viktor and Petro had rescued us. I understood why Yuri had wanted to move on alone – because Dariya would have recognised his face.

Yuri Grigorovich stared, and I knew he was thinking he had only two options. He could no longer pretend to be anything other than what he was. I had seen that look on his face; I had seen his true nature. The child thief's only choice now was to either raise his rifle and shoot or try for the cover of the closest tree. But he was injured and tired, and neither option would be easy for him. His game was over.

And when he began to turn, to raise his rifle at me, I shot him once in the chest.

I looked up as I ejected the cartridge, pushing the bolt back home, driving another into the chamber, and I saw Yuri fall back, losing his grip on the rifle. He went down, nothing more than a dark mark on the snow, and I sighted on him once more, ready to fire again, but there was no sign of movement.

I lay in the snow for many heartbeats, watching the shape through the scope. And when it moved, I tightened my finger on the trigger once more.

Yuri drew one leg up so his knee was pointing to the sky, and he brought his arms to his sides, pressing down to push himself up. But the effort was too great, and each time his head rose, his muscles and his strength deserted him. Each time he half sat up, his arms buckled and he collapsed again.

I watched him for longer still, letting him suffer. Then, keeping the rifle pointed at his shape, I struggled to my knees, working against the now dull pain in my back as I crossed the distance between us. My feet dragged through the deep snow, and I came to where Yuri lay.

I kicked his rifle away, touching the barrel of my own to the thick material of Yuri's coat, and I stared down at him.

Yuri was still alive. I could see where the bullet had hit him, piercing the right side of his chest, and I guessed from the laboured breathing that his lungs were damaged. He was probably bleeding into them, slowly flooding them with the one thing that was supposed to keep him alive. He was drowning in his own blood.

He made a shallow rasping with each intake of cold air, and each exhalation was accompanied by a wet bubbling sound. His eyes were wide open and I could see fear in them. After everything he had done, Yuri was afraid of dying.

Blood came into his mouth and touched his lips, spilled from the corner and ran down his chin.

'It was always you?' I said.

Something like a smile passed Yuri's lips.

I glanced back at the first man I'd shot, then turned and went to him. I rolled him over and saw he was one of the soldiers who had been guarding the column of prisoners. Anatoly, he had called himself. The young man who could hardly remember the face of his own wife.

'And the other one?' I said, going back to Yuri. 'You killed him?'

Yuri blinked hard.

'I don't understand. Why would you do it? Why would you do any of it?'

Yuri opened his mouth further and attempted to form words, but his voice was quiet.

'What? You want to say something?'

He nodded, so I crouched closer to him.

'You were the best,' he said.

'What does that mean?'

Yuri closed his eyes. 'The last one was good, but you were better.'

'What does it mean? Why did you do this?'

'Don't you miss it?' Yuri whispered. 'The excitement of hunting another man? Fighting? Killing?'

'No.'

'Liar. It was in your actions when you followed me. In your voice when we were prisoners together. I see it now in your eyes.' He stopped, his chest rising high, trying to take a breath into lungs that were drowning. 'Being arrested was bad luck for me.' His words caught in his throat and he coughed. A weak, wet sound.

'Why did you go to Sushne? Why not stay in the hut? Why not wait for me?'

'The soldiers.'

'What about them?' Then I understood. 'You went home to rescue your own belongings. The man you killed, the one who came to the hut, he told you they were there. He knew you and he told you what was happening, so you murdered him and went to the village to get your things. But they caught you. *They* caught *you*.' I shook my head at him. 'After all that time, everything that happened, you were arrested by boys dressed as soldiers. You must have hated that.' I laughed at the irony of it, let Yuri hear the mockery in my voice. 'All those tricks meant nothing. Your clever game was broken by communist boys. All of it was for *nothing*.'

'Not nothing. First the girl was in the village. Then you.' Something like a smile came to his face. 'I *knew*. I knew who you were but you knew nothing. And after. Among the other prisoners. You and her. It was . . . exciting. Knowing.'

'Exciting? Torturing a little girl? That's exciting to you? How many other children did you murder?'

'Many. But she was going to taste so good.' He turned his head away from me.

I stood and looked down at him, hating him. Then I kicked him, and it felt good, so I did it again, using whatever strength I had left. It was like kicking a sack of dirt, but it gave me release so I kicked him again and again, just as the villagers from Vyriv had kicked the stranger before they lynched him. I insulted him, shouted at him, and then I stopped and spat on him. 'You killed my son.'

I put my rifle to Yuri's forehead and looked into his eyes. 'You killed my son.'

Something like a smile came back to Yuri's lips. His breath rasped. 'Kill me.'

'Of course I'm going to kill you.' I began to tighten my finger on the trigger, bracing for the kick of the rifle, for the loud report, for the result of shooting this animal in the head.

Yuri closed his eyes and smiled.

I stayed my finger on the trigger. 'It's what you want.'

He opened his eyes.

'You want me to kill you.'

'Yes.'

I took the rifle away. 'It's too good for you. Too quick. Maybe I should shoot your knees. Put bullets through your hips.'

I squatted beside Yuri and took out my knife. I used its keen edge to split his trousers from cuff to crotch and then leaned right in so my mouth was close to his ear. 'Maybe I should strip the flesh from your legs, how about that?' I shifted so that I could look into Yuri's eyes. 'Or I could scalp you.' I put the blade against his forehead and pressed hard enough to bring blood. 'Isn't that what you like to do to those poor children?' I drew the knife across his skin. 'You used them as bait in your dirty game, and when the fun was all finished, you scalped them and butchered them.'

Yuri blinked hard, squeezing his eyes shut and then opening them.

'But I won't do that.' I took the knife away, wiping the blood on Yuri's coat. 'I'm not like you. I'm not a monster. But I *am* going to let you drown in your own blood. I'm going to let you die slowly. In pain.'

I sat down beside Yuri and took the packet of cigarettes from my pocket. I lit one and took a long drag. I put my head in my hands for a moment and thought it strange that I felt no satisfaction Yuri was going to die. I felt only sadness for those who had suffered at his hands. And there was a great emptiness in my heart that had once been filled by my son.

I looked at Yuri, watching the movement of his body as he drew breath and exhaled it. Drew and exhaled. Drew and exhaled. The rattle in his throat continued. The rasp of his approaching death.

When I next spoke, the smoke wafted through my teeth and from my nostrils. 'I'm going to watch you die. I'm going to watch the life drain out of you, and then I'm going to bury my son.'

Close by, the crow alighted on a branch, growing more used to our presence. It called its harsh call and turned its head this way and that as if studying us.

'And when you're dead, the crows will eat your eyes. You'll be a blind man in hell.'

34

I watched Yuri's laboured breaths until he was still. He didn't speak again, and when he was dead, I left him exactly as he was, open-eyed and slack-jawed.

I buried Petro in the place where he had fallen to the child thief's bullet and spent the night in a rough shelter, close to my youngest son for the last time.

At dawn I headed home to Vyriv, following the tracks of Viktor's horse, coming to the rise overlooking the village, where among the trees I found my living son. Aleksandra and Dariya stood close to him, but there were others there too. Evgeni, Dimitri, and those who had been freed from the column of prisoners.

I spoke to none of them. I came into the trees and walked among them, going to Dariya. I got down on my knees in front of her and put my hands on her shoulders.

'He's dead,' I said. And I pulled her to me and held her for a long time.

35

We remained hidden until the sun was gone and the moon cut an opening in the clear sky. We lit no fires. We gave no sign we were there. And in the darkness, I walked to the top of the slope and stood, looking out at Vyriv. The collection of houses was nothing more than a muddle of dark shapes in the night. There were one or two lights, but not many.

Viktor came to my side, along with Evgeni and Dimitri, who were holding the rifles they'd taken from the soldiers.

'We're going to make it, aren't we, Papa?'

'Of course we're going to make it,' I said. 'I'll get your mother and Lara – Svetlana too – and we'll leave.'

'*You'll* get them?' Viktor said. 'You mean *we* will.'

I knew Viktor would protest, but there was no way I would let him come into Vyriv. However Viktor tried to persuade me, I was already determined not to give in. 'It's better if I go alone. I'll be quicker and quieter that way. You can stay up here and cover me with this.' I took the child thief's rifle from my shoulder and held it out to my son.

'You'll need it,' Viktor said.

'Not down there.' From Viktor's belt I pulled the pistol with the red nine carved into the handle. 'This will be better.'

'I'm not letting you go down there on your own,' Viktor said.

'You have to. I can't risk another son.'

'It's not a risk. You might need me, and—'

'What I need is for you to watch me from here.' I pushed the rifle into Viktor's hands. 'If I'm followed, I'll need you right here

343

to shoot at anyone behind me.' I looked at Dimitri and Evgeni. 'All of you.'

'I won't stay,' Viktor protested. 'I'm coming with you. I can't cover you from here, it's too dark for the scope, and you can't see any of the village centre. You have no idea how many men might be down there.'

'They won't notice me if I'm alone.' I stepped closer to my son so our noses were almost touching. I lowered my voice and spoke through tight lips. 'I already have to explain to your mother that I lost one son; I won't let that be two. Do as I ask, Viktor. Please.'

'Your father's right,' Evgeni said. 'You should stay.'

'It's none of your business,' Viktor snapped, but I grabbed his shoulders and shook him, forcing him to look into my eyes.

'Think what would've happened if we'd all been taken to Sushne. We'd be on our way to a labour camp now, or shot dead and lying in a ditch. But you were there to stop it from happening. So we can't both go down there. We just *can't*. Because if we do, who will be left to help us?'

Viktor stared at me.

'No one,' I said. 'There'd be no one.' I released my grip. 'And there has to be someone here for Dariya.'

'She has Aleksandra.'

'It should be you.'

Viktor watched me, searching for any sign that I might change my mind, but saw none, so he turned his back on me and took a few steps away before stopping. 'An hour,' he said. 'One hour and I'll come looking for you.'

'One hour,' I agreed. 'OK.'

Viktor shook his head once and walked a few paces along the ridge, not wanting to speak to me any more. He was angry I wouldn't allow him to go with me, but his feelings were more to do with the situation than me. He understood the reasons why I wanted him to stay away from Vyriv.

'I'll go with you,' Evgeni said beside me. 'I've nothing to lose.'

I continued to watch my son.

344

'And you might need help. After everything you've been through, Luka, you're tired and—'

'I'm fine. I feel strong.'

'You look like shit.'

I turned to Evgeni and wondered if it was like looking into a mirror. Even in the dim light I could see that Evgeni's face was drawn, his shoulders hunched, his whole demeanour that of a man close to defeat.

'You know, they might not even be down there,' I told him. 'I haven't said this to Viktor, but they might have shipped them out already.'

Evgeni glanced down at Vyriv. 'There are lights.'

'Some. But they may have marched the people off to the same place they were taking us. I'm going down there, but my wife and daughter might not even be there.'

'Do you think they know about our escape?'

'It's possible.'

'So they might be waiting for us?'

'I have to consider it.'

'Let me come with you.'

'No.' I was tempted to accept Evgeni's offer of help. I was exhausted, with almost no fight left in me. The only thing keeping me going right now was the thought of being with Natalia and Lara again. There would be advantages in taking Evgeni with me, but there would be disadvantages too. 'You're no soldier,' I said. 'And I wasn't lying when I told Viktor I'd be quicker and quieter alone. I want you to stay here – and make sure Viktor does too. If I'm not back in an hour, you should all leave.'

'Leave? But you told Viktor—'

'I know what I told him, but if I don't come back in an hour, it means I'm not coming back.'

'He'd never listen to us.'

'You'll have to make him.'

'No. What if the place is crawling with soldiers like Sushne? It might take longer than an hour just to find them.'

I sighed and shook my head. 'It won't be.'

'But if it is?'

'Then I'll come for help.'

'You promise?'

'Yes. I promise.'

I didn't look back as I descended the gentle slope towards Vyriv. I fixed my eyes on the barn and tried not to imagine the worst of what I might find. I was as afraid now as I had ever been in my life. Behind me my son, ahead of me my wife and daughter. My family was so close, and yet it felt as if they were as far apart as the seasons, all of us just a breath from being lost to each other.

When I reached the fence, I didn't pause. I climbed straight over and headed for the shadow cast by the barn, the closest building and the first real cover. In my hand I gripped the pistol I'd found on the stranger's sled, the one Viktor had used to shoot Yakov from his horse.

The barn doors moved on their hinges when I pressed against them, and from inside I heard the gentle snickering of a horse. I froze, scanning the area around the back of the house, and the fear that had gripped me as I came down the slope began to fade, pushed aside by the instinct gained from years of fighting and hardship.

The horse confirmed the presence of soldiers. No one in the village owned one, and no one had a barn as large as mine. So the soldiers had put their horses in here to protect them from the worst of the cold. I felt for the fastening, finding the lock had been forced off, and I opened the door enough to look inside.

The cow was gone, but in its place there were two horses. Only two. There had been more horses in Sushne, I had seen at least six. There had been cart tracks too, but here there were none, so I was reassured that Vyriv had not been garrisoned in the same way. It made sense – Vyriv was smaller, with fewer people. The soldiers would be here a short while, clear out the village and leave. The presence of soldiers also made me believe that the villagers were probably still here.

I closed the doors and moved to the corner of the barn, leaning out to look across at the rear window of my home, ignoring the memory of when I had last been there with my daughter, watching the men going out to search for Dariya the day they hanged the stranger.

I crouched low, moving quickly, crossing the space between barn and home, pushing my back against the wall below the window, allowing my breathing to settle. I hoped I would be strong enough to do what I needed to.

Turning and rising up to peer into the bedroom, there was enough light to see the beds were empty, but there was a weak glow leaking under the closed door that opened into the living area. I imagined Natalia and Lara sitting at the table, waiting for me to return, and my heart ached with the need to see them. In an almost uncontrollable surge of emotion, I wanted to rush round to the front door and burst in to lift my daughter in my arms, but I tightened a fist around the butt of the pistol and forced the emotion away.

Instead, I crept to the corner of the house and edged along the side wall until I could lean out and look into the centre of the village. It was almost as if the houses were deserted. Only one or two windows were lit with the faint orange glow of candlelight. In the centre of the village, beside the oak, directly beneath the branch that had been used to hang the stranger, two soldiers stood, rifles on their shoulders, smoking cigarettes, stamping their feet. Their demeanour was casual and indifferent, as if they didn't expect trouble from the people of Vyriv.

Seeing the few lights and the relaxed soldiers, it occurred to me that I might be wrong about the villagers still being here. Perhaps they had already been taken away and the soldiers had remained only to finish their business before moving on. But I thought about the light I'd seen beneath the door in my house, and I somehow knew that Natalia and Lara were safe. I knew they were in there, right now, awaiting their fate.

I returned to the rear of the building and took out my knife, pushing the strong blade into the crack between the window and the frame, twisting, forcing it open just far enough to put my fingers in and pull it towards me. The pop and creak was slight, but to me it was as loud as a gunshot, and when the window swung open, I dropped to the ground and shuffled away, raising the pistol, waiting.

But no one came.

I waited a while longer, then edged back and stood up to look into the bedroom. Everything was as before.

Dressed as I was, I was too bulky to climb through the window, so I took off my coat and gloves and pulled myself up, dropping quietly onto the bed and stopping again, listening for any sound. I wanted Natalia and Lara to be in the other room, but it might not be them. I had to consider that possibility. Even so, the thought of being this close to them was almost unbearable and, once again, I had to resist the urge to rush straight through. I closed my eyes and took a deep breath, preparing, sharpening my mind to react appropriately to whatever I might find in the room beyond.

I went to the door, lifting the pistol, and turned the handle, pushing it open just a crack.

The weak light came from three candles in a chipped holder on the table. Beside it was a bottle of *horilka* and a cluster of tin cups, most of them dented. The only other object on the table was a peaked cap that I had seen before. It looked almost as if it might be new; the royal-blue crown was clean, the red band was not yet marked and the Soviet star was pristine.

I stepped into the room, raising the pistol.

36

For a long while we stared at each other.

Lermentov remained at the far end of the table, both hands on the surface, while I froze with arms outstretched, the pistol aimed at the OGPU policeman.

To one side of the front door a young soldier, still in his coat, grabbed for the rifle slung over his shoulder.

'Leave it,' I said. 'I'll kill you both.'

The soldier stopped what he was doing and looked over to his superior. Lermentov nodded once, almost in resignation, as he lifted one hand to indicate the soldier should do as instructed. The movement was slow and weary.

'I didn't expect to see you again,' Lermentov said. 'How did you escape?'

I took a step forward, fighting the instinct to shoot and kill the man who had treated me so badly. 'Where're my wife and daughter?' I took another step, coming into the light cast from the candle, wondering if there was any possibility of a positive outcome to this situation.

'You won't shoot me,' Lermentov said. 'It would only bring more soldiers, and then what would happen to Natalia and Lara?'

'They're here?'

'Yes.' He shifted his eyes to the front door and nodded gently, summoning the guard. 'Bring me his weapon.'

The soldier took a few nervous steps towards me, but I stood firm with the pistol pointed directly at Lermentov's head. 'Stay where you are.'

The soldier stopped.

'What are you going to do, Luka Mikhailovich?' Lermentov leaned back. 'Maybe you think you're going to march me outside and force me to release your wife and daughter?'

'I could.' I hadn't yet hit on a solution for resolving this situation, but Lermentov might have just given me one.

'Except there're other soldiers out there—'

'Two.'

Lermentov shrugged. 'Well, there aren't many, but there are more than two, so you'd have to hope none of them was keen enough to try their luck at you – maybe even kill both of us for the glory of the motherland. You know how dedicated to the cause they can be.' He shook his head. 'Or even if you did force me to release them, what then? You think you wouldn't be followed? No, the only way you're going to see them again is if I allow it.'

'How do I even know they're here?' I tried to harden my resolve. 'Maybe I should just kill you anyway.'

'Can you afford to take the risk? After everything you've been through to find that little girl, to escape and come back to your family? No, I don't think you'd throw it all away now. Not if there's even the slightest chance of reunion. You've come too far, Luka; survived too much.' Lermentov relaxed even more now, there was less of an edge to his voice and I wondered if he was drunk again. 'Where is she, by the way? The girl?'

'Safe from you,' I said without lowering the gun.

'I have no reason to harm her.' He nodded to the soldier. 'Take the weapon, comrade. He won't resist.'

The soldier reached out slowly and put his hands on the pistol. I gripped it tight, standing firm, but knew Lermentov was right – shooting him would only bring more men, and I was of no use to Natalia and Lara if I was dead.

'Put it down,' Lermentov said, 'and I will allow you to see them.'

I watched him.

'I swear it.'

I released the pistol, defeated. There was anger in me, but it was tainted with the knowledge that I was beaten. One man could not fight against so large a machine; I had told Viktor as much. I could only hope that Lermentov would make good on his promise and that, up on the hillside, Evgeni and Dimitri would persuade Viktor to turn away and leave.

'I'll take that,' Lermentov held out a hand without standing up, and he waited for the soldier to hand him the weapon. 'German,' he said looking at me. 'Should I ask where it came from?'

I didn't reply, so Lermentov leaned over and spoke quietly to the soldier without taking his eyes off me. When he was finished, the soldier nodded and left us alone, closing the front door behind him.

It was quiet in the room, no sound from outside.

'How did you escape?' Lermentov asked, placing the pistol on the table, close to his right hand. 'I've spoken to your wife so I know what a resourceful man you are, but . . . well, I have to ask.'

'You already know, otherwise why are you here?'

'Oh, you think I was expecting you? No.' Lermentov opened out his hands. 'I always come when they find a new village in my area.'

'But why are you in my house?'

Lermentov shrugged. 'I don't know. Maybe it's because there's something about you, Luka Mikhailovich, something that stayed with me. You're a memorable man.'

I stared at the policeman.

'I can't imagine how you must be feeling right now,' he said. 'You've come all this way only to find me waiting for you. It must be very frustrating. But I can't help admiring your tenacity. You've come a long way. What about the other prisoners?'

I didn't answer.

'You freed them too?'

There was too much confusion for me to think clearly. Anger, despair, surrender and abandon. I'd failed and all I could do now was wrestle with the muddle of thoughts, try to put the emotions away so I could find a way out of this situation, or at least think of a way to warn Viktor and the others.

'There's really nothing you can do,' Lermentov told me. 'You might as well sit down.'

I stayed as I was.

'Fine,' he said. 'Fine. You know, you're either the bravest or the stupidest man I've ever met. I think I may have even said that to you once before, have I not?' He reached for the bottle before pulling over two dented tin cups. He poured *horilka* into them, indicating that one of them was for me. 'Your family,' he said before tipping back his head and drinking the contents in one go.

'What do you want?' I asked. 'If you need workers, take *me*. Let my wife and daughter go.'

'I could take you all. I could take everyone in this village.' Lermentov refilled his cup and raised it in another toast. 'Your health.' When he had drunk, he wiped his lips. 'For God's sake, why don't you just sit down?' He took up the pistol and pointed it at me. 'Sit.'

I pulled out the chair at the other end of the table and sat down. 'I thought you dogs don't believe in God.'

Using one hand, Lermentov poured *horilka* into his cup and pushed the other one across to me. 'Drink with me.'

I took the cup and drank the contents, feeling the alcohol burn my throat.

Lermentov nodded his approval and drank, then placed the pistol back on the tabletop. 'I don't know what anyone believes in now, Luka Mikhailovich. God, communism, our great leader. It seems like everything's gone to shit. Everyone's forgotten who they are and what the damn revolution was for. It's like we're barely human any more.' Lermentov poured another generous measure into his cup. This time he drank without toasting.

I continued to watch him. He was obviously drunk and his reactions would be slow. I reconsidered taking the policeman as a hostage. Lermentov had dissuaded me from it before, made me see danger I hadn't considered, but now it seemed possible again. I saw no other option.

'You'd never make it,' Lermentov said, putting his hand on the weapon. 'I can see how your mind's working. You wouldn't get away. Anyway, there's no need. I'm going to let you see your wife and daughter.' He watched for my reaction. 'I just told that soldier to bring them here.'

'Why?'

'You know, you were right about me.' His words were slow, heavy with alcohol. 'There was a time back in Sushne when I thought you could see right through me.'

'What are you talking about?'

'I have a daughter, and that made me hate you *so* much. I wanted to punish you for everything I felt. I really thought you'd hurt that child. I thought you'd cut her.'

I looked at him, hating him and everything he stood for. 'That's no excuse for what you did to me. And you did the same thing to others for no reason.'

'We live in hard times.'

'Made harder by men like you.'

Lermentov nodded and looked away to the corner of the room. 'We do what we have to.'

'Don't pretend you have to behave the way you do,' I said. 'That's no excuse for the things you've done. You sent Dariya away to work.'

'So she could be with you.'

'And you left Kostya in the bell tower to die. You're—'

'And what have you done, Luka Mikhailovich?' Lermentov raised his voice, the words slurring together. 'How many wars have you fought? How many men have you murdered and how many villages have you burned? How many times have *you* forgotten who you are?' He stopped and took a breath, speaking the next words in a near-whisper. 'Even good men can do bad things.'

I put my hands on the table and stared at him. 'I only ever did what I thought was right. What I had to do to survive.'

Lermentov nodded and sat back. 'The same excuse we all use.'

'It's different.' But I remembered some of the things I'd done and wondered if Lermentov wasn't right: if we didn't all just do what we had to do to survive. *Even good men can do bad things.*

'It's not *so* different,' he said. 'You think I'm any safer from men like me than you are? It's kulaks now, but how long will it be before we look inwards? No one trusts anyone. The police are no different.'

'That's the world you people made,' I told him, and the silence that followed was interrupted by a knock at the door.

'You ready?' Lermentov asked.

'For what?' I turned to look as the latch dropped and the door opened. The soldier who stood framed by darkness moved to one side and Natalia stepped into what had been our home.

Seeing her almost took my breath away, and I felt both joy and sadness in my heart. Joy at her presence, but sadness at the thought of what was to come. But for now we looked at each other unable to believe we were together again. For now all that mattered was that moment.

'Papa,' Lara said, appearing from behind her mother and running straight to me. She threw her arms around my legs and squeezed them tight as I put down a hand to pull her to me. I held my other hand out to Natalia and she came closer so all three of us were reunited. She put her fingers on my face as if to re-assure herself I was really there, and her eyes filled with tears.

'You found her,' Lara said. 'The man told us you found Dariya.'

'Yes,' I said, seeing Svetlana come into the room.

Once she was inside, Lermentov ordered the soldier to leave. He saluted the policeman and closed the door behind him.

'What about Viktor and Petro?' Natalia asked. 'Where are they?'

'Somewhere safe.' I looked across at Lermentov, who was still sitting behind the table with the pistol in his hand. I couldn't tell Natalia where Viktor was, not with the policeman there, and I couldn't bring myself to tell her the truth about Petro. This was not the time. Soon she would be taken from me and our family would be fragmented for the last time, so it was better for her to think both her sons were safe from this nightmare. She didn't need to know.

Lermentov kept his eyes on me and stood. 'You have until morning,' he said.

'Before what?' I asked.

'This village is going to be cleared.' He put the pistol on the table and went to the door, turning to look at me standing with my family. 'If I were you, I'd gather what you can and leave. Just the four of you.'

'You're letting us go?'

'It would be safer if you leave before I remember what I'm supposed to be. A man like you, with your skills, I think you might even make it to Poland.'

'Is this a trick?'

'No.' The policeman put his hand on the latch and opened the door.

'But why?'

Lermentov stopped without turning round. 'Perhaps I forgot who I really am for a while,' he said. 'Or maybe it works both ways: maybe even bad men can do good things.'

Then he stepped out into the cold and closed the door behind him.

About the Author

Dan Smith grew up following his parents across the world. He has been writing short stories for as long as he can remember and has been published in the anthology *Matter 4*, shortlisted for the Royal Literary Fund mentor scheme, the Northern Writers' Award, the 2010 Brit Writers' Published Author of the Year Award and the Best First Novel Award. He lives in Newcastle with his family. Find out more about Dan at www.dansmithsbooks.com